IT BEGINS AS A ROUTINE BUSINESS TRANSACTION....

Three men on a deserted road outside Rome wait for a black Mercedes carrying British businessman Geoffrey Harrison. Within seconds their prey is bound and blindfolded—another statistic in a country where kidnapping is a growth industry. No one is worried. Everyone knows the rules. The ransom will be paid; the prisoner released.

IT BECOMES AN INTERNATIONAL TIME BOMB

When the prisoner is suddenly kidnapped from his abductors by a young fanatic with only one totally impossible, unreasonable demand. Suddenly all bets are off, all hell breaks loose, and no one can predict the outcome of . . .

THE HARRISON AFFAIR

"HIGHLY PROFESSIONAL: FULL OF ACTION, FULL OF PEOPLE, FULL OF SUSPENSE."
—*Library Journal*

"TAUT ACTION . . . SOLID, INTELLIGENT . . . A CUT ABOVE THAT OF MOST TERRORIST FICTIONEERS."
—*Kirkus Reviews*

THE
HARRISON
AFFAIR

Gerald Seymour

A DELL BOOK

Published by
Dell Publishing Co., Inc.
1 Dag Hammarskjold Plaza
New York, New York 10017

Dell ® TM 681510, Dell Publishing Co., Inc.

ISBN: 0-440-13566-4

Reprinted by arrangement with Summit Books, a Simon
& Schuster Division of Gulf & Western Corporation.

Printed in the United States of America

First Dell printing—June 1981

To Gillian, Nicholas and James

1

An hour now they had been in position. The car was nestled off the road under a blanket of high, mushroomed pine branches. It was back from the main route and in a parking space that later would be used by those who came to play tennis on the courts behind. The place was quiet and unobserved, as they wanted it.

Not that the car was here by chance, nothing in these matters was casual and unplanned and spontaneous. For a clear fortnight the men had toured this discreet web of sidestreets, watching and eyeing and considering the location that would afford them the greatest advantage, accepting and rejecting the alternatives and the options, weighing the chances of attack and escape. They had not chosen this place till all were satisfied, and then they had reported back and another had come on the morning of the previous day and had heard from them their description of what would happen and nodded his head, slapping them lightly on the shoulders to affirm his agreement and accolade.

So the ambush was set, the trap was sprung, the

wires taut, and the men could scrutinize their wrist-watches, bright with chrome and status, and wonder whether the prey would be punctual or tardy.

In front of their car the road ran down a gentle hill toward the main six-lane route into and from the city, which it joined at an intersection two hundred and fifty yards from them. Under the pines the road was shadowed and gray, the potholes and rainwater tracks in dark relief. There was no chance that when he came in his car he would be speeding. He'd be doing thirty kilometers at most, because he would be safe-guarding the expensive framework of his Mercedes, creeping between the ruts, avoiding the hazards, and as unaware and unsuspicious as they all were.

The car in which the men sat had been stolen three weeks earlier, taken from outside a hotel in the center of Anzio, away to the south of Rome. By the time the loss had been reported, written in the ledger book by the *polizia*, the Alfetta had already been fitted with new number plates, likewise stolen, but from a car owned in Arezzo to the north. The number plates had originally belonged to a Mirafiori Fiat. The calcula-tion was that the marriage of the stolen car and the stolen number plates would be too complex for any casual check by the *Polizia Stradale*. The paperwork of insurance and tax had been matched to the vehi-cle's new identity by men who specialize in such work.

Three men were in the car, all sharing the lank, coarse hair and mahogany-sheened faces of the deep south, of the toe of Italy. Men of Calabria, of the rug-ged and daunting Aspromonte mountains. This was their game, their playtime. Their experience qualified them for such occasions. Men who traveled from the lofty villages down to the big city to effect the grab and then fled back to the safety of their families, their community, where they lived uncharted and unknown

to the police computers. The smell in the car was of
the crudely packed MS cigarettes that they smoked
incessantly, drawn to their mouths by roughened fingers which carried the blister scars of work in the
fields, and mingling with the tobacco was the night-
old stench of the Perroni beer they had consumed the
evening before. Men close to middle age. The one
who sat in front of the steering wheel had the proud
hair on his forehead receding in spite of the many and
varied ways he combed it, and the one who sat beside
him carried traces of gray at his temples highlighted
by the grease he anointed himself with, and the lone
one in the back wore a wide belly strapped beneath
his leather belt.

There was little talk in the car as the minute hands
of the watches moved on toward seven-thirty. They
had nothing to communicate, conversation was futile
and wasted breath. The man in the back drew from a
satchel that rested on the floor between his legs the
stocking masks that they would wear, purchased the
previous afternoon in the Standa supermarket and
pierced with a knife for eye and mouth vents. Without
a word, he passed two forward to his companions,
then dived again into the bag. A snub-barreled Beretta pistol for the driver, who probably had no need
for a gun at all, as his work was to drive. For himself
and the front passenger there were squat submachine
guns made angular as he fitted the magazine sticks.
The quiet in the car was fractured by the heavy metallic clacking of the weapons being armed. Last to be
taken from the bag was the hammer, a shiny var-
nished handle of new wood weighted with its gray-
painted iron head.

They had a man to lift this time. A man of their
own age, their own fitness, their own skill. It would
be harder than the last one, because that had been a
child. Just a child toddling to kindergarten in Aven-

tino with the Eritrean maid. She'd screamed at the
sight of them, the black whore, and collapsed in a
dead faint on the pavement and the dog shit by the
time they'd reached the child, and the brat hadn't
struggled, had almost run with them to the car. The
car had been stationary no more than fifteen seconds
before they were moving again with the kid on the
floor and out of sight and only the noise of the keen-
ing wail of the maid to let anyone know that anything
had happened. *Duecento cinquante millioni* they'd paid
out, the parents. Good as gold, placid as sheep, shut
the door on the investigations of the *polizia* and the
carabinieri, cooperated as they'd been told to, sold the
shares, went and tapped the grandfather up in Gen-
ova just as it had been planned they would. Nice and
clean and organized. Good quick payout, used *cinquante mila* notes, and not a uniform in sight. Just the
way it should always be. But how this one would
react there was no way of knowing, whether he'd
fight, whether he'd struggle, whether he was the idiot. . . . The man in the back fingered the hammer-
head, stroking its smoothness with his fingers. And in
all their minds was the thought of the welcome the
big men would provide if there was failure, if the car
came back empty, if the cash investment were not re-
paid . . . no room for failure, no possibility . . . the
big bastard would skin them. From behind his ample
bottom, muffled by his trousers, came the screech of
static noise, and then the call sign. He wriggled
round, heaved his bulk so that it no longer suffocated
the transmitter/receiver radio, pulled the device clear
and to his face. They hadn't used the system before,
but this was advancement, this was progress.

"Yes. Yes."

"Number Two?"

"Yes."

There had been a code, an agreed one, but the suddenness of the transmission had seemed to surprise him and he was aware of the frustration of the men in front at his fumbling. They'd practiced the link often enough in the last week, assured themselves that the receiver would pick up from behind the first block a hundred meters up the hill. He saw the anger on the driver's face.

"Yes, this is Number One."

"He is coming . . . it is the Mercedes and he is alone. Only the one."

For each man in the car the distorted and distant voice brought a syringe of excitement. Each felt the tension rise and writhe through his intestines, felt the snap of stiffness come to the legs, clasped at the security of the guns. Never able to escape it, however many times they were involved, never a familiarity with the moment when the bridge was crossed and spanned, when the only road was forward. He'd skin them if they failed, the big man would.

"Did you hear me, Number One. Did you receive?"

"We hear you, Number Two." Spoken with the gray lips against the built-in microphone.

Big and fat and large and juicy, that was what the big man called it, the *capo*. A foreigner, and with a renowned company behind him, a multinational, and they'd pay up well, pay fast and pay deep. A *milliardi* in this one, that for minimum . . . could be *due milliardi*. Spirals of noughts filling the minds. What was *due milliardi* to a multinational? Nothing. A million and a half dollars, nothing.

The man in the back switched off the radio, its work completed.

Burdening silence filled the car again. All ears strained for the drive of the heavy Mercedes engine. And when it came there was the whine of the low gear, the careful negotiation of the pitfalls of the road. Creeping forward, cutting distance. The growing thunder of the wasp wings as the insect closes on the web the spider has set.

The driver, Vanni, half turned, winked and grimaced, muttered something inaudible and indistinct, gave Mario in the front, Claudio in the back, the curl of a smile.

"Come on." Nerves building in the back.

"Time to get the package." Vanni raised his voice. "Time to go pluck the rooster."

He thrust the gear shift forward, eased his foot onto the accelerator, nudged the car out into the narrowness of the road as all three peered left and upward to the bend.

A black monster of a machine. The Mercedes, sleek and washed. A machine that justified its existence only on the freedom of the autostrada but which was now confined and crippled on the broken surfaces. Clawing toward them.

Earsplitting in the confines of the car, Claudio shouted.

"Go, Vanni. Go."

The Alfetta surged forward. Swinging right with the tires protesting across the loose roadside gravel. The wrench of the brakes took Mario and Claudio unawares, punching them in their seats. Thirty meters in front of the Mercedes the Alfetta bucked to a stop across the road, blocking it, closing it. The drumroll of action as the passengers dragged the stockings over their heads, reducing their features to nondescript contours. This was a moment for Vanni to savor—the visible anger of the driver as he closed on them. He knew the man's background, knew he had been nineteen months in the country, and saw framed in his overhead mirror the caricature of the Italian gesture of annoyance. The flick of the wrist, the point of the fingers, as if this was a sufficient protest, as if this were a common drivers' altercation.

Vanni heard the door beside him and the one behind him crash open. As he spun in his seat to see the scene better there was the impact of splintering glass, vicious and vulgar. He saw Claudio, hammer in one hand, machine pistol in the other, at the driver's door, and Mario beside him and wrenching it open. A moment of pathetic struggle and Mario had the collar of the man's jacket and was pulling him irresistibly clear. Making it hard for himself, wriggling, the stupid bastard, but then the men usually did. Vanni felt a shiver in his seat, involuntary and unwelcome, as he saw a car turn on the bend of the hill, begin its descent. Unseen by Mario and Claudio. Both wrestling with the idiot and on the point of victory. He reached for the pistol from his lap, heart pumping, the cry of warning gorging his throat.

Just a woman. Just a signora from the hill in her little car, hair neatly coiffeured, who would be on her way to the Condotti for early-morning shopping before the sun was up. He eased his fingers from the gun and back to their places on the gear shift and the wheel. She'd sit there till it was over. A woman wouldn't hurt them. Hear nothing, see nothing, know nothing.

The man still struggled as if the shrill of the brakes behind him had provided the faint hope of salvation, and then Mario's fist caught him flush on the jutting chin, and the light, the resistance, died.

All finished.

The man spread-eagled over the back seat and floor of the Alfetta, Mario and Claudio towering over him, and there was a shout for Vanni to be on his way. Critical to get clear before the *polizia* blocked the roads, stifled their escape. First fifteen minutes, critical and vital. Vanni wrenched at the wheel, muscles rising in his forearms as he spun left at the junction, flicked his fingers to the traffic horn, dared another to cut him out, and won through with his bravado. From the back came first a groveling whimper and then nothing but the movement of his friends and the breathing of their prey as the stench of the chloroform drifted forward.

The crisis for Vanni would soon be over. Clear of the immediate scene, the principal hazards would disperse. A few hundred meters on the narrow Tor di Quinto, then faster for two kilometers on the two-lane Foro Olympico, before he slowed at the lights of the Salaria junction, and then left on the main road leading to the north and the autostrada away from the city. He could have driven it with his eyes covered. There was no necessity now for speed, no need for haste, just steady distance. He must not attract attention, or invite notice, and there was no reason why he should, if he did not fall into the panic pit. He felt Claudio's fingers tighten on the collar of his shirt and press against the flesh of his shoulder; ignoring him, he kept his attention for the road as he pulled out behind a truck, passed it, moved back into the slower lane.

Claudio would not sense his mood. He was a big man, heavy in weight and grip, and with a dulled speed of thought unable to judge the moment when he should speak, when he should bide his time. Past the truck, safe and clear and cruising. Claudio did not look down at the prone body, easy in its sleep, the head resting on his lap, the torso and legs on the carpet floor enmeshed between Mario's shins.

"Brave boy, Vanni. You took us clear and did it well. How long till the garage?" He should have known the answer himself; they had made the journey four times in the previous week; they knew to within three minutes the time it would take to cover the distance. But Claudio wanted to talk, always wanted to talk, a man to whom silence was punishment. He could be removed from his cigarettes, his beer, and his women, but he would die if he were left to the cruelty of his own company. Vanni appreciated the loneliness of a man who must be spoken to and talked with at all times.

"Four or five minutes. Past the BMW depot and the Bank sports place . . . just past there."

"He fought us, you know. When we had to take him from the car."

"You took him well, Claudio. You gave him no chance."

"If he had gone on, then I would have hit him with the hammer."

"You don't know the sap in your arm," Vanni chuckled. "They'd pay little for a corpse."

"How long did you say to the garage?"

"Three more minutes, a little less than when you last asked. Idiot of Calabria, are you frightened of losing us? You would like to come with us on the train this afternoon? Poor Claudio, you must endure a night of the boredom and the tedium of Rome. You must be patient, as the *capo* said. A bad night for the whores, eh Claudio?"

"We could all have traveled together."

"Not what the *capo* said. Travel separately, break the group. Give Claudio his night between the thighs. Don't you go hurting those girls, big boy." Vanni laughed softly; it was part of the game, the prowess of Claudio the lover. If a girl spoke to the buffoon, he'd fall on his arse in fright.

"I would like to be back in Palmi," Claudio said simply.

"Calabria can wait for you just one day more. Calabria will survive without you."

"It's a bastard trip—on your own."

"You will find someone to talk to, you'll find some fat cow who thinks you're a great man. But don't go flashing her, not your money anyway, not *cinque millioni*." And the laughter faded. "That's how they get you, Claudio, how the *polizia* take you, when you have the money running free in your palm."

"Perhaps Claudio should put his money in the bank," murmured Mario.

"And have some criminal bastard walk in with a shooter and take it? Never! Don't do that, Claudio."

They laughed together, heaving their bodies in the seats. Exaggerated, childish humor, because through that came a relaxation from the tension that had taken three weeks to build and fester since the outline of the plan was first put to them.

Beyond the Rieti turnoff they went right and drove on a rough track skirting a recently completed four-floor block of apartments and toward the garages that lay to the rear, partly shielded from the upper windows by a line of vigorous conifers. There was a van waiting there, old and with its paintwork scratched from frequent scarrings and the rust showing at the mudguards and road dirt coating the small windows set in the rear doors. Two men lounged, elbows on the hood, waiting for the arrival of the Alfetta. Vanni did not hear what was said as Mario and Claudio carried the crumpled, drugged form of their prisoner from the back seat to the opened rear doors of the van. It would be of little interest, the passing of a moment between men hitherto unknown to each other, who would not meet again. When the doors were closed, an envelope passed between fingers, and Claudio slapped the men on their backs and kissed their cheeks, and his face was wreathed in happiness, and Mario handed the satchel to new owners.

Mario led the way back to the car, then paused by the open door to watch the men fasten the back of their van with a padlock and drive away. There was a certain wistfulness on his features as if he regretted that his own part in the matter were now completed. When Claudio joined him, he looked away from the retreating vehicle and slid back into his seat. Then the vultures were at the envelope, ripping at it, tearing it apart till the bundles in the pretty, colored elastic bands were falling on their knees. One hundred notes for each. Some hardly used in transactions, others elderly and spoiled from passage of time and frequency of handling. Silence reigned while each counted his bounty, flicking the tops of the notes to a rhythm of counting.

Vanni loaded his money into the folds of his wallet, pulled a small key from his pocket, climbed from the car and walked to one of the garage doors. He unlocked it, then returned to the car and motioned for Mario and Claudio to leave. He drove the car into the garage, satisfied himsef that the doors prevented a casual glance from the building from seeing his work, and spent five slow minutes wiping clean the plastic and wood surfaces of the interior with his handkerchief and then, when he was satisfied, the outer doors. When he was finished he came out into the warmth and slammed the garage doors shut. The garage had been rented by telephone, a letter with a bogus address containing cash had provided the deposit and confirmation. He threw the key far onto the flat roof, where it clattered momentarily. The rent had six weeks to run, time enough for the Alfetta to rest there, and by the time an irate landlord pried open the doors, all other traces of the group would have been covered.

Together the three men walked out past the apartments and to the main road and then along the pavement to the green-painted bus stop sign. It was the safest way into the city and ultimately to the railway station.

* * *

On that morning, in a flat across two Roman hills, the first of the occupants to wake was the boy Giancarlo. Lithe on his bare feet, he padded across the carpet of the living room, sleep still heavy and confusing to his eyes, blurring the shapes and images of the furnishings. He avoided the low tables and velvet-seated chairs, stumbling on a light cord as he pulled a shirt over his young, undeveloped shoulders. He had shaken Franca gently and with the care and wonderment and awe of a boy who wakes for the first time in a woman's bed and is frightened that the tumult and emotion of the night will be relegated by dawn to a fantasy and dream. He had scratched his fingers across her collarbone and pulled quietly at the lobe of her ear, and whispered her name, and that it was time. He had looked down on her face, gazed intoxicated on the shoulder skin and the contour of the drawn-up sheet, and left her.

A small apartment they lived in. The one living room. The bathroom that was a box which crammed in a toilet, a bidet, and a shower unit. The kitchen with a sink buried under abandoned plates and a stove that had not seen a damp cloth round the burners for more than a week. The bedroom where Enrico still slept noisily and where there was the unused bed that till last night had been Giancarlo's. And there was Franca's room with the single narrow divan, her clothes draped as haphazard carpeting across the woodblock floor. A small hallway and a door with three locks and a peephole, and a metal bar with chain that enabled the door to be opened an inch for additional checking of a visitor. It was a good apartment for their needs.

The requirements of Franca Tantardini, Enrico Panicucci, and Giancarlo Battestini were not great, not complex. It was determined that they should live among the *borghese*, in a middle-class area where

there was wealth, prosperity, where lives were shuttered, self-reliant affairs and closed to the inquisitive.
Vigna Clara hill suited them well, left them secure
and unnoticed in the heart of enemy territory. They
were anonymous in a land of Ferraris and Mercedes
and Jaguars, among the servants and the spoiled children, and the long holidays through the summer, and
the formidable foreign bank accounts. There was a
basement garage and an elevator that could carry
them out of sight to their own door in the attic of the
building, affording them the possibility of cloaking
their movements, coming and going without observation. Not that they went out much; they did not roam
the streets because that was dangerous and put them
at risk. Better that they should spend their hours
cooped between the walls, profiting from seclusion,
reducing the threat of casual recognition by the *polizia*. Expensive, of course, to live there. Four hundred
and seventy-five thousand a month they paid, but
there was money in the movement. Enough money
was available to meet the basic precautions of survival, and they settled in cash on the first day of the
month and did not ask for the contract to be registered and witnessed and the sum to figure on their
landlord's tax return. There was no difficulty finding
premises that were private and discreet.

Giancarlo was a boy with two terms of psychology
study at the University of Rome behind him, and nine
more months in the Regina Coeli jail, locked in a
damp cell low down by the Tiber River. Still a boy,
little more than a child, but bedded now, bedded by a
woman in every way his senior. She was eight years
older than he was, so that he had seen in the first
creeping light of the bedroom the needle lines at her
neck and mouth and the faint trembling of the weight
at her buttocks as she had turned in her sleep, resting
on his arm, uncovered and uncaring till he had pulled

the sheet about her. Eight years of seniority in the movement, and that he knew of too, because her picture was in the mind of every carload of the *Squadra Mobile,* and her name was on the lips of the *capo della squadra antiterrorismo* when he called his conferences at the Viminale, in the Ministry of the Interior. Eight years of importance to the movement; that too Giancarlo knew of, because the assignment of Enrico and himself was to guard and protect her, to maintain her freedom.

The bright, expansive heat drove through the slatted shutters, bathing the furniture in zebra shades of color, illuminating the filled ashtrays and the empty supermarket wine bottles and the uncleared plates with the pasta sauce still clinging to them, and the spread-eagled newspapers. The light flickered on the glass of the pictures with which the room was hung, expensive and modern and rectangular in their motifs, not of their choosing, but provided with the premises, and which hurt their sensitivities as they whiled away the cramped hours waiting for instructions and orders of reconnaisance and planning and ultimately of attack. All of it, all of the surroundings grated on the boy, disturbed him, nurturing his disgust for the apartment in which they lived. They should not have been in a place like this, not with the plumage and trappings of the enemy, and the comforts and ornaments of those they fought against. But Giancarlo was twenty years old and new to the movement, and he was quick to learn to keep his silence at the contradictions.

He heard the noise of her feet tripping to the bedroom door, swung round, and in haste dragged his shirttails into the waist of his trousers and fastened the top button and heaved at the zipper. She stood in the open doorway and there was the look of a cat about her mouth and her slow, distant smile. A towel

was draped uselessly around her waist, and above its
line were the drooping bronzed breasts where Giancarlo's curls had rested; they hung heavily because she
forswore the use of a brassiere under her daily uniform of a straining blouse. Wonderful to the boy, a
dream image. His hands were still on the zipper.

"Put it away, little boy, before you run dry." She
rippled with her laughter.

Giancarlo blushed. Tore his eyes from her to the silent, unmoving door to Enrico's room.

"Don't be jealous, little fox." She read him, and
there was the trace of mocking, the suspicion of scorn.
"Enrico won't take my little fox away, Enrico won't
supplant him."

She came across the room to Giancarlo, straight and
direct, and circled her arms around his neck and nuzzled at his ear, pecked and bit at it, and he stayed
motionless because he thought that if he moved the
towel would fall, and it was morning and the room
was bright.

"Now we've made a man of you, Giancarlo, don't
behave like a man. Don't be tedious and possessive
and middle-aged . . . not after just once."

He kissed her almost curtly on the forehead where
it rested against his mouth, and she giggled.

"I worship you, Franca."

"Then make some coffee, and heat the bread if it's
stale, and get that pig Enrico out of his bed, and don't
go boasting to him. Those can be the first labors of
your worship."

She disentangled herself, and he felt a trembling in
his legs and the tightness in his arms, and close to his
nostrils was the damp, lived-with scent of her hair. He
watched her glide to the bedroom, flouncing and
swinging her hips, her hair rippling on her shoulder
muscles. An officer of the Nuclei Armati Proletaria,
organizer and undisputed leader of a cell, a symbol of

resistance, her liberty was a hammered nail in the cross of the state. She gave him a little wave with a small and delicate fist as the towel fell from her waist, and there was the flash of whitened skin and the moment of darkened hair and the tinkle of her laugh before the door closed on her. A sweet and gentle little fist that he had known for its softness and persuasion, divorced from the clamped grip of a week ago as it held the Beretta P38 and pumped the shells into the legs of the falling, screaming personnel officer outside the factory gate.

Giancarlo hammered at Enrico's door. He battered on through the stream of obscenities and protest till he heard the muffled voice cleared of sleep and the tread lumbering for the door.

Enrico's face appeared, the leer spreading. "Keep you warm, boy, did she? Ready to go back to your Mama now? Going to sleep all afternoon . . ."

Giancarlo dragged the door closed, flushed, and hurried for the kitchen to fill the kettle, rinse the mugs, and test with his hands the state of the two-day-old bread.

He went to Franca's bedroom, walking with care to avoid stepping on her clothes, staring at the indented mattress and the striped sheets. He slid to his knees and dragged from the hiding place under the bed the cheap plastic suitcase which always rested there, unfastened the straps and pulled the lid back. This was the arsenal of the *covo*—three machine guns of Czech manufacture, two pistols, magazines, loose cartridges, batteries, wires of red and blue cord, the little plastic bag which held the detonators. He moved aside the metal-cased box with its dials and telescopic aerial that was marketed openly for radio-controlled airplanes and boats and which they utilized for the triggering of remote explosions. Buried at the bottom was his own P38. The rallying cry of the young peo-

ple of anger and dispute—*P trent' otto*—available, reli-
able, the symbol of the fight with the spreading tentacles of fascism. P38, I love you. The token of
manhood, of the coming age. P38, we fight together.
And when Franca ordered him he would be ready. He
squinted his eyes down the gunsight. P38, my friend.
Enrico could get his own, bastard. He fastened the
straps again and pushed the bag away under the bed,
brushing his hand against her pants, clenching them
in his fingers, carrying them to his lips. A whole day
to wait before he would be back there, lying like a
dog on his back in surrender, feeling the pressures on
his body.

Time to get the *rossetti* out of the oven and find the
instant coffee.

She was standing at the doorway.

"Impatient, little fox?"

"I had been at the case," Giancarlo floundered. "If
we are to be at the Post when it opens . . ." Her
smile faded.

"Right. We should not be late there. Enrico is
ready?"

"He will not be long. We have time for coffee."

It was an abomination, an ordeal, to drink the man-
ufactured "instant brand," but the bars where they
could drink the real were too dangerous. She used to
joke that the absence of bar coffee in the mornings
was the ultimate sacrifice of her life.

"Get him moving. He has enough time to sleep in
the rest of the day, all the hours of the day." The kindness, the motherliness, had fled from her, the authority had taken over, the softness and the warmth and
the smell washed away with the shower water.

They must go to the Post to pay the quarterly telephone bill. Bills should always be paid promptly, she
said. If there are delays there is suspicion, and checks
are made and investigations are instituted. If they

went early, were there when the Post opened, then they would head the line at the *Conti Correnti* counter where the bills must be met in cash, and they would hang around for the least time, minimize the vulnerability. There was no need for her to go with Enrico and Giancarlo, but the apartment bred its own culture of claustrophobia, wearing and nagging at her patience.

"Hurry him up," she snapped, wriggling the jeans up the length of her thighs.

Stretching herself in the bed, arching her body under the silk of the pink nightgown, irritation and annoyance surfacing on her cream-whitened face, Violet Harrison attempted to identify the source of the noise. She had wanted to sleep another hour at least, a minimum of another hour. She rolled over in the double bed, seeking to press her face into the depth of the pillows, looking for an escape from the penetration of the sound that enveloped and cascaded round the room. Geoffrey had gone out quietly enough, put his shoes on in the hall, hadn't disturbed her. She had barely felt the snap of his quick kiss on her cheek before he left for the office, and the sprinkling of toast crumbs from his mouth.

She did not have to wake yet, not till Maria came and cleared the kitchen and washed up the plates from last night, and the lazy cow didn't appear before nine. God, it was hot! Not eight o'clock and already there was sweat on her forehead and at her neck and under her arms. Bloody Geoffrey, too mean to install air conditioning in the flat. She'd asked for it enough times, and he'd hedged and delayed and said the summer was too short and prattled about the expense and how long would they be there anyway. He didn't spend his day in a Turkish bath, he didn't have to walk around with a stain in the armpit and an itch in his pants. Air conditioning at the office, but not at home. No, that wasn't necessary. Bloody Geoffrey . . .

And the noise was still there.

. . . She'd go to the beach this morning. At least there was a wind at the beach. Not much of it, precious little. But some sort of cool from off the sea, and the boy might be there. He'd said he would be. Cheeky little devil, little blighter. Old enough to be his. . . . Enough problems without the clichés, Violet. All sinew and flat stomach and those ridiculous little curly hairs on his shins and thighs, chattering his compliments, encroaching on her towel. Enough to get his face slapped on an English summer beach. And going off and buying ice cream, three bloody flavors, my dear, and licking his own in that way. Dirty little boy. But she was a big girl now. Big enough, Violet Harrison, to take care of herself, and have a dash of amusement too. Needed something to liven things, stuck in this bloody flat. Geoffrey out all day and coming home and moaning how tired he was and what a boring day he'd had, and the Italians didn't know the way to run an office, and why hadn't she learned to cook pasta the way it was in the *ristorante* at lunchtime, and couldn't she use less electricity and save a bit on the petrol for her car. Why shouldn't she have a little taste of the fun, a little nibble?

Still that bloody noise down in the road. Couldn't erase it, not without getting out of bed and closing the window.

It took her a full minute to identify the source of the intrusion that had broken her rest. Sirens baying out their immediacy.

In response to a woman's emergency call, the first police cars were arriving at the scene of the kidnapping of Geoffrey Harrison.

2

The cars were Enrico's responsibility.

This week it was a Fiat 128, the fortnight before a *cinquecento* that was hardly large enough for the three of them, before that a Mirafiori, before that an Alfasud. Enrico's specialty. He would drift away from the apartment, be gone three or four hours, and then open the front door smiling away his success and urging Franca to come to the basement garage to inspect his handiwork. Usually it was night when he made the switches, with no preference between the city center and the distant southern suburbs. Good and clean and quick, and Franca would nod in appreciation and squeeze his arm and even the gorilla, even Enrico, would weaken and allow a trace of pleasure.

He was well satisfied with the 128, lucky to have found a car with a painstaking owner and an overhauled engine. Fast in acceleration, lively to the touch of his feet at the controls. Coming down off Vigna Clara, heading for the Corsa Francia, they seemed like three affluent young people, the right image, the right camouflage, blending into their surroundings. And if Giancarlo sitting hunched in the

back was unshaven, poorly dressed, he was not con-
spicuous because few of the sons of the *borghese* who
had their apartments on the hill would have bothered
with a razor in high summer; and if Franca, sitting in
the front passenger seat, had her hair tied with a
creased scarf, neither was that of importance because
the daughters of the rich did not display their finery
so early in the morning. Enrico drove fast and with
ease and confidence, understanding the mechanism of
the car, rejoicing in the freedom of escape from the
confines of the apartment. Too fast for Franca. She
slapped her hand on his wrist, shouted for him to be
more careful as he passed on the inside, wove among
the traffic, honked his way past the more sedate drivers.

"Don't be a fool, Enrico. If we touch something . . ."

"We never have, we won't now."

Enrico's familiar uncurbed response to correction.
As always, Giancarlo was perplexed that he treated
Franca with such small deference. Wouldn't grovel,
wouldn't dip his head in apology. Always ready with a
rejoinder. Brooding and generally uncommunicative,
as if breeding a private, secret hatred that he would
not share. His moments of humanity and humor were
fleeting. Giancarlo wondered what Enrico had
thought of the unmade bed, his absence in the night
hours, wondered if it stirred the pulse, kicked at the
indifference that Enrico presented to all around him.
He doubted it would. Self-sufficient, self-reliant, an
emotional eunuch with his shoulders rounded over the
wheel. Three weeks Giancarlo had been at the *covo*,
three weeks as guard at the safe house of the prize of
the moment, but Enrico had been with her many
months. There must be a trust and understanding between him and Franca, a tolerance between her and
this strange padding animal who left her side only

when she slept. It was beyond Giancarlo to unravel it;
this was a relationship too complex, too eccentric for
his comprehension.

The three young people in a car that carried a license plate and a valid tax disc on the windshield
merged without effort into the soft, flatulent society
with which they were at war. Two days earlier Franca
had exclaimed with triumph, shouted for Giancarlo
and Enrico to come to the side of her chair, and read
to them a statistic from the newspaper. In Italy, she
had declaimed, the increase of political violence over
the previous year's figures was greater than in any
country in the world.

"Even Argentina we lead, even the people in the
Monteneros. So we're wounding the pigs, hurting
them. And this year we wound them more, we hurt
them harder."

She had played her part in the compilation of those
figures, had not been backward in advancing herself,
and had earned the accolade bestowed on her by the
magazines and tabloids of "Public Enemy Number
One (Women)," and shrieked with laughter when she
read it for the first time.

"Chauvinist bastards. Typical of them that whatever I do I cannot be labeled as the greatest threat,
because I am a woman. They would choke rather than
admit that a woman can do them the greatest damage.
My title has to be embroidered with a category."

Eight times in the past twelve months she had led
the strike squads, the action commandos. Target am-
bushes. Bullets blasted into the lower limbs because
the sentence of maiming was thought more devastating on the psychology of the enemy than death. Eight
times, and still no sign that many beyond the hierarchy of the colossus knew of her existence, or cared.
Eight times, and still no indication that the uprising of
the proletariat forces was imminent. When she

thought like that, in the late evening when the apartment was subdued, when Enrico was sleeping, then she came for the boys who were Enrico's constant but changing companions. That was when she demanded the pawing, clumsy association with the juvenile, that her mood might be broken, her despair smashed under the weight of a young body.

These were hard and dangerous times for the movement. The odor of risk was in the air, constant after the kidnapping and execution of Aldo Moro, the mobilization of the forces of the state, the harrying of the groups. The gesture on the grand scale by the *Brigatisti* had been the taking of Moro and the use of the People's Court to try him and pass sentence. But there were many who disputed that this was the way to fight, who counseled caution, argued against the massive strike, and favored instead the process of wearing erosion. More men were rallied against them now; there was more awareness, more sophistication. It was a time for the groups to burrow deeper, and when they surfaced on the street it was in the knowledge that the risks were greater, the possibility of failure increased.

Swerving across the traffic lanes, Enrico brought the car to rest spanning the gutter, half on the pavement, half in the road. Franca wore a watch on her wrist, but still asked the question with the flow of irritation in her voice.

"How long till it opens?"

Enrico, accustomed to her, did not reply.

"Two minutes, perhaps three, if they begin on time," Giancarlo said.

"Well, we can't sit here all morning. Let's get there."

She slipped the door open, swung her feet out, and stretched on the pavement, leaving the boy to struggle at getting her seat forward so that he could follow her. As she started to walk away, Enrico was hurrying

after her because his place was at her side and she
should not walk without him. To Giancarlo her stride
was light and perfect in the taut and faded jeans. And
she should walk well, thought the boy, because she
does not carry the cold, clear shape of the P38 against
her flesh, buried beneath a shirt and trouser belt. Not
that Giancarlo would have been without his gun, not
now that it was his companion and possession. The
gun was more than a package of chewing gum, more
than a pack of Marlboros. Something that he could no
longer live without, something that had manipulated
itself as an extension of his personality. It owned a
divinity to Giancarlo, the P38 with its simplicity of
mechanism, its gas routes and magazine, its hair trigger, its power.

"No need for us all to be in there," she said when
Giancarlo was at her side, Enrico on the other flank,
and they were close to the Post doorway. "Get yourself across the road to the papers. And buy plenty if
we're to be stuck in the apartment for the rest of the
day."

He didn't wish to leave her side, to be parted, not
so soon, even if only for trifling moments. But it was
an instruction, a dismissal.

Giancarlo turned away. He faced the wide and
scurrying lanes of early morning traffic, looked for
the opening that would enable him to reach the raised
center bank of the Corsa Francia. There was a newspaper stand on the far side and nearly opposite the
Post. There was no hurry for him because however
early you come to the Post there will always be a man
there before you: The pathetic fools who are paid to
take the bills and the money for gas and telephone
and electricity because it is beneath the dignity of the
borghese to stand and wait in a line. He saw the opening, a slowing in the traffic, and launched himself
through the welter of hoods and bumpers and spirited

horns and spinning wheels. A hesitation in the center.
Another delay before the passage was clear to him
and he was off again, skipping, young-footed, across
the remaining roadway to the stand with its ebullience and gaudy decoration of magazine covers and
paperback books. He had not looked at Franca and
did not see the slowly cruising car of the *Squadra Mobile* far out in the traffic flow of the road behind him.
Giancarlo was unaware of the moment of surging danger, the startled gape of recognition on the face of the
Vice Brigadiere as he riveted on the features of the
woman, half in profile at the entrance to the Post and
waiting for the lifting of the steel shutter. Giancarlo
did not know as he took his place in the line to be
served that the policeman had savagely urged his
driver to maintain speed, create no warning as he rifled through the folder of photographs kept perma-
nently in the glove compartment of the car.

The boy was still shuffling forward as the first radio message was beamed to the Questura in central
Rome.

Giancarlo stood, hands in his pockets, mind on a
woman, as the radio transmissions hit the air. Cars
scrambling, accelerating. Guns armed and cocked.
Giancarlo searched his memories, finding again the
breasts and thighs of Franca. He did not protest as
the woman in the cream coat pushed past him without
ceremony. An opportunity was given him to sneer and
laugh that she should be discomfited. He knew the
newspapers he should buy: *L'Unita* of the PCI, the
Communists; *La Stampa* of Turin and the paper of
Fiat and Agnelli; *Republica* of the Socialists; *Popolo*
of the right; and *Messagero* of the left. Necessary always, Franca said, to have *Messagero* so that they
could browse through the "Chronaca di Roma" section
and read of the successes of their colleagues in different and separated cells, learn where the Molotovs had

landed in the night, what enemy had been hit, what friend taken. Five papers, a thousand lire. Giancarlo scratched in the hip pocket of his trousers for the money, filling his fist with a dribble of coins and the crumpled notes that he would need, counting out the money, standing his ground against the pushing of the man behind him. He would ask Franca to replace it, it was she who kept the cell's money, in the small wall safe in her room with the combination lock and the documents that could change their identities, and the files on targets of future attacks. She should replace the money—a thousand lire, three bottles of beer, if he went to the bar in the evening. It was all right for him to go out after the darkness, only Franca who should not. But he would not be drinking beer that evening, he would be sitting on the rug at the feet of the woman and close to her, rubbing his shoulder against her knee, resting his elbow on her thigh, waiting for the indications of her tiredness, her willingness for bed. He had been to the bar the night before, after their meal, and come back to find her drooped in the chair and Enrico sprawled and sleeping opposite her on the sofa with his feet on the cushions. She had said nothing, just taken his hand and turned off the lights and led him like a lamb to her room, and still not spoken as her hands had slipped down the length of his shirt to his waist.

The agony of waiting for her would be unendurable.

Giancarlo paid his money, stepped back from the counter with the folded newspapers and scanned the front page of *Messagero*. Carillo of Spain and Berlinguer of Italy were meeting in Rome, a Eurocommunist summit, middle-class, middle-aged, a betrayal of the true proletariat. A former minister of shipping was accused of having his hand in the till, what you'd expect from the bastard Democrazia Christiana. The steering

committee of the Socialists was sitting down with the
DC, games being played, circles of words. A banker
arrested for tax evasion. All the sickness, all the fetid
corruption was here, all the cancer of the world they
struggled to usurp. And then he found the headlines
that would bring the smile and the cold mirth to
Franca; the successes and the triumphs. One of their
own, Antonio de Laurentis of Napoli, missing inside
the maximum security jail on Favignana Island, described as "most dangerous," a leader of the NAP inside the prison, and they'd lost him. An executive of
Fiat shot in the legs in Turin, the thirty-seventh of the
year to have the people's sentence inflicted and the
calendar not past eight months.

He tucked the papers under his arm and looked out
across the road to the Post. Franca would be furious,
icy, if he kept her waiting. Cars were heavily parked
now around their 128. Two yellow Alfettas there and
a gray Alfasud, close to their own car. He wondered
whether they'd be able to get out. God, she'd be angry if they were boxed. Over the top of the traffic,
solid and impassable to him, Giancarlo saw Enrico
emerge from the doorway, cautious and wary. Two
paces behind him, Franca, cool, commanding. His
woman. Christ, she walked well, with the loping
stride, never an eye left or right.

And then the blur of movement. Shatteringly fast.
Too quick for the boy to comprehend. Franca and En-
rico were five, six meters from the entrance to the
Post. The doors of the three intruding cars flew open.
Men running, shouting. The moment of clarity for
Giancarlo came when he saw the guns in their hands.
The two at the front sprinted forward, then dived for
the crouch with the automatics held straight-arm to
the front. Enrico twisted his arm back for the hanging
flap of the shirttail and the concealed Beretta.

Across the traffic and pavement void Giancarlo

heard the shriek of the doomed Enrico. The cry for
the woman to run. The scream of the stag that will
stand against the dogs to give time for the hind to
hasten to the thickets. But her eyes were faster than
his, her mind quicker and better able to assess the
realities of the moment. As his gun came up to face
the aggressors she made the quicksilver decision of
survival. The boy saw her head duck and disappear
behind the roofs of the passing cars, and then in a gap
in the procession there was the vision of her, prone on
her stomach, hands on her head.

Enrico would not see her, would believe in his last
sand-running moments that his sacrifice had achieved
its purpose. Even as he fired he was cut down by the
swarm of bullets aimed at him. A thunderclap of gun-
fire. Enrico fell, hacked by the pain and rupture of
the bullets, writhing on the pavement as if trying to
shake away a great agony, rolling and rolling from his
back to his belly. The men ran forward, still suspicious that their enemy might bite, might hurt. There
was a trail of blood from Enrico's mouth, another two
from his chest that meandered together and then separated, and more crimson paths etching from his shattered legs. But his life lingered and a hand scrabbled
at the dirt to get nearer to the gun that had fallen
beyond reach. The men who towered above him wore
jeans and casual slacks and sweat shirts, and some
were unshaven or bearded or wore their hair long on
their shoulders. Nothing to tell them, to separate
them, from Enrico and Giancarlo. These were the men
of the *squadra antiterrorismo*, undercover, dedicated,
as hard and ruthless as those they opposed. A single
shot destroyed the frenzy of Enrico's groping hands.

An execution bullet. Just as it had been said it was
when the *carabinieri* dropped La Muscio on the
church steps near the Colloseo. Bastards, bastard pigs.

A man beside Giancarlo crossed himself in haste, a

private gesture in the glare of a public moment. Down
the road a woman bent in sickness. A priest in long
cassock abandoned his car in the road and ran forward. Two of the men covered the figure of Franca,
their guns roaming close to her head.

A terrible pain coursed through the boy as his
hands stayed clamped on the folded newspapers and
would not waver toward the gun buried in the flesh
of his buttock. He watched, part of the gathering
crowd, the bystander. He willed himself to run forward and shoot, because that was the job the movement had chosen for him, protector and bodyguard of
Franca Tantardini. He knew that if he did so his
blood would stream in the deep gutter, company for
Enrico. No thrust in his legs, no jolt in his arms, he
was a part of those who stayed and waited for the
show to end.

They pulled the woman, unresisting and limp, to
her feet, and dragged her to a car. Two had their
hands on her upper arms, another walked in front
with his fist caught in the long, blond strands of her
hair. There was a kick that missed her shins. He could
see that her eyes were open but bewildered, unrecog-
nizing as she went to the opened car door.

Would she have seen the boy she had opened herself to a short night before?

Would she have seen him?

He wanted to wave, give a sign, shout out that he
had not abandoned her. How to show that, Giancarlo?
Enrico dead, and Giancarlo alive and breathing, because he had stepped back, he had dissociated. How
to show it, Giancarlo? The car revved its engine and
its horn was raucous as it pulled out into the open
road, another Alfetta close in escort behind. The cars
swung across the central island, lurching and shaken,
and completed their turns in front of where Giancarlo
stood. The crowd around him pressed forward that

they should better see the face of the woman, and the
boy was among them. And then they were gone, and
one of the men held a machine gun at the car window.
A fanfare of sirens, an explosion of engine power. For
a few moments only he was able to follow the passage
of the cars in the growing traffic before they were
lost to him, and the sight of Enrico was taken from
him by a moving bus.

Deep in a gathering shame, numbed by the scope of
his failure, Giancarlo turned his back and began
slowly to walk away along the pavement. Twice he
bumped into men who hurried toward him, fearful
that they had missed the excitement and that there
was nothing remaining for them to see but the de-
scended theater curtain. Giancarlo was careful not to
run, just walked away, not thinking where he should
go, where he should hide. Too logical, such ideas for
his fractured thoughts to cope with. Left to him was
the image of the stunned, deep golden eyes of Franca
who was handcuffed and for whom a boy had not
stepped forward.

She had called him her little fox and scratched with
her nails at his body, and kissed him far down on the
flatness of his stomach, she had governed and tutored
him, and he drifted from the place, his feet leaded,
unseeing with the moisture in his eyelids.

The British Embassy in Rome occupies a prime site
of land set back from high railings and lawns and a
stone-skirted artificial lake at 80a Via XX Settembre.
The building itself, supported by pillars of gray cement and with arrow-slit windows, was conceived by
a noted English architect after the previous occupant
of the grounds had been destroyed by the gelignite of
Jewish terrorists . . . or guerrillas . . . or freedom
fighters, a stopover in their search for a homeland.
The architect had fashioned his designs at a time

when the representatives of the Queen in this city
were numerous and influential. Expense and expediency had whittled down the staff list. Many diplomats now doubled on two jobs which formerly had
been separate and independent.

The First Secretary who handled matters of political importance in Italian affairs had also taken under
his umbrella the area of liaison with the Questura and
the Viminale. Politics and security, the aesthetic and
the earthy, strange bed partners. That Michael Charlesworth's two previous foreign postings had been in
Vientiane and Rejkavik was a source of astonishment
neither to himself nor his colleagues. He was expected
to master the local intricacies of a situation inside
three years, and once accomplished he would antici-
pate, and be correct in his assumption, that he would
be sent to a country about which he had only the
most superficial knowledge. After Iceland and the
tangled arguments of the Cod War fracas with the island's fishing interests ranged against the need of his
countrymen to eat northern-water fish from old newspapers, the Roman politics and police had a certain
charm. He was not dissatisfied.

Charlesworth had demanded and won a raise in
rent allowance from his Ambassador and had been
able to set up a home with his wife in a high-ceilinged
apartment within earshot, but not sight, of the Piazza
del Popolo in the *centro storico*. The garaging of a car
there was next to impossible and while his wife's veteran *cinquecento* was parked beneath the conde-
scending eyes of the *Vigili Urbani* in the piazza, he
himself cycled to work on the machine he had first
used twenty years earlier as a Cambridge undergradu-
ate. The sight of the dark stripe-suited Englishman
peddling hard along the Corso d'Italia and the Via
Piave with collapsible umbrella and attaché case
clamped to the carrier over the mudguard of the rear

wheel was a pleasing sight to Italian motorists, who from respect for his efforts gave him a circumspection not readily available. Once the slopes of the Borghese Gardens had been topped, the bicycle provided Charlesworth with fast and intrepid transport, and often he was the first of the senior diplomatic staff to his desk.

A salute from the gatekeeper, the parking and pad-locking of the machine, the shaking free of trouser cuffs from the clips, a wave to security in the ground-floor hall, a gallop up two flights of stairs, and he was striding along the back second-floor corridor. Fully three doors away he heard the telephone ringing from his office. Fast with the key into the lock, swinging the door open to confront the noise, abandoning the briefcase and umbrella to the floor, he lunged for the receiver.

"*Pronto*," panting a little, not the way he liked to be.

"Signor Charlesworth?"

"Yes."

"*La Questura. Dottore Giuseppe Carboni . . . momento.*"

Delay. First a crossed line. Apology, rampant click-ing and interruption on the line before Charlesworth heard the Questura switchboard announce with pride to Carboni that the task was accomplished, the con-nection successful. They were not friends, the police-man and Michael Charlesworth, but known to each other, acquainted. Carboni would know that Charles-worth was happier in English, that language courses were not always victorious. With a faint American ac-cent Carboni spoke.

"Charlesworth, that is you?"

"Yes." Caution. No man is happy talking to the po-lice, least of all to foreign police at fourteen minutes past eight in the morning.

"I have bad news for you, my friend. Bad news to give you for which I am sorry. You have a businessman in the city, a resident, a man called Harrison. He is the financial comptroller of ICH in EUR, International Chemical Holdings. They are at Viale Pasteur in EUR, many of the multinationals favor that area . . ." What's the silly blighter done, thought Charlesworth resigned, socked a copper, drunk himself stupid? No, couldn't be that, not if Carboni was calling, not if it was at that level. ". . . I regret very much, Charlesworth, to have to tell you that Geoffrey Harrison was kidnapped this morning. Armed men, forced from his car near his home."

"Christ," muttered Charlesworth, low but audible.

"I understand your feelings. He is the first of the foreign residents, the first of the foreign commercials to be affected by this plague."

"I know."

"We are doing everything we can. There are road blocks . . ." The distant voice tailed and died, as if Carboni knew the futility of boasting to this man. He came again. "But you know, Charlesworth, these people are very organized, very sophisticated. It is unlikely, and you will understand me, it is unlikely that what we can do will be sufficient."

"I know," said Charlesworth. An honest man he was talking to, and what to say that wouldn't be churlish. "I am confident that you will exercise all your agencies in this matter, completely confident."

"You can help me, Charlesworth. I have called you early, it is not half an hour since the attack, and we have not yet been to the family. We have not spoken to his wife. Perhaps she does not speak Italian, perhaps she speaks only English, we thought it better if someone from the embassy be with her first, to give her the news."

The dose prescribed for diplomats seeking night-

mares was purveying ill tidings to their own nationals
far from home. A stinking, lousy job and indefinite
involvement. "That was very considerate of you."

"It is better also that you have a doctor go to her
this morning. In many cases we find that necessary in
the first hours. It is a shock . . . you will understand."

"Yes."

"I do not want to lecture at this stage, because soon
you will be busy, and I am busy myself in this matter,
but you should make a contact with Harrison's em-
ployer. It is a London-based company, I believe. If
they have taken the employee of a multinational they
will be asking for more than poor Harrison's bank balance can provide. They will believe they are ransom-
ing the company. It could be expensive, Charlesworth."

"You would like me to alert the company to this situation?" Charlesworth scribbled hard on his memo
note pad.

"They must make their attitude clear, and quickly.
When the contact is made they must know what attitude they will take."

"What a way to start the bloody day. Well, they'll
ask me this, and it may color their judgments, you
would presume that this is the work of a professional,
an experienced gang?"

There was a faint laugh, quavering over the telephone line before Carboni replied, "How can I say,
Charlesworth? You read our newspapers, you watch
the *Telegiornale* in the evening. You know what we
are up against. You know how many times the gangs
are successful, how many times we beat them. We do
not hide the figures, you know that, too. If you look at
the results you will see that a few of the gangs are
amateur . . . you English, always you want to reduce
everything to sport . . . and we catch those ones.

Does that give us a winning score? I would like to say so, but I cannot. It is very hard to beat the professionals. And you should tell to Harrison's firm when you speak with them that the greater are the police efforts to release him, then so too is the greater risk to his life. They should not forget that."

Charlesworth sucked at his pencil top. "You would expect the company to pay what they are asked to?"

"We should talk of that later. Perhaps it is premature at this moment." A gentle correction, made with kindness, but a correction nevertheless. Not manners to talk of the will and the beneficiaries while the corpse is still warm. "But I do not think that we would expect the family or the company of a foreigner to adopt a differing procedure to that taken by our own families when they are faced with identical problems."

The invitation to pay. It wouldn't be made clearer than that. The invitation not to be stubborn and principled. Pragmatism winning through, and a bloody awful scene for a policeman to have to get his nose into.

"There may be some difficulty. We don't do it like that in England."

"But you are not in England, Charlesworth," a hint of impatience from Carboni. "And in England you have not always been successful. I remember two cases, two ransom demands unmet, two victims found, two deaths. It is not a straightforward area of decision, and not one which we can debate. Later perhaps, but now I think there are other things that you wish to do."

"I appreciate greatly what you have done, Dottore."

"It is nothing." Carboni rang off.

Five minutes later Charlesworth was in the ground-floor hall of the embassy waiting for the arrival of the

Ambassador. Still shrill in his ears the piercing protests of the woman he had telephoned.

Who was going to pay?

Didn't they know they hadn't any money?

Nothing in the bank, just a few savings.

Who was going to take responsibility?

Not a conversation that Charlesworth had relished,
and his calming noises had been shouted out till he'd
said he had to go because he must see the Ambassador. No more blustering after that; just a deep sobbing, a pain echoing down the wire to him, as if some
dam of control and inhibition had been broken.

Where are you, you poor sod? What are they doing
to you? Must be a terrible loneliness, mind-bending,
horrific. And damn all for comfort. Doesn't even know
that idiots like Michael Charlesworth and Giuseppe
Carboni are flapping their wings and running in circles. Better he didn't know it, make him turn over and
give up. And what chance of the Ambassador being in
before nine? What bloody chance?

They'd tied him expertly as they would have done a
lively bullock going to slaughter. Not a casual job, not
just whipped a length of rope round his legs and left
it to chance.

Geoffrey Harrison had lain perhaps twenty minutes
on the coarse sacking on the van floor before he had
tried to move his ankles and wrists. The effect of the
chloroform was dissipating, the shock of capture and
the numbness of disorientation sliding. The nobbled
bones on the insides of his ankles, wrapped in cord,
caught hard against each other, digging at the flesh. A
set of metal handcuffs on the wrists, set too tight for
him, pressing on the veins. Tape, adhesive and broad,
was across his mouth and forced him to breathe
through his nose and reduced any sounds he could
make to a jumbled, incomprehensible moan. One man

had trussed him swiftly before the chloroform had gone to be replaced by the desperate passiveness of terror in an alien surrounding. And they'd hooded him, reducing his horizons to the limited things he could touch and smell. The hood was cool and damp, as if it had spent the night in the grass and been subject to the light dew and been retrieved before the coming of the drying warmth of the early sun. Because of the handcuffs behind his back, he lay on his right side, where the undulations of the road surface caused his shoulder to impact through the sacking against the ribbed metal floor.

They seemed to move at a constant speed, as if far from the reach of traffic lights and road junctions, and many times Harrison heard the whine of overtaking engines; occasionally the van shuddered, as if under strain, and pulled out to the left. Just once they stopped for a short time and he heard voices, a rapid exchange, before the van was moving again, riding through its gears, getting under way and back to the undisturbed progress. He thought about and conjured a route along the Raccordo Annulare, with its festoons of white and pink oleander between the central divider, and imagined the halt must have been at the toll gate for entry to an autostrada. Could be north on the Florence road, or west for L'Aquila and the Adriatic coast, or south for Naples. Could be any bloody direction, any road the animals wanted to use. Had thought he'd been clever and superior in his intellect to make the calculations, and then came the wave of antipathy, carried on the wing. What did it matter, which direction they took? Did it matter a damn? Not an iota, Geoffrey. A futile and petty exercise because the control of his destiny was removed. Turned him into a bloody vegetable. Anger summoned for the first time, and the fury spent itself straining against the ankle cords, striving to bite with his teeth against the tape across his mouth. Created a force and a power that struggled even as the tears rose and welled. In one convulsion, one final effort to win even the minimum of freedom for any of his limbs, he arched his back, forced his muscles.

Couldn't shift. Couldn't move. Couldn't change anything.

Pack it in, Geoffrey, you're being bloody pathetic. Once more?

Forget it. They don't come with machine guns and chloroform and then find, surprise, surprise, that they don't know how to tie knots.

As he sagged back, his head thumped on the metal floor above the reach of the sacking and he lay still with the ache and the throb in his temples and the smell of the hood in his nose. Lay still because he could do nothing else.

3

The immediate sense of survival was uppermost now in the mind of Giancarlo.

The instinct of the stoat or the weasel that has lost its mate and must abandon its den, move on. But the creature has no knowledge, no instinct of where it should go, only that it must creep with stealth away from the scene of the vengeance of its enemies. He wanted to run, to outstrip the pedestrians who cluttered and barred the pavements, but his training won. He did not hurry. He strolled, because he must blend and forsake the identity bestowed on him by the P38.

The noise and confusion and shouting of the beginning of a new day swamped him. The horns of impatient motorists. The crashing intrusion of the *alimentari* shutters rising in their doorways and windows to display the cheeses and hams and tins and bottles. The arguments that spilled from the bars. Confident, secure sounds, belonging and with a place and a right to be there, swarming around Giancarlo. The boy tried to shut inside himself his concentration and avoid the cancer of these people who swept and surged past him. He belonged to no part of them.

Since the NAP had drifted into existence in the early nineteen seventies, coalesced from a meeting of minds and aspirations to an organization, it had derived its principal security from the cell system. Nothing new, nothing revolutionary in that; laid down by Mao and Ho and Guevara. Standard in the theoretical treatises. Separated in their cells, the members had no need for the identity of other names, for the location of other houses. It was essential procedure, and when one was taken, then the wound to the movement could be swiftly cauterized. Franca was their cell leader. She alone knew the hidden places where munitions and materials were stored, the telephone numbers of the policy committee, and the lists of addresses. She had not shared with Enrico, much less with the boy, the probationer, because neither required such information.

He could not go back to the flat, not the previous one where he had lived with a girl and two boys, as that had been closed and abandoned. He could not tour the cars and streets of Pietralata behind the Tiburtina station and ask for them by name, wouldn't know where to begin, and who to ask. Made him shudder as he walked, the depths of the isolation that the movement had so successfully cloaked him with.

Where among the streaming, scrambling crowds that passed on either side of him did he find the nod and handshake of recognition? Frightening to the boy, because without Franca he was truly alone. Storm clouds rising, sails full, rudder flapping, and the rocks high and sharp and waiting for him.

Giancarlo Battestini, twenty years old.

Short and without weight, a physical nonentity. A body that looked perpetually starved, a face that seemed forever hungry, a boy that a woman would want to take in and fatten because she would have a

fear that unless she hurried he might wither and fade.
Dark hair above the growth of his cheeks that was
curled and untidy. A sallow, wan complexion as if
the sun had not sought him out, avoided the lusterless
skin. Acne spots at his chin and the sides of his mouth
that were red and angry against the surrounding flesh
and to which his fingers moved with embarrassed frequency. The pale and puckered line across the bridge
of his nose that deviated on across the upper cheek-
bone under his right eye was his major distinguishing
mark. The *polizia* of the *Primo Celere* to thank for the
scar, the baton charge across the Ponte Garibaldi
when the boy had slipped in headlong flight and
turned his ankle. He had been a student then, enrolled
two terms at the University of Rome, choosing the
study of psychology for no better reason than that the
course was a long one and his father could pay for
four years of education. And what else was there to
do?

The university with its bulging inefficiency had
seemed to Giancarlo a paradise of liberation. Lectures
too clogged to attend unless you took a seat or standing place a full hour before the professor came. Tu-
torials that were late or canceled. Exams that were
postponed. A hostel within walking distance in the Viale Regina Elena where the talk was long and bold
and brave.

Heady battles they had fought around the university that winter. The Autonomia in the vanguard, they
had driven the *polizia* back from the front facade of
arches and across the street to their trucks. They had
expelled by force Luciano Lama, the big union man
of the PCI, who had come to talk to them on modera-
tion and conformity and responsibility; thrown him
out, the turncoat Communist in his suit and polished
shoes. Six hundred formed the core of the Autonomia,
the separatists, and Giancarlo had first hung round

their fringe, then attended their meetings, and finally
sidled toward the leaders and stammered his pledge
of support. Warm acceptance had followed. A paradise indeed to the boy from the seaside at Pescara
where his father owned a shop and carried a stock of
fine cotton dresses and blouses and skirts in summer,
and wool and leather and suede in winter.

Hit and run. Strike and retreat. Formidable the *polizia* looked with their white bullet-proof tunics hanging to their knees and their stovepipe face masks behind which they felt a false invulnerability. But they
could not run in their new and expensive equipment,
could only fire the gas and beat the clubs on the plastic shields. They were loath to follow the kids, the
Pied Pipers, when the range of the pistols and the gas
diminished.

A scarf tight across his face for protection both
from press photographs and the gas, Giancarlo had
never before experienced such orgasmic, pained excitement as when he had sprinted forward on the
bridge and launched the bottle with its liter of gasoline and smoldering rag at the *Primo Celere* huddled
behind their armored jeep. A shriek of noise had
erupted as the bottle splintered. The flame scattered.
There was a roar of approval from behind as the boy
stood his ground in defiance while the gas shells flour-
ished about him. Then the retaliation. Twenty of them
running, and Giancarlo had turned for his escape. The
desperate, terrifying moment when the ground was
rising, space under his feet, control lost, and in his
ears the drumming of the boots that were in pursuit.
His hands covering his head were pulled away as they
put the baton in, and there was blood cool across his
face and sweet in his mouth, and blows to the leg,
kicks to the belly. Voices from the south, from the
peasant south, from the servants of the Democrazia

Christiana, from the workers who had been bought and were too stupid to know it.

Two months in the Regina Coeli jail awaiting his court appearance.

Seven months imprisonment for throwing the Molotov to be served in the Queen of Heaven.

A whore of a place that jail. Intolerable heat and stench through that first summer when he had bunked in a cell with two others. Devoid of draft and privacy, assimilated into a world of homosexuality, thieving, deprivation. Food inedible, boredom impossible, company illiterate. Hatred and loathing bit deep in the boy when he was the guest of the Queen of Heaven. Hatred and loathing of those who had put him there, of the *polizia* who had clubbed him and spat in his face in the truck and laughed in their dialect at the little, humbled *intelletuale*.

Giancarlo sought his counterstrike and found the potential for revenge in the top floor cells of the B wing where the men of the Nuclei Armati Proletaria were incarcerated, some on remand, some sentenced. They could read in the boy's eyes and the twist of his lower lip that here was a progeny who could be useful and exploited. He learned in those heated, sweating cells the theory and the practice, the expertise and the strategy of urban guerrilla conflict. A new recruit, a new volunteer. The men gave him diagrams to memorize of the mechanism of weapons, lectured him in the study of concealment and ambush, droned at him of the politics of their struggle, hectored him with the case histories of corruption and malpractice in government and capitalist business. These men would not see the fruits of their work, but took comfort that they had found one so malleable, so supple to their will. They were pleased with what they saw. Word of his friendship spread along the landings of his own wing. The homosexuals did not sidle close and flash their

hands at his genitals, the thieves left undisturbed the
bag under his bunk where he kept his few personal
possessions, the *agenti* did not bully.

In the months in jail he passed from the student of
casual and fashionable protest to the political militant.

His parents never visited him in the Queen of
Heaven. He had not seen them since they had stood at
the back of the court, half masked from his sight by
the guard's shoulders. Anger on his father's face, tears
running the mascara on his mother's cheeks. His father wore a Sunday suit, his mother dressed in a black
coat as if that would impress the magistrate. The
chains on his wrists had been long and loose, and they
gave him the opportunity to raise his right arm,
clenched fist, the salute of the left, the gesture of the
fighter. Screw them. Give them something to think
about when they took the autostrada back across the
mountains to Pescara. And his picture would be in the
Adriatic paper and would be seen by the ladies who
came to buy from the shop and they would whisper
and titter behind their hands. In all his time in the jail
he received only one letter, written in the spider hand
of his brother Fabrizio, a graduate lawyer and five
years his elder. There was a room for him at home,
Mama still kept his bedroom as it had been before he
had gone to Rome. Papa would find work for him.
There could be a new start, he would be forgiven.
Methodically, Giancarlo had torn the single sheet of
paper into many pieces that flaked to the cell floor.

When the time came for Giancarlo's release he was
clear on the instructions that had been given him from
the men in B wing. He had walked out through the
steel gates and onto the Lungotevere and not looked
back at the crumbling plaster of the high ochre-
stained walls. The car was waiting as he had been
told it would, and a girl had moved across the back
seat to make room for him. First names they called

themselves by, and they took him for a coffee and poured a measure of Scotch whisky into the foaming milk of the *cappuchino* and brought him cigarettes that were imported and expensive.

Half a year, now, of being hunted, half a year of running and caution and care, and he had wondered what was the life expectancy of freedom, thought of how long his wings would stay unclipped by cell bars and locked doors.

Once he had been in the same flat as the one they called the Chief. Seen his profile through an opened door, bushy-bearded, short, vital in the eyes and mouth, and who stayed now on the island prison of Asinara and who, they said, had been betrayed.

Once he had strayed into the bedroom of a *covo* carrying the cigarettes he had been sent to buy and looking for the man who had dispatched him and recognized the sleeping form of the one they said was expert with explosives, and he also, they said, had been betrayed to a life sentence on the island.

Once he had been taken to stand for a moment on the steps of a church where Antonio La Muscio and Maria Vianale had sat and eaten plums on a summer evening, and he now in his grave with half a *carabinieri* magazine to put him there, and the fruit unfinished, and La Vianale rotting in the jail at Messina.

Hard and dangerous times, only recently made safer by the skill and calm of Franca.

But as the net grew closer, shrinking around the group, Franca had disowned the safety of inactivity.

"Two hundred and fifty political prisoners of the left in the jails, and they believe we are close to the moment of our destruction, that is what they say on the RAI, that is what they say at the DC congress. So we must fight, demonstrate beyond their concealment that we are not crushed, not neutered."

Franca did not talk in the slogans of the kids of his

first *covo*. She had no use for the parrot words of "enemies of the proletariat," the "forces of repression,"
"capitalist exploitation." Confused the boy because
they had become a part of his life, a habit of his
tongue, cemented to his vocabulary. She vented her
anger without words, displayed her dedication with
the squeezed, arctic index finger of her right hand.
Three bedridden victims in the Policlinico, another in
a private room of the nursing home on the Trionfale,
they were her vengeance. Men who might never walk
again, would not run with their children, and one
among them who would not sleep with and satisfy his
wife.

Inevitable that it must end. The risks too great, the
pace too heady, the struggle unequal.

Giancarlo crossed a road, not looking for the cars,
nor for the green-lit *Avanti* sign, not hearing the
shriek of the brakes, ignorant of the bellowed insult.
Perhaps he would have brought her flowers that evening. Perhaps he would have gone to the piazza and
bought from the gypsy woman some violets or a sprig
of pansies. Nothing gaudy, nothing that would win a
sneer from her. Simple flowers from the fields that
she might smile and her face soften, that would erase
the harshness of her mouth which he had first seen as
she walked from the shooting of the personnel officer.

And flowers would not help her now, not the flowers of the boy who had declined to step forward, who
had walked away.

There was a hunger already in his stomach and little chance to appease it. His wallet still lay in the
room beside his unused bed on the small table. There
was some loose change in his hip pocket and the *min-
iassegni* notes that were worth not more than a
hundred and a hundred and fifty lira apiece. In total
he had enough for a bowl of pasta or a sandwich, and
a coffee or a beer, and after that nothing. He must

keep two hundred lira free for the afternoon paper when it came to the newsstands. *Paese Sera* or *Momento Sera*, he must read what they wrote, find what information they carried. His wallet was in the flat. His wallet that he touched and handled through the day, held with the pores of his fingers, the contour whirls that were only his own and that the police fingerprint dust would find and feed to the files. They had taken his fingerprints months back in the police station after his arrest.

They will have your name by the afternoon, Giancarlo, and your photograph. All they want about you, they will have.

Time to begin to think again, to throw off the weight of depression and self-examination. Stupid bastard, take ahold. Behave like a man of the NAP. Save yourself and survive.

Where to start?

The university.

In the vacation, in the summer? When there is no one there?

Where else? Where else do you go to, Giancarlo? Home to Mama, to tell her it was all a mistake, that you met bad people . . . ?

Perhaps there would be someone at the university.

The university offered the prime opportunity to him of an unquestioned bed among the students of the Autonomia whom he had known many months before. He had not been there since his release and he would have to exercise all care as he approached the faculties. A campus heavy with informers and policemen who carried books and mingled. But if he could find the right boys, then they would hide him, and they would respect him because he had graduated from the sit-ins and the lock-ins and the Molotovs to the real war of the fully fledged, of the men. They would look after him at the university.

* * *

Because he reported directly to the Minister of the
Interior, Francesco Vellosi's office was on the second
floor of the lowering gray stonework of the Viminale.
His subordinates were found either a kilometer away
at the Questura, or far to the west in the Criminalpol
building at EUR. But the *capo della squadra antiterrorismo* was required to be close to the seat of power,
just down the corridor from it, which served to emphasize the recognition of the threat to the country
posed by the rash of urban guerrilla groups. A fine
room he occupied, reached through high double doors
of polished wood with an ornate ceiling from which
hung electric bulbs set in a shivering chandelier of
light, oil paintings on the walls, a wide desk with an
inlaid leather top, easy chairs for the visitors, a coffee
table for magazines and ashtrays, a photograph of the
President, and signed, that hung between the tall twin
windows. Francesco Vellosi, thirty years in the police,
detested it, and would have given much to have exchanged the brilliance of the surroundings for a shirtsleeves working area. The room took the sun in the
afternoons, but on this July morning the brightness
had not yet reached it.

The radio telephone in his armor-plated car had
warned Vellosi when midway between his bachelor
flat and place of work that his men had met with a
major and significant success that morning, and waiting for him when he had bustled into the office had
been the initial incident report and photostats of the
files held on Franca Tantardini and Enrico Panicucci.

Vellosi gutted the paperwork with enthusiasm. A
bad winter and spring they had had, built on the de-
pressive foundation of the loss the previous year of
Aldo Moro. There had been arrests, some significant,
some worthless, but the plague of bombings and shoot-
ings had kept at its headlong pace, prompting the dis-

quiet of the deputies in the chamber of the Democrazia Christiana, the ridicule of the newspapers, and the
perpetual demand of his Minister for solutions. Always they came to Vellosi, hurrying in pursuit of the
news of a new outrage. He was long tired of trying to
find the politician or the senior civil servant who
would take the responsibility for what he called the
necessary methods, the hard and ruthless crackdown
that he believed necessary; he was still looking for his
man.

Here at last was good news, and he would issue his
own order that the photographers should have a good
look at the Tantardini woman. The national habit of
self-denigration went too deep, was on display too often, and it was good when the opportunity presented
itself to boast a little and swagger with success.

A tall, heavily built boar of a man, the roughness of
his figure modified by the cut of his jacket, the elegance of his silk tie, Vellosi shouted his acknowledgment across the room to the light tap at his door. The
men who entered the presence were from a different
cast. Two in tattered suede boots, two in canvas training shoes, faded jeans, a variety of T-shirt colors, an
absence of razors. The hard men whose faces seemed
relaxed while the eyes were ever alert and alive and
bright. Vellosi's lions, the men who fought the war far
below the surface of the city's life. The sewer rats, because that was where they had to exist if they were to
find the rodent pest.

The four eased a careful way across the thickened
carpet, and when he gestured to them, sat with care
on the chairs that were deep and comfortable. They
were the officers of the squad that had taken the
woman, destroyed the animal Panicucci, and they had
come to receive their plaudits, tell first hand of the
exploit, and bring a little milk and honey to the days
of Vellosi in the Viminale.

He wriggled with pleasure in his seat as the work of the morning was recounted. Nothing omitted, nothing spared, so that he could savor and live in his mind the moment that Panicucci and the woman had emerged from the Post. As it should be, and he'd wheel them in to shake the hand of the Minister and blunt the back-stab knives that were always honing for him. He limited himself for the briefest of interruptions, preferring to let the steady river of the story bathe him in the triumph of his squad.

The telephone interrupted the reverie.

Vellosi's face showed his annoyance at the interference; that of a man who has optimism and is on the couch with his girl when the doorbell sounds. He waved his hand to halt the flow, would return to it as soon as the business of the call was dispatched. It was the Questura.

Had Vellosi's men been certain when they took the woman that there was not another boy with her? Had they missed one?

The *covo* had been found, the address taken from the telephone slip just paid by the Tantardini woman. The *polizia* had visited the flat and found inside the clothes of another boy, far too small for those of Panicucci. There was a woman on the second floor of the block, sick, and from the moment she was dressed in the morning, she would sit and watch from her window the passing street; when the *ragazzi* drove their car from the garage there were always three, and three that morning. Fingerprinting had begun, there was another set and fresh, not to be confused with Tantardini's and Panicucci's. The *polizia* had been careful to check with the woman at the window the time of the departure of the car from the block and compare it with the timing of the incident at the Post. It was their opinion that there had been no time for a substantial deviation to drop off a second male.

A cold sponge was squeezed over Vellosi.

"Have you a description of this second man?"

"The woman says that he is not a man, just a boy really. There are many identity cards in the flat, one of the photographs may be genuine, but we are working on a photo-fit now. Your own people are there now, no doubt they will brief you. The boy, we think, is eighteen years, perhaps nineteen. We thought you would like to know."

"You are very kind," Vellosi said quietly, then hammered the telephone down.

He ranged his eyes over the men in front of him, brought them sitting upright and awkward on the edge of their seats.

"We missed one." Spoken with a coldness, the pleasure eroded from the session.

"There was no one else at the Post. The car had no driver waiting in it, only the two came out. They were well clear of the doorway when we moved." Defense from a man who an hour earlier had faced the barrel of a Beretta and who had out-thought, out-maneuvered his opponent and fired for his own survival.

"Three came from the flat. The car went straight to the Post."

The inquisition was resented. "He was not there when we came. And after the shooting there were some of our people who watched the crowd as is standard. Nobody ran from the scene."

Vellosi shrugged, resigned. Like eels, these people, always one of them to wriggle away, impose himself between the finest meshes. Always one of a group so that you could never cut off the head and know that the body was beyond another spawning. "He is very young, this one that we have lost."

Three of the men stayed silent, peeved that the moment of accolade had turned to recrimination. The fourth spoke up, undaunted by his superior's grimness. "If it is a boy, then it will have been her runner, there to fetch and carry for her and to serve in the whore's bed. Always she has one like that. Panicucci she did not use, only the young ones she liked. It is well known in the NAP."

"If you are right, it is not a great loss."

"It is an irritation, nothing more. The fat cat we have, the gorilla we have killed, that the flea is out is only a nuisance."

Not yet ten o'clock and there were smiles as Vellosi produced the bottle from the lower drawer of his desk, and then reached again for the small cut-glass tumblers. Too early for champagne, but Scotch was right. The brat had broken the pattern of perfection, but the best of the day had gone before.

Only a nuisance, only an irritation, the missing of the boy.

He knew they had been traveling many hours because the van floor on which he lay was warmed by the outside sun even through the layer of sacking. The air around Geoffrey Harrison was thick with gasoline fumes, pricking against his skin as if all the cool and freshness of the morning's start had been expelled. Painfully hot under the weight of the hood over his head, he sometimes had begun to pant for air with accompanying hallucinations that his lungs might not cope, that he might suffocate in the dark put around him. Occasionally he heard two slight voices in conversation, but the words, even had he been able to understand them, were muffled by the engine noise. Two different tones, that was all he could distinguish. And they talked infrequently, the two men riding in the seats in front. Long periods of quiet between them and then a brief flurry of chatter, as if something that they passed took their fancy, attracted their eyes.

The motion of the van was constant, leaving nothing from its progress to arouse him, releasing him to his thoughts, abandoning him to his fantasies. It was as if he were a package of freight being transported to a far destination by two men who had neither interest in nor concern for him and thought only of their delivery time.

Many times Harrison had read in the *Daily News* and the *Daily American* and in the Italian papers, which he struggled with in the office, of the techniques practiced by the flourishing Italian kidnap gangs. In the bar of the Olgiata Golf Club, little America, little Midwest, where there were Tom Collins and Bourbon mixes he had joined the drift of conversation when the foreigners had talked of the Italian disease. Different setting, different values; easy then to relate all sickness to the bloody inefficiency of Italians, and what else to expect when you're halfway to the Middle East. Well down the road to Damascus here, right? Wasn't it a scandal, the transatlantic executives would say, that a fellow can get picked off the street and have to cough up a million dollars, however many noughts that was in lira, to get himself back to his wife and kids? And wasn't it about time that something was done about it? Couldn't happen at home, of course—not in London, not in Los Angeles . . . not in Birmingham, not in Boston. And there'd always be one there, elbow at the bar and the face puffed with authority, to drop his voice beneath the reach of the Italian members, and lean forward and whisper, "Wouldn't happen if old Musso was running the place. And it's what they need again. A damn great shock up the ass, and someone like Musso to give it to them. Not exactly Musso, because he was an idiot, but someone with a damn great stick." Simple answers, more drinks, and none of them had an idea. He wondered whether they'd remember him; young Harrison, quite a junior fellow, didn't make it up this way that

often, always hanging on the edge of a chat, and a
wife with bright lipstick. Just a drinking member.

Perhaps you're lucky, Geoffrey, perhaps you're
lucky you didn't struggle. Put up a bit of a show, but
not much. Just enough for vague self-respect. Remember the picture in the paper of the man from Milan,
Geoffrey, the man who'd fought back and mixed it.
Stone dead, cold dead, and in a box with the wife in
black and the kids holding her hands walking behind.
At least you're bloody alive. Because they don't muck
about, these people, not governed by Queensberry nor
any other set of rules. Hard, vicious bastards. Remember the black and white images on the television in
the living room; the body of little Christina, eighteen
years old, being dragged out of the rubbish heap and
the ransom had been paid. Remember the race-course
king; made the front pages, trussed like a chicken and
a hood on him, just like you are now except that he
had a hunk of cement to float him down in the lake
near Como. Remember the boy in the village in Calabria with his ear sliced away to encourage his father
to dip deeper into the family savings . . .

Horrible bastards.

Someone would have to pay. Someone would have
to pay if he were to come through, see the sunlight
again, breathe the air. The company would have to
pay, fourteen bloody years he'd bent his back for
them. These people knew how much you had, didn't
fool about with the wrong man, didn't set out to tap
an empty bank balance. Weren't beginners, weren't
learning the trade. They'd know where the money
was, what the company could spill. Go to Board level,
wouldn't it. Up to the Chairman and the Managing
Director, all the Rolls Royce and Bentley brigade. It
would be the decision of men who'd never met Geoffrey Harrison, never heard of him, never known his

existence. They'd weigh the issues, consider the position.

Pray God there isn't some pompous fool in there.

What do you mean?

Well, some stupid ass with a good lunch inside him and letters after his name who wants to talk about the principle of paying.

What do you mean?

Well, if some ape says it's not right to pay, that you have to stand up to these people, that if you give way now, what do you do the next time.

They wouldn't say that, would they, not really say that?

They're not where you are, Geoffrey. They're in a board room, not in handcuffs. They may have cut themselves shaving, but they haven't had a bloody great fist slammed in. Some of them are bloody geriatric. All they know about the sodding country is what they see on a balance sheet.

They wouldn't be so stupid, they couldn't. Don't they know people get chopped if there's no payola, don't they know that?

Calm it. Not bloody helping is it? They'll know it, and if they don't there'll be someone there to tell them.

You're sure?

I'm sure, I'm certain.

How can you know?

I'm certain because I have to believe that, otherwise we go stark bloody mad, straight insane.

The sun, without remorse or hindrance, playing on its roof, baking the closed interior, the van headed at a steady and unremarkable one hundred and ten kilometers per hour southward along the Autostrada del Sol.

4

His Excellency, the Ambassador of Her Brittanic Majesty, who had known the tap of her sword on his right shoulder and who had kissed her hand and valued his audience, was a man who admired discipline of action and protocol of approach. He had not concerned himself with disguising his distaste at what he regarded as the breathy intervention of young Charlesworth when he was only one foot out of his official burnished transport. He had been short with his First Secretary, permitted only the briefest of resumés, failed to raise his eyebrows in either shock or astonishment. And as he had marched away, smiling at the doorman, with Charlesworth snapping like a lapdog at his heels, he had suggested that something on paper by lunchtime would satisfy his requirements for information.

Charlesworth cursed himself for his flustered account as he strode down the drive to the security lodge, for his failure to interest his superior, regretting that he had allowed himself to be put down as a bubbling child is by an overburdened parent. He recalled that the Ambassador was hosting a luncheon party that day; the newly appointed Foreign Minister would

be at his right hand, the guest of honor. Present would
be the senior members of the diplomatic corps, a
smattering of ranking civil servants, the best bone
china and the silverware out from the cupboard. The
Ambassador had his priorities, Charlesworth growled
to himself. The soup shouldn't be too salted, the plates
must be warm, the wine chilled, the conversation
clever. Too much on his mind to worry about the fears
of a hysterical woman, and a man trussed and perhaps
half-dead who was experiencing the greatest degree of
terror he had known in his life. Far too busy for such
sordidness, and a piece of paper with some aptly chosen words presented before the sherry flowed would
be sufficient.

Charlesworth dived out into the road beyond the
regimented railings of the embassy, scanning the
traffic that burst through the arches of the ancient,
reddened brick city wall. Getting a taxi would need
the luck of old Jupiter. And luck was with him, the
yellow Fiat snaking to the pavement, and he waved
frantically and hurried toward its stopping point. He
saw the face in the back, mauve and pink shades that
were equal. "Buster" Henderson: Military Cross in
Korea God knows how many years ago and for doing
something nobody sane would have entertained; military attaché, half colonel. Always took a cab in, and
one home in the afternoon as well. Charlesworth
didn't know how he could afford it, not that and the
gin as well.

"In a hurry, young man?" Charlesworth detested the
way the older staff regarded him as a juvenile. "Flap
on is there? Eyeties declared war on us . . . ?" A
boom of laughter. Must have been the life and soul of
some gory cavalry mess east of the Rhine.

"One of our people had been kidnapped this morning."

"One of the embassy chaps?" Henderson was waiting for the change from his *dieci mila* lire note.

"No, it's not the end of the world, not one of ours. It's a businessman, a fellow who works out here. I've to get up to his wife."

"Poor bastard," said Henderson quietly. His wallet was open, the notes being carefully put away in order of value, damn all of a tip. "Poor devil, rather him . . ."

"Could be rather a shambles for us. It's the first time that a foreigner has been lifted. Well, only the Getty boy, and that was different, I suppose."

Henderson held the door open for Charlesworth. "You'll be handling our end, eh? Well, if you get a bit overwhelmed, give us a shout. Damn all I have to worry about at the moment, diary's empty these next three days. Don't hang about if you want a hand, if you want to talk it over."

"Thank you . . . thank you very much. It's most kind . . . Buster." Charlesworth had never called him that before, never really had a conversation with the army officer on any more substantive subject than whether it would rain on QBP day, whether they'd have to retire to the marquee for the annual Queen's Birthday Party celebrations. Silly little thing, the offer of help, but he was grateful, grateful because he was stepping on stones that he did not know.

"Poor devil, rather him . . ." Charlesworth heard Half Colonel "Buster" Henderson mutter as he closed the taxi door on himself.

He walked in what shade he could find, unable now to control the speed of his legs as they pumped a way along the uneven flagstones, hurrying when he knew he should be calm, pacing the long streets when he should be controlled, because the coolness he had first sought was disappearing and ebbing from his grasp. Giancarlo, feeling the stress and lead weight of the fugitive.

Not that the shade offered him solace. The stinking, brutalizing heat of the morning penetrated the air, sucked into it, broke open his skin and thrust out the sweat rivers that soaked and irritated the boy. No wind down at street level. Just the furnace and the car exhausts. He tramped on for the sanctuary of the university, where a face might be familiar, where the environs would be known, where there would be an end to the perpetual swinging of his head for a first glimpse of the coasting police cars. The other side of a counterfeit coin, a new experience for the boy, Giancarlo. Never before had he known the feeling of being hunted, of being loose and adrift from the companionship of the group, of being cast outside the protective womb casing of the NAP.

When Giancarlo had walked at the side of Franca Tantardini, the NAP had seemed to him a great and powerful organization. Limitless authority and potential gushed when he had been close to her and the words had cascaded from her tongue of victory and success and triumph. But the sheen of safety was stripped from the boy. Enrico was dead, washing his face in his own blood, and Franca was taken. He fled toward the reassurance of the nursery, the safety of the crèche, to the university.

Tired legs, sore feet, a heaving chest, he stumbled from tiredness as he passed the huge, drawn-out complex of the hospital. The signs of *Pronto Soccorso*, which guided the racing, siren-loud ambulances to where they should bring their emergencies, were at his right arm. Where they brought Franca's victims. Where they deposited the men with the gunshot wounds for the first immediate lifesaving operation to counter the work of the P38. The boy saw the men

who waited in their short white coats and the nurses
in their belted dresses, and who lounged under the
trees expectant for the screaming of the ambulance
approach that would send them scurrying in preparation to Casualty Reception.

Going past the Policlinico, Giancarlo knew with the
sureness of the first lightning flash in a storm why
they would hate him, why they would track him, why
they would spend a lifetime edging toward his back.
No forgiveness, no charity, not while men lay in pain
on the metal bed frames of the Policlinico, and
shouted in the night for their wives. A great army
they would bring against him, and a mind with a limitless and unbroken memory.

A boy who was as nothing. Devoid of possessions,
importance, status.

Armed with a P38 and a magazine of eight shells.
Devoid of plan and program and blueprint.

Armed with a detestation of cruel force against the
system that rallied now to crush him.

Devoid of friendship and accomplices and the
strength of a leader to guide.

Armed with the love of a girl who had taken him
into herself. Armed with the love of Franca Tantardini. Must have loved him. She must have wanted
him, Giancarlo Battestini, or he would not have
known her bed and her warmth and her murmurs and
her fingers. She must have loved him. If it took a
week or a month or a year, he would take her from
them. Repossess her freedom, the freedom of the bird
to escape the cage walls. Because she had loved him.

Dwarfing the boy were the great white stone walls
and archway of the university. Designed for immortal-
ity, designed to stand for a thousand years as proof to
a grateful worker class of the power wielded by the
black shirt and the leather boot. Giancarlo took in the
daubed slogans of the spray paint aerosols, bright col-

ors of graffiti that disfigured the impression of om-
nipotence but only as high as a student's arm could
rise. Above the reach of the protestor was the clean-
cut stone of the rejected regime. The slogans of the
Autonomia were here at shoulder height. The painted
outline of the closed fist with the first and second fingers extended—the *P trent' otto*. Here were daubed
the cries of hate against the ministers of government,
the parties of democracy, the *polizia*, the *carabinieri*,
the *borghese*. He had arrived at the place where succor might be found.

Stretching away in front of him was the wide avenue between the Science and Medical Faculties and
the Administration buildings. Many closed doors,
many shuttered windows, because the academic year
and examinations had terminated six weeks earlier.
But there would be some students here. Those who
had taken a cause and rejected the cloying parental
hold over the family holiday, they would have stayed.
Giancarlo broke into a run. He lifted the weariness
from his legs, lengthened his stride, till he was sprint-
ing down the gentle hill.

At crawl speed, the taxi, the driver displaying caution rare in his vocation, nudged up the hill and
rounded the three police cars that straddled in front
of the Mercedes. Charlesworth saw the driver's side
window shattered, frozen glass littered in the gravel
surface of the road.

The *polizia*, in blue mauve trousers with the thin
maroon cord astride their thighs and open blue shirts
and caps pushed back on their foreheads, were working around the smitten vehicle. They dabbed on fingerprint dust, and a tin in which plaster glistened
wetly, and which would be used if the impression of a
tire grip needed recording, was beside them. Too
warm for the *polizia* to move with exertion, and the

lack of energy was augmented by the very familiarity
of the scene. There was nothing new, nothing particular in the procedures at "scene of crime" for a kidnap.
As the taxi circumvented the blockage, Charlesworth
saw two men in civilian suits, and they were the only
ones who mattered. Only two. Not the young boys in
their crumpled uniforms recruited from the *mezzo
giorno* who knew less of crime than a Neapolitan pick-
pocket or a Milanese burglar, and wore the uniform
because that was the only escape from the region of
unemployment. Just two, the trained ones who took
the privilege of wearing their own clothes, enough to
make him heave and throw up. Dear old Carboni,
with his courtesy and his compromise, who had promised nothing, no bromide consolation, he knew the
limitations of his force. And why should they bust a
gut—because a man who's been lifted has a blue passport with a lion rampant and English scroll inside the
front flap? Carboni had marked Charlesworth's card,
said there should be a payoff, that they should get the
misery over, forget the games. So what's in it for a
policeman, standing on his big flat feet, when more
money will be paid than he'll see in a lifetime, and it
won't be missed, won't be noticed, and his own chief
says that's the way to do business?

He paid the driver, stepped out of the taxi, and
looked around him.

A wide street on a sloping hill. Apartments that
owned areas of neat lawn in front and flower bushes
that had been tended and cropped and watered that
morning by the porters. Blocks of five floors with
deep terraces and canvas awnings and jungles of foliage. The ladies' cars parked bumper to bumper; the
little runabout city autos. Dust floated softly down
onto Charlesworth's jacket and the maid in the
starched apron stared him out as she shook her mop.
Not much poverty here, not much malaise from the

economic crisis, not up here on the hill. And there was the reaction to the affluence for him to see, provided by those who crept up the slope under cover of night; spray-painted swastikas, the daubed *Morte al Fascisti*, that could never be scrubbed from the marble veneer surfaces.

Didn't do badly, the old multinationals, for their people. If International Chemical Holdings had put their man in here, then they were solvent, they had no liquidity problems. And the bastards would have known that or Geoffrey Harrison would be sitting at his desk right now, clobbering his secretary for the lateness of the post, straightening his tie for his next appointment. Money here, and plenty of it, and these people knew where to sniff in the air for it, where to strike, where the dividend was assured.

Charlesworth walked into the hallway of the block, paused at the porter's nook where a man with a saddened and troubled face sat, mentioned the name, and was told which floor. A slow elevator creaked and swayed upward. Two policemen lolled against the wall beside the door of the apartment. They straightened when they saw the diplomat, not dramatically, but enough to swing the holstered pistols that hung from waist belts. Charlesworth said nothing, merely nodded, and pressed the bell.

Soft, slippered feet shuffled to the door. An age passed while four sets of locks were unfastened. The door opened an inch and a half, as far as a chain would allow. Like a bloody fortress, he thought. But they all lived like that on the hill and damn all good it did them when the vultures began to circle. It was dark inside and he could see nothing through the gap.

"Who is it?" A small voice, invisible and inanimate.

"It's Charlesworth, Michael Charlesworth. From the embassy."

A pause, and then the door was closed. He heard

the button on the end of the chain being withdrawn from its socket. The door opened again, sufficient to admit him.

"I'm Violet Harrison. Thank you for coming."

He turned, almost startled, two steps inside the hall, as if he had not expected the voice to materialize from behind. A quick movement that betrayed his unease. She came out of the shadows and her hand took his elbow and maneuvered him toward the living room where the blinds were drawn and the low table lights lit. He followed meekly behind the tented swirl of her trailing cotton dressing gown with the big flowers embroidered across the shapes of her back and her buttocks and legs. He stole a glance at the silhouette against a light and dug his nails into the palm of a hand. Would have thought she'd have dressed by now, on a morning like this, with a bloody deluge of visitors about to come tripping in. You'd have thought the woman would have put some clothes on.

He saw her the first time when she reached her chair and angled her face at him. Might not have dressed, but she'd made her face up, had worked at it long enough to give the tears scope to smudge and spoil her efforts. She would have been crying from the time he telephoned. The eyelids were puffy and bulging red above the dark, broad-painted eye shadow. A small, tight, turned-up nose that had taken the sun and the freckles offset her cheeks which were smooth and bronzed. Attractive but not remarkable. Well shaped but not beautiful. His eyes flickered over her, unwilling but compelled, and she gazed back at him, no hint of embarrassment. Charlesworth looked away, the blush rising in him. Been caught like a schoolboy hadn't he? Been seen peering in the Soho bookshop window during school holidays. Been noticed ogling a woman who wore a sheer nightdress and a light cotton wrap.

"I'm very sorry for what has happened, Mrs. Harrison," he said.

"Would you like some coffee . . . there's only instant."

"You're very kind, but no. Thank you."

"There's tea, I can make a cup," A small, far voice.

"No thanks. Thank you again, but I won't. Would you like me to put the kettle on for you? Can I make you some tea?"

"I don't want any tea. Would you like a cigarette?" Still staring at his eyes, raking and examining them.

"It's very nice of you, but I don't. I don't smoke." He felt he should apologize because he didn't want Nescafé, didn't want teabags, didn't want a cigarette.

She sat down, away into an armchair, flanked by the tables that carried last night's glasses and last night's coffee cups, with a flurry of shin and knee glimpsing out. He followed into a chair across the central rug, felt himself going down into far-settling cushions, the sort that you drown in and then forever feel ill at ease in because you're too low and can't dominate the conversation, and your nose is halfway to the carpet. She was still looking into him, boring and penetrating.

"Mrs. Harrison, first I should tell you who I am. I have responsibility for political affairs at the embassy, but I also double on matters affecting the police, relations between the British community in Rome and the Italian police. Those, that is, that aren't covered by the Consular Department . . ." Come on, Charlesworth, you're not doing your own testimonial; not applying for the job either. " . . . So I was called this morning by a fellow called Carboni, he's one of the bigger men at the Questura. There wasn't very much known then, it was just a few minutes after your husband had been seized. Doctor Carboni gave me a solemn assurance that everything possible was being done to secure your husband's early release."

"And that's bugger all," she said slowly and with deliberation.

Charlesworth rocked back, rode it, but the blow had done damage, confused and deflected what was building in his mind. "I can only repeat . . ." he hesitated. They didn't use that sort of language, the embassy secretaries and his wife's friends. First Secretary of the British Embassy he was, and she should be listening to him, and grateful that he'd taken the time to come out and see her. "What he said was, Doctor Carboni, that everything would be done . . ."

"And what's everything? Half of nothing, if that much."

Charlesworth bridled. "It's not a very sensible attitude to take in the circumstances, Mrs. Harrison. You'd be better . . ."

"I've had my cry, Mr. Charlesworth. I got that over before you came. It won't happen again. You know you don't have to come here with platitudes and a bottle of Librium. I'm pleased you came, grateful to you, but I don't need a shoulder to weep on, and I want to know what's going to happen. What's going to happen, not what a crummy Italian policeman says he's doing. And I want to know who's going to pay."

Bit early wasn't it? Knots hardly settled on the old man's wrists and she was chattering about money. God Almighty. "I can advise you about procedures," Charlesworth ploughed on, coldness undisguised. "I can tell you what has happened in the past, to Italians. I can suggest what I think that you should do, and I can indicate the area where I think the embassy can be of service."

"That's what I want to hear."

"When they write about kidnapping in the Italian papers, they call it a successful growth industry.

That's a fair enough description. Since 1970 there have been more than three hundred cases. What you'd expect, of course, but the people responsible vary enormously. There are the big gangs, big organizations, well lead, well funded, well briefed. Probably originating from the real south, probably with what we'd call the Mafia at their roots. I never quite know what's meant by the Mafia, it's an overused word, something simplistic to cover whatever you want it to. In my book the Mafia means skill and ruthlessness and power and patience. If your husband has been taken by these people, then there will be an initial contact followed by a drawn-out haggle over money, and it will end with a business transaction. Very clinical and quite slow because they will want to know that their tracks are well covered."

"And if it's such a group how will they treat my husband?"

A long time coming, that question, thought Charlesworth. "Probably quite well. They'd keep him fed and dry and marginally comfortable, enough to sustain his health . . . in a basement, perhaps a farmhouse . . ."

"That's as long as they think we're going to pay?"

"Yes."

"And if they aren't sure we're going to pay?"

Charlesworth looked hard at her, slipped behind the swollen eyes, delved beyond the mascara. He wondered how his own wife would be reacting in these circumstances, loved her, and knew for all that she'd be a disaster. Helpless as a bloody ship on the rocks and thrashing around for someone to blame. She was different from this woman. Different because Violet Harrison didn't wear her concern and her care on her shoulders. Hadn't even put her knickers on for the great day. Didn't sound as if it meant a damn to her beyond the inconvenience.

"Then they'll kill him."

She didn't react beyond the flutter of the eyebrows, a slight and fractional quiver at the mouth, but nothing that he would have noticed if he hadn't been watching her, absorbing her face.

"And if we go to the police and throw it all into their lap, give it to your Mr. Carboni, what then?"

"If the kidnappers see that through an indiscretion or a clumsiness we have offered full cooperation with the police, and if they feel that endangers their security, then they will kill him." He turned the knife because the realization of how much he disliked the woman, how alien she was to his background, seeped through him. "I put it to you, Mrs. Harrison, that the people who have your husband will not hesitate to murder him if that serves their purpose better than keeping him alive."

He paused, allowed the message to sink and spread, find its own water level. He found his advantage growing. The signs of fear were shown by the slight pant in her chest, the motion of the fingers.

"And even if we pay, if the company pays, we still have no guarantee . . ."

He anticipated her. "There are never guarantees in these matters." That was about as strongly as he had the stomach to put it. Couldn't bring himself to tell her of Luisa di Capua, whose husband had been dead two months before the body was found, and who had received the last ransom note a day before the discovery. "No guarantees, we would just have to hope."

He won a shrill, short laugh from her.

"How much will they ask, Mr. Charlesworth? How much is my Geoffrey worth on the Italian market?"

"They'll ask for more than they'll be happy to end up with. Starters would probably be around five million dollars, and they'll settle for perhaps two. Not less than one million."

"Which I don't have." She was faster now, and

louder, and the control was fracturing. "I don't have it, do you understand that? Geoffrey doesn't, his parents don't. We don't own that sort of money."

"It's not really your husband that's being ransomed, it's his company. The group will expect the company to pay."

"And they're tight bastards," she spat across at him. "Tight and mean and penny-pinching."

He remembered the exterior of the block, allowed himself to fade a glance across the interior fittings of the flat.

"I'm sure they will look favorably when they have had the situation explained to them. I had intended to speak to them after I had seen you. I thought that might be valuable to them."

"So what happens now? What do I do?"

The questions rolled from her, as if Charlesworth were some all-knowing guru on the subject of kidnap reaction. "We have to await the first contact, probably by telephone. Then it can take quite a time for them to decide what arrangements they want to make for payment."

"So what do I do, sit by the bloody telephone, sit by it all day? And I don't even speak the bloody language, just what I need round the shops in the morning. I don't speak their bloody language. I won't know what they're bloody well saying." Shouting for the first time, dipping into hysteria. Charlesworth fidgeted in the deep chair, willed the session to end.

"We can have it said in the papers that your husband's office is standing by to receive a message."

"But they're all bloody Italians . . . what the hell do they know about it?"

"A damn sight more than we do, because they live with it every day of the year. Because every one of your husband's senior colleagues knows this can hap-

pen to him any time, and a few of them will ring their
wives each morning just as soon as they've sat down
at their desks, just so that the women will know
they've made it safely. They know more about this
than you do, and I do, and your husband's company
in London will. If your husband is to come out of this
alive you'll need the help of all his friends in that office. All of those 'bloody Italians,' you'll need all of
their help."

He was out of the chair, backside clear of the cushions, fingers gripping for leverage into the uphol-
stered armrests. Poor old show, Charlesworth. A stupid, ignorant cow she may be, but not your job to
pass judgment. He sagged back, ashamed that he had
battered the remnants of the calm, destroyed the very
thing that he had come to maintain. The color had
fled her face, which had taken on a pallid glow in the
shock of his counterattack. Not a whimper from her.
Only the eyes to give the message, those of someone
who has just stepped from a car accident in which the
driver or passenger has died and who knows dimly of
catastrophe but does not have the power to identify
and evaluate the debris.

"Mrs. Harrison, you mustn't think yourself alone.
Many people will now be working for your husband's
release. You must believe in that."

He stood up, shuffled a little, edged toward the
door.

She looked up at him from her chair, cheeks very
pale below the saucer eyes, knees apart and the gown
gaping. "I hate this bloody place," she said. "I've
hated it from the day we arrived. I've hated every
hour of it. He'd told me we wouldn't have to stay
here, not more than another year, he'd promised me
we'd go home. And now you want to go, Mr. Charlesworth, well don't hang round because of me. Thank

you again for coming, thank you for your advice, thank you for your help, and thanks to bloody everybody."

"I'll get a doctor to come round. He'll have something for you. It's a very great shock, what has happened."

"Don't bother, don't inconvenience anyone."

"I'll send a doctor round."

"Don't bother, I'll be a good girl. I'll sit beside the telephone and wait."

"Haven't you got a friend who could come and stay with you?"

The old laugh back again, high and clear and tinkling. "Friends in this bloody hole, you're joking, of course?"

Charlesworth hurried to the door, mumbled over his shoulder, "I'll be in touch, and don't hesitate to call me at the embassy, the number's in the book."

Trying to master the different locks delayed his flight sufficiently for him to hear her call from the remoteness of the living room. "You'll come again, Mr. Charlesworth? You'll come again and see me?"

He pulled the door brutally shut behind him, erasing from his ears the trickle of her laughter.

Some five minutes the *colonello* spent attempting to marshal the moving waves of photographers and reporters into a straight line. He threatened, pleaded, negotiated the issue of how many paces the prisoner should walk in front of the lenses and microphones before he was finally satisfied with his arrangements in the square internal courtyard of the Questura.

"And remember, no interviews. Interviews are absolutely forbidden."

He shouted the last exhortation for discipline before the wave of his arm to the *polizia* who stood shaded in a distant doorway.

When she emerged, Franca Tantardini held her head high, jutted her chin, thrust her eyes unwaveringly into the sun. The chains at her wrists dangled against her knees as she walked. Her jeans and blouse were smeared with the street dirt of the pavement outside the Post. To her right the *polizia* linked arms to hold back the press of cameramen. An officer gripped tightly at each of her elbows; not the men who had taken her, not the men who had killed Enrico Panicucci, because those were anonymous and undercover and would not be photographed. These were men in uniform, spruced, with combed and greased hair and polished shoes, who preened themselves and swelled with importance. She ignored the babble of shouted questions and walked on until she was level with the place where the crowd was densest, the pushing at the police shoulders most acute, the cameras closest. A glance she spared for the scrimmaging, then ripped her right arm clear of her escort's hold, swung it aloft into the air, clenched her fist in salute, seemed to hover a smile at the chatter of the camera shutters. The policeman regained his hold, dragged her arm down, she was pulled through a doorway, lost from sight. Show completed. Police taking their kudos, cameramen their pictures. Satisfaction of all parties. A triumphal procession of victor and vanquished, and smoothly done.

From an upper window, unnoticed by the journalists, Francesco Vellosi had watched the courtyard parade. At his side stood an Under Secretary of the Interior Ministry.

"Still defiant, *la leonessa*. Magnificent, even in defeat," the Under Secretary murmured.

"A year in Messina, perhaps two, then she'll be tamed," responded Vellosi.

"Magnificent, quite magnificent. Such hate, such pride."

"We should have shot her on the street." And there was a cold and bitter snarl at Vellosi's lips.

The computer trace on the third set of fingerprints found by police in the *covo* was fast and efficient. But then the equipment was German, modern and expensive, the sort of item on which government, harassed and defensive, was prepared to lavish its money in the fight against the urban activist. The printout on the teleprinter was clear and concise.

```
CRIMINALPOL EUR ROMA
XXXXXXX  25 7 80  XXXXX  REF:  A419/B78
BATTESTINI GIANCARLO MARCO      BORN
    12 3 60
82C VIA PESARO PESCARA
RIOTOUS ASSEMBLY      SENTENCED 7 MONTHS
    11 5 79
PHOTOGRAPHED FINGERPRINTED 9 3 79
```

More information would follow later, but a name and a picture would be waiting on Francesco Vellosi's desk when he returned from the Questura. Another identity, another set of features, another case history would settle on the top of his mountain of files of wanted persons.

5

It had taken many minutes of the new motion of the van before Geoffrey Harrison was sufficiently aroused to realize that they no longer traveled on the smooth worn surface of the autostrada.

The tang of the chloroform was just a memory now, one receding aspect of the morning nightmare. The swell of the moisture across his limbs and torso had become acceptable with familiarity, was no longer unendurable. The breathing through the hood became more possible as time went on, the harsh smell of the carbon monoxide from the engine could be ignored. It was a long time since he had tried to struggle with his bonds and he had given up the ambition to loosen the tapes. With the greater calmness came a greater comfort. No tears, no fight, no desperation. No reason for him to compete anymore, just a need to lie back, prone and supple, and let it all float across him, to obliterate the more vicious fantasies that hovered near his imagination. There was nothing that he could do to change his situation, nothing that was within his potential. And so he lay there, feeling the jar and jolt and shift of the van wheels, and gaining from the bruising impacts the knowledge that they had moved to a slower, indirect road.

He thought of Violet, poor old Violet.

She'd know by now, she'd have heard, and the police would be swarming round the flat and she'd be shouting at them and crying, and unless someone came who spoke English she wouldn't have a damn of an idea what they were talking about. Poor old Violet, who'd wrung it out of him that they wouldn't stay past next summer—two and a half years she'd have existed then, and she'd said that was her limit, that was enough. Should have adjusted, shouldn't she? Should have compromised and made something of it.

Of course it was different from England, but people go abroad and people cope. She should have been able to find some friends to coffee mornings with, go walk about the ruins with. Didn't seem to make the effort though, did she? And didn't seem interested, not in anything, not in his job, not in his business colleagues, not in the few foreigners who lived within walking distance of the flat. Never accepted living in a flat and not having neighbors she could lean over a fence and gossip with, never accepted that people who spoke a different language were still human beings and intelligent and kindly and funny, and that if they weren't British it didn't mean they wiped their backsides with their hands.

Bloody ridiculous it was, old Violet locked up in her castle on the hill and not letting the drawbridge down.

Tried hard enough, hadn't he? Yes, Geoffrey. Well what the hell else could be done? Couldn't throw her out the front door with a street map and shout down the terraces that she mustn't be back before six. He remembered when her parents had come to visit from Stoke on Trent. Never been out of England before. Didn't know whether they should put their teeth in

the water at night. Didn't hold with all the wine at the
meals. Didn't master the coils of spaghetti falling off
their forks when he took them all out to dinner. Set
them back, the pair of them, that visit, argued about
it endlessly after the old people had gone; him telling
her she should make more effort and not live like a
bloody mole and what an advantage and opportunity
she had; her telling him she hated it, wanted out and
to England. Poor old Violet. Him telling her to get
interested in the city, get off her bottom and visit the
Vatican and the Foro Italico; her telling him she was
buggered if she would be ordered to tramp round mu-
seums. Poor old Violet. Must have been out of her
mind with boredom. And she didn't even hit the bottle because he looked each night when he came home,
checked the gin level and the Martini Bianco level,
and the Tio Pepe level. She didn't even drink the time
away. Only thing she seemed to like was getting down
to the beach, and that was bloody ridiculous too.
There was a nice quiet pool just down the road for her
to use, and some very decent families using it. But she
preferred the beach and a hell of a drive down to Ostia and all the filth and the oil to sit on, pressed in
close by those Italians burning themselves nigger
brown. A total bloody mystery. Getting the sand in
her hair, not speaking to anyone. Poor old Violet, poor
bored old Violet. Hadn't thought about her for a long
time, had he? Not like this, not examining her day.
Well, he didn't have time, did he? Someone had to put
the clothes on her back, the food in her fridge. A
damn good job he had in Rome. Better prospects, better pay than he could have hoped for in London. He
wished she'd see that. Working damned hard he was,
and he could do without the abuse when he flopped
home in the evenings.

They were slow, rambling thoughts, indulgent and
close, lulling him from the crisis, until there was an-

other change in the engine pitch and he felt the movement of the gears, the slowing of the engine, the ap-
plication of brakes. The van bumped crazily on rough
ground. A dead stop. Voices that were clearer with
the motor cut. The complacency was evacuated, the
trembling resurgent, because this was frightening to
the man who was bound and gagged and hooded and
who had no horizons of sight. A way of existence that
had become settled, achieved a tranquillity, was rup-
tured.

The van left the autostrada halfway between Cassino and Capua, bypassed the small town of Vairano
Scalo, avoiding the single, wide street and central piazza. They had turned east on a winding, open hill
road which would eventually reach the village of Pietramelara, the home of few more than a thousand people with shuttered minds and uninquisitive tongues,
who would not question the presence of a strange vehicle with distant number plates that might rest for
half an hour among the trees and off the road short of
their community.

Harrison felt himself bracing his muscles as if
trying to push his way farther back into the interior of
the van, crawl on his buttocks away from the rear
door. He heard the slamming at the front and the
gouging scratch of feet on the ground walking along
the length of the side walls, and then the noise of a
lock being turned and a handle being tugged. When
the door opened there was a slight smudge of light
filtering through the weave of the hood and the floor
of the van bucked under a new weight. He felt the
shape, alien and revolting to him, brush against his
knees and thighs, and then there were hands at the
hood, scrabbling close to his chin, at the back of his
neck as the cloth was drawn back across his face. He

wanted to scream, wanted to vomit, to expel the fear. Taut, tensed, terrorized. The smell of garlic was close to his nose, and the odor of a farm.

The light, brilliant, blinding, flooded over him, hurting so that he screwed his face and tried to twist away. But he was not just turning from the intrusive sun, but also from the man who was hunched, bent double under the low roof, and who now loomed above him. Boots close to his head, hard, roughened, unpolished, cracked with wear. Trousers that were old and patched and shapeless, grease-stained. A shirt of red check material, sleeves turned high on muscled forearms. And dominating, compelling his eyes, was the hood, black cloth with eye slits and the crudely cut hole that simulated the position of the mouth. Nowhere for Harrison to writhe to. Nowhere for him to find refuge. The hands, coarse and blistered, thrust to the tapes across his mouth. One savage pull ripped and tore them clear and left the skin as a vast, single abrasion. He coughed hard, spluttered with his face smarting, his eyes heavy with tears at the sharpness of the pain.

No word from the man above who screwed up and tossed away the jumble of adhesive tape. There was another silhouetted against the light of the doorway, and Harrison saw him pass forward a roll of bread that bulged with lettuce and tomato and ham. Big and fat and filling it would have been if he were hungry. The bread was placed against his mouth. He bit and swallowed. Bit again, swallowed again. Around him an awareness of the surroundings grew. The tastes were of the far countryside, distant and removed from the city that was his home. The air was closed to urban sounds, open only to the calls of the birds that were loose and roaming at their will. Harrison ate half the roll, could stomach no more and shook his head, and the man threw it casually behind him, successful in his aim, avoiding his friend. They let him swig from a bottle of water; *aqua minerale* and lively with gas and bubbles from the movement of the van. One drink and then the bottle was withdrawn. He lay numbly still, unresisting, as his face was again taped. Instinctively he pleaded with his eyes because they were the only vehicle of argument left to him, but the hood was returned to its place. Back in this realm of darkness, his stomach ground on the food it had taken down, his bowels were loose and confused by the content of what he had eaten. He heard the back door close, the lock applied, the men walking back to the front of the van. The engine started.

No threat, no kindness. No cruelty, no comfort.

Men without any sensitivity. Vicious bastards, without emotion, without charity. To take a blindfold off a man who was terrorized, holding his muscles to keep his pants clean, to rip the gag from his mouth and then offer him nothing, nothing in communication, nothing as one human being to another. The one who fed him had worn on his left hand, the hand that held the bread, had worn on his third finger the wide gold band of a wedding ring. He had a wife whom he would hold close to him and sweat and grunt his passion against, the children who would call to him and laugh. The bastard, the fucking bastard, who could extinguish the compassion, drown it, and say not a word, give not a sign to a fellow creature who was in pain and suffering and alone.

So help me God, if ever I have the chance I'll kill that bastard. Beat his head with a stone, smash and pound and break it. While he pleads, while he cries, while the blood spatters. So help me God, I want to kill him, I want to hear him scream.

You've never hit anyone in your life, Geoffrey, you wouldn't know how.

The van moved off.

* * *

They drove slowly into the village of Pietramelara.
The driver found what he was looking for without difficulty. A bar with the circular sign of a telephone
dial that heralded the presence of a coin box machine.
He left his passenger in the seat, nodded respectfully
to the village priest hurrying home for his lunch, accepted the smile of greeting. Conversation in the bar
was not interrupted. The driver pulled from his
pocket a clutch of *gettoni* coins, the tokens necessary
for the call. He took from the breast pocket of his
shirt a packet of cigarettes, and deciphered the number written on the inside of the cardboard lining. Six
gettoni he required for Rome. He remembered the
zero six prefix then carefully repeated the seven figure number from the packet. When the answer came
he spoke quickly, gave only his first name and that of
the village and his estimation that the journey would
be completed in eight hours.

Had there been difficulties?

There had been none.

The call was terminated by the other party. The
driver did not know to whom he was speaking. He
walked back to the van anxious to be on his way. He
faced a long drive, far into the very toe of the Italian
boot, into the mountain country of Calabria. And tonight he would sleep in his own cottage, sleep against
the cool stomach of his woman.

The contact of the driver would permit the organization in the group that had kidnapped Geoffrey Harrison to make their first contact with the Englishman's
home. They now knew that their merchandise was far
beyond the reach of rescue by the *polizia*, that the
cordons and roadblocks were way outstripped.

Claudio stood with his hands in his pockets among
the little groups of waving Romans. A varied sadness

painted all those who watched the train, the ana-
conda, snake away from the long platform of the Terminii, bending at the first far curve, engine already
lost. Mario and Vanni gone, settled into their seats in
the gray carriage that carried the sign of Reggio Calabria, nine hundred kilometers to the south. Their
going left Claudio without a companion, condemned
to wait away the night, contain his resentment that he
was not with his friends. Time to be killed and frittered as a man does when he is in a strange city that
has no heart, no belonging for him.

Once he waved, without conviction, lifting his arm
and waggling his fingers at the train as it diminished
and blended with the softness of the heat haze that
distorted and tricked.

There had been temptation as Mario and Vanni had
walked along the platform to follow and join, but fear
of the men of the organization was enough to cast the
apple from big Claudio's mouth. Some before had discarded the instructions of the organization, trifled
with their orders. All had been awarded a fine funeral, two and more priests to celebrate the Mass,
many boys to sing in the choir, enough flowers to
cover all the stones in the cemetery, enough tears to
make a dead man believe he was mourned. Claudio
had stayed behind and waved and would catch tomorrow's train.

He swung his eyes away from the converging,
empty track and headed for the bar and the first of a
new session of Perroni beers, which would help him
watch the hour and minute hands of his watch.

Later he would find a room near the station.

Sometimes hurrying, sometimes slowly when the
lethargy bred from failure was on him, Giancarlo
searched among the familiar places, the rooms and
corridors where he expected to find his friends. He

had gone to the Faculty of Letters where the walls were bright in a technicolor of protest paint and wandered the high plaster-coated corridors, past the stripped notice boards, past the locked lecture theaters, into the quiet of the library. To some who were relaxed and lounging in chairs he had spoken. Not with confidence, but sidled toward them. Mentioned a name and seen a head shaken. Moved on, another name, shoulders shrugged in response. On from the Faculty of Letters to the Faculty of Social Science and further echoing and deserted corridors which rang with his thin-soled shoes and in which reverberated the laughter of those who belonged and knew their place.

Hopeless for him to ask the question directly.

Where are the people of the Autonomia? Where can I find any member of the group of the Autonomia? Not information that would be given to a stranger, not in casual conversation. He plodded on, wet and constricted in his clothes, dampened and caught in his unhappiness. On from the Faculty of Social Sciences, heading for the Faculty of Physics. Two hours Giancarlo paced the university complex. There was no one that he knew among the students who sat and talked in the sunshine, or walked with their bundles of books, or who crouched over the printed words of their study texts. No one that could send him with a smile and a gabble of directions to where he might discover the people of the Autonomia.

Still careful, still watchful, he hesitated by the door of the Faculty of Physics, pausing in the shadow by the great opened doors, short of the sun-bright steps that led down into the central yard of the university. Traversed with his eyes, as a fox will when it sniffs the early air before leaving its den. Giancarlo quivered, stiffened, focused on the gray gunmetal Alfasud parked back and out of the light, far into the shade of

the trees. The car was distinctive because of its radio
aerial, high and set above the right rear wheel, and
the three men sprawled in the seats. Bearded, two of
them, clean-shaven the third, but all of them of too
great an age to be students at the university. He
watched the car for many minutes, hidden by shadow
as it was, observing the men fidget and shift in response to the discomfort of their seats, assimilating
their mood, their state of preparedness. Nothing ex-
ceptional that the police should be there, he told himself, the place crawled with the pigs and their informers, and there was no urgency about these men as
they watched the young people move across their vision. Dumb bastards, because even if they had his
name and his picture they telegraphed their presence
by their age, by their location.

Had they his name yet?

Not so quickly, surely, not within the few hours, not
already. Confidence and depression, ebullience and
fear, competed for place in the mind of the boy as he
scurried for a side entrance and cover among the
parked buses at the Tiburtina *termini.* Rampant in his
imagination was the sight of the three men low in the
seats of their car. The one with his newspaper, the one
with his arm trailing through the open window with
the dangled cigarette, the one with the barely opened
eyes. They had made him run, hastened the end of his
fruitless, wasted search, and that was how it would
always be till the shooting time, till he no longer
needed to scan the cars and the faces for the *polizia.*

Pig bastards. There would be a moment when he
stood his ground. A moment when they would know
of him. When, Giancarlo? There was a pain at the
boy's eyes, and agony behind the lids, because this
was a public place among the buses and the people
who waited and they would not see him weep.

He climbed onto a bus. Chose it not for its routing,

but because it was one that did not have a conductor to collect money and hand out tickets, and relied instead on a machine and the honesty of passengers.

Heart pumping, blood coursing, the little boy who had lost his protection and was running.

The girl in faded jeans and a flowing, wrist-buttoned blouse came quickly to the top of the high steps at the entrance to the Faculty of Social Sciences. She paused there, raking the open ground in front of her with her eyes, then jogged down the steps and across the parking lot toward the gray Alfasud. It was not remarkable that she could identify the unmarked police car, any student could have done that. As she approached the car she saw the interest of the occupants awaken, the cigarette stubbed, the newspaper dropped, the backs straightened. At the driver's open window she hesitated as the men's eyes soaked into her, and this was a public place for an informant to work.

"You are looking for a boy?"

The cool smile from the front passenger in response, the lighting of another cigarette.

"Dark curly hair—jeans and a shirt—not tall, thin."

The man in the back seat flipped casually at a note pad in which were scribbled words.

"A boy like that came into the library, it was just a few minutes ago. He was nervous, you could see that, in his voice, in his hands . . ."

The notebook was passed to the front, examined with a secrecy as if the knowledge written there were to be denied to the girl.

". . . he asked a friend if two boys were in the university. The boys are both of the Autonomia, both are arrested, after the last fight, more than three months ago."

She was answered. The front passenger drew his

Beretta pistol from the glove drawer and armed it, the man in the back groped to the floor for a short-barreled machine gun. The man snapped a question, "Where did he go?"

"I don't know. There is the student's lounge, he went in that direction . . ."

The girl had to step back as the car doors whipped open. Handguns pocketed, the machine gun closed from view under a light jacket, the three policemen ran for the Faculty entrance.

They searched methodically for an hour in the public places of the university, while more men of the anti-terrorist squad arrived to augment their efforts. There were curses of frustration at the failure of the hunt, but satisfaction could be drawn from the knowledge that the identification, if it were genuine, showed that the kid was short of a *covo*. It would not be long before the boy was taken, not if he were scouting the university for friends more than twelve weeks in the cells.

That night the university and its hostels would be watched. Men would be detailed to stand in their silence in the shadows and doorways. Pray God, the bastard returns.

By telephone the message from Pietramelara was relayed to the *capo*. That the initial moments of the kidnapping of the Englishman had met with success he knew from the radio beside his desk. The communiqué bearing the fruits of his enterprise had been broadcast with commendable speed by the RAI networks.

How they help us, he thought, how they facilitate our business. And now the cargo was moving beyond the scope of the road checks. Soon he would authorize the initial approaches to the family and the company, and set in motion the financial procedures in the matter laid down by his specialist accountant. A fat, choice haul, and the lifting sharp and surgical.

It was not for a man of the prominence of the *capo* to burden himself with the machinery of the extortion of ransom, a team he paid to do that, paid them well that tracks should be smothered and hidden. He let himself out of his office, locked his door from a wide ring of keys, and crossed the pavement to his car. For the long journeys to the south and the hill village where his wife and children lived, he used the Dino Ferrari that would eat into the kilometers to the Golfo de Policastro, where he would break the journey back to his family. Beside the sea, in the sprouting coastal resorts, his business was fueled by the new and flourishing source of revenue. He cut a good figure as he climbed with an athleticism into the low-slung sports car. To the superficial watcher, there was nothing in his bearing or his dress to link him with profitable crime, painstakingly organized, ruthlessly executed. He would be at the resort area by early evening, in time to take a functionary of the regional planning office to dinner, and when the man was drunk and grateful for the attention, the *capo* would leave him and motor on to his villa in the Aspromonte.

He drove aggressively from the curbside, attracting notice. To those who saw his going, there was the feeling that this was a man on whom the sun shone with favor.

Violet Harrison had no clear intention of going to the beach at Ostia that afternoon. Nothing definite in her mind, no commitment to escape from the funereal movements of her maid, but there had to be an alternative to sitting and smoking and drinking coffee and straining for the telephone's first ecstatic ring. She had taken the three newest bikinis from the drawer of the chest in her bedroom—one in yellow, one in black, the third in pink with white dots—and laid them with a neatness that was not usually hers out on the bedspread, and looked at their flimsy defiance.

"Bit on the small side, isn't it?" Geoffrey had laughed. "Bit of a risk running round in that in these parts." That was last week and he'd slapped her bottom, kissed her on the cheek, and never mentioned it again. But written all over his bloody face, "What's an Old Girl like you wanting a Teenager's fripperies for?" He'd settled in his chair with a drink in his hand and a folder of accounts on his lap. "Bit on the small side . . ." and he'd held her most recent purchase, pink with white dots, in between his fingers, dangling. She'd found it in the boutique window down past the market, wanted it, urged herself to buy it. She'd ignored the supercilious stare of the shop girl, tall and manicured and straight-backed, a haughty bitch who said with her eyes what her husband had spoken five hours later.

Violet Harrison had only worn the pink and white bikini once, just the day before, while she lay on the beach at Ostia and listened to the virulent run of conversation around her. Couldn't understand a word they said, to her it was a medley of silly chatter and giggling and exuberance that made her content. But it made a state of independence for her, a secret hideout. Among the people and litter from the ice cream wrappers and the beer bottles and Pepsi cartons, it was her place, unknown to the cool and monied world of the inhabitants of Collina Fleming. Marvelous she felt there, bloody marvelous, and the sun burned into her skin, and the sand flicked across her face and went unnoticed. The nearest thing to happiness and guiltless pleasure. And then the silly kid had started talking to her. All part of the game, wasn't it? All part of the scenario of escape and freedom. A silly little kid

trying to pick up an English matron, old enough to
be . . . his aunt, anyway. Trying to pick her up as if
she were an *au-pair* on an afternoon out. And he'd
said he'd be there that afternoon.

It's not my bloody fault, Geoffrey.

What am I supposed to do? Dress in black tights
and put polaroid specs on so that people can't see that
I haven't cried for four hours? Put flowers round the
living room and wear soft shoes so I'll make no noise
when I pace up and down, and keep the bloody place
looking like a funeral parlor.

What do you want me to do? Sit here all day, sit
here and weep, and ask Mummie to come out and
hold my hand and make mugs of tea. I don't mean
that, Geoffrey, not like that. I don't mean you any
harm. I can't just sit here, you understand that, I can't
just eke it all out. I'm not strong enough, that's what I
mean . . . I'm not a public person's wife.

But I'm not going to go anyway. I mean it, I'm not
going to the beach. I'm going to stay here and wait for
the telephone, that's what I have to do, isn't it? I have
to suffer with you because you're out there, somewhere. Are you frightened, Geoffrey? . . . A man
came to see me, some idiot from the embassy, and he
said they wouldn't hurt you. Well, he didn't quite say
that, but they won't actually hurt you if everything
goes well, if nothing is wrong. That's what he said.

She grabbed the bikini from the bed cover on
which had rested the little cotton triangles, the linking
cords, the fastening straps. Crushed them in her fist
and hurled the pieces toward the corner that housed
the neat formation of Geoffrey's shoes.

She started to run from the bedroom, drawn always
faster by the piercing, siren call of the telephone.
Crashing through doors, slipping on the smoothed
floor surface. The caller was patient, allowed the bell

to ring out its summons, let the persistence of the
noise swamp the flat, cutting the walls, floating to the
crannies.

Again the air conditioning was not working.

Michael Charlesworth sat in his office, jacket
draped over his chair, tie loosened, top three shirt buttons undone. Sweat coated the paper in front of him,
running the ink where he'd written with his biro, and
beside his elbow the telephone was still wet from his
palm print. A great quiet in a building usually leaking
with noise; the Ambassador and his guests at lunch,
attachés and first and second secretaries disappeared
to the shaded restaurants near the Porta Pia and the
Via Nomentana. The typists had covered their machines, the clerks locked their filing cabinets. Charlesworth scribbled on fiercely.

He had started with a list of his immediates. A call
to Carboni at the Questura, to ensure the message was
discreetly fed to the afternoon newspapers that Harrison's office was standing ready to receive contact. He
had barely put the phone down when Violet Harrison
rang; she had seemed detached, distant. Enough for
him to wonder if a doctor had called with sedatives.
She had spoken of a message and a man who talked
only in Italian, and she had shouted and he had
shouted, each obliterating the words of the other.
There was a great calmness about her, as if a narcotic
were at work, and a politeness as she had told Charlesworth that she was going out for a few hours.

"I can't just sit here," she said, matter-of-fact, un-
troubled by crisis. "I can't just hang about. I think you
understand."

He had tried to reach the Ambassador, sent a spirit-
less message through to the personal secretary, and received the reply he anticipated.

"If nothing has changed the Old Man would be

happy to see you about five. He wouldn't want to be disturbed before that. At least, not unless it's a case of life and death, you know."

A nice girl, the personal secretary, long and leggy and combed and sweet, projecting out of cotton print dresses, but fierce and loyal in her protectiveness. And what was a case of life and death? A guy on his back, crapping himself and bound so that he lay in his filth, and savage bastards round him who'd kill if it was to their advantage. Life and death? Not in the Old Man's terms, not reason enough to spoil a good lunch. And there wasn't anything new, not if he were honest about it. Just that a woman was having a plucky try and likely to succeed at a nice and public nervous breakdown, not a special woman who knew an MP back home with clout, or who'd figure on the embassy scones and tea invitation list. But Michael Charlesworth hadn't provided the granite pillar for Violet Harrison to support herself against, not the shoulder, nor the handkerchief. A dreadful woman, awful manners, disastrous sense of occasion, but worthy of some small charity—yes, Michael Charlesworth? His teeth played on his lower lip as he heaved in his chair and grabbed again for the telephone.

"It's ten minutes since I asked for that London call, sweetheart. Ten minutes, and that's too long." He called her Miss Foreman normally.

"I can't help it, Mr. Charlesworth. The operator on International won't answer. You know how it is." The syrup voice of a lady who knitted and took holidays in Welsh hotels off-season, and thought of Italians as dirty, and wished she were twenty years younger, not too old to be loved.

"Can't you just dial it for me, darling . . . ?"

"You know that's not allowed, Mr. Charlesworth."

"You can dial it for me." Wearying of the game.

"You'll have to sign for it. One of the girls will have

to come up to second when she's free and get your signature . . ."

"Just get me the call." Charlesworth's temper fraying, ragged.

"As soon as we've looked out a priority form and a girl's available I'll send her up."

"Get me that bloody call, get it now. Dial it. A man's bloody life may depend . . ."

"You don't have to swear, there's no need for offensiveness."

"Just get me the call, darling. I'll sign the priority later, but it's important that I speak to London and that cretins like you don't waste any more of my time."

The earpiece exploded in the sounds of switchboard mechanics. Plugs extracted, plugs inserted. Numbers dialed and whirring on their arcs. The ringing tone. He'd never spoken to Miss Gladys Foreman MBE like that. Doubted if anyone ever had, not in three decades anyway. Like urinating right across the lounge carpet at a standup buffet at the Residence.

Two rings and the plastic, automated voice of a faraway girl.

"International Chemical Holdings. Can I help you please?"

"It's the British Embassy in Rome. Michael Charlesworth speaking. I need to talk with the Managing Director."

Delays, reroutings, a false start and the call retrieved. Charlesworth sat at his desk, soaking the sunlight, telling a secretary that he was damned if he was going to precis his message and that he wanted her master, and she should pull her bloody finger and get off the line. Yes, he could wait a moment, he could wait all day, why not? Different whether the other blighter could, whether Geoffrey Harrison could.

"Adams speaking. What can I do for you, Mr.

Charlesworth?" Sir David Adams, captain of industry, clipped voice, a brusqueness that demanded information and warned against wasted time.

"It's good of you to speak to me. I have to tell you that your representative in Rome, Mr. Geoffrey Harrison, was kidnapped this morning, on his way to your office." Charlesworth paused, cleared his throat, a guttural clatter, then launched into the few available facts, recounted his conversations with the Questura. Not a great deal to say, and the inadequacy hurt.

"I've read in the newspapers of these happenings, but I confess I was under the impression this was an Italian problem, a domestic one." A sharp voice distorted to a high pitch by the static of the communication.

"Your man is the first of the foreign business community."

"And it could be expensive?"

"Very expensive, Sir David." Lurched to the heart of the issue, hadn't he?

"To get him back, what sort of figure might we be talking about?"

"The asking price might by anything up to four or five million dollars." That'll set him swinging in his black leather chair. "There might be a possibility of negotiation, but it won't be easy for a company like yours to plead poverty."

"And if we don't pay?"

"Then you are in for a long widow's pension. Mrs. Harrison is a young woman."

"Well, that's a Board decision. And in the meantime, what action should we take?"

"The only thing you have to do is to get that decision taken, and fast. It could go very hard for Mr. Harrison if the group that hold him thought you were prevaricating. As you probably realize, in this country there is a tradition of paying up, they would not respond well to the breaking of that custom."

Don't ever say I didn't root for you, Geoffrey Harrison. Don't ever say I didn't go in there with two feet kicking. A silence on the line, the big man chewing on it, deliberating. A slow smile winning across Michael Charlesworth's face.

When Sir David Adams spoke again, the chisel had blunted in his voice. "It's a great deal of money, Mr. Charlesworth. My Board would have to be very certain that it's totally necessary to pay the sort of sum you mention. They won't like it. And there's a question of principle too; there's a tradition in this country that we don't crumble to blackmail."

"Then you would have to make the decision that on a point of principle you were prepared to sacrifice the life of Mr. Harrison. Of course, it might not come to that, but the possibility, perhaps the probability, exists."

"You are very frank, Mr. Charlesworth." There was the trace of disapproval in the scraped gravel tones. "If we suppose, and only suppose, that we were to pay a very considerable sum, then who would control the arrangements?"

"It would be best done by your office in Rome. The embassy couldn't get involved."

Charlesworth heard the low laugh in response. Ten minutes they'd been talking, ten minutes in querying the profit and loss columns, and whether a ransom should be paid. Principle or expediency. A martyr for the greater good of the majority or a shame-laden deal for the return of one man. Perhaps, Charlesworth thought, he'd minimized the issues at stake. Perhaps a line had to be drawn. No deals, no bargains, no compromise, there would be many willing to shout that clarion call. If you gave in once, if you slipped one time into the shadows with a suitcase of used bank notes and a string of Zurich bank-account numbers, then how many other poor bastards were going to follow the road of Geoffrey Harrison? Not his business, though, not his concern, because as he'd said most clearly, the embassy couldn't be involved, would stand detached from the affray within its glass walls and watch and murmur occasional interest. That was why Sir David Adams, Managing Director of International Chemical Holdings in the City of London could laugh lightly at him, without humor, without rancor, at the moment of dismissal.

"You've been very kind, Mr. Charlesworth. I'll get one of my people on the plane this evening. I'd like him to be in touch with you."

The call was terminated.

Michael Charlesworth flopped back into the small comforts offered by the plastic padding of his chair. A time for reflection. He must call Miss Foreman, he must apologize, and there would be some flowers for her basement bunker tomorrow, in the morning. And then the bell again, the bloody telephone.

The Questura had been informed from the offices of ICH in Viale Pasteur that a demand of two million dollars for the return of Geoffrey Harrison had been received. There should be no contact with the police, further details of arrangement for payment would follow through intermediaries. Dottore Carboni was not in his office at present but he had requested that the information be passed to Signor Charlesworth. There were mutual thanks and politeness.

Two million dollars. More than a million in sterling at whatever the fluctuating rate. Four million Swiss francs. Cascades of figures. And less than he'd thought it would be, as if those who had taken Harrison had settled for a bargain basement price and would not haggle and barter, but expect settlement without delay.

Michael Charlesworth changed his mind. He would apologize in person to Gladys Foreman. He fastened his shirt buttons, straightened his tie, slipped on his jacket, and walked slowly out of his office. He wondered what the man looked like, Geoffrey Harrison, how his voice sounded, whether he'd be good company for dinner, if he told a good joke. He felt himself inextricably involved with a man he did not know, could not picture and might never meet, unless a company on the other side of the continent jettisoned an issue of principle and made available more money than he could decently imagine.

6

The Terminii was a good place for Giancarlo to come to.

A great, extended, white stone frontage before which the buses parked, the taxis queued, the traders hawked gaudy toys and shiny shoes and polished belts, and where thousands streamed each morning and afternoon on their way to and from the business of the city. Shops and bars and restaurants and even a subterranean aquarium catered to those who had time to pass. Vast, sprawling, a dinosaur dedicated to the days before the private car and the growth of the autostrada. Businessmen were there, neat and watching the departure board for the evening expresses to Torino and Milano and Napoli. Families of impatient mothers and fretful children waited for connections to the resorts of Rimini and Ricci and the towns south of Bari. Soldiers and sailors and airmen looked for the trains that would carry them to far distant barracks or back to their homes, the routine of conscription broken for a few short days. Gypsy girls in ankle-length wraparound skirts and with painful faces of destitution held out paper cups for money. Noise and move-

ment, and blurred features and the mingling of ac-
cents of Lombardia, Piedmonte, Umbria and Lazio
and Toscana.

Tired, famished, with a throat desert-dry, he stalked
slowly and still with care and watchfulness, onto the
main concourse. A good place for Giancarlo because
there were many here. Too many people, too many
scuffling feet for the *polizia* to notice one small boy.
The training of the NAP was well etched in the youth
so that places of concealment were second nature as
he sought to camouflage his presence. With his weariness had come no sense of defeat, not the will to
cringe and concede, only a confusion as to how he
might best strike back at those who had taken Franca
Tantardini. A white scabbed face, bristle on his
cheeks, hair hanging, eyes sunken. Past the stalls for
the children's toys, past the stands of newspapers and
magazines and books, oblivious of the broadcast news
of platform changes and delays, he walked the wide
length of the concourse.

The second time that he passed the big bar, the one
that faced the platforms, he saw the man who awakened recognition.

It took Giancarlo many more dragging steps as he
wracked his memory to identify the fatted face,
threatening body, dropped shoulders of the man who
leaned on his elbows with a glass in his hand and
gazed out of the bar.

The one they called *gigante*, the huge one, that was
the man in the bar. The boy conjured the image of
him in the prison on the iron steps that led between
the landings, his great strides which echoed down the
yawning corridors, of men stepping back from his
path and skirting his strength. All had conceded precedence to the *gigante*, all except the NAP men on B
wing. Claudio, he could place even his name. Not his
other name, only the first one, the given one. Clau-

dio—treated with respect in the Regina Coeli because his fist was the width of a pizza portion and his temper short and his sensitivity slight. To the boy he seemed gross in his stomach, looked to have taken his food, and from the tilt of the glass, his beer was not the early one of the day.

Giancarlo turned on his heel, retraced his way till he came and stood at the doorway of the bar which was open to lure the faint breeze into the heated interior. Stood stationary waiting for the head to rise and the gaze to fasten. The boy stood statue-still until the sleep-lost, narrow eyes of the big man rolled across the doorway and past him, and then swept backward as if awakened. Giancarlo smiled and slipped forward.

"*Ciao*, Claudio," the boy said quietly, close to him.

The big man stiffened, the prodded bullock, as if recognition ruffled and unsettled him.

"It's a long time, Claudio, but I think you remember me."

He read the uncertainty in the other's face, watched the war going on between the frown lines of his shallow forehead, the fight to put a name and a place to the boy who had accosted him. Giancarlo prompted.

"At the Queen of Heaven, Claudio. Do you not remember me, do you not remember my friends? My friends were in the political wing, and I was under their protection."

"I've not seen you before." Something in the denial that was weak and furtive, and the big man looking round, peering about him.

"But I know your name. And I could tell you the number on the cell door, perhaps even I could tell you the names of those who slept there with you." A half smile played at Giancarlo's lips, and an ebb tide of relaxation was running in him. It was the first time in the day, through the long hours since the Post, that he felt an intuition of advantage. "If we had coffee and we talked, then you might remember more of me and of my friends. My friends were in the political wing, they were people of influence in the Queen of Heaven, they still hold that influence." His voice died away, the message of menace inherent in the boast of his pedigree.

Claudio laughed with a ripple of nervousness and he looked past the boy as if to be certain that he was alone, that a trap was not set for him. He walked away without explanation to the girl at the cash desk, shouldered his way past others. Giancarlo saw a thickened wad of notes emerge from the hip pocket, saw the hands that trembled and scuffed at the notes before the *mille* lira note was produced. Money, endless rolls of it, enough to quicken the attention of the boy. As a pilot fish clings to a shark that he may feed from the droppings at its jaws, so Giancarlo stayed close to the reluctant Claudio.

"You will have a beer with me," said Claudio when he was back from the bar.

Slow and stilted, the man and the boy circled each other in sporadic conversation over the first beer. Claudio seeking to determine what the other wanted of him, Giancarlo working at the crannies of information and looking for advantage and the area of profit. A second beer, and a third, and Claudio's head was rolling from the intake, his words sluggish and with a creeping edge of confidence leading him forward. By the fourth bottle of tight, gassed Perroni, Claudio's arm was across Giancarlo's bent shoulder, and together they scanned the front page of the afternoon paper. A pudgy, scarred finger, grime to the quick of the nail, stabbed at the report on the front page of the kidnapping of a British businessman as he had left his home that morning.

When Giancarlo looked sharply into the big man's face there was a dissolve of giggles.

The boy struggled to stay alert, to hose out the beer that flowed in him. Seeking the information that might lead to power over his drinking companion. Claudio was from the south, Giancarlo's memory told him, the fact confirmed by the thickened accent of Calabria, and he was waiting for a train from Rome and there was the music of his laughter and his attention to a kidnapping. Here was a source of money, a source of protection, because the big man was running too, was also a fugitive and had betrayed himself.

"But we are not the most news today," muttered Claudio, a tinge of disappointment, an actor denied limelight. "Because they have taken one of yours. They have taken a whore of the NAP. They took her this morning and that is what excited the *polizia*." Giancarlo kept his peace, and the finger was moving again, dabbing down and smudging with dirt the picture of Franca Tantardini. "A leader of the NAP they call her, and the one that guarded her dead. Silly bitch, to have been out, in the open. Silly cow. Did you know her, boy? She looks worth knowing."

"I had met her." Giancarlo keeping the casualness of his words. "But there are many like her and she will be avenged. They will not hold her in prison, her friends will release her. They cannot hold our people." In the picture Franca's head was high and her blouse tight, and the camera had caught the sting of the nipple and the clasp of the manacles at her wrists.

"That's shit, boy. When they have her, they hold her. Good-looking bitch," mouthed Claudio. And then it was as if a clarity had come to him and the beer vapor was dispatched and the interest crawled like a spider's path across his face. "That is why you are running. Why you are here without food, without money, sponging from an old peasant. It is because they have taken her."

Giancarlo looked back at him, unwavering, deep into the blood streams of his eyes. "It is why I seek the help of a friend."

"You were with the girl?"

"I need the help of a friend."

"Because they have taken her, you have no place?"

"I have no place to go."

"In a city, in Rome, you have nowhere to cover yourself?"

"I am alone," said Giancarlo.

"But there are friends, there are others."

"We do not have that structure. We have the cell grouping. We are separated because that is the rule of the NAP."

Around their ears the noise and chaos of the bar reigned. Arms pressing against them, orders shouted to the white-shirted men behind the bar. But they had created their island, were immune to disturbance.

"Perhaps you should go home," something softer from the big man. "You should go back to your family. Bury yourself away, let the thing pass."

"I am hunted. I was with her when she was taken, and the other who was with her was killed by the pigs. They are searching for me." The supremacy over Claudio was lost, frittered away. Giancarlo searching for comfort, and turning for it to a hardened, brute animal. "I have walked all day. I have nowhere to go."

"I remember you, boy, because you were the one that went always to their cells. You had their protection." The arm was tight on Giancarlo's shoulders and the breath of garlic bread and sausage and beer was close to his nostrils. "So you became a man in the movement, something of substance, and now you turn to a Calabrian idiot for help, a man from the farms, one you would have dismissed as an ignorant and stupid pig."

"I would not dismiss you as an ignorant and stupid one. You have money in your pocket. You are not the victim of exploitation and oppression."

"You have eyes, then, my little lost one." Something cold and bovine in Claudio's face. "You watch a man when he has too much beer."

Giancarlo smiled with a richness and warmth, and cracked the frozen stare. More beers, and Claudio spoke of a hotel room, but of a meal first. Playing the grand host, he would be provider, he said, for a few hours of shelter and safety. Giancarlo wondered why, laid the reasoning of the other man at the bottles of the beer that he had drunk, and acquiesced.

The Mafia and its attendant tentacles were hated and despised by the politicized groups such as the NAP. To the organizations of the extreme left, organized crime represented the total and complete control of the working classes, its survival dependent on fear and repression inflicted on the lesser and weaker, and its helpers were the senior and corrupt officials in administration. In the revolutionary war of Giancarlo, high on the list of enemies would be the gangs that operated for money and chattels. Venality was despicable. So Claudio was Giancarlo's opponent, but the boy would use him for his purposes. If Claudio had been sober, if his limited wits had been alerted, he would not have countenanced the liaison, but he was oiled now in alcohol and his native and naive cunning for self-preservation was shorn from him.

Churning in the boy's mind was the bud of an idea. Something that needed to be cultivated and pruned if it were to show a bloom. A way to win back from the bastards his Franca. A desperate, deep yearning for her, for her body, the bright laugh and the brazen love. Franca, Franca, a muted shout, and they went into the humid night air.

The political activist and the kidnap gorilla, arms unequally around each other, bloated by beer, headed together from the Terminii in search of a plate of spaghetti.

Caught now in traffic on the Raccordo Annulare, both lanes blocked, Violet Harrison cursed and shouted her abuse at the unhearing, uncaring audience. One hundred meters she had crawled in the last eight minutes. On the back seat of the car was the plastic bag with the towel thrown angrily inside so that on her return it would be creased and untidy, and beneath it the pink polka-dot bikini, buried and unworn.

She had willed herself to stand her ground in the flat, to sit beside the telephone because that was the proper and right thing for her to do, the proper and right place for her to be. But the desire for self-preservation had won the field. She had capitulated to the gnawing opponent of lonely misery, abandoned the apartment, driven to the beach.

A ludicrous sight she must have seemed, that much she knew. A woman, a foreigner, pacing the length of the sand, her feet slipping and stumbling in their insecurity. Scanning with her eyes, peering at the boys with the golden torsos and bared legs and muscled shoulders. Seeking to keep an assignation, and showing to all who cared to watch the torment and humiliation of not finding him whom she had chosen to meet. A grown woman with a fertile womb, and thighs that were thickening, and a waist no longer slender, and a throat that showed the time ravages, and she had succumbed and come back to the beach to talk to a boy whose name she did not know. Angry tears ran without hindrance on her cheeks by the time that she had climbed back into the car and surged away in the glowering dusk.

Perhaps if she had come at the time she was always at the beach, perhaps he would have been there. Bloody boy, as if he had no knowledge of what she had sacrificed to come to find him. Couldn't have known the pain he inflicted or he would have been there. Bloody child.

"I'm sorry, Geoffrey. As God is my witness, I can't help myself. I even ironed the bikini."

Michael Charlesworth cycled home without enthusiasm, taking no pleasure from the ease with which he skirted the piled-up, slow-moving cars and ignored the impatient defiles. Normally he reveled in the freedom of the bicycle, but not on this evening.

His meeting with the Ambassador had been predictable. The aftermath of the lunch and flowing hospitality had left His Excellency with scant reserves of attention for matters outside the strict protocol of functions exercised by the embassy.

"In a criminal kidnapping there can be no area of responsibility for us," the Ambassador had remarked, his cigar tapering between his fingers. It's a matter for this poor devil's company. Their decision as to whether to pay, and how to conduct their negotiations. Personally I don't think they've any option in the matter, local conditions being what they are. The company can afford it, and let's hope they get it over as quickly as is decently possible. And don't forget the legal problems. If they're not discreet they can run into all sorts of internal problems with the law here. It's not that I'm unsympathetic, just that it's a fraught area, and not one for us. So I see no need for our feet to go in any deeper, and we should let the matter rest in the hands of those directly involved."

So the bowl of water had been brought to the throne and the hands had been rinsed. The Old Man was right, of course, invariably was. Paying out ransom money could be assessed as aiding and abetting a felony; thin ice for diplomatic boots to risk. But the ice wasn't thick under Geoffrey Harrison, and him without his woollies and a life jacket. Poor bastard. Geoffrey Harrison could scratch Michael Charlesworth off his list of angels.

He flung out his left arm, failed to turn his head, swerved across two traffic lanes, ignored the scream of tires and brakes. Their country, so do it their way. Local conditions, he thought. Local conditions, the catch phrase of the day.

Through the afternoon and early evening Francesco Vellosi had wrestled with the temptation, until at the time he would usually have left the Viminale for his home, he had finally asked his private secretary to warn the Questura that he was coming to their offices and that he wanted to sit in on the interrogation of Franca Tantardini. There was no place on such an occasion for a man in his position, nothing that he could usefully learn by his presence that could not as satisfactorily be taken from the transcripts that would await him in the morning. But the admiration of the under secretary, the reverence in which the civil servant had clothed the distant chained figure as she had been paraded for the photographers, had haunted him through the day. Most of those taken were humbled figures by the time their photographs had been executed in the basement cells, bravery leaking, the struggle and fervor of the revolution drained. It was the same with both factions, with the red fascists and the black fascists, the maniacs of the extreme left and the extreme right. But to Vellosi this girl had been particular, unique. Haughty and proud, as if beaten only in a skirmish, not a battle. Vellosi was an experienced and dedicated policeman, who had learned his trade in the hard schools of Milano and Reggio, his favor was sought after, his presence the delight of a dinner-party hostess. He was a man regarded with envy by his colleagues because of his competence and singleminded determination. Yet the sight of the woman in the warm Questura yard had unsettled Vellosi. Two years they had hunted her, countless man-hours had been expended in following snippets of information, watching buildings, in frustration and disappointment. Two years of the treadmill, and now that they had her there was none of the satisfaction that the capture should have brought.

In the back of his car, mindful of the escort vehicle behind him without which it was deemed unsafe for him to travel, Vellosi pondered the catechism he had set himself. What made the Tantardini woman turn aside from a world that the majority were grateful to accept? Where did the web of conformity burst? Where did the grotesque mutation spawn? There were more than five hundred of them, red and black, in the jails. Mostly minnows, mostly idiots, mostly the cruel oddities of life who saw in violence and maiming the only outlet they might capture in their desire to be heard of, shouted about.

But not this woman. Too intelligent, too trained, too vicious to be classified with the herd. From a good family in Bergamo. From a convent school. From money and opportunity. . . . The real and worthy opponent, the one who taxed and exhausted Francesco Vellosi. A woman who could make a man bend and crawl and suffer. She could grind me, this one, he thought, could squeeze and suck me dry between her legs, with her brain. And there was little to confront her with, nothing to frighten her, no instrument with which to break her.

"Mauro, I've said it before today and I say it again. We should have shot the bitch on the pavement." He spoke quietly to his driver, the trusted ear for his musings. "More people have been killed, crippled, in the name of Renato Curchio than ever were attacked while he was at liberty. More of these bastard kids are motivated by the name of La Vianale than ever before we took her. We will build another rallying point when we lock up Franca Tantardini. We can put her down in Messina, throw the key away, and it will change nothing. If we segregate her from other prisoners, then it's called inhuman treatment, mental torture. If we put her with the pack, it's too easy for her, she'll be over the wall. Each month she's in Messina the *Radicali* will be yelling her name in the Camera. All ways we approach it we lose. Eh, Mauro?"

It was not the driver's place to reply. He nodded agreement. His attention was on the road, always watchful for a car closing too fast on the open side, looking to his mirror that the escort should not have become separated.

"They have called for a demonstration tonight," Vellosi continued his monologue. "The students, the unemployed, the men of the Democrazia Proletaria, the children of the Autonomia. A medley of the discontented. The Questura has banned it, no march nor meeting is permitted, but the rats will be out once they have the night to hide them. The murder of Enrico Panicucci is the rallying cry. They will break some limbs and smash some shops and burn some cars and scream about the violence of the state. And Tantardini's name will be heard in the *centro storico* and the ones that shout it would not have heard of her before this morning's radio. Mauro, I feel I should weep for Italy."

The driver, sensing the discourse was exhausted, again nodded, decisively and with agreement. Perhaps if the Dottore had a wife and children then he would be changed, not bleed so copiously. But Vellosi was

alone, and his home was his office and his furniture
was his filing cabinet, and his family were the young
men he sent onto the streets at darkness to fight his
war. The cars swept into the back entrance to the
Questura, recognized and saluted by the officer on
the barrier.

Francesco Vellosi was not a man to be kept waiting.
A welcoming party of three shook his hand as he
emerged from his car. If the Dottore would follow
them they would lead to the interrogation room. Tantardini was eating in the cell block. She had been
questioned once, a shrug of the shoulders and a gri-
mace to demonstrate how much had been learned.
The session was about to be resumed. Vellosi followed
his guides through pale-lit corridors, down steps, past
guards. Down into the bowels of the building. More
handshakes at the entrance to the designated room
and then Vellosi's escort abandoned him. He was left
with his own people, the ones prepared to dirty their
hands while those who had brought him this far could
retreat from the subterranean world of violence and
counterviolence and breathe again the real air that
was not conducted by aging generators and fans.
There were two men in the room, both known to Vellosi because they were his appointees; hard men, and
efficient and devoid of soul. Skillful in interrogation,
impatient of prevarication, these were their creden-
tials. And what other criteria could be used in recruitment? What other men could be found to soil their
fingers in defense of a gross and obese society? The
excitement was running for Vellosi because these
were his colleagues, and in their company he was at
ease.

He gestured his readiness and sat himself on a bare
wooden chair in the shadow of the door where he
would face the interrogators. The prisoner would not
see him as the lights shone in her eyes, where she

would be confronted by her questioners, her back
would be to him. Vellosi heard the far distant and
then encroaching tramp of weighted shoes, and he
found himself arched and taut as the woman, eclips-
ing the lights, was brought through the door. She blazoned her indifference, casually flopped down in a
chair in front of the lone table. This was the enemy,
dangerous, menacing, and all for him to watch were
the angular shoulder blades of a good-looking woman,
her hair circled by a cheap cotton scarf. Dirty jeans
and unwashed blouse, no lipstick and a sneer to sub-
stantiate the threat. Where were her tanks, and her
APCs? Where was her army and her regiments and
platoons, where was her serial number and her rank?
Deadstill Vellosi stayed because that way she had no
reason to turn and face him. That way he was the voyeur, the intruder at a private party.

One interrogator lounged across the table from her.
The second man farther back behind him with the file
and the notepad on his knees. There was no paper laid
out on the table, because the man who would ask
questions and seek to find flaws in her defiance must
demonstrate his knowledge, must have no need for
typed reports, must dominate if he were to succeed.

"You have had your food, Tantardini?" He spoke
conversationally, without rancor.

Vellosi heard her snort, the derision that communicated tension.

"You have no complaints about the food?"

No response.

"And you have not been hurt, you have not been
tortured?"

Vellosi saw her shrug. Noncommittal, as if the question were unimportant. Now the woman had no audience, but would be a changed person in the cockpit of
the public courtroom.

"We have not treated you in any way that violates

the constitution? We have behaved, Tantardini, is that right?" He mocked her gently, feeling his way forward, amused.

Again the shrug.

"And that is not as you would have expected? Am I correct? That is not what the communiqués will state, am I correct?"

No response.

"But then we play by different rules from yours."

She drove back at him, seeking to destroy the smugness and complacency reflected on his face. "If you do not hurt me it is because you are afraid. There is no compassion in lackeys like yourself. There is no kindness among you pigs. Fear governs you. Fear of the reach of our arm. The society that you are servile to cannot protect you. If you lay a hand on me, a finger, a nail, then we will strike you down. That is why you give me food. That is why you do not touch me."

"We are afraid of no one, Tantardini. Least of all the little ones, like yourself. Perhaps we are cautious of the strength of the *Brigate Rosse*, cautious only, perhaps we treat them with care. But the NAP does not match the *Brigate Rosse*, the NAP is trivial and without muscle."

"You hunt us hard. If we have no muscle, you spend much time on us."

The interrogator smiled, still sparring, still dancing far apart, as if unwilling yet to clash with the gloves. Then he leaned forward and his grin faded.

"In twenty-five years' time, Tantardini, how old will you be?"

Vellosi could see the outline of the woman's neck, could see the smooth bright skin of youth.

"You have the files, you have the information," she replied.

"You will be old, Tantardini. Old and withered and barren. In twenty-five years there will be new generations. Young men and women will grow and take their places in society and they will never have heard of La Tantardini. You will be a dinosaur to them. An ancient creature, verging on extinction."

Perhaps he has hurt her, perhaps that is the way to her. Vellosi sat very still, breathing quickly, satisfied she was unaware of his presence. There was no response from her.

"That is the future, that is what you have to consider, Tantardini. Twenty-five years to brood on your revolution." The interrogator droned on. "You'll be a senile hag, a dowager of anarchy, when you are released. A tedious symbol of a phase in our history, courted by a few sociologists, dug out for documentaries by the RAI. And all will marvel at your stupidity. That is the future, Tantardini."

"Will you say that when the bullets strike your legs?" she hissed, the cobra at bay. "When the comrades are at you, when there are no chains at their wrists. Will you make speeches to me then?"

"There will be no bullets. Because you and your kind will be buried behind the walls of Messina and Asinara and Favignana. Removed from the reach of ordinary and decent people . . ."

"You will die in your own blood. It will not be in the legs, it will be to kill." She shouted now, her voice echoing across the room. Vellosi saw the veins leaping at her neck, straining down into the collar of her blouse. Fierce and untamed, *la leonessa,* as the civil servant had christened her.

"La Vianale cursed her judge, but I think he is well and with his family tonight, and that it is now two years that her threat has been empty and hollow." The interrogator spoke quietly.

"Be careful my friend. Do not look for paper victories, for victories that you can boast of. We have an arm of strength. We will follow you, we will find you."

"And where will you find your army? Where will you recruit your children, from which kindergarten?"

"You will find the answer. You will find it one morning as you kiss your wife. As you walk back from school from setting the children down. You will see the power of the proletarian masses."

"That's shit, Tantardini. Proletarian masses, it means nothing. Revolutionary warfare, nothing. Struggle of the workers, nothing. It's gibberish, boring and rejected gibberish."

"You will see." Her voice was a whisper and there was a chill in the room that clutched at the man who wrote the notes behind the interrogator and which made him thankful that he was far from the front line, a noncombatant, obscure and unrecognized.

"It's shit, Tantardini, because you have no army. You go to war with sick children. What have you to throw against me? Giancarlo Battestini, is that the hero who will strike . . ."

The pain fled her face. She shrieked with laughter, pealed it round the faces of the watching men. "Giancarlo? Is that what you think we are made of? Little Giancarlo?"

"We have his name, we have his fingerprints, his photograph. Where will he go, Tantardini?"

"What do you want with him, little Giancarlo? His capture won't win you a war."

Angered for the first time, resenting the dismissal of a situation he had worked toward with care and precision, the interrogator slammed his fist to the table. "We want the boy. Tantardini, Panicucci, Battestini, we want the package."

She jeered back at him. "He is nothing, not to us, not to you. A little bed wetter, looking for a mother. A thrower of Molotovs. Good for demonstrations."

"Good enough for your bed," he chanced.

"Even you might be good enough for my bed. Even

you, little pig, if there was darkness, if you washed your mouth."

"He was with you at the shooting of Cesare Fulni, at the factory."

"Sitting in the car, watching, messing his pants, masturbating most likely." She laughed again, as if in enjoyment.

Vellosi smiled, deeply and safe in his privacy. She was a worthy enemy.

"Where will he go?" The interrogator flustered and unsettled.

"If you want Giancarlo go and stand outside his mother's door, wait till it is cold, wait till he is hungry."

The interrogator shook his shoulders, closed his eyes, seemed to mutter an obscenity. His fingers were clamped together, knuckles showing white. "Twenty-five years, Franca. For a man or a woman it is a lifetime. You know you can help us, and we can help you."

"You begin to bore me."

Vellosi saw the hate summoned to the man's narrowed lips.

"I will come one day each year and stand over the exercise yard and I will watch you, and then you will tell me whether I bore you."

"I will look for you. And on the day that you have broken the rendezvous, then I will laugh. You will hear me, pig, however deep you are buried, however far is your grave. You will hear me. You do not frighten me because already you are running."

"You stupid little whore."

She waved her hand carelessly at him. "I am tired. You do not interest me and I would like to go now. I would like to go back to my room."

She stood up, proud and erect, and seemed to Vellosi to mesmerize her questioner because he came round the table and opened the door for her. She was gone without a backward glance, leaving the room abandoned and without a presence.

The interrogator looked sheepishly at his chief. "The boy, sweet little Giancarlo, she would have eaten him, bitten him down to the bone."

"A very serious lady," replied Francesco Vellosi with as composed a face as he could muster. "She will have given her little bed wetter and Molotov thrower a night he will not quickly forget."

7

Four undemanding years Archie Carpenter had been on the sprawling staff list of International Chemical Holdings. Four years in which his life revolved around negotiated office hours, a stipulated lunch break, five weeks annual holiday, and days off for working public holidays. A "soft old number, Archie" his onetime friends in the Special Branch of the metropolitan police called him when the old ties proved too strong and he hunted them out in the pub behind the Yard for a grouse and a gossip. He had settled for a predictable backwater in an unremarkable current. So it had been a traumatic evening. First, he had been summoned to the Managing Director's suite of offices. He'd stood with a puzzlement on his face through a briefing on the kidnapping of Geoffrey Harrison and its company implications. On the way out, the personnel director had handed him an open-dated return ticket to Rome. In a fluster he had been ushered to the front entrance where a company car waited to speed him to Heathrow. Last onto the plane.

But he wasn't in Rome. Hadn't arrived at his destination. Archie Carpenter was in front of the departure board at Linate, Milan's international airport. Strike in Rome, he'd been told. Cockpit crew, and he was lucky to have reached this far. There might be a flight later and he must wait as everybody else was waiting. He'd asked repeatedly whether he should have a seat on the first flight to leave for Fiumicino. He was smiled at and had learned in twenty minutes that the shrugged shoulder of a man in uniform meant everything or nothing. All done up for the party, dressed in a fancy crinoline, and nowhere to go. He paced, cursing, through the scurrying crowds of fellow travelers, always returning to the crush around the board. Four years ago he wouldn't have been flapping, would have made his assessment and either sat back and let the tide take him or jumped off his backside and done something about it, like a self-drive hire car, or a taxi down to the Central Station and an express to the capital. But improvisation was on the way out, the mechanics of initiative were rusty, and so he tramped the concourse and breathed his abuse.

A Detective Chief Inspector in Special Branch had been Archie Carpenter's lofty ranking in the Metropolitan Police when he had moved over into "industry," as his wife liked to spell it out to the neighbors. All the big firms in the city had been frantic for security-trained personnel to advise them on protection from the rash of Provisional IRA bombings in London. Frightened half to death they'd been at the prospect of letter bombs in the mail bags, of explosive devices in the corridors and the underground garage, looking for chaps with a confident jargon and who seemed to know what they were at. ICH, a multinational colossus, offices and factories halfway round the world, had one small plant outside Ballymena, County Antrim, in Northern Ireland. The Board of Directors had determined that this put the vast conglomerate at risk and was sufficient reason to lure Archie

Carpenter from sixteen hours a day, five days a week of plodding with the Branch. They had popped him into a nice, clean, air-conditioned office with a secretary to write his letters, a pension when he was senile, and nine thousand a year for his bank account. Had seemed like one long holiday. No more surveillance on winter evenings, no more meetings of the political loonies to drift into, no more Irish pubs to swill Guinness in, no more tetchy Arabs to stand alongside with a Smith and Wesson rammed in his belt. It had taken him a month to seal Chemical House, to put a system into operation that reduced the always faint threat to a minimum, and after that it had been more than comfortable with little to worry him beyond the occasional pilfering from the typists' lockers, and the one great drama of the loss of a set of board room minutes. He didn't complain, didn't want it to change.

He wasn't a small man. Had a good set of shoulders on him, and a stomach to go with it from four years of canteen lunches. But they availed him nothing when the herd of would-be passengers responded to the loudspeaker announcement and surged for the standby check-in counter. Slight little girls bouncing him aside, chaps with concave chests pushing him half off his feet. Never seen anything like it.

"Wait a minute. Excuse me, won't you. You don't have to push like that, you know," helped him not at all.

Archie Carpenter's anger rose, the tired flush driving up his cheeks, and he thrust with the best of them and was almost ashamed at the progress. The gaps opened for his sharp, driving kneecaps and the heave of his elbows, and there were pained stares. Bit heavy, perhaps, but I didn't start it, darling, did I? So don't curl your bloody lip and flick your fingers. A little victory it had been, and one worth winning if there wasn't anything else about to compete for.

Ticket and boarding card in his hand, step a little lighter, Archie Carpenter headed for the security gates dividing the concourse from the departure lounges. His face twisted in distaste at the sight of the *polizia*, slacks that looked as if they'd been sat in for a week, dowdy pointed shoes, and those bloody great machine pistols. What were they going to do with them? In a crowded space like an airport lounge, what was going to happen if they let one of those things off? Be a massacre, a Bloody Sunday, a Saint Valentine's Day job. Needed marksmen, didn't they? Chaps who'd be selective, not wallpaper merchants. First impressions, Archie, and they're the worst. Fair enough, sunshine, but if that's the mob that has to bust out Harrison, then draw the curtain and forget it. He'd carried a gun a dozen times in eight years with the Branch, always under a jacket, and it hurt him, professionally, to see these kids with their hardware lolling against their chests.

No moon and a heavy darkness round them, the Alitalia DC-9 lifted off. They'd be hours late into Rome, and then all the joke of the money change queue and finding whether he'd been met and if the hotel had a booking. Stop bloody moaning, Archie. Off on your holidays, aren't you? Remember what the wife said. Her mum had brought back from Viareggio some nice leather purses, be good for Christmas presents for the family, must not forget to bring something like that. I'm not going for my health, for a saunter round, darling. But you'll have some time off. Not for a shopping spree. Well, what are you going for? Haven't time to tell you now, darling, but it's all a bit messy and the plane's leaving five minutes ago. And he hadn't any clean underwear. He'd rung off, gently put down the telephone in the Chemical House hallway. Would have shaken the poor old sweetheart. Weren't many fellows in Churchill Avenue, Motspur

Park, who charged off abroad without as much as a
toothbrush to hold onto.

All a bit messy, Archie Carpenter.

No drinks on the flight. Cockpit crew strike ended.
Cabin crew strike continuing.

The Managing Director had been explicit enough.
They'd pay up and pay quickly. Head Office didn't
want it lingering. The locals would set it up and he
was there to oversee the arrangements and report
back. Going to cause a bit of pain, paying out that
sort of cash. Surprised him really, that they'd made up
their minds so fast and hadn't thought of brazening it
out.

Fifty minutes of sitting cramped in his seat and
nothing to read but personnel's photostat file on Geoffrey Harrison with a six-digit number stamped on the
outside. In the file was a blownup passport photograph of the man, dated eighteen months earlier. He
looked to be a reasonable enough chap, pleasant nondescript sort of face, the sort people always had problems describing afterward. But then, Archie Carpenter
thought, that's what he probably is, pleasant and nondescript. Why should he be anything else?

They had stripped the hood from him before he
was brought from the van, opening a vast relief at the
freedom from the musk of the material that had
strained and scratched at his throat. The plaster, too,
had been pulled away from his mouth, just as they
had done hours earlier when they had fed him. The
tape around his legs had been loosened and the blood
flowed, quick and tingling, to his feet.

All that Geoffrey Harrison had seen of his new
prison had been from the beam of the flashlight that
one of the masked men had carried as they pushed
him along a way between small stones and across sun-
dried earth, until they had come after a few meters to

the shadowed outline of a farmer's shed. The beam
had played vaguely on a small, sturdy building, where
the mortar was crumbling from between the rough-
hewn stones, replaced by dangling grass weed. Win-
dowless and with twin doors at each end, a shallow
and sloping corrugated roof. They had hurried him
through the door and the light had discovered a ladder set against piled hay bales. No words from his
captors, only the instruction of the jabbed fist that he
should climb, and immediately that he started to
move there was the weight and shudder of another
man on the rungs below him, steadying and supporting because his hands were still fastened at his back.

Between the roof and the upper level of the hayloft
was a space some four feet in height. The man in the
darkness behind shoved Harrison forward and he
crawled ahead along the noisy and shifting floor of
bales. Then there was a hand at his shoulder to stop
him. His wrist was taken in a vice grip. One ring of
the handcuff's was unlocked. He looked upward as
the man worked in haste by the flashlight. The hand
that was still imprisoned was jerked high and the
ratchet action of the handcuff closed on a steel chain
that hung from a beam to which the roofing iron was
nailed. A chain of the width and strength to subdue
an Alsatian dog.

Geoffrey Harrison had been brought to the safe
house. He had been hidden in a distant barn long unused for anything except storage of winter fodder for
cattle. The barn lay a hundred meters off a dirt track
that in turn was a tributary of the high-banked paved
road a kilometer away that linked the town of Palmi
with the village of Castellace in the pimpled foothills
of the Aspromonte. Through the day and the greater
part of the night the van had traveled more than nine
hundred kilometers.

To the northeast of the barn was the village of San

Martino, to the southeast the village of Castellace. To
the northwest were Melicucca and San Procopio, to
the southwest was the community of Cosoleto. From
the rooftop of the barn it would have been possible to
identify the separated lights of the villages, lonely and
glowing places of habitation. This was the country of
lightly rolling, rockstrewn hills decorated with the
cover of olive groves, the territory of shepherds who
minded small sheep flocks and herds of goat and who
carried shotguns and shunned the company of strangers. These were the wild hill lands of Calabria that
claimed a fierce independence, the highest crime rate
per capita in the Republic, the lowest arrest rate. A
primitive, feudal, battened-down society.

The low voices of two men were Harrison's company as he lay on the bales, the talk of men who are
well known to each other and who speak merely because they have time on their hands and long hours to
pass.

As a formality he ran his left hand over the handcuff, and then tested with his fingers the route of the
chain over the bar, and groped without hope at the
padlock that held it there. No possibility of movement, no prospect of loosening either his wrist or the
chain attachment. But it had been a cursory examina-
tion, that of a man numbed with exhaustion, who had
burned deep into the core of his emotion.

On the warm softness of the hay he was soon
asleep, curled on his side with his knees pressed up
against his chest. His mind closed to all around him,
permitting neither dream or nightmare, he found a
peace, stirring hardly at all, his breathing calm and
regular.

The clashes spread far through the *centro storico* of
the capital city. Under cover of darkness the gangs of

young people, small and uncoordinated, smashed a trail of broken shop windows and burned-out cars. The night air echoed with the crack of Molotovs on the cobbles, the howl of police sirens and reports of the *carabinieri* rifles that threw the gas shells into the narrow streets. A night full of the noise of street battle and the cries of "Death to the Fascists," "Death to the assassins of Panicucci," and "Freedom for Tantardini."

Twenty-nine arrests, five *polizia* injured, eleven shops damaged and eighteen cars. And the name of Franca Tantardini had been heard and would be seen, when morning came to the city, written large on the walls in dripping paint.

His guests gone, the dinner table of the executive suite in ICH House cleared, Sir David Adams retreated to his office. During the week he frequently worked late, his justification for prohibiting business interferences during weekends at his country retreat. The principal officers of the company had learned to expect his staccato tones on the telephone at any hour before he cleared his desk and walked across to his Barbican flat for the trifle of sleep that he needed.

His target on this evening was his personnel director who took the call on a bedside extension line. The conversation was typically to the point.

"The man we sent to Rome, he got away all right?"

"Yes, Sir David. I checked with Alitalia, he was diverted to Milan, but he managed an onward to Rome."

"Have you called Harrison's wife?"

"Couldn't get through. I tried before I left the office, but this fellow Carpenter will do that."

"He'll be in touch with her?"

"First thing in the morning."

"How's Harrison going to stand up to all this? The

man from the embassy who called me was pretty blunt in his scenario."

"I've been through Harrison's file, Sir David. Doesn't tell us much. He's a damn good record with the company . . . well that's obvious for him to have had the posting. He's a figures man . . ."

"I know all that. What's he going to be like under this sort of pressure, how's he going to take it?"

"He's fine under business pressure . . ."

The personnel director heard a sigh of annoyance whistle at his ear.

"Is he an outdoor type, does he have any outdoor hobbies listed on his file?"

"Not really, Sir David. He listed 'reading' . . ."

There was a snort on the line. "You know what that means. That he comes home, switches on television, drinks three gins, and gets to his bed and his sleep. A man who offers reading as a hobby is a recreational eunuch in my book."

"What are you implying?"

"That the poor blighter is totally unfit for the hoop he's going to be put through. I'll see you in the morning." Sir David Adams rang off.

In a restaurant in the northern outskirts of Rome, secure and far from the running street fight, Giuseppe Carboni shuffled his ample wife around the cleared dance floor. The tables and chairs had been pushed back against the walls to make space for the entertainment. A gypsy fiddler, a young man with a bright accordion, and his father with a guitar provided the music for the assortment of guests. It was a gathering of friends, an annual occasion, and one valued by Carboni. The kidnapping of Geoffrey Harrison provided no reason for him to stay away from the evening of fancy dress enjoyment.

He had come dressed as a ghost, his wife and her sewing machine concocting from an old white sheet and a pillow slip with eye slits the costume that had caused loud acclamation on his entry. She was robed in the dress of a Sardinian peasant girl. They had eaten well and drunk deep from the Friuli wine, and the night would serve as a scant escape from the dreary piling of reports on his desk at the Questura. And there was advantage for Carboni in such company. An under secretary of the Interior Ministry, in a mouse's habit with tail hanging from his rump, was dancing close to his shoulder. Across the floor a deputy of the Democrazia Christiana, and one spoken of as ambitious and well connected, clutched at the hips of a girl both blond and beautiful and attired solely in a toga created from the Stars and Stripes. Good company for Carboni to be keeping; and what good to be achieved from sitting in his apartment with an ear poised for the telephone? Too early in the Harrison matter for intervention. Always it was easier to work when the money had been paid, when there were not tearful wives and stone-faced legal men complaining in high places that the life of their dear one and their client was endangered by police investigation.

He bobbed his head at the under secretary, smirked beneath his pillow case at the deputy, and propelled his wife forward. There were few enough of these evenings when he was safe from disturbance and aggravation. He bowed to the man in property who wore the fading theatrical uniform of a Napoleonic dragoon and who was said to be a holiday companion at the villa of the President of the Council of Ministers. Diamonds catching brightly in the guttering candle-light, the crisp cackle of laughter, the sweet ring of the violin chords. Movement and life and pleasure, and the white-coated waiters weaved among the guests dispensing brandy tumblers and glasses of sam-

bucca and amaro. The man in property was beside
him, more smiles, and a hand released from his wife's
waist so that Carboni could greet the interloper.

"Please forgive me, Signora Carboni, please excuse
me. May I take your husband for a moment . . . ?"

"He dances badly," she tinkled.

The man in property kissed her hand, laughed with
her. "It is the cross of marrying a policeman, always
there is someone to take him to the side and whisper
in his ear. My extreme apologies for the interruption."

"You have the gratitude of my feet."

The ghost and the dragoon huddled together in a
corner, far from earshot, achieving among the sounds
of talk and music a certain privacy.

"Dottore Caboni, first my apologies."

"For nothing."

"You are busy at this time with the new plague, the
blight over us all. You are involved in inquiries into
the kidnappings."

"It is the principal aspect of our work, though less
intense here than in the north."

"And always the problem is to find the major figures, am I right? They are the hard ones."

"They will protect themselves well, they cover their
activities with care."

"Perhaps it is nothing, perhaps it is not my business . . ." How they all began when they wished to
plant poison in a policeman's ear . . . "but something
has been brought to my attention. It has come from
the legal section of my firm, we have some bright
young men there, and it was something that aroused
their interest, and that involved a competitor."

Predictable, too, thought Carboni, but the man
must be heard out, if it were not to reach the head of
government that a policeman had not reacted to the
advice of a friend.

"A year ago I was in competition for a site of chalets on the Golfo de Policastro, near Sapri, and the man against me was called Mazzotti, Antonio Mazzotti. Around two hundred millions were needed to settle the matter, and Mazzotti outbid me. He took the site, I took my money elsewhere. But the Mazzotti could not fulfill his commitments, it was said he could not raise the capital, that he was too greatly extended, and I am assured he sold at a loss. It is a difficult game, property, Dottore, many burn their fingers. We thought nothing more of him, another amateur. Then two weeks ago I was in competition for a place to the south of Sapri, at the Marina de Maratea. There was another location where it was possible to build some chalets . . . but my money was insufficient. Then yesterday my boys in the legal section told me that the purchaser was Mazzotti. Well, it is possible in business to have fast recovery, but he paid in bank draft the greater proportion of the sum. From an outside bank, outside Italy. The money has run back sharply to the hands of this Mazzotti. I set my people to find out more and they tell me this afternoon that he is from the village of Cosoleto in Calabria. He is from the bandit land. I ask myself, is there anything wrong with a man from the hills having brains and working hard and advancing himself? Nothing, I tell myself. Nothing. But it was in foreign draft that he paid, Dottore. That you will agree is not usual."

"It is not usual," Carboni agreed. He hoped the man had finished, wished only to get back to the music. "And I would have thought it a matter for the Guardia di Finanze if there have been irregularities of transfer."

"You do not follow me. I do not care where the fellow salts his money, I am interested where he acquires it, and how its source springs up so quickly."

"You are very kind to have taken so much trouble."

"I have told no one else of my detective work," a light laugh.

"In the morning I will make some inquiries, but you understand I have a great preoccupation with the kidnapping of the Englishman."

"I would not wish my name to be advanced in this matter."

"You have my word," said Carboni, and was gone to the side of his wife. Something or nothing, and time in the morning to run a check on Antonio Mazzotti. Time in the morning to discover whether there were grounds for suspicion or whether a disgruntled businessman was using the influence of the network of privilege to hinder an opponent who had twice outwitted him.

Giuseppe Carboni scooped the pillow slip over his head and downed a cooled glass of Stock brandy, wiped his face, dropped again his disguise, and resumed with his wife a circuit of the dance floor.

When they reached the second-floor room, puffing because they came by the turning staircase as there was no elevator in a *pensione* such as this, Giancarlo stood back, witnessing the drunken effort of Claudio to fit the room key in the door lock. They had taken their beds in a small and private place between the Piazza Vittorio Emmanuele and the Piazza Dante with a barren front hall and a chipped reception desk that carried signs demanding prepayment of money and the decree that rooms could not be rented by the hour. The *portiere* asked no questions, explained that the room must be vacated by noon, pocketed the eight thousand lire handed him by Claudio and presumed them to be from the growing homosexual clan.

On the landing, waiting behind the fumbling Claudio, Giancarlo looked down at his sodden jeans, dark and stained below the knees, and his canvas shoes

that oozed the wine he had poured away under the
table in the pizzeria. He had eaten hugely, drunk next
to nothing, was now sobered and alert and ready for
the confrontation that he had chosen. The Calabrian
needed a full minute, interspersed with oaths, to unfasten the door and reveal the room. Bare and func-
tional. A wooden table with chair. A wooden single-
door wardrobe. A thin framed print of old Rome. Two
single beds separated by a low table on which rested
a closed Bible and a small lamp. Claudio pitched forward, as if it were immaterial to him that the door
was still open, and began pulling with a ferocious
clumsiness at his clothes, dragging them from his back
and arms and legs before sinking heavily in his underpants onto the gray bedspread. Giancarlo extracted
the key from the outside lock, closed the door behind
him, and then locked it again before pocketing the
key.

Cold and detached, no longer running, no longer in
flight, Giancarlo looked down with contempt at the
sprawled figure on the bed, ranged his eyes over the
hair-encased legs and the stomach of rolled fat and on
up to the opened mouth that sucked hard for air. He
stood a long time to be certain in his mind that the
building was at peace and the other residents asleep.
An animal, he seemed to Giancarlo, an illiterate animal. The pig had called his Franca a whore, the pig
would suffer. With a deliberation he had not owned
before, as if sudden age and manhood had fallen to
him, he reached under his shirttail and pulled the P38
from his belt. On the balls of his feet and keeping his
silence, he moved across the linoleum and stopped
two meters from the bed. Close enough to Claudio,
and beyond the reach of his arms.

"Claudio, can you hear me?" a strained whisper.

In response, only the convulsed breathing.

"Claudio, I want to talk to you."

A belly-deep grunted protest of irritation.

"Claudio, you must wake up. I have questions for you, pig."

A little louder now. Insufficient to turn the face of Claudio, enough to annoy and to cause him to wriggle his shoulders in anger, as if trying to rid himself of the presence of a flea.

"Claudio, wake yourself."

The eyes opened and were wide and staring and confused because close to them was the outstretched hand that held the pistol, and the message from the boy's gaze was implicit even through the mist of Station beer and pizzeria wine.

"Claudio, you should know that you are very close to death. I am near to killing you, there as you lie on your back. You save yourself only if you tell me what I want to know. You understand, Claudio?"

The voice droned at the dulled mind of the prostrate man, dripping its message, spoken by a parent who has an ultimatum on behavior to deliver to a child. The bedsprings whined as the bulk of the man began to shift and stir, moving backward toward the headrest, creating distance from the pistol. Giancarlo watched him trying for focus and comprehension, substituting the vague dream for the reality of the P38 and the slight figure who held it. The boy pressed on, dominating, sensing the moment was right.

"There is nowhere to go, no one to save you. I will kill you, Claudio, if you do not tell me what I ask you. Kill you so that the blood runs from you."

The boy felt detached from his words, separated from the sounds that his ears could hear. No word from the pig.

"It is the P38, Claudio. The weapon of the fighters of the NAP. It is loaded and there are bullets. I have only to draw back the trigger. Only to do that and you are dead, and rotting and fly-infested. Am I clear, Claudio?"

The boy could not recognize himself, could not recognize the strength of his grip upon the gun.

"It is the P38. Many have died by this gun. There would be no hesitation, not in sending a Calabrian pig to his earth hole."

"What do you want?"

"I want an answer."

"Don't play with me, boy."

"If I want to play with you, Claudio, then I will do so. If I want to tease you, then I will. If I want to hurt you, then you cannot protect yourself. You have nothing but the information that I want from you. Give it to me and you live. It is that or the P38."

The boy watched the man strain in the night stillness for a vibration of life from the building, cocked ears, seeking something that might give him hope of rescue, and saw the dumb man collapse at the realization that the *pensione* slept, was cloaked in night. The big body crumbled back flat onto the bed as if defeated and the coiled springs tolled under the mattress.

"What do you want?"

He is ready, thought Giancarlo, as ready as he will ever be.

"I want to know where the man is hidden who was taken this morning." The message came in a flurry, as a transitory shower of snow falls on the high places of the Appennines, quick and brisk and blanketing. "If you want to live, Claudio, you must tell me where to find him."

Easier now for Claudio. Easier because there was something that he could bite at. Half a smile at his face, because the drink was still with him and he lacked the control to hide the first frail amusement.

"How would I know that?"

"You will know it. Because if you do not, you will die."

"I am not told such things."

"Then you are dead, Claudio. Dead because you are stupid, dead because you did not know."

From the toes of his feet, moving with the swaying speed of the snake, Giancarlo rocked forward, never losing his balance which was perfect and symmetrical. His right arm lunged, blurred in its aggression till the foresight of the gun was against the man's ear. Momentarily it rested there, then raked back across the fear-driven, quivering face and the sharp needle of the sight gouged a ribbon welt through the jungle of bristle and hair. Claudio snatched at the gun and grasped only at the air and was late and defeated, while the blood welled and spilled from the road hewn across his cheek.

"Do not die from stupidity and idiocy, Claudio. Do not die because you did not understand that I am no longer the child who was protected in the Queen of Heaven. Tell me where they took the man. Tell me." The demand for an answer, harsh and compelling, winning through the exhaustion and the drink, abetted by the blood trickle beneath the man's hand.

"They do not tell me such things."

"Inadequate, Claudio . . . to save yourself."

"I don't know. In God's name, I don't know."

Giancarlo saw the struggle for survival, the two extremes of the pendulum. If he spoke now the immediate risk to the pig's life would be removed, but replaced in the fullness of time by the threat of the retribution that the organization would bring down on his dulled head should betrayal be his temporary salvation. The boy sensed the conflict, the alternating fortunes of the two armies waging combat in the man's mind.

"Then in your ignorance you die."

Noisily because it was not a refined mechanism, Giancarlo drew back the hammer of the pistol with his thumb. Reverberating around the room, a sound that was sinister, irretrievable. Claudio was half up on the bed, pushed from his elbows, his hand flown from the wound. Eyes, saucerlarge and peering into the dimness, perspiration in bright rivers on his forehead. Dismal and pathetic and beaten, his attention committed to the rigid, unmoving barrel aimed at the center of his rib cage.

"They will have taken him to the *mezzo giorno*," Claudio whispered his response, the man who is behind the velvet curtain of the confessional and who has much to tell the Father and is afraid lest any other should hear his words.

"The *mezzo giorno* is half the country. Where in the south has he gone?"

Giancarlo held the trapped rat in his cage, offering it as yet no escape.

"They will have gone to the Aspromonte . . ."

"The Aspromonte stretch a hundred kilometers across Calabria. What will you have me do? Walk the length of them and shout and call and search in each farmhouse, each barn, each cave? You do not satisfy me, Claudio." Spoken with the chill and deep cold of the ice on the hills in winter.

"We are a family in the Aspromonte. There are many of us. Some do one part of it, others take different work in the business. They sent me to Rome to take him. There was a cousin and a nephew of the cousin that were to drive him to the Aspromonte where he would be held. There is another who will guard him . . ."

"Where will they guard him?" The gun, hammer arched, inched closer to Claudio's head.

"God's truth, on the soul of the Virgin, I do not know where they will hold him."

The boy saw the despair written boldly, sensed that he was prying open the area of truth. "Who is the man who will guard him?" The first minimal trace of kindness in the boy's voice.

"He is the brother to my wife. He is Alberto Sammartino."

"Where does he live?"

"On the Acquaro road and near to Cosoleto."

"I do not know those names."

"It is the big road that comes into the mountains from Sinopli and that runs on toward Delianuova. Between Acquaro and Cosoleto is one kilometer. There is an olive orchard on the left side, about four hundred meters from Cosoleto, where the road begins to climb to the village. You will see the house set back from the road, there are many dogs there and some sheep. Once the house was white. His car is yellow, an Alfa. If you go there you will find him."

"And he will be guarding the Englishman?"

"That was what had been arranged."

"Perhaps you try only to trick me."

"On the Virgin, I swear it."

"You are a pig, Claudio. A sniveling coward pig. You swear on the Virgin and you betray the family of your wife, and you tell all to a boy. In the NAP we would die rather than leave our friends."

"What will you do with me now?" A whipped dog, one that does not know whether its punishment is completed, whether it is still possible to regain affection. On a lower floor a lavatory flushed.

"I will tie you up and I will leave you here." The automatic response. "Turn over to your face on the pillow. Your hands behind your back."

Giancarlo watched the man curl himself to his stomach. In his vision for a moment was the shamed grin of self-preservation on Claudio's face, because he had won through with nothing more than a scratch across his cheek. Gone then, lost in the pillow and its grease coat.

When the man was still, Giancarlo moved quickly forward. Poised himself, stiffened his muscles. He swung down the handle of the pistol with all his resources of strength onto the sun-darkened balding patch at the apex of Claudio's skull. One desperate rearing convulsion that caused the boy to adjust his aim. The breaking of eggs, the shrieking of the bedsprings, and the tremor of breathing that has lost its pattern and will fade.

Giancarlo stepped back. An aching silence encircled him as he listened. Not the creak of a floorboard, not the pressure of a foot on a staircase step. All in their beds and tangled with their whores and boys. Blood on the wall behind the bed, spattered as if the molecules had parted on an explosive impact, was running from drops in downward lines across the painted plaster, and above their farthest orbit, untainted, was the smiling and restful face of the Madonna in her plastic frame with the cherubic child. The boy did not look at Claudio again.

He cleared the hip pocket from the strewn trousers on the floor and went on tiptoe to the door. He turned the key, carried outside with him the *non disturbare* sign, attached it to the outer door handle, locked the door again and slipped away down the stairs. To the *portiere* he said that his friend would sleep late, that he himself was taking an early coach to Milano. The man nodded, scarce aroused from his dozing sleep at the desk.

Far into the night and with little traffic to impede him as he crossed the streets, the wraith, Giancarlo Battestini, headed for the Terminii.

8

What in Christ's name am I doing here?

The first thoughts of Archie Carpenter. He was naked under a sheet, illuminated by the light that
pierced the plastic blind slats. He flailed his arms at
the hanging cloud of cigarette smoke, spat out the
reek of brandy from the glasses that littered the dressing table and windowsill.

Archie Carpenter sat up in bed, putting his memory
together. Half the bloody night he'd spent with the
men from ICH. All the way from the airport in the
limousine he'd listened and they'd talked, he'd asked
and they'd briefed. Convincing the big man from
Chemical House of their competence, that's how he
saw it. They'd taken care of his bags at the hotel with
a finger snap and tramped into his room, rung down
for a bottle of cognac, and kept up the barrage till
past three. He'd slept less than four hours, and he had
to show for it a headache and the clear knowledge
that the intervention of Archie Carpenter had no
chance of affecting Geoffrey Harrison's problems. He
climbed out of bed and felt the weakness in his legs
and the mind-bending pain behind his temples. Half

midnight, at the latest, they wound things up in Motspur Park. With babysitters at a pound an hour there
wasn't much time after the ice cream and fruit salad
to sit on your arse and chat about the rate of income
tax. And the brandy didn't flow, not out there in the
suburbs, not at seven pounds a bottle. A quick splash
after coffee and the Mums and Dads were on their
way. Not that the Carpenters had kids . . . that's another trial, Archie. Not for now, old sunshine.

He'd need a shower to flush it out of him.

Beside his bed, under a filled ashtray, was his diary. He thumbed through for the number the Managing Director had given him. A chap called Charlesworth, from the embassy and said to be helpful. He
dialed, listened to the telephone ringing, took a time
to answer. What you'd expect at this time in the morning.

"*Pronto,* Charlesworth."

"My name's Carpenter. Archie Carpenter of ICH.
I'm the company's Security Director . . ." since when
had he had a title like that? But it sounded right, just
sort of slipped out like a palmed visiting card . . .
"they've asked me to come out here and see what's
going on. With this fellow Harrison, I mean."

"It's nice of you to ring, but I'm a bit out of touch
since yesterday evening."

"They said in London you'd put yourself out in this
business. I was asked to pass on the thanks of the
company."

"That's very kind of you, it was nothing."

"They thought it was. I have to go out to the EUR
place, wherever that is, and I have to go visit Harrison's missus, so I'd like to meet up with you before
that. First thing."

Carpenter was aware of a hesitation on the line. A

natural enough request, but it had sparked prevarication.

"I don't think there's very much I can tell you."

"I'd like to hear views other than from the company people. They're Italians, every last one of them. I'd like your views."

"There really isn't much that I can tell you."

"Not in the line of duty?" Carpenter clipped in, cold, awake, the brandy disgorged.

"I double between political and security. Security doesn't warrant a great deal of time, and the desk is pretty loaded with the political stuff at the moment. My plate's more than full."

"So is Harrison's." A flare of anger from Carpenter. What was the bloody fool at? "He's British isn't he? Entitled to a bit of help from the embassy."

"He is," the cautious reply. "But there's debate in the shop about how much help."

"You've lost me."

"I'm sorry then."

Carpenter closed his eyes, grimaced. Begin again, Archie boy. Start all over again.

"Mr. Charlesworth, let's not waste each other's time. I'm not a moron, and I've kidnapping coming out of my ears after last night with the locals. I know it's not straightforward. I understand the threat that exists, that Harrison's on the edge. I know it's not just a matter of sitting in the front parlor and waiting for the shareholders to cough up so Harrison can come back and kiss his sweet wife hello. I know the risks for Harrison. They told me about Ambrosio, shot because a mask slipped and he saw his captors. I heard how they chopped Michelangelo Ambrosio. They told me about de Capua. Now on to the other side of things. I did eight years in Special Branch before I moved to ICH. My rank at Scotland Yard was Chief Inspector. This isn't the time for a 'need to know' show."

A laugh on the line. "Thanks for the speech, Mr. Carpenter."

"What's the problem then?"

"I wouldn't want what I say repeated."

"I've signed the bloody Official Secrets Act, Mr. Charlesworth, just as you have."

"It's a tedious matter of keeping our hands clean. Theoretically its a criminal offense to pay ransom money and would be damaging to us if we could be linked with such a felony. In the Ambassador's view this is a private matter between ICH and a gang of Italian criminals. He doesn't want us to be seen to be condoning the extortion of money, and he feels that any public involvement could give the impression that we're bending the knee to criminal action. If Harrison worked for Whitehall we wouldn't be paying, it's as simple as that."

"And a chat in your office . . ."

"That's involvement in the Ambassador's eyes."

"That's bloody ridiculous." Carpenter barked into the telephone.

"I agree, particularly in a country where ransom payment is the normal way of extrication. If you're that well briefed you'll have heard of a man called Pommarici in Milano. He's a prosecutor and has tried to freeze kidnap victims' assets to prevent payment. He lost . . . the families said he was endangering the lives of their loved ones. It all went back to the jungle. So what it adds up to is that the embassy has no role to play. Off the record we can help, but not if it's visible. Do you read me?"

Carpenter slopped back onto his bed. "I read you, Mr. Charlesworth."

"Give me a ring this afternoon. We'll have an early bite in town."

"I'd like that," Carpenter said and rang off. Poor bloody Harrison, but how inconsiderate of him. To get himself kidnapped and embarrass HMG. Not a very good show, my old love.

The wooden shutters, bent and paint-peeled but still capable of restricting light, stayed late across the upper window of the narrow terraced home of Vanni, the driver. The noises, provided by children and cars in the cobbled street behind the main road through Cosoleto, merely lulled the man as he lay in the drowsy pleasure of his bed.

It had been close to midnight when he had returned to his home, and there was the radiance in his worn face to tell his wife that the journey had been profitable. She had not asked what the work had been, what the danger, what the stake, but had busied herself first in the kitchen, then against the muscles of his stomach in the great bed that had been her mother's. And when he had slept she had slid from the sheets and looked with a glowing excitement at the hard roll of banknotes before replacing them in the hip pocket of the trousers thrown with abandon on a chair. A good man he was to her, and a kind man.

While she worked in the kitchen beneath, Vanni was content to idle the early morning hours. Not time yet for him to dress, throw on a freshly ironed shirt, put a sheen on his shoes, and drive his car into Palmi for a coffee and a talk with Mario who would make a similar journey if ever he woke—she was an animal, Mario's woman, consumed in the brute passion of the Sicilians. A coffee with Mario, if he had satisfied his woman, if he had the sap to leave his bed.

And when Claudio had returned on the morning *rapido*, then perhaps they all would be summoned to the villa of the *capo* to take a glass of Campari and talk of the olive trees, the goat herds, and the death of an old man of the village. They would not speak of anything that was immediate and close to them, but

they would smile at their mutual knowledge, and each
in his own way reflect a peculiar glory.

At least another hour Vanni could keep to his bed.

At Criminalpol, where the Rome police forensic effort is mounted, the first particles of evidence were
being gathered in the scientific analysis section.

Brought from the central telephone exchange were
recordings of all calls received by ICH in EUR and of
those directed to the private number of the Harrisons.
One of the most far-reaching advances in the hunt for
the kidnappers had been the development of a voice
bank programmed for the computer to match similari-
ties. The same man, the electronics decided, who had
called ICH with the ransom demand had also made
the abortive call to Mrs. Harrison. Nothing peculiar in
that. The stir of interest among the technicians came
when they fed to the brain scores of recordings made
from previous interceptions, and sought a similarity
with their latest material. On the readout screens the
file on the Marchetti case was flashed. Eight and a
half months earlier. A four-year-old boy. Taken from a
foreign-national nanny in the Aventino district of
Rome. No arrests. No clues left on site. A ransom payment of *due cento cinquante millioni* paid. Marked
notes. No sign of ransom money. The Marchetti communication and the calls on the Harrison case had
been made by the same man. Vocal interpretation lo-
cated an accent from the extreme south.

The night work of machines. The recordings were
sent by line to the Questura to await the arrival of
Giuseppe Carboni.

The *Agente di Custodie* hurried from the prison officers' mess to the main gate of the Asinara jail. He
had not eaten the breakfast provided for the men
coming off night shift after they had supervised the

first feeding of the prisoners. The weight of the message that he must telephone to the contact number bore down on him, spiriting up the fear waves of nausea.

His recruitment as a pigeon for the leading members of the NAP held on Asinara when they wished to communicate with the outside world had been a long drawn-out affair. As a badger will sniff and dig for choice roots, so members of the group at liberty, had discovered the turmoil that the *agente* and his family lived with as they devoted themselves to the care of their ailing *spina bifida* baby. Reports had come back of crippling doctors' bills in the town of Sassari on the Sardinian mainland to the south of the prison island. There had been word of the inability of the father to pay for visits to Roma or Milano for consultation with specialists.

The *agente* had been ripe for plucking. There was money for his wife, used notes in envelopes. He was no longer in debt and muttered instead and without conviction to the medical men of the help of a distant relative. Not that the child could improve, only that the conscience of the parents might be easier. The numbers that he must telephone changed frequently, and the cryptic messages that he must pass on became a deluge.

On Asinara is the maximum security cage of the Italian forces of justice; escape was deemed impossible. It is the resting place of the most dedicated of the male urban guerrilla community, the receptacle for those found guilty of armed insurrection against the state. Originally a prison colony, then a jail for the liberal few who opposed Mussolini's fascism, the jail drifted to disrepair before the refurbishment that was necessary for the incarceration of the new enemy. The renovation had been from the drawing board of the magistrate, Riccardo Palma; he had done his work

well, and died for it. But through the *agente*, the
words of the chief of staff of the NAP could pass beyond the locked cell doors, along the watched corridors with their high closed circuit cameras, through
the puny exercise yards, piercing the lattice of the
electrically controlled double gates and their
dynamite-proof bars. The message had been given to
the *agente* as he lined the prisoners in a queue for
their food, slipped in his hand, drowned in the sweat
sea of his palm.

Beyond the gates and heading for his home, the free
house of the prison service where only anxiety and
pain awaited him, he had read the message on the
scrap of torn paper.

Per La Tantardini. Rappresaglia. Numero quattro.
For Tantardini. Reprisal. Number four.

The *agente*, held in the clutch of compromise,
walked in a tortured daze that fled him as the pale
broken face of his wife greeted his arrival at the front
door. His child was dying, his wife was failing, and
who cared, who helped. He kissed her perfunctorily,
went to their room to change out of uniform, and then
looked in silence through the half-open door at the
child asleep on her cot. In his own clothes and without explanation he strode down into the hamlet to telephone the number he had been given at Porto Torres
across the narrow channel on Sardinia. Within one
day, perhaps two, he would witness on the little black
and white television screen in the corner of the living
room the results of his courier work.

The swollen pressure of his bladder finally awoke
Geoffrey Harrison. He stretched himself, jerking at
the handcuff, wrenching at his wrist, aware immediately of the inhibitions of his slept-in clothes. Still the
suit that he had dressed in for the drive to the office,
still with the tie at his neck, and only the top button

undone as a concession to the circumstances. The sun
had not yet played on the roof of the barn and he was
cold, shivering. His socks smelled, pervading the limited space between the rafters and the bales; the ny-
lon ones that he always wore in the summer and that
he changed when he came home in the early evening.

Didn't speak the language, did he? Had never taken
a Berlitz. He could only order a meal and greet his
office colleagues at the start of the day. So what to
shout to the men in the other half of the barn? He
wanted to urinate, wanted to squat and relieve himelf,
and didn't know how to say it. Basic human function,
basic human language. He couldn't mess his trousers.
That was revulsion, and so from necessity came the
shout. Couldn't have an accident.

"Hey. Down there. Come here." In English, as if because of his urgency they would understand him.
They'll come, Geoffrey, they'll want to know why the
prisoner shouts. "Come here."

He heard the sudden movement, and the voices of
two men who were closer. A creaking from the swing
of the barn door, which was hidden from him by the
bales, and the ladder top slid into position and shook
from a man's weight. A gun first, black and ugly, held
in a firm grip and following it the contortion of a
hood with eye slits. Eerie and awful in the half light
before it gave way to the recognizable shape of shoulders and a man's trunk. The gesture of the gun was
unmistakable. He obeyed the order of the waved barrel and stumbled back as far as the chair would allow.
He pointed down to his zip, then across with his free
hand to his buttocks. A grotesque mime. And the
hooded head shook and was gone, lost below the lip
of the hay.

There was noisy chuckles from below and then a
farm bucket arched up from an unseen hand. Old and
rusted and once of galvanized steel. A folded wad of

newspaper pages followed. He was left to a slight privacy as he pulled the bucket toward him, turned his
back on the ladder, and fingered at his belt. Humiliated and hurt, one arm aloft and fastened, he contorted his body over the bucket. He speeded his functions, willing his bladder and bowels to be emptied,
before the slitted eyes returned to laugh at his
dropped pants and his bared thighs and genitals. How
half the world does it, Geoffrey, so get used to it.
Don't think I can bloody well take it, not every day,
not like this. God, what a bloody stink. The sandwich . . . all stink and wind. He groped down for the
paper; damp with the morning dew, must have been
outside through the night, and it tore soggily in his
hands. He wanted to cry, wanted to weep and be pit-
ied. Harrison cleaned himself as best he could, tears
smarting, pulled at his underwear and trousers,
zipped himself and fastened the belt.

"I've finished. You can come and take it."

Movement and repetition. The ladder moved as before and the gun and the hood reappeared. He
pointed to the bucket.

"I've used it. You can take it away."

Just a belly laugh from the covered face and a
jumping in merriment of the shoulders, and the hood
sinking and going, and the muffled call of fun and
entertainment. A bloody great joke, Geoffrey. Do you
see it, do you see why he's splitting himself? You
asked for the bucket, they've given it to you, given it
for keeps. They've given you a little present. It's going
to sit there, a couple of yards away. Stinking and rotten and foul. Own pee, own shit, own waste. You've
given them a bloody good laugh.

"Come here. Come back." All the command that he
could summon. The tone of an order, unmistakable,
and enough to arrest the disappearance of the hood.
The laugh was cut.

"Come here."

The head came upward, revealed again the shoulders. Geoffrey Harrison leaned back on his left foot, then swung himself forward as far as the chain permitted. He drove his right instep against the bucket, saw it rise and explode, career against the shoulder of the man, spill its load across his mask and faded cotton shirt. Strained and dripping.

"You can have it back," Harrison giggled, "You can have it again now."

What in God's name did you do that for?

They'll bloody murder you, Geoffrey Harrison, they'll half tear you apart for that.

It's what they're for, those bastards, to be crapped and peed on.

Right, dead right. When you've a bloody army at your back. You're an idiot, Geoffrey Harrison.

I don't know why I did it.

You won't do it again.

They came together for him. The other man leading, the one with the smears on his shirt and hood a rung on the ladder behind. No words, no consultation, no verbal reproach. Nothing but the beat of their fists and the drumming of their boots against his face and chest, and the softness of his lower belly and his thighs and shins. They worked on him as if he were a suspended punching bag, hanging from the beam. They spent their strength against him till they panted and gasped from their effort, and he was limp and defenseless and no longer capable of even minimal self-protection. Vicious, angered creatures, because the act of defiance was unfamiliar and the bully had risen in them, sweet and safe. Harrison crumpled down onto the hay floor feeling the pain that echoed in his body, yearning for release; wishing for death. The worst was at his rib cage, covered now in slow funnels of agony. When did you ever do anything like

that in your life before, Geoffrey? Never before,
never stood up, not to be counted. And no bastard
here this morning with his calculator. No one there to
see him, to cheer and applaud. Just some mice under
his feet, and the stink of his body, and the knowledge
that there was a man close by who loathed him and
would cut off his life with as little ceremony as pick-
ing the muck from his nostrils.

He worked a smile over the pain of his jaw and
gazed at the emptied bucket. He'd tell Violet about it,
tell her it blow by blow. Not what they did to him
afterward, but up till then, and his foot still ached.

He struggled upright, knees shaking, stomach in
torment.

"You're animals," he shouted. "Slobbering, miserable swine. Fit to shovel shit, you know that." The
scream wobbled under the low cut of the rafters. "Get
down in your shit and wash yourselves, you pigs. Rub
your faces in it, because that's what makes pigs
happy. Pig shit, pig thick."

And then he listened, braced for a new onslaught,
and heard the murmur of their voices. They took no
notice of him, ignored him. He knew that he could
shout till he lifted the roof and that they had no fear
of it. He was separated from every civilization that he
knew of.

Without hunger, without thirst, numbed by the an-
nihilation of the big Calabresi, Giancarlo sat on a
bench in the Terminii, waiting the hours away. Close
to exhaustion, near to drifting in fitful sleep, hands
masking his face, elbows digging at his legs, he
thought of Franca.

There had been girls in Pescara, the daughters of
the friends of father and mother. Flowing skirts,
starched blouses and knee boots, and the clucking approval of mother as she brought the cream cakes out.

The ones that giggled and knew nothing, existed with
emptied minds. Crucifixes of gold at their necks and
anger in their mouths if he reached for buttons or zips
or snaps.

There had been girls at the university. Brighter and
more adult stars who regarded him as an adolescent.
There he was someone who could make up the numbers for the cinema or the beach, but who was
shunned when it was dark, when the clinching began.
The spots, the acne, and the tittle behind the hand. It
should have been different with the Autonomia, but
the girls would not grovel for a novice, for a recruit,
and Giancarlo had to prove himself and win the acclamation. Far out in the front of the crowd, running forward with the fire eating into the rag at the hilt of the
milk bottle, arching the Molotov into the air. The battle for approval, and his ankle had turned. Would they
even remember him now, the girls of the Autonomia?
Giancarlo Battestini had no experience other than in
the arms, between the thighs, wrapped warm by
Franca. It was the crucible of his knowledge. A long
time he thought of her.

Franca with the breasts golden and devoid of the
rim of suntan, Franca with the cherry-pip nipples,
with the flattened belly holed by a single crater,
Franca with the wild forest that had tangled and
caught his fingers. The one who had chosen him. Darling, darling, sweet Franca. In his ears was the sound
of her breathing, the beat of her movement on the
bed, her cry as she had spent herself.

I am coming, Franca. I am coming to take you from
them, he whispered to himself.

Thinking of Franca as the station began to live
again, to move and function, participate in a new day.
Thinking of Franca, he walked to the ticket counter
and paid the single fare on the *rapido* to Reggio.
Thinking of Franca as he climbed up to a first-class

carriage. Away from the herd of Neapolitans and Sicilians with their bundles and salads and children and
hallucinating noise of discussion and counterdiscus-
sion. No other passengers in the compartment. Thinking of Franca as the train pulled away from the low
platform and crawled between the sidings and junctions and high flats draped in the day's first washing.
The boy slumped back, slid his heels onto the seat in
front, and felt the pressure of the P38 against his
back.

Out across the flatlands to the south of the city,
carving through the grass fields and the close-packed
vineyards, skirting the small towns of Cisterna de La-
tina and Sezze away on the hills, and Terracina at the
coast, the train quickened its pace. Blurring the tele-
graph poles, homing and seeking out the dust-dry
mountains and the bright skies of the Aspromonte.

"Believe in me, Franca. Believe in me because I am
coming." The boy spoke aloud above the rash of
wheels on the welded track. "Tomorrow they will
know of me. Tomorrow they will know my name. Tomorrow you will be proud of your little fox."

9

At the Questura there were barely disguised smiles from the uniformed men who watched Dottore Giuseppe Carboni disgorged from his car. The evidence of the night before was plain. Bulldog bagged eyes, blotched cheeks, a razor-nicked chin, a tie not hoisted. He swept uneasily through the door, searching straight ahead of him as if wary of impediments and took the elevator instead of risking the flight of stairs. Carboni had greetings for none of those who saluted and welcomed him along the second-floor corridor. Ignoring them all, he was thankful to make the haven of his desk without public humiliation. They would think he had been drinking all night, would not know, as they whispered and clucked in disapproval, that he had left the party before two, and back at his flat, had collapsed in a chair with a tumbler of whisky that he might better search his memory for patterns and procedures in his latest kidnap burden. Never time for thought, for analysis, once he was at work with the telephone ringing and the stream of visitors, humble and distinguished. And a tumbler had become two and merged into half a bottle as he picked into the recesses of the problem before him. He had stayed up till his wife, magnificent in her flowing nightdress, had dragged him to her bed, and little enough chance of sleep then.

He sank heavily into his chair and buzzed the connecting speaker for his aide. A moment and the man was there, sleek and oiled and ready with an armful of files, battered brown folders encasing a hillock of typed paperwork. What did the Dottore intend the priority of the day to be?

Carboni winced, the stab of pain ringing in his head. "The Harrison affair. There is nothing else."

"We have the tapings of the calls to Mrs. Harrison and to ICH. The one to Harrison's wife was futile. She couldn't understand what she was being told and rang off." There was a sneer at the mouth of Carboni's assistant. "The first tangible steps toward extortion were made in a message to his company. Also, from Criminalpol, there is voice analysis. They believe there is similarity here with the communication of the Marchetti kidnapping, the child."

"Just the one message to the company?"

"A single message, the establishment of lines of approach."

"Leave me with the tapes," said Carboni, eyes closed, head spinning, wishing deliverance from intelligent and confident young men.

When he was alone he played the cassette many times. Hands over his face, shutting out the noise through the open windows of the traffic below, concentrating his effort on the brief and staccato message. A callow, rasping voice he heard, and the policeman did not need the help of the memorandum that was attached to the package to know that this voice came from the toe of the country, from Calabria, from the land of the Mafiosi chieftains. Where else? A humble, inarticulate voice, reading a message that had been written for him, which was normal. Then there was the tape of the first call to the Marchetti family to be heard. A match, didn't take a computer to tell him that.

Time now for work on the telephone. He mopped at his neck with his handkerchief. Half an hour in his office and his shirt was soaked.

Calls to his subordinates drew blanks. No further eyewitnesses had been produced since he had left for home the previous evening. There was nothing to feed into the machines beyond the very basics of description supplied by the single woman on Collina Fleming, bulk and height and a general clothing description. No faces, no fingerprints, no escape car yet traced. No information had emerged from the tenuous links with the underworld maintained by the discreeter elements of the antikidnap squad. No word and none expected because to inform in these matters was the sure and fast way to a wooden box. Not for the first time since he had reached his lofty eminence, Giuseppe Carboni pondered the value of his work. The servant of a society that stepped back from commitment and involvement. The servant, neither trusted nor appreciated, and struggling for standards that those who lodged even in the higher places renounced. Lockheed, Friuli, Esso Italiana, Belice, even the Quirinale, even the presidency. Scandals; nasty and deceitful, and the guilty were from the chief echelons of the great Mama Italia. So, who wanted law, who wanted order? The ache was back at his head, the throb of a hungover man, wetted with disillusion. He could take his pension. He could go on his way, and the President would hang a medal round his neck, and his parting would be unseen, unimportant.

Carboni smacked his pudgy hand down on the desk, felt the shockwaves vibrate back up to his elbow, enjoyed the affliction. There was time for a few

more of the great ones to go behind bars, time for a
few more handcuffs to be wrapped on the wrists of
those who at last would show shame as the doors of
the Regina Coeli closed on them. Abruptly he pressed
the intercom button and heard the silken voice of his
assistant.

"A man called Antonio Mazzotti, originally he is
from Cosoleto in Calabria." He had slipped away
from the priority of the day because he did not know
how to harness the energy he wished to expend for
Harrison's freedom. "He has an office in Rome and
deals in property speculation. He has made some development deals in the Golfo di Policastro. I want the
telephone number of his office. Just the number and I
will call it myself."

"It will be attended to, Dottore."

"And not this evening, not this afternoon," Carboni
growled. "I want it this morning."

"Of course, Dottore. And the firm of Harrison rang.
They would like an Archibald Carpenter to see you.
He is the Security Director of ICH head office, from
London . . ."

"Around twelve I could see him."

"I will let the company know."

"And the number of this man, Mazzotti, no delay."

"Of course not, Dottore." The voice dripped. Carboni hated him, would have him shifted. "Dottore, the
news is coming of another kidnapping. From Parioli."

"I cannot handle it. Someone else will have to."

"They have taken the nephew of a considerable industrialist . . ."

"I told you, I have enough to concern me."

" . . . an industrialist who is generous to the Democrazia Christiana with funds."

Carboni sighed in annoyance and resignation. "Get
my car to the door, and when I am back I want that

number on my desk, and I want this Carpenter here at twelve."

"Of course, Dottore."

Vengefully Carboni slapped the intercom button to the "off" position, locked his desk, and headed for the corridor.

Far out on the Nomentana Nuova, shadowed by the high-rise apartments that the planners had dubbed "Popular" was a simple row of garages of precast concrete with swinging, warped doors. The garages were skirted by waste ground, discarded rubbish, and stray dogs. Few were in use, for the occupants of the flats found them too far from their front doors and out of sight to their windows and therefore unsafe from the work of thieves and vandals. One was a chosen burrow of a NAP cell, rented through an intermediary, not to house a car, but to provide storage and meeting space. There were guns here. Quarry explosives stolen by sympathizers. Boxes full of car license plates. Sleeping bags and a camping stove, and the mimeo machine on which the communiqués were run off. None of the possessions of the cell would have been visible if the doors had been carelessly opened, because time had been lavished on the garage. If the dirt on the floor were brushed away, the outline of a trap door became apparent. They had carved through the cement and underneath had dug out a tomb some two meters wide, two and a half meters long, and a meter and a half high. A narrow plumbing pipe to the surface brought them air. This was the hideaway in times of great danger, and this was where three young men sheltered, for it was just a day since La Tantardini had been taken and they had abandoned their safe house. Though she was a leader, who could say whether she would talk to her interrogators? Dark and closed, the pit provided a lair to the men who breathed the damp and musty air. There was the son of a banker, the son of a landowner, the son of a professor of economics at the University of Trento.

Above them, muffled through the thickness of the cement, came four sharp raps at the closed wooden doors of the garage. It was a sign they recognized, the signal that a courier had visited them. An envelope had been pushed far from sight under the cover of the doorway, the message it held dispatched four hours earlier from the island of Asinara.

For Tantardini. Reprisal. Number Four.

In the pit, among the cell's papers, would be the code sheet that would identify Number Four, the target the young men must reach for. They would wait several minutes in the calm of the darkness before levering aside the entrance and crawling upward to find and read the communication.

Through the morning, as the sun rose and blazed with its full force on the tin roof above him, they left Harrison to himself. No food, no water, and he hadn't the stomach and courage to call for either.

There were pains in many parts of his body, slow and creeping and twisting at the bruised muscle layers.

Deep in sweat, heavy in self-pity, slumped on the hay and straw, conscious of his own rising smells, he ebbed away the hours without hope, without anticipation.

Giancarlo was half asleep, meandering in the demistate between dream and consciousness, relaxed and settled, the plan in his mind evaluated and approved. Small and lone and hungry for the action he had decided upon, he was sprawled between the padded seat back and the hard face of the window's glass.

The sights beyond the comfort of the speeding train were ignored.

It would be hot that day in Pescara, hot and shrouded in a sea-top mist, and noisy and dusty from the car wheels and the tramping of the thousands who would have come to roast themselves on the thin sand line between promenade and water. The shop would be open and his father wheedling with the lady customers. Perhaps his father would know by now, would know of his boy. Perhaps the *polizia* would have come, pained and apologetic because this was a respectable citizen. His father would curse him, his mother cry in her handkerchief. Would he shut the shop if the *polizia* came and announced with due solemnity that little Giancarlo was with the NAP and living in a *covo* with a feared terrorist, the most dangerous woman in the land and their lad cohabiting? They would hate him. Hate him for what he had done to them. And the base rock of their hatred would be their majestic, colossal absence of understanding of why he had taken his road.

Stupid, pathetic, insignificant, little crawling fleas, Giancarlo rolled the words round his tongue. Groveling servants, in perpetual obeisance to a system that was rotten and outworn. Savagely he recalled the wedding of his elder brother. Hair oil and incense, an intoning, doddering priest, a hotel reception on the seafront that neither the groom's nor the bride's father could afford. New suits and hair trims for the men, new dresses for the women and jewelry out from the wall safes. An exhibition of waste and deception, and Giancarlo had left early, walked across the town, and locked himself in his room and lain in the darkness until his father, much later, hammered at the door and shouted of the offense given to aunts and cousins and friends. The boy had despised his father for it, despised him for the chastity belt of conformity. Governing them was the necessity of normality; the mayor must come to the apartment each year, the bishop to the shop, and after Mass in April the shining new BMW must be blessed by the priest and a fee given. Their knees buckled, their hands together ran damp with nervousness when a town hall official visited to safeguard his votes; a rotten little creep with his hand in the till, and they treated him like Christ Almighty. The relationship was past repair. Past patching and bandaging. Past medication. A divided family.

The boy mouthed his insults, sometimes aloud, sometimes without sound, working off, as an athlete sheds weight in roadwork, the ease that had held him during the early hours of the journey. The society of *clientilismo*: whom his father knew in business, had been to school with, was owed a favor by, the way toward a job for a growing boy. The society of the *bustarelle*: the little envelopes of old banknotes that smoothed and purred their way round the town hall. The society of *evasione*: avoidance of commitment to the weak, the ethic of selfishness and personal preservation. That was their society, and he had vowed that the break was final, and the bond of family blood was inadequate to change his determination.

The train rolled on, Napoli left behind.

A boy who had killed and found that no special experience, and who sometimes smiled and sometimes laughed and who had no companion. Giancarlo Battestini on the *rapido* to Reggio.

The screams of the cleaning woman carried far down the column of the staircase well.

The shrieks brought the day porter of the *pensione* as fast up the steps as his age and infirmity would permit, and when he arrived panting at the upper landing the woman was still bent to the door keyhole, the clean, folded sheets on the floor beneath her feet, her bucket in one hand, her sweeping broom in the other. He had fished the passkey from his pocket, opened the door, taken a cursory look, mouthed a prayer, and pushed the woman back from the door. He had locked the room again and without explanation scrambled down the stairs to raise management and authority.

Amid sirens the *carabinieri* arrived, running from the car, leaving the winking blue light revolving, pacing through the hall in a clatter of heavy boots, and pounding on the stairs past the opened rooms of those who had been roused and wondered at the intrusion.

The barest glance at the battered head and the accompanying bloodstains was sufficient to convince the *mareschiallo* that hope of life and survival was long past. One man he sent to the car to radio for the necessary assistance, another he detailed to stand by the door and prevent entry by the gathering crowd on the landing—salesmen, servicemen on leave and the prostitutes who had kept their company during the night. By the time the *mareschiallo* had found the dead man's identity card there were more sirens in the air, warning all those who heard of further misery, the reckoning time for an unfortunate.

Below on the street, another gathering. Little on their faces that betrayed the commodity of sympathy. The day porter stood among them, a man much in demand at this time, with the story to tell of what he had seen.

A blue Fiat 132 limousine brought Archie Carpenter from International Chemical Holdings through the old battered dignity of central Rome to the formidable front archway of the Questura. Like a bloody great museum, he'd thought. More churches per square yard than any place he knew, cupolas and domes by the dozen. The history, the markets, the

shops, the women, bloody fantastic the whole place.
Oozing chic, steady class, he'd felt; dirty and sophisticated, filthy and smart. And now this place, police
headquarters for the city. A great, gray, stone heap,
coated in pigeon dirt. Flag limp and refusing to stir on
the pole above.

He gave Carboni's name at the front desk and
showed the official the name written on paper. Had
to do that because they'd looked blank when he
opened his mouth. But the name seemed to mean
something because heels clicked together and there
were obsequies and ushering arms toward the lift.

Archie Carpenter laughed behind his hand.
Wouldn't be like this if one of their lot came over to
the Yard. Be made to sit for half an hour while they
sorted out his accreditation, checked through to his
appointment, made him fill out a form with three car-
bons. And no chance of getting called "Dottore," no
bloody chance. All a bit strange, but then it had been
strange all morning—from the embassy man who
wouldn't talk, to the time when he'd gone into an
empty office at ICH and dialed the number they'd
given him for Violet Harrison.

Yes, he could come round if he wanted to. If there
was something that he had to say to her, then he
should come round, otherwise she'd be going out. Carpenter had stuck at it. He had to see her, Head Office
was particularly keen that he should personally make
sure everything possible was being done for her.
Well, in that case, she'd said, he'd better come and
she'd stay at home. Like she was doing him a favor,
and would about six o'clock be right, and they could
have a drink.

Well, not what you'd expect, was it, Archie?

Down the corridors they went, Carpenter a pace
behind his escort, bisecting the endless central carpet,
worn and faded, hearing all about him the slow crack

of typewriters, turning his eyes away when two men came out of an office in front and gave each other a big smacker on the cheeks. Round a corner, down another corridor, like a charity hike.

And then he was there. A young man was shaking his hand and prattling in the local and Carpenter was smiling and nodding, catching on with the manners. Then the inner door of the office burst open. The man who came through the door was short, grossly overweight, but moving with the speed of a crocodile on the scent of fresh meat toward his young subordinate. Papers and a cassette recorder were gripped in his left hand, the other remained free for a waving accompaniment to the waterfall of words. Carpenter understood not a phrase, stood rooted to the carpet. Both of them hammering away, and at the body work, arms round the shoulders, heads close enough to recognize the toothpaste. Something had gone well. Was acting as if he'd drawn the favorite in the Irish Sweepstakes, the little fellow with the big belly.

A change of gear, an effortless switch to English, and the recorder and paperwork parceled out to his subordinate, Giuseppe Carboni introduced himself.

"I am Carboni. And you are Carpenter? Good. You come from London, from ICH? Excellent. You come at the right moment. Everything is well. Come into my room."

Can't be bad, thought Carpenter, and followed the disappearing figure into the inner office. Looked around him, swayed a bit. Massive and tasteful, furnished and carpeted. Prints on the wall of old Rome, velvet drapes on the windows, a framed portrait of the President on a desk half submerged in an Everest of files. He sat himself down opposite the desk.

"Carpenter, this morning I am proud. This morning I am very happy and I will tell you why . . ."

Carpenter inclined his head, had the routine

straight now, gave him a flash of teeth. Roll on, let the dam break.

". . . Let me tell you that from yesterday morning when I first heard of what had happened to your Mr. Harrison, from the time I first telephoned to the embassy, this has been a case that has worried and disturbed me. To be frank, there are not many of these kidnappings that greatly affect me. Most of the people who are taken are excessively rich, and you will have read of how much money they can pay for their release. And after they have been freed many are investigated with enthusiasm by the Guardia de Finanze, our fiscal police. One wonders how it is, in a modern society, that individuals can legally accumulate such funds, the hundreds of thousands of dollars necessary to win freedom. They give us little help these people, not the families during the imprisonment, not the victim after return. They shut us out so that we must work from the side, from the edge. When our record of arrests is decried, then I sweat, Carpenter, because we work with only one hand free."

"I understand," said Carpenter. He had heard this, and it stank and ran against all his police training. Intolerable.

"When it is children or teenage girls, the innocent parties, then it hurts more. But your Mr. Harrison, he is an ordinary businessman, I do not seek to denigrate him, but an ordinary fellow. Not important, not rich, not prepared. The shock for him, the ordeal, may be catastrophic for his psychology. You know, Carpenter, I was up half the night worrying about this man . . ."

"Why?" Carpenter cut in, partly from impatience at having the news that provoked the ebullience withheld from him, partly because the syrup was too thick. Benedictine, when he wanted Scotch.

"You laugh at me, you laugh at me because you do not believe I am serious. You have not been a policeman for twenty-eight years in Italy. Had you been, then you would know my feelings. Harrison is clean, Harrison is not tainted, Harrison observes legality. He is in our country as a baby, a baby without clothes, without malice, and he deserves our protection, which is why I work to bring him back."

"Thank you," Carpenter spoke with simplicity. He believed he understood and warmed to the barely shaven, perspiring man across the desk from him.

"You have come to supervise the payment of extraordinary sums for Harrison's release. Why else would you come? . . .

Carpenter flushed.

". . . It does not embarrass me, it was my own advice to your embassy. What I have to tell you is that it may not be necessary. It may not be required."

The jolt shuddered through Archie Carpenter. Straight-backed in his chair, peering forward.

"We try to use modern methods here. We try not to justify the image that you have of us. We do not sleep through the afternoon, we are not lazy and stupid. We have a certain skill, Carpenter. We have the tapes of the telephone calls to Mrs. Harrison and to ICH. The computer gobbles them up. Then we feed other calls into the machine, from other events. And we have made a match. We have two cases where the contact was the same man. You understand police work?"

"I did eight years with Special Branch in London, with the metropolitan police. What you'd see as the political wing." Carpenter spoke with a certain pride.

"I know what is Special Branch."

Carpenter flashed his molars, creased his cheeks.

Carboni acknowledged, then launched himself again. "So I have a match and that tells me that I am not dealing with a first-time-out group. I am working against an organization that has been in the field. It tells me a little, it tells me something. Just now I am talking to a man from the business office of a fellow whom I have been asked to investigate. You know the situation. Many times when you have my position people come with a whisper from the ear. Look at this man, they say, look at him and think about him. Is everything correct about him? And if he is a Calabresi, if he is from the south and has much cash, then you look closely. I rang the office of a property speculator in Rome this morning, but he is not available, he is away on business. I must speak to his junior."

Carboni paused, master of theater, paused and waited until Carpenter willed him on. Seemed to fill his lungs, as if the ten minutes of near continuous talk had vacuumed them.

"Carpenter, we need fortune in this business. You know that, we need luck. This morning we have been blessed. You saw me in the office when I hugged that little prig—I detest the man, arrogant and sneering—and I hugged him because to my ear the voice of the man that says his master is in Calabria is the same as that of the man who called the office of Harrison."

Carpenter bobbed his head in praise. "Congratulations, sincerely, Mr. Carboni, my congratulations. You have a wrap-up."

"It is not definite, of course. I await the confirmation of the machines." A coyness across the desk.

"But you have no doubts."

"In my own mind there are none."

"I say again, congratulations."

"But we must move with care and discretion, Carpenter. You understand that we go into surveillance and taping. Caution is required if we want your Harrison returned. . . ."

Sharply, an intrusion on the men's concentration, the telephone rang. Carboni reached for it and even where Carpenter sat he could hear the strident talk.

Carboni scribbled on his notepad as the Englishman's excitement dissipated and waned. He had not wanted the spell of success broken and now had to endure interruption of the sweet flow. Carboni had written on and covered two sheets of paper before, without courtesies, he put the telephone down.

"Don't look worried, Carpenter. Complications, yes. But those that thicken the mixture. A man has been found dead in a small hotel close to the railway station. He had been clubbed to death. We have the tele-print of his history. He was held briefly on a kidnapping charge, but the principal witness declined to testify at his trial, the prosecution was lost. He comes from the village of Cosoleto, in the far south, in Calabria. The man that I tried to telephone this morning, he is from that village too. There is a web forming, Carpenter. A web is sticky and difficult to extract from, even for those who have made it."

"I think you'd prefer that nobody's hopes were raised yet. Not in London, not with the family."

Carboni shrugged, sending a quiver through his body and eased his fingers through the rare strands of his forehead hair. "I have given you much in confidence."

"I'm grateful to you because you've given me much of your time. If I could see you tomorrow I'd be more than pleased." Archie rose out of his chair, would love to have stayed because the atmosphere of investigation was infectious, and for too long he had been away from the microbe.

"Come tomorrow at the same time," said Carboni and laughed, deep and satisfied. The man who has enjoyed a lively whore, spent his money and regretted nothing. "Come tomorrow and I will have something to tell you."

"We should put some champagne on ice." Carpenter trying to match the mood.

"From this morning, I don't drink." Carboni laughed again and gripped Carpenter's hand with the damp warmth of friendship.

For two and a half years Francesco Vellosi had traveled with the escort of a loaded Alfetta, three men of his own squad always in place behind him as he made the four daily journeys to and from the Viminale and his flat. Sun and frost, summer and winter, they dogged his movements. He had people coming for drinks that evening at home, he told Mauro, in his clipped, even voice. But he would be returning to his desk later. Would Mauro fix the movements and coordination of the escort? A flicker of the eyes went with the request.

For Vellosi there was now time for a brief rest before his guests arrived. He would not permit them to stay late, not with the papers piling on his desk. When he was inside the front door and passed to the responsibility of the guard that lived with him, the motor escort withdrew. Because he would later return to his office, there were curses from the men who accompanied him and who would again suffer a broken evening.

10

The shadows had gone now, called away by the sun that sank beyond the orange orchard over to his right. The lines had lengthened, reached their extremity and disappeared, leaving in their wake the haze of the first darkness of the evening. With their going, a cold settled fast among the trees and bushes that Giancarlo had taken for his watching place. The building in front of him was no more than a blackened outline, indistinct in shape, difficult to focus on. Around him the noises of the night were mustering, swelling in competition. The barking of a far-distant farm dog, the droning of the bees frantic for a last feed from the wild honeysuckle, the engine whine of the skeleton mosquitos, the croak of an owl unseen in a high tree. The boy did not move as though fearing that any motion of his body might alert those whom he knew stayed unaware and unsuspicious in the barn that was less than a hundred meters from him. This was not the moment to rush forward. Better to let the darkness cling more tightly to the land, throw its blanket more finally across the fields and olive patches and the rock outcrops which were submerging in the dusk. The

ideas of Giancarlo, convoluted and hesitant when conceived in the rocking pace of the *rapido*, were now
near to fulfillment. Wild and ill-thought-out at their
birth, they now seemed to him to own a pattern and a
value. Worth a smile, little fox, worth a grin.

Unchallenged he had walked out of the small station with its wide platforms on the Reggio esplanade,
gulped at the sea-blown air, and mingled with the
stream of descending passengers. If there were watching *polizia* at the barrier, Giancarlo had not seen
them, and there had been no shouted command to
halt. Among the people laden with suitcases and
stringbags he had walked from the station. The
streams of humanity had flowed in their differing directions, dividing again and again till he was alone. In
a *tabacci* he purchased a map of Calabria. The names
were clear and well remembered. Sinopli . . .
Delianuova . . . Acquaro . . . Cosoleto. He found
them where the red ribbons of the roads began to
twist into the uplands of the Aspromonte, beyond the
green-shaded coastal strip, far into the deeper sand
and brown of the rising ground.

In early afternoon and with the time of siesta
weighty on the evacuated streets, Giancarlo had found
his car, among the whitewashed houses, parked haphazardly, as if the owner were late for an important
meeting, not just impatient for his lunch. The *mezzo
giorno*, the land of the half day. Washing hung down,
bleached and stiffened, from the balcony of a house
under which a red Fiat 127 was abandoned. Right
outside the front door, keys in the ignition. Shutters
fastened to protect the cool interior, not a child
crying, not a grandmother complaining, not a radio
tuned to music. He slipped into the driving seat, eased
off the hand brake and coasted slowly away down the
incline, waiting till he was clear of the corner before
firing the engine.

He headed north for the long, reaching viaduct where the Mafiosi men had made their fortunes in extortion from those who needed to move in materials and equipment and found it cheaper to concede the dues than to fight. He drove slowly because that was the style of the Calabrian after lunch, and his need was as acute as ever to avoid drawing attention. His face was sufficient of a problem, white with the pallor of prison and confinement in the *covo;* not the complexion of the south, not the burned and dark-wood tan of those who owned this country. He drifted past the turnoff signs to Gallico and Carnitello, and climbed high with the road above the sea channel that separated the Sicilian island from the mainland. For a moment he slowed and stared hard away to his left, his gaze held on the sprawl of Messina away across the azure of the water.

Messina, blurred and indistinct, lay white in the sun among the spreading green and rust of parks and waste ground; Messina, where they had built the jail for the women. This was where they had taken La Vianale, where Curcio's Nadia had waited for her trial, where, if he did not succeed, his Franca would decay and crumble. He could not see the prison, not across eight kilometers of reflecting sea, but it was there, a spur and a goad to whip him on.

The car increased speed, the foot of the boy stamped on the accelerator. Past the road on the left to Scilla, and on the right to Gambarie. Through the booming length of rock-cut tunnels, and on into the interior. Sinopli and Delianuova were signed to the right and he pulled the little Fiat away from the comfort of the dual highway and started the winding negotiation of the hill road. Through Santa Eufemia d'Aspromonte, a barren and meager community where his coming scattered only the chickens feeding in the road gravel, and his going raised barely an eyebrow of

attention from the elderly who sat in black skirts and
suits in front of their homes. Through Sinopli where
he hooted for the right to pass a bus that struggled in
an exhaust cloud on the main street, and where the
shops were still padlocked, and it was too hot, too
sickly clammy for the *ragazzi* to have brought out
their plastic footballs.

Bitter country now. Laden with rock and precipice,
covered with the toughened scrub and trees that grew
from little earth. In low gear, rising and descending,
Giancarlo drove on, until he was over the old and narrow stone bridge across the Vasi and into Acquaro.
Perhaps some saw him go through the village, but he
was unaware of them, studying by turns the map laid
out on the front passenger seat, and the perils of the
curving route. A half kilometer farther on he stopped.
There was a lay-by, and a heap of gravel to which the
workmen would come in the winter when there was
ice to make the road safe for motorists. Farther back
was a turn-in among the trees where perhaps the
hunting parties parked their cars on Sundays or the
young men took the virgins when they could no longer
suffer the claustrophobia of the family in the front
room and the watch of the Madonna above the fire-
place. Giancarlo grinned to himself. Wrong day for
hunters, too early in the evening for virgins. This was
a place for him to park, hidden from the road. He
drove as far between the trees as the track permitted.

From habit, in the quiet of his seat, Giancarlo
checked over the P38, stroked its silk barrel length,
and wiped the faint stains at the handle on his shirt
waist. Eight bullets only, eight to do so much with.
He climbed lightly from the car, eased the pistol back
into his belt, and was lost in the close foliage.

He skirted the road, leaving it what he judged to be
a hundred meters to his left, seeking the thickness of
the wood, easing onto the toes of his canvas shoes,

thankful for the cover. It took him only a few minutes
to find the vantage point. The once-white house, from
which paint and plaster alike peeled, was served by a
rutted track. A hovel to Giancarlo, a place for sheep
and cows. Medieval, had it not been for the car
parked outside the only door. This was the home of a
contadino, a peasant, and a wife moved beside the
building with a bucket, and his half-clothed children
played with a spar of wood. The boy settled himself
comfortably on the mold of generations of fallen
leaves and watched and waited for the husband of the
sister of Claudio.

Not long. Not long enough to try him.

A big man, and balding above a flat weather-
beaten forehead. Cheeks that were not shaved, trousers that were held at the waist with a string, a shirt
that was torn at the armpit. *Contadino*, Giancarlo spat
the word. But of the proletariat, surely? He smiled
mirthlessly. A servant of the bosses . . . ? The boy
agreed, satisfied in the ideology equation. The man
carried a plastic bag and walked down the track from
his house to the road, paused there and traversed his
eyes in a sweep that included the boy's hiding place.
The man had passed close to where Giancarlo lay. Before his sounds subsided Giancarlo was after him, ears
cocked and attuned to the distant noises in front, eyes
fastened on the dried twigs and oak leaves which he
must not break or rustle.

The tree line covered the rim of a slight hill, beyond it was a roughened field indented from the cattle's wet spring grazing. On the far side of the open
ground Giancarlo saw the stone-built barn with its
rain-reddened tin roof and two doors facing him. The
man he had followed was met by one who had come
from the right side door and who carried a single-
barreled shotgun, the weapon of the country people.
They talked, a brief discourse before the bag was

handed over, and a gust of laughter carried to the boy. As the man retraced his steps, Giancarlo melted among the trees and undergrowth, unseen, unheard.

When it was safe he came slowly forward to the dry-stone wall that skirted the field, and picked his watching place. A boundless pride swept through the boy. He wanted to stand up and shout defiance and exultation. Giancarlo Battestini, remember the name, because he had found the Englishman of the multinationals and would exploit him, as the foreign companies exploited the proletariat.

Later Giancarlo would begin his advance, edge closer to the building. Later. Now was the time for him to rest, and to relax if that were possible. And to dream . . . and the images of the thighs, warm and muscled in moisture, and of the curling growth and the breasts where his head had lain blasted and echoed through the mind of the boy. Alone on the ground, the myriad of earth creatures converging on him, he shuddered and knew he would not sleep.

Archie Carpenter had been shown round the flat. He'd made the right noises and stood hesitantly at the bedroom door casting a quick eye over the wide pink coverlet, studied the pictures, paced the corridors with his hands joined behind his back in the pose of royal males factory visiting, and expressed his opinion as to what a fine place it was. She was a queer one, this Violet Harrison, making it all seem so natural as she marched him over the marble floors, pointing to this and that, offering a limited history of the furniture. She'd poured him a drink. Gin, with hardly enough tonic to notice, and splashed some ice cubes in. He'd seen her hand shaking and known it was all a damn great sham. All the poise, all the silly chat, just a counterfeit. That's when the sympathy had started

to roll, watching the trembling fist and the way the
finger talons clutched at the bottle.

Loose and slim in the full flow of her dress as she
sat on a sofa. The sort of woman you could take to
your chest, Archie, sort of nuzzle against, and it would
be all soft and wouldn't hurt anywhere. He wasn't
looking at her eyes when he started to speak, just at
the cleavage, where the freckles ran down. His suit
was tight and hot and too thick for Roman summer.
Bloody strange dress she'd put on for a time like this.

"You have to know, Mrs. Harrison, that the company is doing all it can to get Geoffrey back to you.
As quickly as humanly possible he'll be home again."

"That's very kind," she said, and her words were not
easy to follow, wasn't the first drink she'd had that
day.

"Everything possible," Carpenter hurtled on. "The
Board will rubber-stamp the Managing Director's decision to pay. He wants you to know that the company
will pay whatever is required to get your husband
back. There's nothing on that count for you to worry
about."

"Thank you," she said. Raised her eyebrows at him
as if trying to show how impressed she was that the
Board should make such a commitment.

Bloody marvelous, he thought. What a pair and not
a trace of sweat on her where the neckline cut down
and him dripping wet like a horse at the Derby finish.
"There's not a great deal that we can do at the moment, but your husband's colleagues at ICH in Rome
are geared to take calls and make the financial arrangements. It'll probably all be outside the country,
which makes it smoother." He paused, drank it all in,
watched the shift of the material as she crossed her
legs. "But you have to soldier on for a bit, Mrs. Harrison, for quite a few days. It takes time, this sort of
thing, we cannot settle it in a matter of hours."

"I understand that, Mr. Carpenter."

"You're taking it very well."

"I'm just trying to go on as I usually would, as if Geoffrey were away on a business trip, something like that." She leaned forward slightly in her chair.

What to say now, what ground to stumble over? Carpenter swallowed. "Was there anything you wanted, anything I could help with?"

"I doubt it, Mr. Carpenter."

"It may take a few days, but we're working on two fronts. We can pay, that's no problem. At the same time the police are cooperating and have a major and discreet recovery effort under way, they have their best men on the case and . . ."

"I don't really need to know that, do I?" she asked quietly.

Carpenter bridled. "I thought you'd want to hear what was happening." Cool it, Archie, she's under stress. A brave front and damn all underneath.

"So what you're offering me is that after a week or two I'll know whether Geoffrey is going to walk through the door, or whether I'm never going to see him again."

"I think we should look on the bright side of things, Mrs. Harrison." Out of training, Archie. Bloody years since he'd been a beat copper in uniform and knocking on doors with a solemn face to tell the wife that her old man's come off his motorbike and that if she doesn't hurry she'll see him in the hospital chapel.

Violet Harrison seemed to sag, and the tears came, and then the deeper sobs, and the protest in the choked voice. "You don't know anything. Nothing at all. . . . Mister bloody Carpenter. You treat me like a bloody child . . . let's all have a drink, let's believe it isn't for real. . . . What do you know about his place, sweet fuck all of nothing . . . you don't know where my husband is, you don't know how to get him back.

All you talk about is 'everything possible,' and 'major effort,' 'best men on the case.' It's just bloody bromide, Mister bloody Carpenter . . ."

"That's not fair, Mrs. Harrison, and don't swear at me . . ."

"And don't you come marching in here oozing your platitudes, telling me everything is going to be marvelous . . ."

"Too bloody right I won't. There's people that don't know when someone's trying to help them." Carpenter's voice rose, his neck flushed. He pushed himself up from the seat, gulping at the remains of his drink. "When someone comes and tries to give a hand there's no call for foul language." He couldn't get smoothly out of the deep chair, couldn't make a quick and decent exit with dignity. By the time he was on his feet she was between him and the door and the tears were wet on her face, gleaming in the sheen of her makeup.

"I think I'd better go," he said, mumbling his words, conscious of his failure to complete his task.

She stood very close to him, barring his way, seemed a frail little thing for all the bravura of her language, and looked straight into his face. Her head was turned up toward him, with a small neat mouth, and her arms hung inert down to her hips.

"I think I'd better go . . . don't you? I don't think I can help anymore."

"If you think you ought to." Brown hazel eyes, deep-set and misted, and around them the morass of freckles that he followed the patterns of, followed where they led.

"Geoffrey's bloody useless, you know." Her hand came up, wiping hastily across her face, smudged the cosmetic grease, and the smile was there again. Curtained herself from him, just as she had done when she showed him round the flat, taken a public stance. There was a little laugh, bright in his ear. "I'm not

shocking you, am I, Mr. Carpenter? Quite bloody useless, to me anyway. I don't mean to shock you, but
people ought to understand each other. Don't you
think so?"

One hand was sliding under his jacket, fingers ri-
fling at the damp texture of his shirt, the other played
at the uppermost buttons of her dress.

"Don't let's mess about, Mr. Carpenter. You know
the geography of this flat, you know where my
room is. Oughtn't you to be taking me there now?" Her
nails dug into the small of his back, a small bone button slipped from its hole, the spirals of excitement
climbed at his spine. "Come on, Mr. Carpenter. You
can't do anything for Geoffrey, I can't do anything for
Geoffrey, so let's not pretend. Let's pass the time."
There was pressure on his back ribs, drawing him
closer. The mouth and the pink, painted lips mesmer-
izing him. He could smell her breath, could smell that
she smoked, but she must have used toothpaste just
before he came, peppermint.

"I can't stay," Carpenter said, a hoarseness in his
throat. Out of his depth, floundering in deep water,
and not a life raft in bloody miles. "I can't stay, I have
to go."

The hands abandoned his back and the buttons and
she stepped aside to leave him space to pass into the
hall.

"No hesitations, Mr. Carpenter?" she murmured behind him. He was fiddling with the door locks, anxious to be on his way and therefore hurrying and in
the process slowing himself; the man who is impatient
and cannot unfasten a brassiere strap. "No second
thoughts?"

Teased, bowed by a shame that he could not recognize as coming from either inadequacy or morality,
Archie Carpenter, nine to fiver, opt out from the
grown-up world, finally opened the door.

"You're a boring bastard, Mr. Carpenter," she called after him. "A proper little bore. If you're the best they can send to get my husband out, then God help the poor darling."

The door slammed. He didn't wait for the lift, but took the stairs two at a time.

In prewar Rome the fascist administration sometimes ordered the lights of the principal government offices to be left burning long after the bureaucracy had gone to their trams and buses; a grateful population would believe that the state was working late and be impressed. The spirit of such deception had long since passed and the prevailing dictates of austerity decreed that unnecessary lights should be extinguished. Giuseppe Carboni was one of only a very few who worked late into that night in the shadowed sepulcher of the Questura. By telephone he had indefinitely postponed his dinner at home as he put off the anathema of communication with the force that he saw as his principal rival, the paramilitary *carabinieri*. The *polizia* and *carabinieri* existed uneasily, at best, as bedfellows between the communal sheets of law and order. Competition was fierce and jealous; the success of either was trumpeted by the senior officers of the twin forces, and a weak executive power was satisfied that neither should become overpowerful. A recipe for inefficiency, and a safeguard against a return to the all-powerful police state that Italy had labored under for twenty-one years.

Carboni's problem, and it had taken him many hours to resolve in his mind, was whether or not he should place in the lap of the opposition his information on the speculator Mazzotti. The man was in the far south, apparently at the village of Cosoleto, and beyond the striking and administrative range of the *polizia* at the Calabrian capital of Reggio. Cosoleto

would come under the jurisdiction of the *carabinieri*
at the small town of Palmi, his maps showed him that.
His option was to allow the man Mazzotti to return
from Calabria back into the Roman district where he
would again be liable to police investigation. But if
the gorilla Claudio were linked to the kidnapping of
Harrison, of the Englishman, then the report of his
killing in Rome would serve only to alert those involved. For another few hours, perhaps, the name of
the dead man could be suppressed, but not beyond
the dawn of the next day. It was immaterial at whose
hand the strongarm had met his death, sufficient for
Carboni that it would be enough to set into play the
fall-back plans of the kidnap group. Not possible for
him to delay in his action, and if he acted now, made
a request for help that was successful, then what
credit would be laid at the door of Giuseppe Carboni?
Trivial plaudits, and victim and criminals in the hands
of the black-uniformed *carabinieri*.

Enough to make a man weep.

He broke the pledge of the morning and poured
himself a Scotch from his cabinet, the bottle reserved
for times of celebration and black depression, then
placed the call to Palmi. Just this once he would do
the noble deed, he promised himself, just this once
break the habit of a professional lifetime.

When the call came the static was heavy on the line,
and Carboni's voice boomed through the quiet offices
and out through the open doors into the emptied corridors of the second floor of the Questura. Many times
he was obliged to repeat himself to the *carabinieri*
capitano, as he was urged for greater explanation. He
stressed the importance of the Harrison affair, the
concern in the matter of high administrative circles in
Rome. Twice the *capitano* had demurred; the action
suggested to him was too delicate for his personal intervention, the Mazzotti family were of local importance,

should there not be authorization from the examining magistrate? Carboni had shouted louder, bellowed bull-like into the telephone. The matter could not rest for authorization, the situation was too fluid to be left till the morning appearance of the magistrate in his office. Perhaps the very vehemence impressed the *carabinieri* officer, perhaps the dream of glory that might be his. He acquiesced. The home of Antonio Mazzotti would be placed under surveillance from three o'clock in the morning. He would be arrested at eight.

"And be careful. I want no suspicions, I want no warnings given to this bastard," Carboni yelled. "A little mistake and my head is hanging. You understand? Hanging on my belly. You have the man Mazzotti in the cells at Palmi and I'll be with the magistrate by nine, and have him brought to Rome. You will reap full praise for your initiative and flexibility and cooperation; it won't be forgotten."

The *capitano* expressed his gratitude to the Dottore.

"Nothing, my son, nothing. Good luck."

Carboni put the telephone down. There was a black sheen on the handpiece and with his shirt cuff he smeared the moisture from his forehead. Rome in high summer, an impossible place to work. He locked his desk, switched off his desk light and headed for the corridor. For a man so gross in stomach and thighs there was something of a spring in his step. The scent sharp in the nose of the professional policeman. The old one, the one above pride and expediency. Time to go home for his supper and his bed.

Uncomfortable, irritated by the sharpness of the hay strands, impeded by the wrist manacle, Geoffrey Harrison had been denied the relief of sleep. They left no light for him, and the darkness had come once the slanting sun shafts no longer bored through the old nail holes of the roof. A long darkness already aggravated by the absence of food. A punishment, he thought, a punishment for kicking the bucket over them. As if the beating wasn't enough. His belly ached and groaned out loud in its deprivation.

He lay full length on his back, the length of chain allowing his right arm to drop loosely on the hay beside his body. Inert, occasionally dozing, eking out minutes and hours and not knowing or caring about their passage.

The voices of his guards came occasionally through the thickness of the dividing wall of the barn. Indistinct and punctuated by laughter and then loud silence. He heard little of them, and since one had walked heavily outside the building and urinated with force there had been nothing. His concentration was sharpened by the whisper of the scurrying feet of rats and mice who had made their nests in the gaps between the hay bales under him. Little bastards, eating and crapping and copulating and spewing out their litters, performing the functions of their limited lives a few feet below his backside. Each movement of the rodents he heard; the vibrations of the microscopic feet, frantic as they went about their business. He wondered what they made of the smell and presence close to their heartland, whether they'd summon the courage or curiosity to investigate the intruder. Perhaps there would be bats tonight; there might have been last night, but the sleep had been too thick for him to have noticed. All the phobias, all the hates and fears of bats rushed past him so that he could examine and analyze the folklore—the scratchers, the tanglers, the disease carriers . . .

There was a new sound.

Harrison stiffened where he lay. Rigid now on his back. Fingers clenched. Eyes peering upward into the unbroken darkness.

A footfall beyond the side wall away from where his guards rested.

Frightened to move, frightened to breathe, Harrison listened.

A soft-soled shoe eased onto the dirt beyond the wall. A step taken slowly, as if the ground were being tested before the weight of a man was committed.

A stranger was coming silently and in stealth to the barn, without warning, without announcement. A person had come before the sun had set and had called from some way off and there had been greetings and conversations. This was not as then.

Another footstep.

Clearer this time, as if nerve and caution were abandoned, as if impetuosity and impatience were rising. Harrison willed him forward. Anyone who came with the hush of feet on the tinder grass and the scraping stones, anyone who came with such secrecy had no love or friendship for the men who waited in the far room of the barn.

Cruel and mocking came the long unbroken silence.

Each noise of the night he could hear he rejected, because the sounds he searched for were lost. The last footstep had been clear. Perhaps the man had taken flight and would stay still and listen before he came on. The perspiration sprang from Harrison's body, flowing to the crevices. Who was it that had come? Who would travel to this place?

A shatter of noise, a warning shout, a blasting pistol shot ripped an echo through the space under Harrison's low ceiling.

In the half light from the dimmed storm lamp, Giancarlo saw the man nearest him pitch forward, the cry in his throat destroyed. For a moment he caught the reflection of the eyes of the second man, a rabbit's in headlights, and then a stool careered in the air toward him and his ducking weave was enough to take the force of the blow on his shoulder and to distort his gathering aim. Like a huge shadow the man 'dived against the wall, but his movements were sluggish and terrorized and without hope. Giancarlo had enough time before the man reached the shortened shotgun. He held the P38 with his two fists, cursed as the barrel wavered and the ache throbbed in his upper arm. The man stole a last glance at him, and reached the final inches for the shotgun. Giancarlo fired, two shots for certainty, into the target that diminished to the earth floor.

Harrison heard the answering whimper, a moan of supplication, perhaps a prayer, before a choked sob sliced it to silence.

He was frozen still, unmoving, uncomprehending.

The leaning door, old and protesting at its hinges, was opened beneath him; the chain was tight between his arm and the roof, denying him escape. What in God's name happens now? Not the noise the police would have made. Not the way it would have been if they were here. Would have been voices all around and shouts and commands and organization. Only the door below him, deep in the darkness, being pried open.

His name was called.

" 'arrison, 'arrison."

Difficult for him to register at first. Slow and tentative, almost a request.

"Where are you, 'arrison?"

A young voice, nervous. A young Italian. They could never get their tongues round his name, not in the office, not at business meetings, not at the shops when he was out with Violet. The fear swelled inside him, the child that lies in the blackness and hears a stranger come. To answer or not, to identify or to remain silent. Pulsing through him, the dangers of the unknown.

"Where are you, 'arrison? Speak, tell me where you are, 'arrison."

His reply was involuntary, blurted out, made not because he had reckoned out the answers, but because there was a plea for response and he had no longer the strength to resist.

"Up here, I am up here."

"I am coming, 'arrison." The tinge of pride was heavy in the stumbled English. The door scraped across the floor. The caution of footsteps was abandoned. "There are more of them, 'arrison? There were two. Are there more?"

"Just two, there were only two."

He heard the sound of the ladder thudding into position against the hay wall, and the noise was fierce as the feet came against the rungs.

"Come down quickly, we should not stay here."

"They have me by a chain, I cannot move." Would the stranger understand, would his English be competent? "I am a prisoner here." Harrison slid into the staccato tempo of the foreigner, believing that was how his own tongue was best understood.

Two hands clawed at his feet and he could make out the slight silhouette shape of a man rising toward him. He cringed backward.

"Don't fear me. Don't be afraid, 'arrison." A soft little voice, barely out of school with the grammar fresh from the reading primers. The fingers, cruising and exploratory, reached along the length of his body. Across Harrison's thigh, scratching at his waist, onward and upward to the pit of his arm and then away out past his elbow to the wrist and the steel grip of the handcuff. A cigarette lighter flicked on, wavering and scarcely effective. But from the kernel of light Geoffrey Harrison could distinguish the face and features of the boy beneath the short thrown shadows. Unshaven, pallid, eyes that were alive and burned bright. A shape to marry to the garlic smell of bread and salad sandwiches.

"Take it."

An order and the lighter was directed toward Harrison's free hand.

"Turn your face away."

Harrison saw the shadowed pistol drawn, squat and revolting, a macabre toy. He bucked his head away as the gun was raised and held steady. Squinted his eyes shut, forced them closed. Tearing at his ears was the noise of the gun, wrenching at his wrist the drag of the chain. The pain burned in the muscle socket of his shoulder, but when his arm swung back to his side it was free.

"It is done," the boy said, and there was the trace of a smile, sparse and cold in the flame of the lighter. He pulled at Harrison's hand, led him toward the ladder. It was a cumbersome descent because Harrison favored his shoulder, and the boy's hands were occupied with the gun and the flick lighter. The pressed earth of the floor was under Harrison's feet and the grip on his arm constant as he was led toward the opaque moon haze of the doorway. They stopped there and the fingers slipped to his wrist and there was a sharp heave at the bullet-broken handcuff ring. A light clatter on the ground.

"The men, those who were watching me . . . ?"

"I killed them." The face invisible, the information inconsequential.

"Both of them?"

"I killed the two of them."

Out in the night air, Harrison shuddered as if the

damp on his forehead were frozen. The waft of fresh wind caught at his hair and flipped it from his eyes. He stumbled on a rock.

"Who are you?"

"It is not of concern to you."

The grip on his wrist was tight and decisive. Harrison remembered the fleeting sight of the pistol. He allowed himself to be dragged away across the uneven, thistled grass of the field.

The eyewitnesses to the attack melted from the pavement with the wailing approach of the ambulance sirens. Few would stay to offer their account and their names and addresses to the investigating police. Out in the middle of the road, slewed across at right angles to the two traffic flows' was the ambushed Alfa of Francesco Vellosi. Mauro, the driver, lay pale in death across his steering wheel, his head close to the holed and frosted windshield. Alone in the back, half down on the floor, was Vellosi, both hands clamped on his pistol and unable to stifle the trembling that invaded his body. The door of reinforced armor plate had saved him. Above his scalp the back passenger windows for all their strengthening were a kaleidoscope of colors reflected from the fractured glass splinters. So fast, so vivid, so terrifying, the moment of assault. Eight years in the *squadro antiterrorismo*, eight years he had spent standing and looking at cars such as his, at bodies such as Mauro's. Yet no real knowledge had accrued of how the moment would find him. Inadequate, everything he could previously have imagined. Not even in the war, in the sand dunes of Sidi Barrani under the artillery of the English, had there been anything as overwhelming as the trapped rat feeling in the closed car with the sprays of automatic fire beating over his head.

The escort car had locked its bonnet under the rear bumper of Vellosi's vehicle. Here they had all survived and now they were scattered with their machine pistols. One in cover behind the opened front passenger door. One away in a shop doorway. The third man in Vellosi's guard stood erect in the middle of the street, lit by the high lights, his gun cradled and ready and pointing to the pavement lest the prone figures should rise and defy the blood trails and the gaping intestinal wounds and again offer a challenge.

Only when the street was busy with police did Vellosi unlock his door and emerge. He seemed old, almost senile, his steps labored and heavy.

"How many of them do we have?" he called across the street to the man who had been his shadow and guard these three years, whose wife cooked for him, whose children he was a godfather of.

"There were three, *capo*. All dead. They stayed beyond their time. When they should have run, they stayed to make certain of you."

He walked into the lit center of the street and his men hurried to close around him, wanting him gone, but reading his mood and unwilling to confront it. He stared down into the faces of the boys, the *ragazzi*, grotesque in their angles, with the killing weapons close to their fists, only the agony left in their eyes, the hate fled and gone. His eyes closed and his cheek muscles hardened as if he summoned strength from a distant force.

"The one there," he pointed to a shape of denim jeans and a blood-flawed shirt. "I have met that boy. I have eaten at his father's house. The boy came in before we sat down at dinner. His father is a banker, the Director of the Contrazzoni Finanziarie of one of the banks in the Via Corso. I know that boy."

He turned reluctantly from the scene, dawdling, and his voice was raised and carried over the street and the pavement and to the few who had gathered and watched him. "The bitch Tantardini, spitting her poison over these children. The wicked, contaminated bitch."

Hemmed in on the back seat of his escort car, Francesco Vellosi left for his desk at the Viminale.

11

With the headlight beams flashing back from the
roadside pine trees, hurling aside the startled shadows, the little two-door Fiat ground its way into the
inky night, leaving behind the cluster of the Cosoleto
lights. Giancarlo forced the motor hard, oblivious of
the howling tires, the crack of the fast-changed gears
and the drift of Harrison's shoulders against his own.
His purpose now was to be rid of the vacuum of the
darkened roads and fields, the silhouetted trees, the
lonely farmhouses. He was a town boy and nurtured
the urban fear of the wide spaces of the country
where familiarity was no longer assumed by a known
street corner, a local shop, or a towering cement land-
mark.

He drove on the narrow road to Seminara, scarcely
aware of the man beside him who was carpeted in
silence, contemplating perhaps the gun that rested on
the shelf of the open glove compartment. The P38,
ready and willing, though its magazine had been de-
pleted in the barn, but still with sufficient cartridges
in its bowels to remain lethal. Through Melicucca
where the town was asleep, where men and women

had taken to their early beds heavy with the wine of the region, the weight of the food, and the priest's condemnation of late hours. Through Melicucca and onward from the village before even the lightest sleepers could have turned and wondered at the speed of the car that violated the quiet of their night. He turned sharp to the left at Santa Anna because that was the route to the coast and the main road.

And the task was only begun. Believe that, Giancarlo. The starting of a journey. The pits, the swamps, all ahead, all gathering. They are nothing, the boy said soundlessly to himself. Nothing. He slowed as they came to Seminara. A town where people might still be alert, where caution must be exercised. He'd studied the map in the field near the barn, knew the town had one street; the mayor's office would be there.

A formidable building it was, decayed and in need of money for repair. Heavy doors tight shut. Sandwiched between lesser structures and close to the central piazza. Illuminated by the street lights. He braked, and the man beside him lunged forward with his hands to break an impact.

"Get out of the car," Giancarlo said. "Get out of the car and put your hands on the roof. And stand still, because the gun watches you."

Harrison climbed out, his shoulder still in pain, did what he was told to do.

Giancarlo watched him straighten, flex himself, and shake his head as if an internal dispute had been resolved. He wondered whether Harrison would run, or whether he was too confused to act. He held the gun in his hand, not with aggression, but with the warning implicit. He would see the P38 and he would not play the idiot. The movements on the pavement of the Englishman were sluggish, those of a netted carp after a protracted struggle. He would have few problems with this man. From the shelf he took a pencil and a scrap of paper on which had been written on one side the gasoline purchases and additions of the car's owner.

"We will not be long, 'arrison. Stand still because it is not sensible that you move. Afterward it will all be explained."

There was no response from the sagging trousers that he could see against the opened door. He began to write with the bold, flourishing hand that had been taught him by a teacher at the Secondary School of Pescara who prided herself on copperplate neatness. The words came quickly to the paper. There had been time enough on the train to formulate the demand that he would make.

> Communique 1, of the Nuclei Armati Proletaria. We hold prisoner the English multinational criminal, Geoffrey Harrison. All those who work for the multinational conspiracy, whether Italian or foreigners, are exploiters of the proletarian revolution, and are the opponents of the aspirations of the workers. The enemy Harrison is now held in a People's Prison. He will be executed at 09.00 CET, the 27th of this month, the day after tomorrow, unless the prisoner of war held in the regime concentration camp, Franca Tantardini, has been freed and flown out of Italy. There will be no further communiques, no further warnings. Unless Tantardini is freed from her torture, the sentence will be carried out without mercy.
>
> In the memory of Panicucci.
>
> Victory to the Proletariat. Victory to the workers. Death and defeat to the *borghese*, the capitalists and the multinationalists.
>
> Nuclei Armati Proletaria.

Giancarlo read over his words, screwing his eyes at the paper in the dim light. As Franca would have wanted it. She would be satisfied with him, well satisfied.

"'arrison, do you have any paper, something that identifies you? An envelope, a driver's license?" He thrust the gun forward so the weight of his message would be augmented, and accepted the thin hip wallet in return. Money there, but he ignored it, and drew out the plastic folder of credit cards. Eurocard, American Express, Diners' Club. American Express was the one he coveted.

"Perhaps you will get it back sometime, 'arrison. With this paper push it under the door. It is important for you that it is found early in the morning. Push it carefully and the card with it, that too is important."

Giancarlo folded the paper and wrote on the outside leaf in large capitals the letters of the symbol of the *Nappisti*. He handed the paper and the credit card to his prisoner and watched him bend to slide the two under the main door to the office of the mayor of Seminara.

"You will drive now, 'arrison, and you will be careful because I am watching you, and because I have the gun. I have killed three men to come this far, you should know that."

Giancarlo Battestini slid across into the passenger seat, vacating the driver's place for Geoffrey Harrison. Their stop in the center of Seminara had delayed them a little more than three minutes.

In the rhythm of the driving, the numbing shock wore away, chipped from the mind of Geoffrey Harrison.

Neither attempted conversation, leaving Harrison free to absorb himself in the driving, while in the darkness beside him the boy wrestled with the map folds and plotted their route and turnings. As the minutes went by the doldrums cleared from Harrison's thoughts. No explanation from the boy, everything left unsaid, unamplified. But he felt that he understood everything, had been given the signs which he now used as the textbook of his assessment. The way the hand had gripped his wrist, that told him much, told him he was incarcerated and under guard. The pistol told him more, evidence of lightning attack, of a ferocity of purpose. There was the warning too, the warning in Seminara, spoken as if it were meant kindly. "I have killed three men to come this far." Three men dead that Harrison should drive in the warm night past signposts to towns he had not heard of, along a road he had never before traveled on. A prisoner a second time. A hostage with a dropped note setting out terms of release.

Yet he felt no fear of the gun and the youth with the bowed head beside him, because the capacity for terror had been exhausted. Patient, he would wait for the promised explanation. Out beyond Laureana, racing alongside the dried-out river bed, Harrison forced the Fiat 127 away from the scenes of the barn at Cosoleto and the men with their hoods and kicking boots and fouled shirts. Hours more till dawn, he reckoned. He had no complaint, only a dulled brain, exerted by the need to hold the car on the road, the dipped lights on the verge. Only rarely did his attention waver, and when he turned he saw that the boy sat with his arms folded, the pistol cupped by an elbow and the barrel facing the space beneath his armpit.

An hour down the road from Seminara, past the sign to Pizzo, the silence broke. "You don't have a cigarette, do you?" Harrison asked.

"I have only a very few."

Frank enough, thought Harrison, marking the bloody card. "I haven't had one for a couple of days, you know. I'd really like one."

"I have only a very few," the boy repeated.

Harrison kept his eyes on the road. "I don't ask what the hell's going on, I don't throw a fit. I wait to be told all about it in your own good, sweet time. All I do is ask for a cigarette . . ."

"You speak too fast for me, I do not understand."

Hiding, the little bastard, behind the language.

"I just said that perhaps we could share a cigarette."

"What do you mean?"

"I mean I could smoke it, and you could smoke it, and as we were doing so you could talk to me."

"We could both smoke the cigarette?"

"I've no known disease."

The boy reached into the breast pocket of his shirt and out of the corner of his eye Harrison saw the red packet emerge. Tight, wasn't he? Not what you'd call the generous type. Inside the car there was the flash of the igniting light, then the slow glow of the cigarette burning, tantalizing and close to him.

"Thank you," Harrison spoke out clearly.

The boy passed the cigarette. First contact, first humanity. Harrison wrapped his lips on the filter end, pulled hard into his lungs, and eased his foot on the accelerator.

"Thank you." Harrison spoke with feeling and nicotine smoke played eddies and tributaries inside the car's confines. "Now it's your turn. There'll be nothing funny, I'll keep quiet, but it's you for the talking. Right?"

Harrison looked quickly away from the road's illuminated markers and the direction lines, gave himself time to absorb the furrow of frown and concentration on the boy's face.

"You should just drive," and there was the first simmering of hostility.

"Give me the cigarette again, please." It was passed to him; one desperate intake, like the swill minutes in the pub back in England when the beers are on the counter and the landlord's calling for empty glasses. "What's your name?"

"Giancarlo."

"And your other name, what's that, Giancarlo?" Harrison spoke as if the question were pure conversation, as if the answer carried only trivial importance.

"You have no need to know that."

"Please yourself. I'll call you Giancarlo. I'm Geoffrey . . ."

"I know what your name is. It is 'arrison. I know your name."

Brutal going. Like running up a bloody sandhill. Remember the shooter, if you don't want the ketchup running out of your armpit.

"How far are you going to want me to drive, Giancarlo?"

"You must drive to Rome." Uncertainty in the boy's voice. Unwilling to be pulled through the clothes wringer with his plan.

"How far's Rome?"

"Perhaps eight hundred kilometers."

"Jesus . . ."

"You will drive all the time. We will only stop when the day comes."

"It's a hell of a way, aren't you taking a turn?"

"I watch you, and the gun watches you. Eh, 'arrison?" The boy mocked him.

"I'm not forgetting the gun, Giancarlo. Believe me I'm not forgetting it." Try another route, Geoffrey. "But you're going to have to talk to me, otherwise I'll be asleep. If that happens it's the ditch for all of us;

Harrison, Giancarlo, and his pistol. We're going to
have to find something to talk about."

"You are tired?" Anxiety. Something not considered.

"Not exactly fresh," Harrison allowed a flicker of
sarcasm. "We should talk—about you for starters."

The car bounced and veered on the uneven road
surface. Even the autostrada, the pride of a motoring
society, was in a creeping state of disrepair. The last
time the section had been resurfaced the contractor
had paid heavily in contributions to the men in smart
suits who interested themselves in such projects. For
the privilege of moving machines and men into the
district he had cut hard into his profit margins. Econ-
omies had been found in the depth of the newly laid
paving which the winter rains had bitten. Harrison
clung to the wheel.

"I told you my name is Giancarlo."

"Right." Harrison did not turn from the windshield
and the road in front. The smells of the two mingled
closely till they were inseparable, unifying them.

"I am twenty years old."

"Right."

"I am not from these parts, nor from Rome."

No need anymore for Harrison to respond. The
floodgates were breaking and the atmosphere in the
little car ensured it.

"I am a fighter, 'arrison. I am a fighter for the rights
and aspirations of the proletariat revolution. In our
group we fight against the corruption and rottenness
of our society. You live here and you know what you
see with your eyes, you are a part of the scum, 'arrison.
You come from the multinational, you control workers
here, but you have no commitment to the Italian
workers. You are a leech to them."

Try and comprehend him, Geoffrey, because it's
not the time for argument.

"We have seen the oppression of the gangsters of the Democrazia Christiana and we fight to destroy them. The Communists who should be the voice of the workers are in the DC pockets." The boy shook as he spoke, as if the very words caused him pain.

"I understand what you say, Giancarlo."

"On the day that you were taken in Rome by those Calabresi pigs, I was with the leader of our cell. We were ambushed by the *polizia*. They took our leader, took her away in their chains and with their guns around her. There was another man with us—Panicucci. Not of our ideology at first, but recruited and loyal, loyal as a fighting lion. They shot Panicucci like a dog."

"Where were you, Giancarlo?"

"Far across the street. She had told me to bring the newspapers. I was too far from her. I could not help . . ."

"I understand." Harrison spoke softly, acute to the failure of the boy. He should not humiliate him.

"I could not help, I could do nothing."

And soon the little bastard will be crying, thought Harrison. If the gun wasn't at his rib cage, Geoffrey Harrison would have been laughing fit to bust. Saga of bloody heroism. Away across the road buying newspapers, what sort of medal do you get for that one? Driving hard past the road to Vibo Valentia, hammering over the bridge and the low reflected waters of the drought-starved Messima River.

"The one that you call the leader, tell me about her."

"She is Franca. She is a lovely woman, 'arrison. She is a lady. Franca Tantardini. She is our leader. She hates them and she fights them. They will torture her in the name of their shitty democratic state. They are bastards and they will hurt her."

"And you love this girl, Giancarlo?"

Deflated the boy, seemed to prick him where the gas was densest.

"I love her," Giancarlo whispered. "I love her, and she loves me too. We have been together in bed."

"I know how you feel, Giancarlo. I understand you."

Bloody liar, Geoffrey. When did you last love a woman? How long? In the early days with Violet, that was something like love, wasn't it? Something like it. . . .

"She is beautiful. She is a real woman. Very beautiful, very strong."

"I understand, Giancarlo."

"I will liberate her from them."

The car swerved on the road, swung out into the fast lane toward the divider. Harrison's hands had tightened on the wheel, his arms had stiffened and were unresponsive, clumsy.

"You are going to liberate her?"

"Together we are going to liberate her, 'arrison."

Harrison stared, eyes gimlet clear, out onto the ever-diminishing road in his lights. Pinch yourself, kick your arse. Push the bedclothes off and get dressed. Just a bloody nightmare. It has to be.

He knew the answer, but he asked the question.

"How are we going to do it, Giancarlo?"

"You sit with me, 'arrison. We sit together. They will give me back my Franca and I will give you back to them."

"It doesn't work like that. Not anymore . . . not after Moro . . ."

"You have to hope it is like that." The cold back in his voice, the ice chill that the boy could summon from the high ground.

"Not after the Moro business. They showed it then . . . they don't bend. No negotiation."

"Then it is bad for you, 'arrison."

"Where were you when Moro was done?"

"At the University of Rome."

". . . weren't there any newspapers there?"

"I know what happened."

Harrison felt his control sliding, and fought it. His eyes were no longer on the road, his head was swung toward the boy. Noses, faces, unshaven cheeks, mouth breath, all barely separated.

"If that's your plan it's lunatic."

"That is my plan."

"They won't give in, a child can see that."

"They will surrender because they are weak and soft, fattened by their excesses. They cannot win against the might of the proletariat. They cannot resist the revolution of the workers. When we have destroyed their system, they will talk of this day."

God, how do you tell him? Harrison said quietly, chopping his words with emphasis, "They won't give in . . ."

The boy screamed, "If they do not return her to me, then I kill you." The wail of the cornered mountain cat, and the spittle flecked Giancarlo's chin.

"Please yourself, then."

Wasn't true, wasn't real, not happening to Geoffrey Harrison. He had to escape from it, had to find a freedom from the snarling hatred. Harrison swung the car hard to the right, stamped his foot on the brake, whistled to himself in tune with the tire screech, and wrenched the car to a halt. The pistol was at his neck, nestled against the vein that ran behind his earlobe.

"Start again," Giancarlo hissed.

"Drive yourself," Harrison muttered, sliding back in his seat, folding his arms across his chest.

"Drive or I will shoot you."

"That's your choice."

"Listen, 'arrison. Listen to what I say." The mouth was close to his ear, competing for proximity with the

gun barrel, and the breath was hot and gusting in the
boy's anger. "At Seminara, at the town hall, I left a
message. It was a communiqué in the name of the Nuclei Armati Proletaria. It will be read with care when
it is found, when the first people come in the morning. With the message is your card. They will know
that I have you, and later in the morning the barn will
be found. It will confirm also that I have taken you
when they find the bodies. I have no more need of
you, 'arrison. I have no more need of you while they
think that I hold you. Am I clear?"

So why doesn't he do it, Harrison wondered. Not
scruple, not compassion. Didn't know and didn't ask.
The gun was harder against his skin and his defiance
sagged. Not going to call his bluff, are you, Geoffrey?
Harrison engaged the gears, flicked the ignition key,
and coasted away.

They would talk again later, but not now, not for
many minutes. Giancarlo lit another cigarette and did
not share it.

Where the *carabinieri* lay close to the two-story villa
of Antonio Mazzotti they could hear without difficulty the stumbling account of the woman close to
hysteria at the front door of the house. She wore a
cotton shift dress and a cardigan round her shoulders,
and rubber boots on her feet as if she had dressed in
haste, and the man she spoke with displayed his
pyjama trousers beneath his dressing-gown robe.
There had been a brief pause when Mazzotti disappeared inside leaving the woman alone with her face
bathed in light, so that the *carabinieri* who knew the
district and its people could recognize her. When Mazzotti came again to the door he was dressed and carried a double-barreled shotgun.

As they hurried down the road and onto the wood
path, the woman had clung to Mazzotti's arm and the

volume of her tale in his ear had covered the following footsteps of the men in camouflage uniforms: She
had heard shots from the barn and knew her husband
had work there that night, she knew he stayed at the
barn for Signor Mazzotti. She had gone there and
could hardly speak of what she had seen there. Now
her wailing was enough to rouse the village dogs.
Mazzotti made no attempt to silence her, as if the enormity of what she described had stunned and shaken
him.

When the *carabinieri* entered the barn, the woman
was prostrate on the body of her husband, her arms
cradling the viciously wounded head, her face pressed
to the coin-sized exit wound in his temple. Mazzotti,
isolated by the flashlights, had dropped his shotgun
to the earth floor. More light poured into the musty
room and searched out and found the second body
owning a face contorted by surprise and terror. Men
had been left to guard the building till dawn, while
the *capitano* hurried with his prisoners to their jeeps.

Within minutes of arriving at the Palmi barracks,
the officer had telephoned Rome, prized the home
number of Giuseppe Carboni from the argumentative
clerk, and was speaking to the policeman in his suburban flat.

Twice Carboni asked the same question, twice he
received the same deadening answer.

"There was a chain from a roof beam with part of a
handcuff attached. This is the place the Englishman
could have been held, but he was not there when we
came."

The *capitano* anticipated praise for the efforts of
his unit that night and received none.

A solitary car, lonely on the road, fast and free on
the *auto del sol*. Closing on the ankle of Italy, the heel
and toe left in its wake. Coming at speed. Geoffrey

Harrison and Giancarlo Battestini headed toward
Rome. Geoffrey and Giancarlo and a *P trent' otto.*

Archie Carpenter was at last asleep. His hotel room
was cruelly hot, but he had lost the spirit to complain
to the management on the problems of his reverberating air conditioner. He'd drunk more than he'd intended at the restaurant.

Michael Charlesworth had been purging his guilt at
the embassy's stance by maintaining a high level in
Carpenter's glass. Gin first, followed by wine, and
after that the acid of the local brandy. The talk had
been of strings that could not be tugged, of restric-
tions on action and initiative.

They had talked late and long on the extraordinary
Mrs. Harrison. Violet, known to them both, who behaved as no one else would that they could imagine in
those circumstances.

"She's impossible. Quite impossible. I just couldn't
talk to her. All I got for the trouble of going up there
was a mouthful of abuse."

"You didn't do as well as me," grinned Carpenter.
"She bloody near raped me."

"That would have been a diversion. She's off her
rocker."

"I'm not going back there, not till we march old
Harrison through the door, shove him at her, and
run."

"I wonder why she didn't fancy me," Charlesworth
had said, and worked again on the brandy bottle.

Violet Harrison, too, was deep in sleep. Still and
calm in the bed that she shared with her husband,
week after week, month after month. She had gone to
bed early, stripping her clothes off after the flight of
the man from Head Office. Had dressed in a new
nightgown, silky and lacetrimmed, that rode high

around her thighs. She wanted to sleep, wanted to rest, that her face might not be lined with tiredness in the morning, that the crow's feet would not be at her eyes.

Geoffrey would understand, Geoffrey would not condemn the desperate night urges. Geoffrey, wherever he was, would not blame her, would not pick up and cast the stone. She would not be late again at the beach.

Her legs wide and sprawled, she slept on a clear, bright, starlit night.

With a small torch to guide them, their bodies heaving, their feet stumbling, Vanni and Mario charged along the trail in the forest toward the rock face above the tree line.

Word of what had happened at the farm barn and the villa of the *capo* raced in a community as small as Cosoleto by a spider's web of gently tapped doors, calls from upper windows across the streets, by telephone among those houses that possessed the instrument. Vanni had flung his clothes on his back, snapped to his wife where he was going, and run from the back door to the home of Mario.

It was a path known to them since their childhood, but the pace of the flight ensured the bruised shins, the torn arms, and the gutteral obscenities. Beyond the trees, the way narrowed to little more than a goat track, necessitating that they must use their hands to pull them higher.

"Who could have been there?"

Vanni struggled on, out of condition, seeing no reason to reply.

"Who knew of the barn?" The persistence of shock and surprise consuming Mario. "It's certain it's not the *carabinieri* . . .?"

Vanni drew the air down his lungs, paused. "Certain."

"Who could have been there?" Mario wrung advantage from the rest, spattered his questions. "No one from the villages here would have dared. They would face the vendetta . . ."

"No one from these parts, no one who knew the *capo* . . ."

"Who could it have been?"

"*Cretino*, how do I know?"

The climb was resumed, slower and subdued, toward a cave beneath an escarpment, the bolt hole of Vanni.

Past five in the morning the discreet banging at his door woke Francesco Vellosi. In the attics of the Viminale were the angled ceiling closets where men in haste could sleep. He had worked late after the attack, calming himself with his papers, and neither he nor his guards were happy that he should drive back to his home. And the death of his driver, the killing of Mauro, had shed him of his desire for the comforts of his apartment. At the second flurry of knocking he had called on the man to enter. Sitting on his bed, naked but for a pale blue undershirt, his hair ragged, his chin alive with the growth of the small hours, he had focused on the messenger who brought blinding light into the room and a buff folder of papers. The man excused himself, was full of apology for the disturbance of the Dottore. The file had been given to him by the men in Operations, in the basements of the building. He knew nothing of the contents, had simply been dispatched on an errand. Vellosi reached from his bed, took the folder, and waved that the messenger should leave. When the door was closed he began to read.

There was a note of explanation, handwritten and

stapled to the long telex signed by the night duty officer, a man known to Vellosi, not one who would waste
the time of the *capo*. Workmen had come at four in
the morning to the offices of the mayor at the town of
Seminara in Calabria. The message reproduced on the
telex was the text of what they had found, along with
a credit card of American Express in the name of
Geoffrey Harrison.

It was the work of a few seconds for him to absorb
the contents of the communiqué. God, how many
more of these things? How much longer the agony
and suffering of these irrelevancies in the life span of
poor, tottering, broken-nosed Italia? After the pain
and division of the last one, after the affair of Moro,
was all this to be inflicted again? Dressing with one
hand, shaving with the battery razor provided
thoughtfully beside the washbasin, Vellosi hurried toward the premature day.

The fools must know there could be no concessions.
If they had not weakened for the elder statesman of
the Republic, how could they crumble now for a businessman, for a foreigner, for a life whose passing
would hold no lasting consequence? Idiots, fools, lu-
natics, these people.

Why?

Because they must know there cannot be surrender.

What if they have judged right? What if their analysis of the malaise and sickness of Italia were more per-
ceptive than that of Francesco Vellosi? What if they
had discerned that the country could not again endure
the strained preoccupation of sitting out ultimatums,
deadlines, and photographs of would-be widows?

Was he confident in the sinew of the state?

Over his body they would free Franca Tantardini.
Let the bitch out to Fiumicino, bend the constitution
for her . . . not as long as he held his job, not as long
as he headed the antiterrorist squad. Badly shaven,

temper rising, he headed for the stairs that would lead him to his office. His aides would be at home in their beds. The dawn meetings with the Minister, with the Procurator, with the *carabinieri* generals, with the men handling the Harrison affair at the Questura, would have to be scheduled by himself.

The route to a coronary, Vellosi told himself, the sure and steady road. He tripped on the narrow steps and shouted aloud in his frustration.

12

The first rays of light pushed across the inland foothills, graying the road in front of Harrison and Giancarlo. A water-color brush dabbed on the land, softening with pastel the darkness. The grim hour of the day when men who have not slept dread the hours of withering brightness which will follow. They wound down from the hills, running from the mountains as if they had caught the sniff of the sea which drew them to the beaches of Salerno.

For more than an hour they had not spoken, each wrapped in his hostile silence. A fearful quiet lulled only by the throb of the small engine.

Harrison wondered whether the boy slept, but the breathing was never regular, and there were the sudden movements beside him that meant lack of comfort, lack of calm. Perhaps, he thought, it would be simple to disarm him. Perhaps. A soldier, a man of action, would risk all on a sudden swerve, a quick breaking and a fast grapple for the P38. But you're neither of those, Geoffrey. The most violent thing he'd ever accomplished in his adult life was to kick that bucket at the guerrillas in the barn. And a smack at Violet once. Just once, not hard. That's all, Geoffrey, all the offensive experience. Not the stuff of heroes, but it wasn't in his chemistry, and for heroes he read bloody idiots.

Geoffrey Harrison had never in his life met the dedicated activist, the political attack weapon. Newspaper photographs, yes, plenty of those. Wanted men, captured and chained men, dead men on the pavement. But all inadequate those images, when it came to this boy. They're not stupid, not this one anyway. He worked out a plan and he executed it. Found you when half the police in the country were on the same job and late at the post. This isn't a gutter kid, not from the shanties down on the Tevere banks. A gutter kid wouldn't argue, he'd have killed for the stopping of the car.

"Giancarlo, I'm very tired. We have to talk about something. If I don't talk we'll go off the road."

There was no sudden start, no stirring at the breaking of the quiet. The boy had not been asleep. The possibility of action had not been there. Harrison felt better for that.

"You are driving very well, we have covered more than half of the distance now. Much more than half." The boy sounded alert, and prepared for conversation.

Harrison blundered in. "Are you a student, Giancarlo?"

"I was, some years ago I was a student." Sufficient as a reply, giving nothing.

"What did you study?" Humor the little pig, humor and amuse him.

"I studied psychology at the University of Rome. I did not complete my first year. When the students of my class were taking their first year examinations, I was held a political prisoner in the Regina Coeli jail. I was part of a struggle group. I was fighting against the *borghese* administration when the fascist police imprisoned me."

Can't they speak another language? Harrison thought. Are they reduced only to compilation of slogans and manifestoes? "Where do you come from, Giancarlo? Where is your home?"

"My home was in the *covo* with Franca. Before that my home was in the B wing of the Regina Coeli, where my friends were."

Harrison spoke without thought. Too tired to pick his words, and his throat was hoarse and sore even from this slight effort. "Where your parents were, where you spent your childhood, that was what I meant by home."

"We use different words, 'arrison. I do not call that my home. I was in chains . . ." Again the warm spittle spread on Harrison's face.

"I'm very tired, Giancarlo. I want to talk so that we don't crash, and I want to understand you. But you don't have to give me that jargon." Harrison yawned, not for effect, nor as a gesture.

Giancarlo laughed out loud, the first time Harrison had heard the rich little treble chime. "You pretend to be a fool, 'arrison. I ask you a question. Answer me the truth and I will know you. Answer me, if you were a boy that lived in Italy . . . if you were from the privilege of the DC, if you had seen the children in the 'popular' quarter in their rags, if you had seen the hospitals, if you had see the rich playing at the villas and with their yachts, if you had seen those things, would you not fight? That is my question, 'arrison, would you not fight?"

The dawn came faster now, the probes of sunlight spearing across the road, and there were other cars on the autostrada that they either passed or that sped by them.

"I would not fight, Giancarlo," Harrison said slowly, with the crushing weariness surging again and his eyes cluttered with headlights. "I would not have the courage to say that I am right, that my word is law. I would need greater authority than a bloody pistol."

"Drive on, and be careful on the road." The attack of the angered wasp. As if a stick had penetrated the nest and thrashed about and roused the ferocity of the swarm. "You will learn my courage, 'arrison. You will learn it at nine o'clock, if the pigs that you slave for have not met . . ."

"Nine tomorrow morning," Harrison spoke distantly, his attention on the taillights in front and the dazzled center mirror above him. "You give them little time."

"Time only for them to express your value."

Away to the left were the lights daubed on the Bay of Naples. Harrison veered to the right and followed the white arrows on the road to the north and Rome.

Another dawn, another bright fresh morning, and Giuseppe Carboni alive with lemon juice in his mouth arrived at the Viminale by taxi.

It was a long time since he had been to the Ministry. No reason for many months for him to desert the unprepossessing Questura. His chin was down on his tie, his eyes on his shoes as he paid off the driver. This was a place where only the idiot felt safe, where the knives were sharp and the criticism cutting. Here the sociologists and the criminologists and the penologists held court, and rule was by university diploma and qualification by breeding and connection, because this was close to power, the real power that the Questura did not know.

Carboni was led up the stairs, a debutante introduced at a dance. His humor was poor, his mind only slightly receptive when he reached the door of Francesco Vellosi who had summoned him.

He knew of Vellosi by title and reputation. A well-known name in the *pubblica sicurezza* with a history of clean firmness to embellish it, the one who had made a start at cleaning the drains of crime in Reggio Calabria, ordered significant arrests, and not bowed to intimidation. But the corridor gossip had it that he delighted in public acclamation and sought out the cameras and microphones and the journalists' notebooks. Carboni himself shunned publicity and was suspicious of fast-won plaudits.

But the man across the desk appealed to him.

Vellosi was in his shirtsleeves, glasses down on his nose, cigarette limp between his lips in the gesture of the tired lover, tie loosened, and his jacket away on a chair across the room. No reek of aftershave, no scent of armpit lotion, and already a well-filled ashtray in front of him. Vellosi was studying the papers that climbed on the desk. Carboni waited, then coughed, the obligatory explanation of his presence.

Vellosi's eyes grabbed at him. "Dottore Carboni, thank you for coming and so soon. I had not expected you for another hour."

"I came immediately that I had dressed."

"As you know, Carboni, from this office I run, I manage, the affairs of the antiterrorist unit." The rapid patter had begun. "If one can make such a delineation, I am concerned with affairs political rather than criminal."

It was to be expected that time would be consumed before they arrived at the reason for the meeting. Carboni was not disturbed. "Obviously, I know the work that is done from this office."

"And now it seems that our paths cross, which is rare. Seldom do criminal activities liase with those of terrorism."

"It has happened," Carboni replied.

"An Englishman has been kidnapped. It happened

two mornings ago. I am correct?" Vellosi's chin was buried in his hands as he gazed hard across the desk. "Tell me, please, Carboni, what was your opinion of that case?"

Something to be wary of, something to herald caution, Carboni paused before speaking. "I have no reason to believe that the kidnapping was not the work of criminals. The style of the attack was similar to that previously used. The limited descriptions of the men who took part indicated an age that is not usually common among the political people, in their thirties or more. A ransom demand was made that we have linked with a previous abduction, a further connection has been found with the office of a speculator in Calabria. There is nothing to make me doubt that it was a criminal affair."

"You have been fortunate, you have come far."

Carboni loosened. The man opposite him talked like a human, without scheme and plot. The superiority of his rank he kept covered. The man from the Questura felt a freedom to express himself. "Last night I was able to ask the *carabinieri* of Palmi near Reggio to keep a watch on this speculator. His name is Mazzotti, from the village of Cosoleto, he has connections in local politics. I acted without a warrant from the magistrate, but the time was not ripe for waiting. If I might digress, a man was found yesterday in a Roman *pensione* battered to death . . . he had a record for kidnapping, his family is from Cosoleto. I return to the point. The *carabinieri* behaved faultlessly." Carboni permitted himself a slow smile, one policeman to another, histories of rivalry with the paramilitary force, mutual understanding on the scale of the compliment. "The *carabinieri* followed Mazzotti to a barn, he was taken there by a woman who had heard sounds in the night. The woman's husband was dead there, shot at close range, another man also had been killed. There were signs of a temporary holding place, flattened-down hay bales, and there was a chain with a mana-cle. A pistol, Vellosi, had been used to break the lock of the handcuff. It had been broken by gunshot. We did not find Harrison, not any trace of him."

Vellosi nodded his head, the picture unveiled, the drape drawn back. "What conclusion, Carboni, did you draw from the information of the *carabinieri*?"

Carboni struggled for eloquence and could not ar-rive at the trite phrase he would have wanted. He opted for simplicity. "Someone came to the barn and killed the two men that he might have Harrison for himself. It was not a rescue since there have been no messages from the south of Harrison's arrival at a po-lice station or a *carabinieri* barracks, I checked before I left home. I cannot draw an ultimate conclusion."

The head of the antiterroist squad hunched forward, voice lowered and conspiratorial, as if in a room such as his there were listening places. "Last night I was attacked. Ambushed as I left my home, and my driver was killed . . ." Vellosi understood from the stunned frowns building and edging across Carboni's forehead that he knew nothing of the evening's horror . . . "I survived unhurt. We have identified the swine that killed my driver. They are *Nappisti*, Carboni. They were young, they were inefficient and they died for it."

"I congratulate you on your escape," Carboni whis-pered.

"I mourn my driver, he was a friend of many years. I believe I was attacked as a reprisal for the capture of the woman Franca Tantardini, taken by my squad in the Corsa Francia. She is an evil bitch, Carboni, a poisoned, evil woman."

Carboni recovered his composure. "It was a fine ef-fort by your people."

"I have told you nothing yet. Hear me out before

you praise me. There is a town, Seminara, in Calabria.
I have no map, but we will find, I am sure, that it is
close to your Cosoleto. Under the mayor's door an
hour ago was found a scribbled statement, not typed,
not neat, from the NAP. A credit card of Harrison was
with the paper. They will kill him tomorrow morning
at nine o'clock if Tantardini has not been freed."

Carboni whistled, an expiry of wind from his lungs.
His pen fumbled between the fingers of his two
hands, his notebook was virgin clean.

"I make an assumption, Carboni. The *Nappisti*
reached your man Claudio. They extracted information. They have taken Harrison from the custody of
Mazzotti. The danger now confronting the Englishman is infinitely greater."

With his head bowed, Carboni sat very still in his
chair as if a heavy blow had struck him. "What has
been done this morning to prevent an escape . . . ?"

"Nothing has been done." A snarl from Vellosi's
mouth and above it the cauterized cheeks, the whitened skin at the temples. "Nothing has been done because until we sat together there was no dialogue on
this issue. I have no army, I have no authority over
the *polizia* and the *carabinieri*. I do not have the numbers to stifle an escape. I have given you the *Nappisti*, and you have given me a location, and now we
can begin."

Carboni spoke with a sadness, unwilling to stamp
on the energy of his superior. "They have five hours
start on us, and they were close to the autostrada and
at night the road is free." His head shook as he multi-
plied kilometers and minutes in his mind. "It could be
hundreds of kilometers in a fast car. The whole of the
mezzo giorno is open to them . . ." He tailed away,
awed by the hopelessness of what he said.

"Blister the local *carabinieri*, the *polizia*, breathe
some fire under their backsides. Get back to your of-

fice now and hunt the facts." Shouting now, consumed by his mission, Vellosi banged on his desk to emphasize each point.

"It is outside my jurisdiction . . ."

"What do you want? A rule book and Harrison dead in a ditch at five minutes past nine tomorrow? Get yourself into the fifth floor at the Questura. All the computers, all the Honeywell machines there, get them moving, let them earn their keep."

Resistance failing, Carboni subsided, "May I make a telephone call, Dottore?"

"Make it and be on your way. It is not you alone who is busy this morning. The Minister will be here in forty minutes . . ."

Carboni was on his feet, magnetized into activity. With quick, sweaty fingers he flicked in his diary of telephone numbers for that of Michael Charlesworth of the British Embassy.

The early sun was denied entry by the drawn drapes to the reception lounge of the Villa Wolkonsky. The more fancied of the room's collection of rare porcelain had been put away the night before, because there had been a small reception and the Ambassador's wife was ever wary of light fingers among her guests. There remained enough to satisfy the curiosity of Charlesworth and Carpenter as they stood close to each other in the gloom. They had come unannounced to the Ambassador's residence, spurred by Giuseppe Carboni's call to Charlesworth which sketched through the night's developments. The diplomat had collected Carpenter from his hotel. A servant in a white coat, not hiding his disapproval of the hour, had admitted them. If we broadcast we're on our way, Charlesworth had said in the car, then the barricades go up, he'll stall till office hours.

The irritation of the Ambassador was undisguised

as he entered the room. A puckered forehead and a jutting chin sandwiched the hawk eyes of annoyance. He wore his familiar, dark striped trousers, but no jacket to drape over the braces that held them firm. His collar was unfastened.

"Good morning, Charlesworth. I understand from the message sent upstairs that you wished to see me on a matter of pressing importance. Let's not waste each other's time."

In the face of the salvo Charlesworth did not falter. "I've brought with me Archie Carpenter. He's the Security Officer of International Chemical Holdings in London . . ."

His Excellency's eyes glinted, a bare greeting.

" . . . I have just been telephoned by Dottore Carboni of the Questura. There have been disturbing and unpleasant developments in the Harrison case . . ."

Carpenter said quietly, "We judged that you should know of these—whatever the inconvenience of the hour."

The Ambassador threw him a glance, then turned back to Charlesworth. "Let's have it, then."

"The police have always believed Harrison was kidnapped by a criminal organization. During the night it seems that this organization was relieved of Harrison. It seems he is now in the hands of the Nuclei Armati Proletaria."

"What do you mean, 'relieved'?"

"It seems that the NAP has forcibly taken Harrison from his original kidnappers," said Charlesworth with patience.

"The police are offering this as a theory? We are to believe this?" Spoken with the killer chop of sarcasm, the bite of ridicule.

"Yes sir," Carpenter again interjected, "we believe it because there are three men on their backs in the morgue to convince us. Two have died of gunshot wounds, the third of a dented skull."

The Ambassador retreated, coughed, wiped his head with a handkerchief, and waved his visitors to chairs. "For what motive has this happened?" he said simply.

Charlesworth took his cue. "The NAP demand that by nine tomorrow morning, Central European Time, the Italian government shall release the captured terrorist, Franca Tantardini . . ."

The Ambassador, sitting far to the front of the intricately carved chair, reeled forward, "Oh my God . . . go on, Charlesworth."

". . . the Italian government shall release Franca Tantardini or Geoffrey Harrison will be killed. In a few minutes the Interior Minister will get his first briefing. I imagine that within twenty you will be called to the Viminale."

Rock-still, his head in his tired, aged hands, the Ambassador contemplated. Neither Charlesworth nor Carpenter interrupted. The buck had been moved on. For a full minute the silence burgeoned around the room causing Charlesworth to feel for the straightness of his tie knot, Carpenter to look at his unpolished shoes and the lace that was loosened.

The Ambassador shook himself as if to dislodge the burden. "It is a decision for the Italian government to make. Any interference, any pressure on our part, would be quite unwarranted. Indeed, any suggestion of action would be quite uncalled for."

"So you wash your hands of Harrison?" Carpenter was flushed as he spoke, temper surging, hands clenched together.

"I don't think that's what the Ambassador meant . . ." Charlesworth cut in unhappily.

"Thank you, Charlesworth, but I can justify my own statements," the Ambassador said. "We don't wash our hands of the fate of Mr. Harrison, as you put it, Mr. Carpenter. We face the reality of local conditions."

"When this was a criminal matter, when there was only money at issue, then we were prepared to deal . . ."

"Your company was prepared to negotiate, Mr. Carpenter. The British Foreign Office remained uninvolved."

"What's so bloody different between a couple of million dollars and freedom for one woman?" All that bloody brandy that Charlesworth had plied him with, couldn't marshal his sentences, couldn't hit at the smug, sober bastard opposite him. The frustration welled in his mind.

"Don't shout at me, Mr. Carpenter." The Ambassador was cold, aloof on his pedestal. "The situation is different indeed. Before, as you rightly say, only money was involved. Now we add principle, and with that the sovereign dignity of the Republic of Italy. It is inconceivable that the government here can bow to so crude a threat and release a public enemy of the stature of the Tantardini woman. It is equally inconceivable that the government of Great Britain should urge such a course."

"I say again, you wash your hands of Geoffrey Harrison. You're prepared to see him sacrificed for the 'dignity of Italy,' whatever bloody nonsense that is . . ." Carpenter looked across to Charlesworth for an ally, but he had been anticipated and the gaze was averted. "Well, thank you gentlemen, thank you for your time. I'm sorry you were disturbed, that the day started badly, and early." Carpenter stood up. "You're putting our man down the bloody bog, and you're pulling the bloody chain on him, and I think it's bloody marvelous."

There was a passionless mask across the Ambassador's features and he stayed far back in his chair. "We merely face reality, Mr. Carpenter, and reality will dictate that if the losers in this matter are to be either Geoffrey Harrison or the Republic of Italy, then it will be Harrison that is lost. If that is the conclusion, then the life of one man is of lesser importance than the lasting damage to the social and political fabric of a great and democratic country. That is how I see it, Mr. Carpenter."

"It's a load of bullshit . . ."

"Your rudeness neither offends me nor helps Harrison."

"I think we should be on our way, Archie," Charlesworth too was standing. "I'll see you later in the office, sir."

When they were out in the sunshine and walking toward the car, Charlesworth saw that there were tears streaming on Archie Carpenter's face.

For several minutes Harrison had been watching the jumping needle of the fuel gauge that bounced against the left corner of the dial, bringing him the knowledge that the tank was emptying. He wondered how the boy would react to the idea that the car would soon be useless, considered whether he should alert him or whether he should simply drive on till the engine coughed and died, barren of petrol. Depends what he wanted from it, whether it was a fight, or whether it was the easy way and safety, however temporary. Tell him now that they were about to stop on the hard shoulder and perhaps the boy wouldn't panic, would work at his options. Allow it to happen and the boy might crumble under a crisis, and that was dangerous because of the presence of the P38.

Same old question, Geoffrey, same old situation. To confront or bend, and no middle road.

Same old answer, Geoffrey. Don't shake it, don't rock it. Don't kick the bucket of muck in his face.

"We won't be going much farther, Giancarlo."

Harrison's softly spoken words boomed inside the quiet of the car. Beside him the boy straightened from his low-slung sitting posture. The gun barrel dug at Harrison's ribs as if demanding explanation.

"We're almost out of petrol."

The boy's head, coated in its curled and tangled hair, darted across Harrison's chest to study the dial. Harrison eased back in his seat, gave him more room, and heard the breathing of Giancarlo speed and rise.

"There's not much more in the old girl, Giancarlo. Perhaps a few more kilometers."

The boy lifted his head, and the hand that did not hold the gun scraped at his chin as if this were a way to summon inspiration and clarity of decision.

"It's not my fault, Giancarlo."

"Silence," the boy snapped back.

Just the breathing to mingle with the steady purr of the little engine, and time, too, for Harrison to think and consider. Behind their different walls the man and the boy entertained the same thoughts. What would a stoppage mean to the security of the journey? What risk would it offer Giancarlo of identification and subsequent pursuit? What possibility of escape would it present to his prisoner? Not only the boy with decisions to make, Geoffrey, you as well. Couldn't be as vigilant, could he, not if they were stopped on the roadside, not if they were pulled into a toll gate, and then going in search of a petrol station? Opportunities were going to loom, opportunities for escape, for flight, for a dash, for a struggle.

Then he'll shoot.

Sure?

Can't be sure but likely.

Worth a try, whether he'll shoot or not?

Perhaps, if the opportunity's there.

You won't do it, you won't take him on, you won't fight.

Perhaps, but only if it presents itself.

"We take the Monte Cassino turnoff," Giancarlo was out of his dream, breaking Harrison's debate.

High above them to the right of the autostrada perched the triumphant monastery. It loomed on the mountaintop, a widow's shrine for women of many far countries whose men had staggered and fallen distant years back under the rain clouds of shrapnel and explosives and bullet swathes. The car plunged past the signs for the turnoff.

Giancarlo raised himself in his seat and pulled from a hip pocket a wad of notes and the autostrada toll ticket taken hundreds of kilometers back from a machine.

"I had not thought of the petrol," the boy laughed with a quick nervousness. A drip of weakness before the tap was turned tighter. " 'arrison, you will not be silly. You will pay the ticket. The gun will be at you, all the time at you. You are not concerned with what will happen to me, you are concerned with what will happen to yourself. If you are silly, then you are dead, whether I am too does not help you. You understand, 'arrison? You understand?"

"Yes, Giancarlo."

Harrison pulled the wheel hard to the right, felt the tires bite beneath him, heard their squeal, and the view of the autostrada diminished in his windshield mirror. He had slowed the car as they wound on the tight bend toward the toll gate. Giancarlo reached back to the seat behind and grabbed at his light windbreaker, arranged it over his lower arm and his fist and the gun, and again pressured the barrel into the softness of Harrison's waist.

"You don't speak."

"What if he talks to me?" Harrison stammered, the
tension exuding from the boy spreading contagiously.

"I will talk to him, if it is necessary . . . if I fire
the pistol from here I kill you, 'arrison."

"I know, Giancarlo."

Perhaps, but only if it presents itself. You know the
answer, Geoffrey. He squeezed his foot onto the
brake as the booths of the tollgate loomed in front of
him. He stopped the car as the hood edged against the
narrow barrier, carefully wound down the window,
and without looking, passed the ticket and a bank
note out into the cool dawn air.

"*Grazie.*"

The voice startled Harrison. Contact again with the
real and the permanent life, contact with the clean
and familiar. His eyes followed his arm but there was
no face in his vision, only a hand that was dark and
hair-covered with a worn greasy palm that took his
money and was gone before snaking back with a fist-
ful of coins. It had not presented itself. The gun
gouged at his flesh, and the man would not even have
seen their faces. The voice beside him was shrill.

"*Una stazione di servizio, per benzina?*" . . . .

"*Cinque centro metri.*"

"*Grazie.*"

"*Prego.*"

The barrier was raised, Harrison edged the car into
gear. The bloody man wouldn't even have seen them.
Shouldn't he have crashed the gears, stalled the engine, dropped the change in the roadway? Shouldn't
he have done something? But the gun was there,
round and penetrating at the skin. All right for those
who don't know, all right for those without experience. Let them come and sit here, let them find their
own answers to cowardice. Within moments the lights
of a service station shone at them in the half light,
diffused with the growing sun.

"You follow my instructions exactly."

"Yes, Giancarlo."

"Go to the far pumps."

Where it was darkest, where the light was masked by the building, Harrison stopped. Giancarlo waited till the hand brake was applied, the gear in neutral before his hand snaked out to rip the keys from the ignition. He snapped open his door, thrust it shut behind him, and jogged around the back of the car till he was at Harrison's door. He held his windbreaker across his waist with an innocence that was above suspicion.

Harrison saw a man in the blue overalls of Agip stroll without urgency toward the car.

"*Venti mila lire de benzina, per favore.*" . .

"*Si.*"

Would he look into the car, would the curiosity bred from the long night hours cause him to turn from the boy who stood beside the driver's door, and wish to examine the occupant? Why should it? Why should he care who drives a car? This has to be the moment, Geoffrey. Now, right now, not next time, not next week.

How?

Fling the door open, crash it into Giancarlo's body. You'd knock him back with it, he'd fall, he'd slip. For how long? Long enough to run. Sure? Well, not sure . . . but it's a chance. And how far do you run before he's on his feet, five meters . . . ? It's the opportunity. Then he shoots and he doesn't miss, not this kid, and who else is here other than a half-asleep idiot with his eyes closed, who will have to play the hero?

Giancarlo passed the man the cash and waited as he walked away, then hissed through the window, "I am going to walk around the car. If you move I will shoot, it is no problem through the glass. Do not move, 'arrison."

Only if it presents itself. Geoffrey Harrison felt the great weakness creeping into his knees and shins, lapping in his stomach. His tongue smeared a dampness across his lips. You'd have been dead, Geoffrey, if you'd tried anything, you know that, don't you? He supposed that he did, supposed that he had been sensible, behaved in the intelligent, responsible way that came from education and experience. Wouldn't have lasted long on that mountainside, not in 1944, Geoffrey, wouldn't have lasted five bloody minutes.

They drove sharply through the small town, rebuilt from the ravages of bombardment into a characterless warren of apartment blocks and factories, and headed north on a narrow road among the rock defiles, ever watched by the great whitestone eye on the mountaintop. They bypassed the somber war cemetery for the German dead of a battle fought before the birth of Giancarlo and Harrison, and then the road's turns became more vicious and the high banks more intrusive.

Three kilometers beyond the rugged message of the graveyard cross, Giancarlo indicated an open field gate through which they should turn. The car lurched over the bare grass covering of the hardened ground and was lost to sight behind a gorse hedge of brilliant yellow flowers. Shepherds might come here, or the men who watched the goat flocks, but the chance was reasonable in Giancarlo's mind. Among the grass and weeds and climbing thistle and the bushes of the hillside they would rest. Rome lay just one hundred and twenty-five kilometers away. They had done well, they had made good time.

With the car stationary, Giancarlo moved briskly. The wire that he had found in the glove compartment in one hand, the pistol in the other, he followed Harrison between the gorse clumps. He ordered him down, pushed him without unkindness onto his stomach, and then kneeling with the gun between his thighs, bound

Harrison's hands across the small of his back. The legs next, working at the ankle, wrapping the wire around them, weaving it tight, binding the knot. He walked a few paces away and urinated noisily in the grass and was watching the rivulets when he realized he had not offered the Englishman the same chance. He shrugged and put it from his mind.

Harrison's eyes were already closed, the breathing deep and regular as the sleep sped to him. Giancarlo watched the slow rise and fall of his shoulders and the gaping mouth that was not irritated by the nibbling of a fly. He put the gun onto the grass and scrabbled with his fingers at the buckle of belt and at the elastic waist of his underpants.

Franca. Darling, sweet, lovely Franca. I am coming, Franca. And we will be together, always together, Franca, and you will love me for what I have done for you. Love me, too, my beautiful. Love me.

Giancarlo subsided on the grass and the sun played on his face and there was a light wind and the sound of the flying creatures. The P38 was close to his hand. And the boy lay still.

13

Giancarlo asleep seemed little more than a child, hurt
by exhaustion and dragged nerves, coiled gently. His
real age was betrayed by the premature haggardness
of his face, the witness to his participation in the affairs of men. His left forearm acted as a shield to the
climbing sun, and his right hand was buried in the
grass, and his fingers lay among the leaves and stalks
and across the handle of the P38.

The boy was dreaming.

The fantasy was of success, the images were of
achievement. Tossed and tumbling through his febrile
mind were the pictures of the moment of triumph he
would win. Sharp pictures, vivid. Men in blue Fiat se-
dans hurrying with escorts of outriders to the public
buildings of the capital, men who pushed their way
past avalanches of cameras and microphones with anger at their mouths. Rooms that were heavy in smoke
and argument where the talk was of Giancarlo Battestini and Franca Tantardini and the NAP. Crisis in the
air. Papers would be set in front of the men and pens
made ready. Official stamps, weighty and embossed
with eagles, would clamp down on the scrawl of the

signatures. The order would be made, Franca would be freed, plucked clear from the enemy by the hand of her boy and her lover. The order would be made, in the dreaming and restless mind of Giancarlo there was no doubt. Because he had done so much . . . he had come so far.

He had done so much, and they could not deny him the pleasure of his prize. There was one more element among the images of the boy sleeping in the field. There was a prison gate, dominating the skyline and shadowing the street beneath, and doors that would swing slowly open, dragged apart against their will by the hands of Giancarlo. There was a column of police cars, sirens and lights bright on a July morning, bringing his Franca free; she sat as a queen among them, contempt in her eyes for the truncheons and Beretta pistols and machine guns. Franca coming to freedom.

It would be the greatest victory ever achieved by the NAP. Loving himself, loving his dream, Giancarlo groped downward with his right hand, urging his thoughts to the diminishing memory of his Franca, conjuring again her body and the sunswept skin.

The spell was broken. The dream gone; a blur of light, a memory and a ripple. Lost and destroyed. Trembling in his anger Giancarlo sat up.

"Giancarlo, Giancarlo," Geoffrey Harrison had called. "I want to pee and I can't the way I am tied."

Harrison saw the fury in the boy's face, the neck veins in tunnel relief. Frightened him, the intensity, the loathing that was communicated across the few meters of stone and burned field flowers.

He slipped back from confrontation. "I have to pee, Giancarlo. It's not much to ask."

The boy stood up, uncertain for a moment on his feet, then collected himself. He traversed with his eyes as if all the ground and surroundings were unfamiliar to him and in need of further checks to establish his security. He examined the long depth of the horizon, breaking the fields and low stone walls and distant farm buildings into sectors that they might be vetted more thoroughly. Harrison could see that the boy was rested, that the sleep had alerted and revived him. He used a bush of gorse and yellow-petaled flowers to cover himself from the road as he looked around. Something slow and workmanlike and hugely sinister, the calm of the boy. Better to have tied a knot in it or soaked his trousers, Harrison thought, than to have woken him.

Giancarlo walked toward him, feet light on the springy grass, avoiding the stones set far into the earth. The hand with the gun was extended, aimed at Harrison's chest.

"Don't worry, don't point it, I'm not playing heroes, Giancarlo."

The boy moved behind Harrison, and he heard the scuff of his feet.

"There's a good lad, Giancarlo, you know how it is. I'm fit to bloody burst, you know . . ."

The blow was fierce, agonizing and without warning. The full force of the canvas toe cap of the shoe on Giancarlo's right foot, digging into the flesh that formed the protective wall for the kidneys. The pain was instant, welding together with the next source as the following kick came in fast and sharp. Three in all, and Harrison slid onto his side.

"You little pig. Vicious . . . bullying . . . little pig." The words were gasped out, strained and hoarse, and the breath was hard to find, thin and unwilling to be drawn into his lungs. More pain, more hurt, because the wounds of the men in the barn were liberated again and aroused and mingled with the new bruising. Harrison looked up into the eyes of the boy and they bounced his gaze back. Something animal, something primitive. Where do they make them, these bloody creatures?

Slowly and with deliberation the boy bent down behind Harrison, the barrel of the pistol indenting the skin where it was smooth and hairless behind the ear. With his free hand Giancarlo untied the bonds. It was the work of a few moments and then Harrison felt the freedom come again to his wrists and ankles, the shock surge of the blood running free. He didn't wait to be told, but rose unsteadily to his feet. He walked a half-dozen paces with a drunken gait and flicked at his zipper. The spurting, draining relief. That's what it had come down to; ten minutes of negotiation, a kick, a gun at the back of his head—all that because he wanted to pee, to spend a penny as Violet would have said. Being pulled down into the cesspool, being animalized. He looked down into the clear, reflecting pool in front of his feet and in a moment of hesitation between surges saw the traces of his own concerned and wrung-out face.

Geoffrey, we want to go home. We're not fighters, old lad, we're not like those who can just sit in a limbo and be, pushed and tugged by the wind. Just a poor, little bloody businessman who doesn't give a stuff about exploitation and revolution and the rights of the proletariat. Just a poor, little, bloody businessman who wants to wrestle with output and production and raw materials, the things that pay for summer holidays and the clothes on Violet's back, and a few quid to go on top of a widowed mother's pension. It's not our war, Geoffrey, not our bloody fight. Harrison shook himself, swayed on his feet, pulled up the zipper, and turned his hips so that he could see behind him. His movements were careful, dedicated to causing no alarm. The boy was watching him, impassive, and with all the emotion of a whitewashed wall. The two of them, devoid of relationship, without mutual sympathy, stared at each other. He'd kill you as he'd stamp on a dragonfly, Geoffrey, and it wouldn't move him, wouldn't halt his sleep afterward. That's why he doesn't communicate, because the bastard doesn't need to.

"What are we going to do now?" Harrison asked in a small voice.

The boy stood out of arm's reach, but close. Another gesture from the arm that held the pistol and they walked the few meters toward the car.

"Where are we going?" Harrison said.

Giancarlo laughed, opening his mouth so that Harrison saw the fillings of his teeth and smelled the stench of his breath. This is the way the Jews went to the cattle trucks in the railway sidings, without a struggle, making obeisance to their guards, thought Harrison. Understand, Geoffrey, how they forsook resistance?

He opened the door of the car, climbed in, and watched Giancarlo walk round the front of the engine. The key was in the ignition, the P38 took up a position by his rib cage, the brake was eased off, the gears engaged.

Harrison headed the car back toward the road.

Its headlights shining vainly in the morning brilliance, a white Alfetta swept down the sloping crescent of the driveway outside the Viminale. An identical car with the smoked, half-inch-thick windows and reinforced bodywork had latched itself close behind, the worrying terrier that must not leave its quarry. Alone among the members of the Italian government, the Interior Minister had discarded the midnight blue fleet of Fiat 132s after the kidnapping of the President of his party. For him and his bodyguards bulletproof transport was decreed. The Minister had said in public that he detested the hermetically sealed capsule in

which he was ferried in high summer from one
quarter of the city to another, but after the chorus of
interservice recrimination that followed the attack on
the vulnerable Moro car and the massacre of his five-
man escort, the Minister's preferences realized little
precedence.

With the siren blaring, scattering the motorists on
Quattro Fontane languidly aside, the Alfetta plied
through the mounting traffic. The driver was
hunched in his concentration, left hand steady on the
wheel, the right resting loosely on the gear stick. Beside the driver, the Minister's senior guard cradled a
short-barreled machine gun on his lap, one magazine
attached, two more on the floor between his feet.

For the Minister and his guest, the British Ambassador, conversation was difficult, each clinging to the
thong straps above the darkened side windows. The
Ambassador was traveling at the Minister's invitation,
his presence hurriedly requested. Would he care to be
briefed on the situation concerning the businessman
Harrison while the Minister was in transit between his
offices and those of the Prime Minister? Somewhere
lost behind them in jammed Roman streets was the
embassy Rolls which would collect the Ambassador
from Palazzo Chigi.

Public men both of them and so they were jacketed.
The Italian sported above his blue shirt a red silk tie.
The Ambassador favored the broad color bands of his
wartime cavalry unit. The two men were stifled with
heat near to suffocation in the closed car, and the
Minister showed his irritation that he should be the
cause of his guest's discomfort. Protests of apology
were waved aside, there was the little clucking of the
tongue that meant the problem was inconsequential.

Unlike many of his colleagues, the Minister spoke
English fluently and with little of the Mediterranean
accent. A lucid and educated man, a professor of law,

an author of books, he explained the night's events to the Ambassador.

"And so, sir, we have at our doors another nightmare. We have another journey into the abyss of despair that after the murder of our friend Aldo Moro we hoped never to see again. For all of us then, in the Council of Ministers and in the Directorate of the Democrazia Christiana, the decision to turn our backs on our friend provoked a bitter and horrible moment. We all prayed hard for guidance then. All of us, sir. We walked across to church from the deliberations at the Piazza Gesu, and as one we went to our knees and prayed for God's guidance. If He gave it to us He manifested Himself in His own and peculiar way. His message bearer was Berlinguer, it was the Secretary General of our Communist party who informed us that the infant understanding between his party and ours could not survive vacillation. The PCI dictated that there could be no concession to the *Brigate Rosse*. The demand that we release thirteen of their nominees from jail was rejected. The chance to save one of the great men of our country was lost. Who can apportion the question of victory and defeat between ourselves and the *Brigatisti?*"

The Minister mopped a smear of sweat from his neck with a handkerchief scented with cologne sufficient to turn the Ambassador's nostrils. The monologue, the exposition of the day's business, continued.

"Now we must make more decisions, and first we must decide whether we follow the same rules as before or whether we offer a different response. The hostage on this occasion is not an Italian, nor is he a public figure who could by some be held accountable for the society in which we live. The hostage now is a guest, and totally without responsibility for the conditions that unhappily prevail in our country . . . I won't elaborate. I turn to the nature of the ransom demanded. One prisoner, one only. Thirteen we could not countenance, but one we might swallow, though the bone would stick. But swallow it we could, if we had to."

The Ambassador rocked pensively in his seat. They had cut down the curved hill from the Quirinale and surged with noise and power across the Piazza Venezia, dispersing the locust swarms of jeaned and T-shirted tourists. Not for him to reply at this stage, not till his specific opinion was required.

The Minister sighed, as if he had hoped for the load to be shared, and realized with regret that he must soldier on.

"We would be very loath to lose your Mr. Harrison, and very loath to lose the Tantardini woman. We believe we should do everything within our power to save Mr. Harrison. The dilemma is whether 'everything in our power' constitutes interference in the judicial process against Tantardini."

The Ambassador peered down at the hands in his lap. "With respect, Minister, that is a decision the Italian government must make."

"You would pass it all to us?"

The Ambassador recited, "Anything else would be the grossest interference in the internal affairs of a longstanding and respected friend."

The Minister smiled, grimly, without enjoyment. "We have very little time, Ambassador. So my question to you will be concise. There should be no misunderstandings."

"I agree."

The Minister savored his question before speaking. The critical one, the reason that he had invited the Ambassador to travel with him. "Is it likely that Her Majesty's Government will make an appeal to us to barter the woman Tantardini with the intention of saving Harrison's life?"

"Most unlikely." The Ambassador was sure and decisive.

"We would not wish to take a course of action and afterward receive a request from Whitehall for a different approach."

"I repeat, Minister; it is most unlikely that we would ask for the freeing of Tantardini."

The Minister looked with his jaded blue eyes at the Ambassador, a dab of surprise at his mouth. "You are a hard people . . . you value principle highly. It does not have much merit in our society."

"My government does not believe in bowing to the coercion of terrorism."

"I put another hypothesis to you. If we refuse to negotiate with the *Nappisti* for the freedom of Tantardini, and if as a consequence Harrison dies, would we be much criticized in Britain for the hard line, *la linea dura* as we would say?"

"Most unlikely." The Ambassador held the Minister's questioning glance, unswerving and without deviation, the reply clear as a pistol shot.

"We are not a strong country, Ambassador, we prefer to circumvent obstacles that fall across our path. We do not have the mentality of your cavalry, we do not raise our sabers and charge our enemy. We seek to avoid him . . ."

The car came to a halt and the driver and bodyguard leaned back to unfasten the locks on the rear doors. Out on the cobbled courtyard of the Palazzo Chigi the Ambassador breathed in the clean, freshened air and dried his hands on his trouser crease.

The Minister had not finished, busily he led the Ambassador into the center of the yard where the sun was bright and where there were none who could overhear their words.

The Minister held the Ambassador's elbow tightly. "Without a request from your government there is no reason for our cabinet even to consider the options over Tantardini. You know what I am saying to you?"

"Of course."

"You value the point of principle?"

"We value that consideration," the Ambassador said quietly and with no relish.

The Minister pressed. "Principle . . . even when the only beneficiary could be the Republic of Italy . . ."

"Still it would be important to us." The Amhassador pulled at his tie, wanting relief from its clutching hold. "A man came to see me earlier this morning, he is a representative of Harrison's firm, and I told him what I have told you. He called me Pilate, he said I was washing my hands of his man. Perhaps he is right. I can only give my opinion, but I think that it will be ratified by London."

The Minister still somber. Still clinging to the Ambassador's arm as if unwilling to break away for his cabinet colleagues waiting upstairs, said, "If we refuse to release Tantardini, I do not think we will see Harrison again."

The Ambassador accepted his opinion, nodded gravely.

"I will relay your thought to Whitehall."

The two men stood together, the Ambassador disproportionately taller. High frescoes in centuries-old paint leered down at them, mocking their transitory plans for history. Both perspired, both were too preoccupied to wash away the moisture beads. "We understand each other, my friend. I will tell my colleagues that the British ask for no deal, no barter, no negotiation . . . and whatever happens we win the victory of principle . . ."

The Ambassador interrupted his short choked laugh. "I am sure that Defense Ministry would send the Special Air Service, the close-quarter attack squad, as they did for Moro. They could be here this afternoon, if it were helpful."

The Minister seemed to snort, give his judgment on an irrelevance, and walked away toward the wide staircase of the Palazzo.

Those who came late that morning to their desks in the Viminale on the second floor found that already the corridors and offices were nests of total activity. Vellosi paced the rooms, querying the necessity of bureaucrats and policemen alike for occupying their premises and their precious telephones, and where he found no satisfaction he commandeered and installed in their place his subordinates. By ten he had secured an additional five rooms all within shouting distance of his own. Technicians from the basements were made busy hoisting the mess of cables and wires, attaching the transmitters and receivers that would secure him instant access to the control center of the Questura and the office of Carboni. Some of the dispossessed hung in the corridors, sleek in their suits and clean shirts, and smiled sweetly at the pace and moment of the working men around them and vowed they would have Vellosi's head served up on a salver were he not to deliver Geoffrey Harrison, free and unharmed, by the next morning. It was not the way that things were done in the Viminale. Noise, rising voices, the ringing of telephone bells, the pleas of radio static all mingled and coalesced in the corridor. Vellosi bounced between the sources of the confusion. He had told an examining magistrate that he was a hindrance and an obstruction, a *carabinieri* general that if he didn't push reinforcements into the Cosoleto area he would face speedy retirement, the persistent editor of the largest Socialist newspaper in the city that his head should be down the toilet bowl and would he clear the line, and sent out for more cigarettes, more coffee, more sandwiches.

At a hectic pace, bewildering to all those who were not central to the knot of the inquiry, the operation and investigation was launched. Those who participated and those who were idle and smirking behind their hands could agree on the one common point. The mood on the second floor of the Viminale was unique. Very few, though, were privy to the telephone conversation between Vellosi and the Minister, who spoke from an anteroom outside the cabinet deliberations at the Palazzo Chigi, only the inner court, the hard men on whom Vellosi leaned for succor and advice.

He had slammed the telephone down, barely a grunt of thanks to the Minister, and confided to those in the room near him.

"They're standing firm, our masters. The men of deviation and compromise are holding a line. The bitch stays with us. Tantardini stays in her cell and rots there."

The four who heard him understood the importance of the political decision, and they smiled to each other in a grim satisfaction and dropped their shoulders and raised their eyebrows and returned to their notepads and their internal telephone directories.

The information began to flow as the team hustled, begged, and screamed into the telephones; shapes and patterns emerging from the kaleidoscope of mysteries and dead ends with which the day had started. Routine is the heart and touchstone of detection. Whether the policeman is from Frankfurt or London or Basle or Vienna or Madrid . . . or Rome. Routine is the road toward his answers and the lone provider of the shortcuts of analysis.

* * *

Antonio Mazzotti was allowed now to sit alone in a cell in the *carabinieri* barracks at Palmi. His right eye was bright with color and the bruises swollen. He had won his freedom from the young *capitano* with a stumbled confession, made between missing teeth, of the ownership of the plan to kidnap Geoffrey Harrison. A man from Cosoleto, a man called Claudio, had been his. With difficulty Antonio Mazzotti had focused on the proferred paper and signed his name to it.

Photographs of the known *Nappisti* at liberty had been spread out on a table for the *portiere* of the *pensione* where Claudio's body had been found. He had not wished to be involved, the elderly man whose job dictated a short tongue and a weak memory. He had turned across many pictures, showing little interest, muttering over and over of the failure of his recollections. The one hesitation, the flicker of curiosity, undid his reluctance. A detective had seen the betrayal of recognition that the *portiere* had tried to hide. The work of a police photographer, and the typed message on the back of the picture gave the name of Giancarlo Battestini.

What name had he used? What identity card had he shown? What had his clothes been? What time had he arrived . . . what time had he left? The questions battered at the old man in his fading uniform until he had broken the reticence born of the sense of survival and told the story the police wanted from him. A link forged, something of value, something priceless to Vellosi. Connection and result, something that he could brood upon and feed from. The knowledge breathed a new activity into the squad of men around him, heaved at their flagging morale and drove them on.

"It's beside the station," Vellsoi stormed down his

telephone to a *maggiore* of the *pubblica sicurezza*.
"Right beside the station this *pensione*, so get the photograph of Battestini down to the ticket counters, get
it among the platform workers. Check him through all
the trains to Reggio yesterday morning. Find the
ticket inspectors on those trains, find their names,
where they are now, and get that picture under their
noses."

So much commitment, so much cajoling and abuse
that for a full minute Giuseppe Carboni stood ignored
in the doorway of Vellosi's office. He bided his time;
the tempo of the music would hesitate and he would
have his moment. And it would be choice, he thought,
choice enough for it to have been worth his while to
abandon his desk at the Questura and come unannounced to the Viminale. Vellosi was on his way for
another prowl along the corridor to chase and jockey
his men when he careened into the solid flesh wall of
the policeman.

"Carboni, my apologies." Vellosi laughed. "We have
been very busy here, we have been going hard . . ."

"Excellent, Vellosi, excellent . . ." a measured reply, tolerant and calm.

". . . you will forgive my hurry, but we have discovered an important connection . . ."

"Excellent."

"The boy of the NAP, Battestini . . . the one we
missed when we took Tantardini, this is the kernal of
this matter, it was he who killed the gorilla in the hotel. We have established that, and this Claudio was
from those that took your Harrison . . . we have not
been idle."

"Excellent."

Vellosi saw the smile on Carboni's face. Felt the
man had picked up a book and found it already
known to him. He saw that his revelation won no recognition of achievement.

"And you are prospering too, Carboni?" Subdued already, Vellosi braced himself. "Tell me."

Carboni led the head of the antiterrorist squad back to his desk. With his heavy rounded fingers he produced from a neat briefcase two sheets of facsimile paper. He laid them on the desk, pushing aside without care the piles of handwritten notes which had accumulated there through the morning. With his forefinger, Carboni punched at the upper sheet.

"This is the statement taken from Battestini by the *polizia* more than eighteen months ago . . . after his arrest for some student fracas; it carries his handwriting at the bottom."

"I have seen it," a curtness from Vellosi.

Carboni pulled clear the under sheet. "This is the statement from the *Nappisti* found at Seminara along with Harrison's card. Observe the writing, Vellosi, observe it closely."

Vellosi's nose was a few inches from the papers as he held them in the light.

"It has been checked. At Criminalpol they ran it through the machines for me. The scientists have no doubt that there is a match, they are firm in their opinion." Carboni savored the moment. It was perhaps the finest of his professional life. He stood among the gods, the princes of the elite force, the cream of the antisubversion fighters, and he told them that which they had not seen for themselves. "Giancarlo Battestini, nineteen years old, born in Pescara, university dropout, probationer of the NAP, he is the one who has taken Geoffrey Harrison. Harrison is in Battestini's hands, and I venture to suggest that is the limit and extent of the conspiracy."

Vellosi dropped back to his chair. A hush, contagious and effective, sprawled across the room and on into the corridor and farther offices. Men in shirtsleeves and holding their cigarettes and plastic coffee beakers crowded to the doorway. "Is it possible for one man . . . not even a man, a boy . . . is it possible for one to have achieved all this?"

"Vellosi, it has happened." The pleasure streamed on Carboni's face. "I won't detain you, but you should know we are sifting the reports of stolen vehicles from the area of the city of Reggio—there are not many, not at the times that fit. Two *cinquecentos*, but they would be too small for the purpose, there was a BMW, but that is a noticed car. Close to the main station at Reggio, a few minutes' walk away, there is reported missing within ninety minutes of the arrival of the *rapido* from Roma a One Two Seven. It has a red color and the registration is going out now. There is the same problem as always with the roadblocks because we do not know where to set them, but if it is on the radio and the lunchtime television, then perhaps . . ."

"Shut up, Carboni," Vellosi spoke quietly. He reached up with both arms, put them around Carboni's neck, and pulled the ill-shaven face toward him. Their cheeks met, the kiss of friends and equals. "You're a genius, Carboni, nothing but a genius."

Carboni blushed, swung on his heel, and left with a little wave of his fingers for farewell. He had stirred Vellosi's ant hole, changed its direction, turned the whole apex of the inquiry.

"Well, don't stand about," Vellosi snapped at his audience. "We've let an amateur show us what's happening, point to what's been staring at us for hours. We have more in a day that we had in a month with Moro. Use it."

But for Moro he had had time. For Harrison he had less than twenty-two hours until the expiry of the ultimatum.

Vellosi scuffed among his papers till he found the photograph of Battestini. He searched into the mouth and the strength of the jaw and the set of the eyes for information, pulled and pummeled at it for understanding. An old friend, a long-serving member of his staff, was at his shoulder, taking his own clues, making his own assessment. The wind and bombast had fled. Francesco Vellosi, another policeman scrabbling to catch up, scratching to make do with diminishing hours, the tools of the trade.

"The little bastard can be anywhere," and Vellosi swore and reached for his coffee which was cold.

Back to the basics he must go, back to deep and quiet thought in the midst of the noise surrounding him, back to analysis of the minimal factual evidence available.

Start again from the beginning. Return to the face of Battestini, drag from those features the response that should be made.

Giancarlo Battestini, imprisoned in Rome after studying in the capital's university, and a member of a NAP cell in that city. Could the boy have links with the far countryside? Likely or unlikely? Vellosi flexed his fingers together. The answer was not required. The boy would know nothing of Calabria. A city boy, a town boy, a foreigner in the *mezzo giorno*.

He turned and called to a colleague who stubbed his cigarette, drained his coffee, and came to him.

"Battestini would not believe he could survive in the countryside, it is beyond his experience. Correct?"

"Correct."

"He would try to return to the city?"

"Possible."

"He is linked only in the files with Rome, he would try to get back here?"

"Perhaps."

"He is divorced from Pescara. He has nothing there. And if he comes back toward Rome he must come by car because he cannot take a prisoner by train."

"Probable."

The momentum carried Vellosi on. "If he comes by road he must decide for himself whether he will attempt speed on the autostrada, or whether he will go for the safer and the slower old roads."

"I think he would choose the autostrada."

Vellosi snapped his fist into the palm of his other hand. "And he must stop . . ."

"For gas."

"He has to stop."

"Certain."

"Either at a station on the autostrada or he must come off and use a toll gate and a station off the main route."

"If he is coming to Rome, if he is coming by car, if he is on the autostrada, then that is correct."

Vellosi thrust his chair away behind him, rose to his full height and shouted. "Work on the gas stations and the autostrada tolls. Each side of Naples. Call Carboni, tell him that too."

His colleague was no longer beside him.

Vellosi slumped back into his seat. There was no one to praise him, no one to smile and slap his back and offer congratulations. To himself he muttered over and over again, "The boy will come back to the city, the boy will return to Rome."

14

While the disparate arms and commands of the security forces strove to drag themselves into a state of intervention, the small, red-coated Fiat slipped unremarked through the toll gate marking the terminal of the autostrada at Roma Sud and away toward the Raccordo Annulare, the belt road skirting the capital. With the passing of the car, common and anonymous through its mass production, through the toll check, the chances of its detection that had before been remote were reduced to the minimal.

The two men had exchanged only desultory conversation, preferring to brood to themselves in the confined space. Geoffrey Harrison, the pain gone from his back, drove in a careless and detached way as if concern and anxiety were no longer with him. His mind numbed, his brain deadened, he performed the automaton tasks of keeping the car in the center lane of the traffic, the speed constant. At two places, the service station and the toll gate, he told himself there had been presented the possibility of breakout from the car. But the will to seek out freedom was reduced and eroded. He had sat meekly in the driving seat, neither looking at nor avoiding the man who secured the fuel tank cap and wiped wetly over the windshield. He had held his silence as the young man at the toll had handed the change through the opened window.

Manipulated and broken, too destroyed to weep, too cudgeled to fight, Harrison guided the car around the east side of the city.

For Violet Harrison the mood of the morning alternated between remorse and defiance.

She had lain in bed, curling slowly over, switching the images of a prisoner husband with those of a dark-chested boy with a flat stomach and sinewed hair-covered legs. Both caused her pain, both snatched at the agony strings.

If she could again find the boy at the beach and forge her liaison, then it would not be the first time, not the second, not the third. It was the usual and climactic way she found relief when the strain soared too high for her. Nothing to do with loving Geoffrey, whatever that meant, nothing to do with being his wife, sharing his life. Irrelevant, all of that. But there had to be a valve somewhere, when the steam boiling point was reached, and this was her release, writhing under a stranger, without obligation, without attachment.

There had been an Irish barman from Evesham in Worcestershire, sought out on the day after Geoffrey, the young industrial trainee, had told her there was a discrepancy in the books and that the branch chief accountant believed him responsible. He had been cleared of suspicion, but only after Violet had spent an afternoon in an autumn field with a man whose name she had never learned.

There had been a West Indian bus driver from Dalston in East London after a Friday night when Geoffrey had come home to report that he had drunk too much that lunchtime and told the head of his department to stuff his job where it would hurt and smell. Geoffrey had apologized on the Monday morning, been accepted back with handshakes and smiles, and had never known of Violet's two hours on a Sunday morning in a railway hotel close to King's Cross, ridden hard by a muscled lad who called her "darlin" and bit her shoulders.

Other crises had come, some greater, some lesser. Same palliative, same escape, and Geoffrey had stayed innocent of them, of that she was sure and grateful. She remembered once she had watched on the television the wife of a British governor of a colony island, just widowed after her husband had been terribly murdered while taking a late evening stroll in the gardens of the Residence. The woman had worn white and sat on a sofa with her daughters and talked to the cameras with composure and dignity. Had it been Violet, she thought, she would have been in the chauffeur's bed. She knew it, hated it, and told herself she did not own the strength to resist. And if Geoffrey did not know, if Geoffrey were not wounded, then what did it matter? Who else's business was it?

There had been no boy in Rome. God knows there were times when she would have wished for one, hoped for the release from an arched back and a driving thrust. But there had been none. Until she had been to the beach she had not given herself even the opportunity, the smoker that rations the daily diet, the drinker who loses the cabinet key. Isolated and cocooned in a flat where the telephone never rang, the door bell never sounded, she had been protected from the predators.

She dressed with studied care, as if anxious not to crease the bikini and the covering dress, as if forgetful that she would be sitting in her car for the hour-long

drive to Ostia or Fregene or Santa Marinella. A
peahen jealous of her scant plumage. The bikini was
new, and the dress, though a month old, had not been
worn. Her hair she combed loosely, sitting at her
dressing-table mirror and aware of the excitement and
the tremble that came with the narcotic, with the con-
templation of the unmentionable. It was the only gesture of independence that Violet Harrison was capable of, to climb into her little car, drive away down
the road, and spend and punish herself of her own
volition, in her own time, in her own panting scenario.
Would Geoffrey have cared if he had known . . . ?
Perhaps, perhaps not. But it didn't matter, because
Geoffrey did not know, Geoffrey was away, bound
like a chicken with the stubble on his face and a gun
at his head. Geoffrey would be thinking of her, hers
would be the face in his mind, as clear and sharp as it
was in the mirror before her. Geoffrey would be leaning on her, conjuring in his mind only the good times.
That was when the remorse always won through from
the defiance. That was when it hurt, when the urge
was strongest, when she was weakest, least able to
struggle.

Smudges of tears gathered below the neat blond hair.
She was aware of the telephone's bell. Long, brilliant rings, calling her to the kitchen. Perhaps it was
Mother from London announcing which flight she
was taking, and was her little poppet all right, and did
she know that it was all over the papers. Perhaps it
was those miserable bastards who had called before
and jabbered in an alien language. The ringing would
not leave her, pulled her off the low chair and
dragged her through the doorway toward its summons. Every step she prayed it would cease its siren
call. Her entreaties were ignored, the telephone rang
on.

"Violet Harrison. Who's that?"

It was Carpenter. Archie Carpenter of ICH.

"Good morning, Mr. Carpenter." A cool voice, the confidence coming fast, because this little man had run from her, the little suburban man.

Had she heard the latest information on her husband?

"I've heard nothing since last night. I don't read the Italian papers. The embassy hasn't called me."

She should know that her husband was now thought to be in the hands of an extremist political group. She should know that demands had been made to the government for the release of a prisoner before nine the next morning. She should know that if the condition was not met, the threat had been made that her husband would be murdered.

Violet rocked on the balls of her feet. Eyes closed, two hands clutching the telephone. The pain seemed to gather at her temples, then sear through deep behind.

Was she still there?

A faint small voice. "I'm here, Mr. Carpenter. I'm listening."

And it was a damned scandal, the whole thing. The embassy wouldn't lift a finger. Did she know that, could she credit it? Geoffrey had been relegated in importance, dismissed and left to the incompetence of an Italian police investigation.

Fear now, and her voice shriller. "But it was all agreed. It was agreed, wasn't it, that the company would pay. It was all out of the Italians' hands."

Different now. Money was one thing. Easy, plenty of it, no problem. Different now, because it was said to be a point of principle. Said to be giving in to terrorism, if the prisoner were to be released.

"Well, what's a fucking principle got to do with Geoffrey? Do they want him dead or what?" She shrieked into the telephone, voice raucous and rising.

They'd say it was the same as in the Schleyer case in Germany, the same as in the Moro case locally. They'd say they can't surrender. They'd use words like blackmail, and phrases like "dignity of the state." Those are the things they'd say, and the embassy would support them, every damned inch.

"But it will mean Geoffrey's killed . . ." The hysteria was rampant, and with it the laughter and the breaking of flimsy control. " . . . They can't just sacrifice him. This bloody place hasn't had a principle in years, it's not a word in the bloody language. They couldn't even spell it here."

Carpenter was going to call Head Office in London. They wouldn't take this lying down. She could rely on that. He'd call back within an hour, she should stay by the telephone.

Her voice had been to its summit, to its pitch, and had tumbled on the reverse slopes, and was now the product of crouched and humiliated shoulders.

"Could you come and see me, Mr. Carpenter?"

Did she want him to come to the flat?

"Could you come and tell me what's happening. Yes, to the flat."

Carpenter was sorry, very sorry indeed. But he had an appointment, an urgent appointment. She would understand, but he had a fair amount on his plate, didn't he? But Carpenter would telephone her as soon as he had something to say, and that would be, he thought, within an hour.

The cycle of her changing mood swung on. The screaming past, the whimpering gone. Cold again with the veneer of assurance. "Don't call again, Mr. Carpenter, because I won't be here. Perhaps I'll be back this evening. Thank you for telling me what's going on. Thank you for telling me what's going to happen to Geoffrey."

Before he could speak again, she had cut Carpenter off the line.

Violet Harrison strode into her bedroom, swept a swimming towel off a bedside chair, and the underclothes that she had discarded on the floor the previous evening. She dropped them into her Via Condotti shopping bag and headed for the elevator and the basement garage.

Forty minutes later, when the red Fiat had moved onto the Raccordo with its center reservation of pink and white oleander bushes, Giancarlo gestured to Harrison that he should turn off to his right. It was the Via Cassia junction and within five miles of his home. Strange to Harrison to be in the midst of tried and trusted surroundings. But the disorientation won through and he obeyed the instruction without question. The silence that for both of them was now safe and losing its awkwardness remained unbroken.

They had made good time. Giancarlo could reflect that the stamina of the driver had been remarkable.

They had given up the speed of the Raccordo for a slow, winding road, heavy with trucks and impatient cars, flanked by the speculative apartments that overburdened the facilities. Several times they stopped in the bumper-to-bumper jams. Harrison sat passively, not knowing where he was being led, declining to ask.

Along the length of the Reggio Calabria to Rome, autostrada patrol cars of the *Polizia Stradale* and *carabinieri* had begun the pin and haystack game of searching for a red Fiat car of the most popular model in use. Scores of motorists found themselves pitched out of 127s, covered by aimed machine guns as they were searched, ordered to produce identity papers while their faces were examined against the photo-

stated likenesses of Battestini and Harrison. The roadblocks were large and impressive, each utilizing a
minimum of a dozen armed men, and were compre-
hensive enough to warrant coverage by the RAI elec-
tronic camera teams.

The concentration of effort and manpower was
blessed. At the toll gate at Monte Cassino, a Fiat of
the right size and color was remembered. A young
man had asked for gas. A small success and one sufficient to whet the appetite as the police concentration
built up in the community of Monte Cassino. The garage owner was quizzed in his office.

Yes, he could tell them who had been manning the
pumps at that time. Yes, he could tell them the address of that man's home. Yes, and also he could tell
them that this man had said the previous evening
when he came on duty that after he finished the night
shift it was his intention to take his grandchildren into
the central mountains. No, he did not know where
they would go, and he had waved expansively at the
big hazed skyline and shrugged.

The helicopters were ordered from Rome. The military twin-engine troop carriers were loaded with
armed men, sweating in the confined spaces on the
baked, makeshift landing pad outside the town. Four-
seater spotter machines were dispatched to fly low
over the high ranges and valleys, brushing the contours. Truckloads of *polizia* were slowly given the co-
ordinates on large scale maps that the whole rugged
area might be sealed.

The white walls of the mountain monastery looked
down upon the hopeless task, while the shouting and
irritation of the flustered staff officers in the commandeered school reflected the feeling that the ter-
rain, rugged and vast, would mock their efforts to
find a boy and his captive and his car.

* * *

But the element of chance born from the routine
moved the chase on, gave it a new impetus, a new
urgency. The chance without which the police could
not hope for success in a manhunt and which had for-
saken them when the center of the country was
scoured for the fated President of the Democrazia
Christiana.

A young man had gone off duty from his work at a
gate on the Roma Sud toll. He had taken the bus
home after a six-hour shift, had doused himself under
the shower, and dressed and sat down at the kitchen
table for cheese and fruit before lying on his bed to
rest. His daughter, just a baby, had been crying, and
therefore he could not be certain he had heard cor-
rectly the description of the two men that had been
broadcast on the radio. The detail, rigidly held to,
from which he would not deviate, caused the men in
uniform and suits to paw at the air in their frustration,
but Giuseppe Carboni, master of his own office, was
at pains to thank the young man for calling his nearest
police station. Past eleven in the morning, time hur-
tling on its way, and Carboni demanded the patience
of those around him. The photograph was produced,
the picture of Geoffrey Harrison, and the young man
nodded and smiled and looked for praise. It was
strange, he said to Carboni, that a man who wore an
expensive shirt should be unshaven with grime at his
neck and his hair untended.

Carboni's room had disintegrated into movement,
leaving the witness to gaze long and hard at the picture.

Telephones, telexes, radios, all into play now to seal
the city of Rome. Close it up, was the order, block the
routes to Aquila to the east, to Firenze to the north.
Tighten a net on the autostradas and damn the lines.
Pull off the men beginning the search of the Monte
Cassino hills, bring them back to the capital. Carboni

set it all in motion, then came back to the young man.

"And there was a boy, just a *ragazzo*, with this man?"

"I think so . . ."

"It is the older man that you are clear on?"

"That was the one who gave me the money. It is difficult to see across the interior of a car from where we sit in the cabins."

A good witness, would not admit to that which he was not certain of. Carboni replaced the photograph of Harrison with that of Giancarlo Battestini. "Could this be the boy? Could this be the passenger?"

"I am sorry, Dottore, but really I did not see the passenger's face."

Carboni persisted. "Anything at all that you can remember of the passenger?"

"He wore jeans . . . and they were tight, that I remember. And his legs were thin. He would have been young . . ." The toll attendant stopped, head low, the frown of concentration. He was tired and his thoughts came slowly. Unseen to him Carboni held up his hand to prevent any interruption from those who were now filtering back into the room. " . . . he paid, the driver that is, and he paid with a big note and when I gave him the change he passed it to the passenger, but the other's hands were beneath a light coat that was between them, I could see that from my cabin, the driver dropped the change onto the top of the coat. They did not say anything, and then he drove away."

Pain at Carboni's face. To the general audience he announced, "That is where the gun was, that is why Harrison drives, because the boy Battestini has the pistol to his body."

The young man from Roma Sud was sent home.

Fuel for the computer, for the dispersal systems of

information, and with each piece of typed paper that slipped from his office, Carboni fussed and plotted. "And tell them to be careful, for God's sake be careful. Tell them that the boy has killed three times in forty-eight hours and will kill again."

There was no smirk at the features of Giuseppe Carboni, no expression of euphoria. Geographically they had run their quarry to a ground comprised of a trivial number of square kilometers, but the ground, he could consider ruefully, was not favorable. One man and a prisoner to hunt for in a conurbation that housed four million citizens.

Chance had taken the sad, worn-down policeman up a road of promise, and had left him at a great crossroads wich boasted no signposts.

He reached for his telephone to ring Francesco Vellosi.

At noon the men held in maximum security on the island of Asinara were unlocked from their cells and permitted under heavy supervision to line up together in the communal canteen for their pasta and meat lunch. Conversation was not forbidden.

The long-term prisoners, those serving from twenty years to the ultimate maximum of *ergastolo*, the natural end of life, all had radio sets in their cells. The news had been carried behind the heavy doors and barred windows of the kidnapping of Geoffrey Harrison, the ultimatum for the freedom of Franca Tantardini, the failed reprisal against Francesco Vellosi.

Several men sidled close to the leader of the NAP. Who was the boy, Battestini, they asked, a name blasted from every news bulletin in the previous hour? How big was the infrastructure organization from which he worked? The *capo*, the movement's spiritual leader in the intellect and violence, had shrugged his shoulders, opened his hands, and said quietly that he had never heard of the boy nor sanctioned the action.

A few had felt he was carrying his secrecy obsessively, but there were those who waited and shuffled forward with their steel trays who understood the bafflement of the man who claimed absolute domination of the NAP from his island cell.

One thing to give orders, another to have them implemented. Many men in the Questura and the Viminale had lent their names and authority to instructions for the sealing of the city. There were contingency plans for such measures that were readily at hand, but a police and paramilitary effort of the scale required is not a facile thing to initiate. Which were the vital routes, which were the areas for the greatest concentration of manpower, where in the streets of the city should the maximum vigilance be gathered? These were questions that demanded time for answers, and time was a lost commodity.

The Fiat had turned off the main Cassia road at the village of La Storta, traveled fifteen more kilometers and then turned again, choosing a narrower route that would skirt the hill town of Bracciano and lead toward the deep, blue-tinted volcanic lake beneath the collection of straggling gray stone houses. The car was forty kilometers now from the heart of the capital and here the country was at peace, and the bombs and killings and kidnappings were matters delivered only by the newspapers and television bulletins. This was a place of small farmers, small shop-keepers, small businessmen, people who valued their tranquillity, drank their wine, and drew their curtains against the wind of brutality and chaos and graft that blew from across the fields and the main road.

Abruptly Giancarlo pointed to an open farm gate

that was set in a wall of stone and blackthorn flowers
to the left side of the road and some four hundred
meters short of the water's edge. The field into which
they drove, jerking over the thick grass, was skirted on
two sides by a wood of heavy-leafed oaks and syca-
mores. Tall shade-bearing trees. It was a great risk
that he had taken, to have traveled this far in daylight, but the boy was sufficiently secure in himself,
sufficiently buoyant after coming so far, to believe
that he had outstripped the *apparati* of the nation. Far
up the side of the field, where it was shielded from
the road, Giancarlo waved his hand for Harrison to
stop. They boy glanced around him and then motioned toward a place close by where the grass of the
field merged with the tree line, a place where the cattle would come in winter to escape the ferocity of the
rainstorms.

There was a darkness and shadow in the interior of
the car as Harrison finally pulled at the brake handle
and switched off the ignition. The place was well chosen. Hidden from the air, hidden from the road, perfect in its safety and in its loneliness. Giancarlo
grabbed decisively at the keys, smiled with a contempt at his driver, and watching him all the time
with the gun ready, cocked, climbed out. He stretched
himself, flexed his barely developed chest, enjoyed
the sun that filtered and dappled between the leaf
ceiling.

"Are you going to kill me here?" Harrison asked.

"Only if by nine o'clock tomorrow morning they
have not given me Franca."

It was the first time that Giancarlo had spoken since
they had left the autostrada.

International Chemical Holdings with representation
in thirty-two countries of the first and third worlds
maintained close links with the Foreign and Common-

wealth office and the Ministry of Overseas Development. Its Board members and principal executives were frequent guests at the black-tie dinners given by government to visiting delegations, they figured cautiously in the New Years and Birthday Honors lists, and to some the workings of the company were regarded as an extension of British foreign policy. An aid package to a newly independent member of the Commonwealth often contained the loan necessary to launch an ICH plant.

Sir David Adams was well known to the Minister both as a businessman aloof from party politics and as a social guest to be valued for his ease and humor in difficult company. On the telephone pad of Sir David's desk in the city tower block was the Foreign Secretary's direct number. He had spent a few brief moments pondering Archie Carpenter's call from Rome before scanning the pad for the number. He had been connected with a private secretary, had requested, and been granted, a few minutes of the Foreign Secretary's time before lunch.

A desolate sort of room, the Minister's working office seemed to Sir David. Not the sort of quarters he'd ever have tolerated for himself. Wretched velvet drapes, and the furniture out of a museum, and a desk large enough for snooker. He'd have had one of those young interior decorator chaps in with a bucket of white paint and some new pictures and something on the floor that represented the nineteen eighties, not the days of dropping tigers at Amritsar. He was not kept waiting sufficiently long for the completion of his refurbishment plans for the office.

They sat opposite each other in lush, high-backed armchairs. There was a Campari soda for the Minister, a gin and French for the managing director. No aides, no stenographers.

"Not to beat about the bush, Minister, the message

from my chap out there came as a bit of a shock. My chap, and he's no fool, has his feet on the ground, says your Ambassador has just about told the Italians that as far as Whitehall is concerned they should run this new phase in the Harrison business just as if our man was any Italian businessman. I find that a bit heavy." Sir David sipped at his glass, enough to dampen his tongue, little more.

"Bit of an oversimplification, David. Not quite the full story." The Foreign Secretary smiled over the bulldog folds of his cheeks. "The actual situation is that a senior member of the Italian cabinet, and this is of course confidential, asked HMG via the Ambassador and at a time when the Italians were having to make early but very important decisions of approach in this matter, whether HMG would be requesting the release of a terrorist to safeguard your fellow. That's not quite the same thing, is it?"

"With respect, it's the germ of the same thing. I'll put it another way and ask you what initiative the British government is taking to secure the release, unharmed, of Geoffrey Harrison?" Another sip, another faint trembling of the liquid line in the glass.

"You should know there can only be one answer. There is no initiative that I can take with regard to the internal politics of Italy . . ."

"You can suggest that it is desirable to get my man back, whether or not that requires unlocking a door for this woman they're holding."

"David, I have a full program of meetings." There was a sternness in the rebuke. "I should have been at one now, but I've relegated it to a junior. When I make the gesture please do me the courtesy of hearing me out."

"Accepted. Apologies, and sincerely meant." An inclined head acknowledged the ministerial rap.

"Italy isn't a business competitor, David. It's not a

rival company. If it collapses, if it goes bankrupt, morally or financially, if it's greatly weakened, the Members of the Commons won't stand up and cheer and wave their order papers as your shareholders would. It's not just a place of funny foreigners, David, of spaghetti and gigolos and bottom pinchers. It's a major power in the West, it's a NATO ally, it's the seventh industrial power in the world. You know all that better than I do. When things are difficult there we draw no pleasure from it. We do our damnedest to support them, and a friend needs support when she's on her knees. The Moro affair nearly crippled them. The state was held at ransom, the very system of democracy was threatened, but they held firm, and in doing so they lost . . . they sacrificed . . . a leader of great standing."

"It's a fine speech, Minister, and it will do you credit in the House on the day my company buries Geoffrey Harrison. You'll send a wreath, I trust . . . ?" The two men eyed each other. The counterpunches had bloodied the noses and the eyes were puffing and there were many rounds to go.

"Not worthy of you, David, and you know better than to taunt me. When the German was missing in Northern Ireland, the one we never found, the Minister of the day didn't have Bonn snapping at him. When Herrema, the Dutchman, was kidnapped in Eire, The Hague was quick to express support for all the measures that Dublin was taking."

"You're still hiding, Minister." Sir David Adams was not one to be easily deflected. He pushed his adversary toward the ropes, leading with his chin, a lifetime's habit. "You're hiding behind a screen of meaningless protocol. I want a young and innocent man back, I want him back with his wife. I don't give a damn for Italian terrorism, nor do I give a damn for Italian democracy. I've done business there and I know the place. I know how much of our payments go to the bank in Milan, how much goes to Zurich. I know about the yachts and the bribes and the villas. I understand why they've an urban guerrilla problem on their doorstep. It's a nasty, clannish society that can't look after itself, and it's not for you to abandon an Englishman in the sewer there in order to start giving those people lessons in principle, or whatever."

"You haven't been listening to me, David." Ice cold, the Foreign Secretary, but the temper concealed beneath the frozen smile. "They sacrificed one of their principal postwar leaders, wrote him off, and on a point of principle."

"We're going in circles."

"We are indeed, but I suggest you are leading."

Sir David gulped at his glass, the impatience winning, half drained it. "I put it to you, Minister, that there is something you can do that doesn't infringe on the question of 'principle' . . ." He rolled over the word, gutting it of all feeling. " . . . You can find out from your friends in Rome the exact importance of this woman. You can find out her importance to guerrilla movement. And let's not stand on too high a pedestal. I know my recent history. Northern Ireland, right? . . . we've emptied Long Kesh when we were after a political initiative, chucked the Provisionals out onto the streets to get on again with their bombing and maiming. What happened to principle then? We've given their leaders safe conduct. We sent the Palestinian girl, Leila Khaled, home from Ealing courtesy of an RAF jet. We're not lily-white. We can bend when it suits us . . ."

"Who's making speeches, David?"

"Don't be flippant, Minister. My fellow has little more than twenty hours to live." The eyes of Sir David Adams, gimlet and boring, offered no concessions. "Italy can live without this woman in a jail, Italy can survive . . ."

He broke off in response to a light knock at the door behind him. Irritation at the interruption registered on both men's faces. The Foreign Secretary glanced at his watch. A young man, shirtsleeves and club tie, glided across the room with a telex copy in his hand. He gave it without explanation to the Minister and withdrew as silently as he had come. There was quiet in the room as the message was read, the Minister's forehead lined, his lips pursed.

"It's the Harrison business, that's why they interrupted." No emotion in the voice, just an aging and a sadness. "He's held by a young psychopath, responsible for three killings in two days. The assessment of the Italians is that he will kill your man without hesitation or compassion should the deadline expire. The woman involved is called Franca Tantardini. She is classified in Rome as a major activist and will face charges of murder, attempted murder, armed insurrection, they're throwing the book at her. Our embassy records the observation that several of the senior and most respected officers of the Italian public security forces would resign should she be released. In addition, the Italian Communist party has endorsed in a statement the government's no-deal approach."

The Foreign Secretary looked across the room to the shadowed face of the industrialist.

"It's not in our hands, David. It is beyond the British government to offer intervention. I am very sorry."

Sir David Adams rose from his chair. A little over six feet in height, a dominating and handsome man, and one unused to failure.

"You won't forget the flowers, Minister?"

And he was gone, leaving his glass half filled on the small table beside the chair.

* * *

Michael Charlesworth from his office and Archie Carpenter from his hotel room had spoken by telephone. Seemed to want to talk to each other, these two men of the differing backgrounds, drawn from divorced social groups, because the feeling of inadequacy was crippling, the feeling of helplessness was overpowering. Both as eunuchs with little to do but listen to the radio as Charlesworth did, and scan the newspapers and gaze at the staring photographs of Battestini plastered on the afternoon editions that Carpenter passed the early afternoon with.

"Shouldn't you be with Violet Harrison?" Charlesworth had asked.

"I called her this morning, said I'd call her back—she said not to bother . . ."

"It's not my job, thank God, holding her hand."

"Not mine either." Carpenter had snapped.

"Perhaps." Charlesworth had let it sink, let the thought drown. He sensed the desperation of the man who had been sent to make decisions, to move mountains, and who was failing. "You'd better come up to my place tonight and have a bite with us."

"I'd like that."

Charlesworth had returned to his radio, moodily flittering between the three RAI services. They portrayed activity and haste and effort, and nothing of substance.

It had taken Giancarlo fully thirty minutes to find the place that satisfied him. He had prodded Geoffrey Harrison through the deeper recesses of the wood, using him as a plough to clear a way between the whippy saplings that clipped back to the eyes and ears and forearms. But the place that pleased him was close to a slight path, where once a giant oak had grown before the wind had taken its leafy canopy and pulled it down, tearing open a great gouge in the earth beneath its raised roots. A shallow pit had been left that would only be found if the searcher stumbled to its very rim.

Giancarlo methodically repeated the drill of earlier in the morning. He bound Harrison's ankles with the wire, and then again tied the wrists behind his back. The spare lengths he used to loop around the stronger roots exposed under the earth roof. If Harrison lay still he could rest on his side in some attitude of comfort. If he moved, if he struggled, then the wire would bite at his flesh and cut and slash it. The boy had thought of this, introducing knots that dictated that the reward for movement was pain. There was one refinement from the morning, the handkerchief from Harrison's trouser pocket, twisted like a rope, was inserted between his teeth, knotted behind his ears. Giancarlo was careful in tying the handkerchief, as if he had no wish to suffocate his prisoner.

When the work was finished he stepped back and admired it. He was going to get some food. Harrison should not worry, he would not be away long.

Within moments he was lost among the line of trees and the shadows and the slanting columns of light.

15

Geoffrey Harrison's field of vision was minimal. It comprised only a slight arch encompassing a score of rising tree trunks, heavy with lime and flaking bark, which soared above the rim of the small crater in which he lay. Above and around him was the motion of the isolated wood; a pair of woodpeckers in pursuit of a jay, cackling protest at the intrusion of the nest-hunting bird; a tiny *pettirose*, its reddened breast thrust forward proudly, that dug and chipped for grubs and insects; a young rabbit that darted in terror among the trees, crazed with fear at a brief encounter with a skillful stoat; the wind in the upper branches that collided with one another high up and beyond the possibility of his eyeline. Action and activity. Those that were free and liberated going about the business of their day while he lay helpless and in fear beneath them.

But his brain was no longer stifled. The very solitude of the wood had livened and awakened him, made him aware of each miniature footfall on the ground, sharpened his senses. The drug effect of the endless miles of autostrada driving was drifting from

his system, and with the withdrawal from the nearing
headlights and the perpetual traffic lanes came the
increasing awareness of his situation. That something
was stirring in him, some desire once again to affect
his future, was clear from the way he tested the skill
with which he had been bound. He tried to move his
arms apart, seeing how tightly the knots were tied,
whether there was a stretch in the plastic-coated wire.
The sweat crawled again on his chest. Several minutes
the effort lasted before the realization came that the
binding had been done well, that it was beyond his
capabilities to loosen the wires.

So what are you going to do, Geoffrey? Going to sit
there like a bloody turkey in its coop, waiting for
Christmas Eve and the oven to heat up? Are you
going to lie on your side and wait for it, and hope it's
quick and doesn't hurt? Should have done something
in the car, or at the petrol stations, or at the toll gates,
or when the traffic stopped them on the Cassia. When
you had the chance, when you were body to body
close in the seats of the car.

And what would he have done about it, precious
Giancarlo?

Might have fired, might not, can't be sure.

But it would have been better than this, better than
sitting the hours out.

Would it have been that easy in the car? He'd kept
the door locked because that way there was one more
movement required before it could have been opened,
and that way there was more delay, more confusion,
more chance for him to shoot.

Idiot, Geoffrey Harrison, bloody idiot. Wouldn't
have mattered how long it took to get the door open
because he'd have been flattened by then, squashed
half out of existence, you're damn near double his
bloody weight, starved little scarecrow.

But you didn't do it, Geoffrey, and there's no

thanks in dreaming, no thanks in playing the bloody hero in the mind. The time was there and you bucked it, preferred to sit in the car and wait and see what happens.

See it now, lad, can't you? Half scared to bloody death already, and there's a pain in your balls and an ache in your chest and you want to cry for yourself. Scared out of your mind.

Too bloody right, and who wouldn't be? Because it's curtains, isn't it? Curtains and finish and they'll be getting the bloody box ready for you and cutting the flowers and choosing the plot, and the chaps in Head Office will have sent their black ties out to the dry cleaners. Through his mind the misery was fueled. No chance in a hundred bloody light-years that Franca would get her marching orders. All in the imagination of the little prig. Couldn't let her out, not a hard-line girl that it had taken months to get the manacles on. But that doesn't leave room, Geoffrey. Leaves you on a prayer and a hope . . . and what had Geoffrey bloody Harrison done, how come that his number was spinning with the lottery balls?

God, he was going to cry again, could feel the tears coming, thirty-six years old and fit to wet himself, and no stake in the place, no commitment.

Wrong again, Geoffrey, you're bleeding the masses, crucifying the workers.

That's lunacy, bloody madness.

Not to this kid, not to little Mister Giancarlo Battestini, and he's going to blow the side of your bloody head off just to prove it's real.

Harrison lay with his eyes tight shut, fighting the welling moisture. The foul taste of the cotton handkerchief suppurated around his back teeth. Nausea rising, and with it the terror that he would be sick and with the gag in position be unable to vomit and then choke in his own mess. What a bloody way to go,

choking in your own filth. Eyes so close together, lids
squeezed so that they were hurt, so that they bruised.

Violet, darling, bloody Violet, my bloody wife, I
want to be with you, darling, I want you to take me
away from here. Violet, please, please, don't leave me
here to them.

Near to his head a small branch cracked.

Harrison flashed open his eyes, swung his body up
and blinked away the tears.

Ten feet from him was a pair of child's knee-high
boots, their shiny skein broken by smears of dried
mud and bramble scratches, the miniature replicas of
an adult's farm wear, and rising out of them were the
little baggy trousers with the knees holed and the material faded with usage and washing. He twisted his
head slowly higher and gulped in the salvation of a
check sports shirt with the buttons haphazardly fastened and the sleeves floppily rolled. There was a
sparse and skinny bronzed neck and a young clean
face that was of the country and exposed to wind.
Harrison sagged back, dropped himself hard against
the earth. Thank God! A bloody ministering angel.
White sheet, wings, and a halo. Thank God! He felt a
shiver, the spasm of relief, running hard in him . . .
but not to hang about, not with Giancarlo gone only
for food. Come on, kid. God, I love you. Come on, but
don't hang about. You're a bloody darling, you know
that. But there's not all day. He looked up again into
the child's face, and wondered why the little one
just stood, stationary and still. Like a Pan statue, three
paces away, not speaking, demonstrating a graveness
at the cheeks, a caution in the eyes. Come on, kid,
don't be frightened, don't. He tried to wriggle his
body so that the bound wrist could be visible, waste
of time, the child could see the gag and the trussed
legs. The little feet backed away, as if the movement
disconcerted him. What's the bloody matter with the

kid? Well, what do you expect, Geoffrey? What did
your mother tell you when you were small and went
out into the fields and woods to play, and along the
street and out of sight of the row of houses that
belonged in their road? Don't talk to strangers, there's
funny people about, don't take sweets from them.

Harrison stared at the boy, stared and tried to understand. Six, perhaps seven years old, deep and serious eyes, a puzzled and concerned mouth, hands that
tugged and pulled the cloth of his trousers. But hesitant in coming forward, as if the man who lay in this
contorted posture was a forbidden apple. As best he
could, through the impediment of the gag, Geoffrey
Harrison tried to smile at the child and beckon with
his head for the boy to come closer, but he won no
response. Be a loner wouldn't he? Won't take chewing
gum from a man he doesn't know. It can't bloody happen to me. Please, not now, God. Please, God, not a
trick like this on me. It was going to take a long time
to win the boy. But time wasn't available, not with
Giancarlo gone only for food. What would the mean
bastard do with the child. Think on that, Geoffrey,
think on that as you try to bring him closer. What does
Giancarlo do with the kid if he finds him here, all
bright eyes and a witness? That's an obscenity, that's
foul. But that's truth, Geoffrey . . . hurry up, kid,
come closer quickly. Not just my life, your life hanging on a cotton thread.

Geoffrey Harrison knew that he had no call on the
child, that this was a private matter between himself
and the boy, Giancarlo. But he beckoned again with
his head and above the cloth at his mouth his cheeks
creased in what he thought of as a welcome greeting.

The child watched him with neither a smile nor
fear, and the small boots stayed rooted, neither slipping forward nor back. It would take a long time and
Giancarlo might return before the work was finished.

* * *

There were many young campers on the wooded hills and beside the lake at Bracciano and the stubble-cheeked boy in the *alimentari* on the waterfront aroused no comment. High summer holiday season, and for many the slopes that were cool and shaded and the deep lake in its volcanic crater represented a more welcome resting ground than the jam of the beaches. For those who had abandoned the city, however temporarily, the news bulletins went unheard, the newspapers unread. In the *alimentari* he attracted no attention as he bought a plastic razor, a can of pressurized shaving soap, and six *rosetti* filled with cheese and tomato slices.

From the *alimentari* he headed for the back lavatory of one of the small trattorias that stretch out on precarious stilts over the gray beach dust. With the cold water and the thickness of his cheek growth and the sharpness of the new blade, he had to exercise care that he did not lacerate his face. It would not be a clean shave but sufficient to change his appearance and tidy him in the minds of any who looked at and examined him. He had once read that the art of successful evasion was a dark suit and a tie; he believed it. Who searches for the fanatic among the closely groomed? He grinned to himself, as if enjoying the self-bestowed title. The "fanatic." Many labels would be handed down from the top table of the Directorate of Democrazia Christiana, and the Central Committee of the PCI, and they had seen nothing yet.

His humor was further improved by the wash, and there were more shops to visit. He bought socks and a light T-shirt that carried a cheaply stenciled rendering of the fifteenth-century castle of Bracciano that dominated the village. His former clothes he stuffed into a rubbish bin. Farther along the pavement he stopped and bought with coins from the newspaper stand the

day's edition of *Messagero*. He looked into Geoffrey
Harrison's picture, holding the page hard in front of
his face. The company portrait, serene and sleek,
harmless and smug, beaming success. On an inside
page was the information that had led him to need a
newspaper, the full story of the hunt with the facts
available till two o'clock that morning and the name
of the policeman who controlled the search. Dottore
Giuseppe Carboni, working for the Questura. Giancarlo's mouth rang with his innate contempt for his
adversary. Among the clatter of loose change in his
pocket were four *gettoni*, enough for his task. He
hunted now for a bar or trattoria that had a closed
phone booth, not willing to be overheard when he
made his telephone call. At a bar he passed there
were two coin telephones for the public, but both
open and fastened to the wall where there would be
no privacy. He walked on till he reached the *ristorante* attached to the sailing club at the end of the
half kilometer esplanade, and this place was suitable
to him. A closed telephone booth in the hallway leading from the street door to the inner eating sanctum.
He had to wait some minutes for the two giggling
girls to finish. Neither bothered to glance at the frail
boy as they plunged out, loud in their shared noise.

This near to the capital the telephone booths were
equipped with Rome directories. He flicked through
the first pages of the scruffed edition of Pagina
Gialle, running with his cleaned fingernail over the
addresses and numbers listed under Commissariati PS.
At the bottom of his page he found the answer. Questura Central—v. di S Vitale 15 (46 86).

This would stir the bastards.

He would carry the fight to them, as Franca would
have wished, carry it right to the doors of the Questura where they sat with their files and their minions
and their computers. They would hear of Giancarlo,

the hacks and lackeys would hear his name. He was
trembling through his body, taut as a whiplash at the
moment that it cracks on a horse's back. The shaking
convulsed his palms and the *gettoni* rattled dully in
his fist.

No nearer, no farther from Harrison, the child had
sat down. He was cross-legged, knees out akimbo with
his elbows resting on them and his hands supporting
his chin, the kindergarten pose, listening to a teacher's
story.

Like you're a bloody animal, Geoffrey, like he's
found a fox half dead in a gin trap, and he has a patience and will wait to see what happens. All the hours
in the world the child had to be patient with, too
young for a watch, for a sense of fleeting time. Harrison's attempts to draw him closer, to engage those
small sharp fingers in the binding knots had failed.
All the nodding and gesturing with his head had been
ignored except for the few times when his most violent contortions had gathered a flash of fear to his
face and the child's slim muscles had stiffened and
prepared for escape. Don't get excited, Harrison had
learned, and for God's sake, even with the eyes, don't
threaten him. The child has to be kept there, his confidence has to be conserved, he has to be wooed.

You want to keep him here, Geoffrey, with Giancarlo coming back? Giancarlo and the *P trent' otto*
coming back with the food, and you're trying to keep
the child here?

God, I don't know, and the moments were marching, the hands would be sliding on the watch face of
his wrist.

Almost a sadness on the child's face as Harrison
peered into its shallow depths. He would be a kid
from a farmhouse, self-sufficient, self-reliant in his entertainment, a creature of the woods, and owing loy-

alty and softness only to his parents. A peasant child.
You'd find one like this on the Yorkshire uplands or
the Devon moors, or on the far west shoreline of Ireland's Donegal. God knows how to communicate with
the blighter. Cannot frighten him, cannot please him.
If there had been a child of his own, but Violet had
said that her figure . . . can't blame bloody Violet,
not her fault you don't know how to talk to a child.

Hope was fleeing from Harrison. His head movements became less frequent, and he had seen that
when he subsided into inertia, then the small attention
was lost and the start of boredom glazed on the child's
eyes. That way he would leave, pick himself off the
earth and wander on his way. That's what he should
do, lie still, bore the kid out, and hope that he was
gone before Giancarlo was back, that was saving the
kid. That was the proper way, that was diving clothed
into an icy pool to pluck a baby out.

God, I don't want him to go. The fear came again,
the horror of being abandoned by this child, and he
nodded again with his head and wore the pantomime
face of the clown in his urgency.

Hating himself, with the fever in his eyes as he
called mutely for the child to come forward, Harrison
strained to hear the footfall of the returning Giancarlo.

"*Pronto*, Questura."

Giancarlo stabbed with his finger at the button that
would release a *gettoni* to fall into the caverns of the
machine.

"Questura . . ."

"Please, the office of Dottore Giuseppe Carboni."

"A moment . . ."

"Thank you."

"For nothing, sir . . ."

A hesitation, the sounds of connection. Perspiration dribbled down Giancarlo's chest.

"Yes . . ."

"May I speak with Dottore Giuseppe Carboni."

"He is most involved at this time. In what connection . . . ?"

"In connection with the Englishman, 'arrison."

"Can I help? I work in Dottore Carboni's office."

"I must speak with him directly. It is important."

There would be a taping of all incoming calls for Carboni. Giancarlo assumed that, but unless suspicions were aroused the trace procedures would not be automatic. He kept his voice calm, regulated.

"A moment . . . who is it who calls?"

Giancarlo flushed. "It does not matter . . ."

"A moment."

More delays and he fed another *gettoni*. He smiled mirthlessly. Not the time to lose the call for lack of coins. His last two rested in his hand. More than sufficient . . . he started, clenched at the receiver.

"Garboni speaking. What can I do for you?"

The voice seemed to come from a great distance, a whispering on the line as if there were a great tiredness and the resignation heavy.

"Listen carefully, Carboni. Do not interrupt. This is the spokesman of the Nuclei Armati Proletaria . . ."

Don't gabble, Giancarlo. Remember that you are kicking them. Remember that you are hurting them as surely as the P38 in Franca's hand.

". . . we hold the Englishman, 'arrison. If Franca Tantardini has not been released and flown out of Italy to the territory of a friendly socialist nation by nine o'clock tomorrow morning, then the multinationalist 'arrison will be executed for his crimes against the proletariat. There is more, Carboni. We will telephone again this evening, and when your name is asked for, then the call must be given to yourself immediately, and in your room must be Franca Tantardini. We will speak to her ourselves. If the connection is not made, if Comrade Tantardini is not there to talk to us, then 'arrison will be killed. The call this evening will come at twenty hours . . ."

Forty seconds on the revolving hands of his watch since he had announced the source of the communication. And the trace system would be in operation. Mad, Giancarlo, mad. It's the behavior of the fool.

". . . Is that understood?"

"Thank you, Giancarlo."

The boy's head jolted forward, fingers white and bloodless on the plastic telephone. A breathy whisper, "How did you know?"

"We know so much, Giancarlo. Giancarlo Battestini. Born Pescara. Father, a clothes shop there. One meter sixty-eight tall. Weight on release from Regina Coeli, sixty-one kilos. Call again, Giancarlo . . ."

Another twenty seconds departed on his watch, lost. Giancarlo snapped, "You will have her there. You will have Comrade Tantardini on this telephone?"

"If it pleases you."

"Do not doubt us. When we say we will kill the man 'arrison, do not doubt us."

"I believe you will kill him, Giancarlo. It would not be clever, but I believe that you are capable . . ."

With his forefinger Giancarlo pulled down the hook beside the telephone box, felt the moment of sliding pressure before the sound that told him the call was terminated. Franca had told him they needed two minutes for a trace. He had not exposed himself to their reach. Time in hand. He walked out of the *ristorante* and into the lively afternoon sun, knees weak, breath summoned fast, his mind a confusion of spattered images. They should have groveled and they had not. They should have bent and they had held. Perhaps in the sinking pit of his stomach there was an alien and unholy presentiment of the imminence of failure.

But the mood was soon discarded. The chin jutted and the eyes glowed and he hurried back on the dust-covered road, retracing his way toward the wood.

It was more than an hour now since the child had come, and the crease lines of interest still wrapped his face.

Harrison no longer moved, no longer attempted to wheedle the small boy closer. Tried, you poor bastard, tried all you knew. The ants were at him. Virile swine, monsters with a singeing bite, hitting and retreating and returning, calling for their friends because the mountain of food was defenseless and amusing. And the kid hadn't spoken one bloody word.

Go away, you little blighter, get lost, get back to your Mama and your tea. You're no bloody use to me. A pretty face the child had, and the frown lines were worn as if by a martyred infant in the colors of a church window. Violet would notice a face like this child's, and she'd enthuse on it and want to tousle his hair and coo to him. Why didn't the child respond? God knows, and he's not caring. He'll be in church, this brat, on Sunday morning, with his hair combed and his face washed, with a red cassock down to shined sandals and white socks, probably be singing his bloody heart out in the choir stall, and he won't even remember the strange shape of the man in the woods with the wild gaze and the body twist of fear. He'll be in church . . . if Giancarlo isn't back soon.

The child started up, the rabbit alerted, slid fast to his feet, easily and with the suppleness of great youth.

For Harrison there was nothing beyond the lethargic motion of the wood.

The child began to move away and Harrison watched fascinated for there was a silence under the boots that glided over the dry minefield of leaves and sticks. His place, thought Harrison, among the animals and the birds and the familiar; probably didn't know what the inside of a schoolroom looked like, because this was his playground. He watched the child go, his slight body suffusing with the pale gray lines of the tree trunks. When he was at the murky edge of vision, Harrison saw him drop to his knees and ease the fronds of a sapling across his face and shoulders. The child had covered less than twenty yards, but when he was settled Harrison had to strain and search with his eyes to find his hiding place.

Into view, trying to move with caution, but failing to secure the quiet places for his feet, came Giancarlo, the source of disturbance.

Giancarlo closed quickly, the gun in his hand, and the brown paper bag held between the crook of his arm and his body. He was alert, hunting between the trees with his eyes, but finding nothing to caution or alarm him. He dropped down into his knee and slipped the pistol into the waist of his trousers. The cleaned face and the bright T-shirt gave him a youth and innocence that Harrison had not seen before.

"Food, and I haven't had mine either. We are both equally starved." There was a little laugh and Giancarlo leaned forward and put his arms behind Harrison's head and unknotted the handkerchief, pulled it clear and dropped it beside him. "Better, yes?"

Harrison spat from the side of his mouth, cleared the spittle. Still bent low, Giancarlo bounced on his toes down into the earth crater and worked quickly and expertly on the wrist cord.

"Still better, yes? Even better?"

Harrison looked far into his face and struggled to comprehend the volatile changes of atmosphere. After the hours of silence in the car, after the kicking of the early morning, the new direction of the wind was too complex for him to comprehend. "What did you get for us to eat?" he asked lamely, rubbing his wrists and restoring the glow of circulation. And what the hell did it matter? What importance did it hold?

"Not much. Some bread, with cheese and salad. It will fill us."

"Very good."

"And I spoke to the man who is trying to find you. A fool at the Questura, I called him by telephone. I told him what would happen if Franca were not freed by tomorrow morning." Giancarlo took a bulging bread roll from the bag, ignored the cheese spillage, and passed it to Harrison. He spoke proudly. "He tried to keep me talking to give them time for a trace, but that's an old trick. You won't hear sirens tonight, 'arrison. I told him also that I would talk direct to Franca this evening and that they should bring her to his office."

A chatty, banal conversation. That of two men who have been buried for too long and for whom the quiet has proved oppressive.

"What did you say would happen if Franca were not freed?" Harrison's words were mumbled through the mass of bread and salad.

"I told them you would be executed."

"That's what you told them?"

"I said that I would kill you."

"And what did they say?" Harrison ate on, the words of both of them too daft, too insane, to be real and of value.

"Carboni is the name of the man who is hunting for you. He was the only one that I spoke to. He said nothing."

"Did he say if Franca would be freed?"

"He did not answer that." Giancarlo smiled. There was a certain warmth, a certain charm in the scrubbed, shaved features. "He did not answer any of my questions. You know, he knew my name, he knew who it was that he was speaking to. He was pleased with that, the man Carboni. I mean it, I mean it very deeply, 'arrison, I would be sorry to kill you. It would not be what I want."

Too much for Geoffrey Harrison to assimilate. As it had been once in the yard behind his father's house as they watched the chickens prowling beside the fence and decided which one would make their meal, and which should survive, and he had tried to communicate to the chosen fowl that there was nothing personal in the choice, no malice.

"It doesn't help you if you shoot me." Harrison trying to be calm, trying to soften and mollify through dialogue.

"Only that each time you make a threat you must carry it out if you are to be believed. You understand that, 'arrison. If I say that I will kill you unless I am given something, then I must do it if I am denied. It is the credibility. You understand that, 'arrison?"

"Why do you tell me this?"

"Because you have the right to know."

Harrison turned his head, a slow and casual movement, traversed across the treefront and caught as a flash, that was there and then gone, the blue and white of the check shirt of the child who had sat where Giancarlo now squatted.

"Will they give you back your Franca, Giancarlo?"

"No . . ." he said simply, and his hand dived again in the bag and he passed another roll across to Harrison. An afterthought . . . "Well, I do not think so. But I must try, right 'arrison? You would agree that I should try?"

With the arrival of Francesco Vellosi from the Viminale, the summit meeting in Carboni's office could

begin. Just preceding the head of the antiterrorist unit
had been the Minister of the Interior and before him
the examining magistrate who had successfully jockeyed among his profession for the nominal role of
heading the investigation.

Tired men, all of them. Harassed and without small
talk. There was argument over priorities at the outset
around the bowed figure of the Minister who knew
the penalty for failure to arrest terrorist outrage was
resignation, and who could not find in the bearing of
the men about him the means to gather in the ailing
initiative.

There were many points for dispute and bicker.

Should any new advice be presented to the Council
of Ministers regarding the decision to refuse consideration of the freeing of Franca Tantardini?

Should Franca Tantardini be permitted to speak by
telephone with the boy Battestini?

At least two *gettoni* had been used on the telephone
communication, the call had come from outside the
Rome city limits, and in the countryside the principal
enforcer of the law were the *carabinieri;* should they
now control any further search operation, or should
the overall decision remain with the *polizia?*

Was it useful to contact the Vatican Secretariat to
explore the possibility of His Holiness issuing a similar
appeal to the rejected call of Paulo Sesto for Aldo Moro's life?

Should the President of the Council of Ministers
broadcast to the nation?

Why had it not been possible to extract greater information from the location of the telephone message?

Much of it unnecessary, much of it time-wasting
and sapping in concentration for the men in the room
who bandied the barbs and dagger thrusts. But then
many had to clear themselves if there was a chance of
failure to be found in tomorrow's dawn. Reputations

could be damaged, perhaps destroyed. Backs must be protected. As one of the most junior men in the hierarchy present, Giuseppe Carboni was finally given what amounted to a free hand. He would be provided with a liaison team to link him with Criminalpol, the *carabinieri* force, and the armed forces. If he succeeded, then those who had set in motion the search operation would be standing to the fore. If he failed, then the shoulders would droop and the heads would turn away, and Carboni would stand alone. When they rose from the meeting the room was quickly emptied, few delayed. It was as if the paint daubs of disaster already swept across the walls. Carboni reflected, as he stood beside his desk smiling weakly at the Minister's departing back, that little had been gained, only time frittered away and lost.

"Look at it another way," said Vellosi, his arm around Carboni's short shoulder. "There is little likelihood of us saving Harrison, and perhaps that is not even the first priority. What matters is that we find this scum . . ."

"You talk as if we have reached a state of war," murmured Carboni.

"What matters is that we find this scum, whether tomorrow, or in a month, or a year, and we kick the shit out of him . . . He never reaches Asinara."

"They are dragging us down, Vellosi."

"That is the ground where we meet them, where we fight them, and where we win."

"If in such times victory is available . . . I am less certain."

"Concern yourself with the present, Carboni. Find me the boy Battestini." Vellosi squeezed his arm and walked on out through the door.

In front of a small trattoria Violet Harrison parked her car. Not tidily, not quietly, but with a splash of movement and rising dust and the protest of an over-extended engine. The parking area for patrons, but she would take a cup of coffee and perhaps half a carafe of white wine, and that would satisfy the white-shirted waiters as to her rights to possession of a table. The veranda of the trattoria was at the back, and she walked through the small construction of timber and corrugated iron roofing and past the kitchen where the fires were being stoked for the lamb and the veal. Beneath a screen of interlaced bamboo she would sit, and from there she could watch, across some scrub grass and shallow shifting hills of sand, the boys who walked on the beach.

She conjured a lie, she seemed relaxed, at peace. But the polaroids on her face hid the sight of her eyes, red and damp. She made her posture to the world, obliterated her inner self, and sat at the table and waited. Occasionally she swung her head and gazed away down the beach, a searchlight roving, hunting all the time, haunting and punishing.

16

Early afternoon in the great slumbering capital.

A wicked heat, clamping on the bodies of the few Romans who moved listlessly on the steaming, paper-strewn streets. Little protection for the walkers even from the high buildings of nineteenth-century elegance on the Corso. The pavements, abandoned by their own citizens, were given over to the perspiring, grumbling tourists. The map clutchers, guidebook scanners, ice cream suckers, groped from ruin to ruin, commenting their admiration for what they saw in shrill Japanese, blaring American, dominant German. Bottoms that were compressed under cut-off jeans, short skirts, trailing dresses, vivid slacks, wobbled and shook among all that was notable of ancient Rome.

Like a stranger in his own community, Giuseppe Carboni threaded an impatient way between the loiterers. He crossed the small square in front of the colonnaded church and hurried up the six shallow steps to the central entrance of the church of San Pietro in Vincoli. The visitors were thick, shoulder to shoulder, huddled close to their guides, serious and solemn-faced as they mopped at the culture and the damp-

ness of their armpits. Here Carboni had been told he
would find Francesco Vellosi. The church of Saint Pe-
ter in Chains is where the bonds of the saint are rever-
ently kept, shining and coated in dark paint inside a
gold and glass-faced cabinet. The central nave was
taken by the groups, soaking in the required information, the age of the construction, the dates of renovation, the history of the tomb of Julius II, the smoothed
sculpture of the bearded and muscled Moses that was
the work of Michelangelo. But in the wings, in the
narrower naves, where the tourists gave ground to the
worshipers, Carboni would find his man. Where the
shadows were thicker, where the tall candles burned
in flickering insecurity, where the women in black
came in from the streets to pray. In the right-hand
nave he saw Vellosi, three rows from the front, and
kneeling hunched on a red hassock. The hard man of
the antiterrorist squad, and now bent in prayer because his driver was slain and would be buried in the
morning. No surprise that Vellosi would choose this
church. On the same steps that Carboni had climbed,
the *carabinieri* had shot to death Antonio La Muscio
and captured the girls La Vianale and Salerno. The
place acted as a symbol to those who fought the underground of subversion and anarchy, it was their
place of triumph and riposte.

Carboni did not intrude. He himself crossed to the
small side altar and waited with hands joined across
his stomach. The voices of the guides seemed distant,
the brush of feet was near eliminated. A place of tran-
quil value. A place to shed, for precious moments, the
fearsome and desperate load the two men carried.
Watching and waiting, curling his toes, ignoring the
passage of time that could not be recouped, Carboni
curled himself. He could be thankful that, if nothing
else, he had escaped from his desk, his aides, his telephone, and the endless computer printouts.

Abruptly, Vellosi jackknifed himself from his knees and back onto his chair. Carboni darted forward and eased himself down beside him. When their eyes met Carboni could see that the man was rested, that the purgative of prayer had refreshed him.

"You forgive me, *capo*, for coming here to find you?"

"Nothing, Carboni. I came to say some words for my Mauro . . ."

"A good place to come to." Carboni spoke softly, with approval.

"Here we killed the rat, exterminated La Muscio . . . it's a good place to come to speak with my friend."

"It is right to remember the success. Catastrophe is burdening, deadening."

There was a wry smile on Vellosi's lips. "Catastrophe we are familiar with, success is the star we seek."

"And too often the cloud obscured the star . . . it is seldom visible."

The two men spoke in church whispers, Vellosi content to idle till Carboni was ready to unveil the purpose of his visit.

A deep sigh from Carboni. The man who will jump into a winter sea from a breakwater and must strip off his robe and discard his towel.

"We talked long enough at the meeting," Carboni plunged. "Long enough to have settled every matter that was outstanding, but at the end we had decided nothing, nothing beyond the fact that Giuseppe Carboni should take responsibility . . ."

"You have expected something different?"

"Perhaps yes, perhaps no." Carboni stared in front of him as he spoke, over the shoulder of the wizened sparrow woman, with her bones angular under the blouse of black, who mouthed quiet words to the altar. "A gathering like that is a farce, a babble of men seeking with one voice to disclaim ultimate responsibility, prepared only to pile it on my shoulders."

"They are broad enough," chuckled Vellosi. "You should work at the Viminale, you would quickly learn then what is normal, what is acceptable."

"Do we let the woman Tantardini speak to the boy?" Carboni sharper now, maneuvering and play-acting completed.

Vellosi too responded, the smile draining, the tide running. A savagery in his voice. "I hate that bitch. Believe me, dear friend, I hate her. I wish to Jesus that we had slaughtered her in the street."

"Understandable and unhelpful."

Vellosi snatched back at him. "What do you need most?"

"Now I have nothing. I know only that Battestini was early this morning in the area of Rome. I know that he has traveled on. I have a car number, but that can have been changed. I have no hope of intervention before tomorrow morning." The ebbing of the bravura.

"So you must have a trace, you must have a location. If the bitch is there and talks to him you give your engineers the possibility . . ."

"She has to speak to him?"

"It is you who must make her." There was a snarl in Vellosi's voice, as if the discussion had reached obscenity. "If I were to ask her she would spit in my face."

Carboni looked around him in response to the protesting coughs of those who objected at raised voices in their worship. He stood up, Vellosi following, and together they walked down the aisle between the colonnade and the chairs. "What would you tell her?"

"That you have to decide for yourself."

"I came for help, Vellosi."

"I cannot aid you. You must read her when you see her. When you meet with her you will know why I cannot help you." The inhibitions of the church quiet were lost on Vellosi. "She is poison, and you must think of the consequences for yourself if you involve her."

Carboni stared back at Vellosi as they stopped at the great opened doors. A small and pudgy figure dwarfed by his colleague of the open and strong face. He weighed his words for a moment. "You are nervous of her. Even from her cell in the Rebibbia she frightens you."

No denials, no stuttered protests. Vellosi said simply, "Be careful, Carboni, remember what I say. Be careful of the bitch."

Through the afternoon little had passed between Geoffrey Harrison and Giancarlo Battestini. Harrison's arms had not been tied again since the food and he lay on his side on the earth of the bunker, his only movements to swat the flies from his face and brush the ants and insects from his body and legs. He might have slept, had certainly dozed in the twilight area. All the while Giancarlo watched him with a casual and intermittent observation and with the gun resting on the leaves close to his hand. The summer sun was high, burning even now through the ceiling of foliage, sufficient to shrivel any wind that might earlier have infiltrated. Sticky, hot, and defeated, Harrison slipped into a vegetable state, his mind devoid of ideas and expectations. No longer did the presence of the check shirt in the undergrowth a few yards beyond and behind Giancarlo win any hope of salvation. Just another witness to his helplessness, another voyeur.

His body functions drove Harrison to speak again.

"It's the call of nature, Giancarlo." Ridiculous that he was embarrassed. Couldn't use the language of the dressing room, of the men's club. Couldn't say . . . I need to take a crap, Giancarlo . . . I want to shit, Giancarlo. Didn't want to say it any other way and feared to foul his trousers. "It's been a long time."

Giancarlo looked at him curiously, as if experiencing some new buttress of his power. The great man of the multinational must ask Giancarlo's permission again, because otherwise he would smell and lose his dignity, and no more be a person of stature and importance. The cat and the mouse. The boy and the butterfly with the broken wing. Giancarlo teased his theatrical disbelief. "Perhaps you are trying to trick me, 'arrison."

"Really, Giancarlo, I have to go. I'm not tricking you."

The boy warmed to the hint of desperation, to the fluttered pleading. "Perhaps you would try to escape from me."

"I promise there is no trick . . . but quickly."

"What do you say then, 'arrison? What were you taught to say when you wanted something?"

"Please, Giancarlo . . ."

The boy grinned, played the sneer at his lips. "And you want to go in the trees where you cannot be seen. You think many are watching you?"

"Please, Giancarlo."

The boy was satisfied. Another victory, another demonstration of strength. Enough and the pleasure was satiated. He left the P38 on the ground and slowly taking his time, maneuvered himself behind Harrison. It was the work of a few seconds to detach the wire that fastened the ankles to the tree roots. "Four or five meters only, 'arrison, no more."

"Aren't you going to loosen my legs?"

Giancarlo was further amused. "Crawl, 'arrison, and watch where your hands move, that they do not go close to my knots."

Once more Harrison gazed away past Giancarlo and toward the hiding place of the child. Still visible to him were the flecks of the shirt between leaves and branches. Anger was rising out of the frustration. The little bastard. On his hands and knees, Harrison crawled, the performing pet, toward a cluster of birch trunks.

"Not too far, 'arrison," the mocking call of derision.

His trailing knees scuffed a trail through the leaves and top surface earth before he was partially hidden by the trees. He lowered his trousers, squatted using his hands to support himself and felt the constriction and pain gush away. God, the bloody relief of it. Bloody freedom. And the bloody smell.

"Please, Giancarlo, do you have any paper?"

There was a ripple of laughter from past the trees. "I have no bidet for you, I have no aerosol for you to spray under your armpits. But paper I have for you."

Subdued, Harrison thanked him and then repeated himself when the bag that had carried the rolls landed close to his feet, thrown with accuracy. He cleaned himself, retrieved his trousers, scuffed some dirt over the soiled paper, and dragged himself back to his captor and his prison. He crawled to the flattened earth in the cavity and lay down, matching his familiar position, pliant and nonresistant, and curled his arms behind his back.

"Close your eyes." A command, and with his legs trussed, what chance? Nothing, just plain nothing. He clenched his eyes shut, and heard only the slight sounds of Giancarlo's feet, and then the hands were cruelly at his wrists and the wire was wound tight and brutally across his flesh, and there was the pressure of a knee in the small of his back.

The weight slid from him and with its going there was again the mocking voice. "You can open your eyes."

Above the horizon of the crater rim, Harrison saw Giancarlo standing, observing, hands on hips. Something mindless, something vacuous about the smile and the mouth and the dulled glare of the eyes.

"You're enjoying yourself, Giancarlo. It's sick to be that way. It means that you are ill . . ."

"Now we have a grand speech." Derison from the boy, the void unbridged by the contact.

"To treat anyone like this, it means you're deranged. You're a bloody lunatic. You know what that means . . . you're mad, Giancarlo, you've flipped your bloody lid." Why say it? Why bother? What bloody difference does it make?

"I understand what you say." But the boy was not roused.

"You've become an animal, Giancarlo. A vicious, infected little . . ."

Giancarlo with studied care turned his back. "I do not listen to speeches. I am not obliged to hear you."

"Why don't you do it now?" The whisper, without fervor, without passion. The words of a second in the boxer's ring when he has seen enough blood, when he is ready to throw in the towel.

"Because it is not time. Because I am not ready."

"I say it again, Giancarlo, you enjoy it. You must have felt like a kid giving yourself a wrist job when you killed the men back in the barn, jerking yourself. What are you going to do when you kill me, take your bloody trousers down . . . ?"

Giancarlo narrowed his eyes, and on his slight forehead the frown deepened in its ruts. His voice came as a rush of breeze among the trees. "You know nothing of us. Nothing. You cannot know why a man goes *sottoterra*, why a man fights to destroy a system that is rotten. You were smug and safe and fat, and you were blind. You know nothing of the struggle of the proletariat."

Half into the dirt, Harrison shouted back, "Bloody clichés. Parrot talk you learned in the drains."

"You do not make it easier for yourself."

Attempting an order and a sternness, Harrison called, "Get it over with."

"I have said to them that it will be at nine o'clock, if I have not my Franca. I will wait till nine. That was my word. Keeping you till then does not threaten me."

Giancarlo walked away a few paces, discarded the conversation, withdrew to his inner recesses, gone from Harrison's reach.

And he's right, Geoffrey, you know nothing of them, nothing at all of the new and embryo species. Nothing of the hate squashed into that mind. And there's no help, no succor, the cavalry don't come this time. Just a bloody carcass already, that's all, Geoffrey. Harrison looked into the green-gray mist of the trellis of sapling branches and leaves, and felt the falling of a greater loneliness. He could not see the child. Perhaps it was his eyes, perhaps he looked to the wrong place, but he could not find the checked shirt though he peered till his eyes ached and hurt him.

A second carafe now stood emptied on the table.

The waiters had served the lunches, waved their patrons away, and stripped the cloths from the chipboard tables. Violet Harrison seemed not to notice and with their inbred politeness they waited on her pleasure as she toyed and sipped at the last glass of wine. She alternated between hope and despair as the young men of the beach sauntered by. Straight-backed, tanned from wind and sun and the flailing blows of the fine grains, cocky assured eyes, combed-down hair. Any would have served her purpose. She saw the boy a long way off the beach, walking between two companions.

Recognized him instantly.

"Could I have my bill, please." She rummaged in her bag for the notes, gestured to the waiter that she required no change, and was on her feet and smiling sweetly.

She walked out from the eating veranda taking for herself what she hoped was a casual saunter and following a line that would intercept with the boy's path. She did not look to her right, the direction from which he was coming, but held her head high and straight and focused on the blue sea's depths and its breaking specks of spume. She strode on, waiting for the greeting, consumed with a growing, creeping nervousness.

"The English lady, good afternoon."

She spun around, gouging at the warm sand beneath her sandals. Not that she could claim surprise, but when his voice came, almost behind her, it cut and burned at her consciousness.

"Oh, it's you." How else did you do it? How to flick up a clever answer when all you were confronting was the stud required for half an hour's brisk and anonymous work?

"I did not expect to see you here again."

"It's a public beach." Don't be frightening him off. Too trite, Violet. God, you'd kick and curse yourself. "I come here quite a lot."

She saw the little gesture of the boy with his hands, the clipping of his forefinger against his thumb, the message to the other two that the principal wished to be left to his opportunities. Close together but untouching, no bridging contact of fingers, no brushing of thighs, they moved together toward the sea.

"You would like to swim, Signora?"

How he'd speak to a friend of his bloody mother, thought Violet. "Not yet, I thought I'd just lie on the beach for a bit."

"Give me your towel."

She dived a hand into her bag and produced it for

him. He spread it out onto the sand, gestured with his
hand for her to sit, and followed her down. Little
room for both of them if they were to share it. His
swimming costume was brief and bulging gro-
tesquely. You understand, Geoffrey. Their hips
touched. You won't cast a rock, Geoffrey.

"My name is Marco."

And Geoffrey wouldn't know. That was the rule.
No blows below the belt for Geoffrey. No knowledge
and therefore no hurt.

"I am Violet."

"That is the name of a flower in English, yes? A
very beautiful flower I think."

I know you are alone, Geoffrey. I too am alone. You
cannot move, you cannot help yourself. I too, Geoffrey.

"I said it the last time we met, and I was right. You
are a very cheeky boy, Marco."

He smiled across the inches of towel at her. The
toothpaste advertisement, the smile of a child taken to
a shop, who knows it is his birthday, knows if he is
patient he will receive his present.

"What time is it, Giancarlo?"

"Past five."

The boy returned to his own chasm of silence.

Much to think of, much to concern himself with.
Less than three hours to the schedule that he had set
himself, that he had insisted on. Less than three hours
till he spoke once more with his darling, with his
Franca. Problems and options bombarded him. If they
met his demand, if they agreed to the exchange,
where should he fly to? Algiers, Libya, Iraq, the People's Republic of South Yemen. Would any of those
places take them? And how to judge a preference, a
boy who had never been out of Italy. How would he
guarantee their safety if an airport rendezvous were

permitted? What was the capability of the antiterrorist pigs, would they seek a shooting gallery, regardless of the prisoner? A great team the *Brigatisti* had for the Moro operation, and they now sat in Asinara, locked in their cells, the failed men. As he weighed each trick in the pack, so grew the realization of the sheer mountain face he must scale. Start with the haven, start there, because with nowhere to go they were lost and in defeat. A country to welcome them and harbor them, start there. An Arab country? What else? But even their own people were now shunned and ignored; he had seen the pictures of the trucks blocking the runways in Algiers and Beghazi and Tripoli, if they would do that when an Arab brother was seeking refuge. . . . Late for the answers to the questions. The time was ripe for answers before Claudio walked to his room in the *pensione*, before the *rapido* flew for Reggio, before the Calabresi whimpered in their terror.

Perhaps all irrelevant.

Did he know there would be no exchange? Was that why he had walked to the telephone booth, demanded to talk with Franca, when if he faced success he would sit in an aircraft with her in a trifle of hours? The agony of the boy piled and steepled.

And if there were to be no exchange, what then would the leadership want of him? He wrestled in the growing purgatory of the dilemma. Where lay the victory in this skirmish? The body of his 'arrison in a ditch, the head blasted with the shell of the P38, that or his prisoner released to walk away on a road with a communique in his pocket to be printed the next morning in *Paese Sera* and *Messagero*? Where lay the victory for the proletariat's revolution? How had the *Brigatisti* advanced when they took the life from Aldo Moro on the slime-covered beach at Focene?

Old enough only for questions, too young to carry

their responses. If he could not conjure the answers, then he would not see his Franca again. Not for twenty years and that was ever. Three days since his hands had traveled her skin, since her golden head had passed across the softness of his belly. To be denied that for a lifetime. The boy felt a gust of pain. There was nothing that was simple, that was facile, and that was why there was a steel in the comrades who fought, in Franca Tantardini and the men in the island jail. And what was the sinew of Giancarlo Battestini, in his twentieth year, lover of Tantardini, son of a *borghese*, member of the NAP? A dozen hours, slow and tardy hours, and he would have that answer.

His hands clutched together, white to the knuckles, Giancarlo waited for the time that he should leave Harrison and make his way again to the lakeside of Bracciano.

In his hotel room Archie Carpenter listened to Michael Charlesworth's clipped and exact résumé.

A voice far away on a bad connection. The situation if anything had deteriorated. Reuters and UPI carried on their wires that a boy, Giancarlo Battestini, categorized as little more than a probationer of the NAP, had telephoned to the Questura to emphasize the terms of his ultimatum.

"I don't know how it is that the Italians allow this sort of information out, but nothing stays secure here. It seems Battestini was full of his threats. There's a fair depression about the way it's going," Charlesworth had said.

Holding himself, the diver conserving his oxygen, Carpenter had heard him out. Then the explosion.

"So what are you all doing about it?"

"What we were doing about it earlier, Archie. It has not changed."

"Sweet damn all."

"You can put it that way," Charlesworth placated. "That way if you want to."

"What other bloody way?" Carpenter had rapped.

"Abuse doesn't help, Archie. You've spoken yourself with the Ambassador, he's explained our situation. I've heard since that London has called him. They back him."

"He's written off my man."

"Histrionics don't help either. I'm sorry, you're sorry, we are all sorry . . . but you'll come and have that meal tonight."

"If you want me to."

"Come on up and help us through a bottle. Did you get in touch with the wife?"

"I rang again, took a bloody effort to, but I tried. There's no answer."

"It's a filthy business, Archie, but don't think you're alone with the hair shirt. It's shared about a bit, you know."

Charlesworth rang off.

Archie Carpenter straightened up his bed, brushed his hair, raised his tie knot and drew on his jacket. He took the elevator downstairs and walked out through the front foyer of the hotel, stepping over the piled suitcases of an arriving tour. He hailed a taxi and asked for the Questura. Early summer evening, the traffic rushing home and guaranteeing him an exciting and lively journey among the pedestrians and across the traffic lanes. Carpenter barely noticed. A telephone call from the inquiry desk had promptly led to his being ushered up the stairs to the offices of Giuseppe Carboni, now transformed into a tactical crisis center.

Shirtsleeves, tobacco smoke, coffee beakers, a three-quarter emptied Scotch bottle, faces lined with weariness, the howl of electric fans, the chatter of teletype machines, and radiating energy, Carboni in the midst, rotund and active.

Carpenter hesitated by the door, was spied out, waved forward.

"Come in, Carpenter. Come and see our humble efforts," Carboni shouted at him.

· This was the old world, the known scents. An emergency room under pressure. This was something for Carpenter to feel and absorb. He felt an interloper, and yet at home, among the men he could find sympathy for. The clock was turned back for him as he came with a diffidence past the desks where the paper mountained, past the photographs stuck with tape to the walls that showed shocked and staring faces, past the telephones that demanded response.

"I don't want to be in the way . . ."

"But you cannot sit in the hotel room any longer?"

"Something like that, Mr. Carboni."

"And you come here because everyone you speak with gives you bad news or no news, and from me you hope for a difference?"

Something lovable about him, Carpenter thought. Overweight, ugly as sin, dirty fingernails, a shirt that should have seen the wash, and a bloody good man.

"It was getting to me, just sitting about . . . you know how it is?"

"I will educate you, Carpenter." Carboni was sliding on his coat, then turning away to bellow what seemed to Carpenter a score of differing instructions simultaneously to varied recipients. "I will show you our enemy. You will witness what we fight against. I know you policemen from England, detailed and organized men, who have believed that you are the best in the world . . ."

"I'm not a policeman anymore."

"You retain the mentality. It has stayed with you." Carboni laughed without a smile, a nervous tic. "The rest of the world are idiots, second-class people. I understand. Well, come with me, my friend. We go across the city to the Rebibbia jail. That is where we hold the Tantardini woman and I must play the taxi driver and bring her here, because that is what little Giancarlo wants and we must please him . . ."

Carpenter sensed the swollen anger in the man, wondered where it could find an outlet. The laugh came again.

" . . . I must please him, because if he does not talk to Tantardini, then your Harrison is dead. I am here to save him, I will do my humble best to save him."

"I hadn't really doubted that, sir." Carpenter let the respect run in his voice, because this was a professional man, this was a caring man.

"So, come and see her. Know your enemy. That is what you say in England? The better you know him, the better you fight him." Carboni caught Carpenter's arm and propelled him back toward the door. "You will see that we risk much at this stage. But don't tell me that it was never like that in London. Don't tell me that always you were supreme."

"We had the black times."

"We have experience, we know the black times. Tonight it is that but darker."

His arm still clamped by Carboni's fist, Carpenter surged down the corridor.

Across the hood of the little red Fiat, with a pliant finger, the child drew the letters of his name in the dirt covering of the paintwork. It had perplexed him at first to find a car edged from the field into the shelter of the trees, and he had skirted it twice before gaining the courage to approach it. He had gazed inside, admired the shiny newness of the seat leather, and let his hand flit to the bright chrome door handle and felt it slide down under pressure. But he did not dare to climb into the car and sit in the driver's seat and hold the steering wheel as he would dearly liked to have done. His fun was in the writing of his name in big and bold wobbly letters.

His interest moved on and he walked away, that task completed, as the sun slipped, and he delayed his journey home to the farm only for that time that it took to pluck some wild flowers for his mother. He had little sense of the hour, but the chill that was rising from the grass, carried by the freshening wind, was enough to dictate his going. He ambled between the chewing cows, holding tightly to the stems of the flowers, admiring their colors. That his mother and father might be wondering where he was, might have a cruel anxiety for him, was beyond the assimilation of his young mind.

17

Together Archie Carpenter and Giuseppe Carboni
stood in the courtyard of the jail, far inside the high
swinging gates, ringed by walls and watchtowers and
men who patrolled catwalks with guns ready in their
hands. The Rebibbia prison, Carboni said, was the
maximum security holding center for the capital city.
A fearsome and odious place, it seemed to Carpenter,
where even in the open, where the wind could blow,
there was the smell of kitchens and lavatories, and a
community in confinement.

"She will be here one more day," intoned Carboni.
"Then we transfer her to Messina to await the courts.
God willing, it will be months before they drag her
into the light again."

"This is not your work, these are not the people you
are normally with?" A gentle query from Carpenter.

"I am a criminal policeman, I do not have a political
background. That is the can of worms for a policeman. But there is much willingness that I should be
the man who takes the weight of this action. There are
others better fitted than I, but they did not raise their
hands." There was a tight, resigned sadness on Car-

boni's face. "But that is how we live here, that is our
society. We do not fall down and wag our tails and
demand to be given the hardest task because that is
the way to honor and promotion, when the risk of failure is greatest. We are survivors, Carpenter. You will
learn that."

He broke off, his attention taken to the side door of
a small building that fronted off a towering five-story
cell block. *Carabinieri* with light machine guns led
the way, officers with medal ribbons followed and
then the prisoner. It was the sound of the chains, intrusive and strange to Carpenter, that alerted him to
the presence of Franca Tantardini, diminutive when
surrounded by so many taller men. A flower that is
choked by weeds. Carpenter shrugged. Stop the
bloody politicizing, Archie. And not a bad looker either. Good pair of hips on her.

No fear on the woman's face. A battleship under
steam, proud and devastating and intimidating. The
face that launched Giancarlo, chucked him far out to
sea.

"An impressive bit of woman, Mister Carboni."

"If you find a psychopath impressive, Carpenter,
then this one would meet your definition."

Overstepped the line, Archie. Taking the guided
tour for granted, as of right. You're the workhouse boy
here, out on a charity ride and taking favors. And remember what they brought you here to see. The
bloody enemy, Archie, the enemy of the state. They
watched as Franca Tantardini was led into the win-
dowless gray van with her jailers, and around them
there was running and movement and the revving of
engines from the escort cars; four of them, back windows lowered, machine guns protruding.

The rear of the van was held open and Carboni
moved rapidly inside, Carpenter following and chas-
tened.

"We are sensitive at this moment . . . about these people."

"Take my apology, it was the remark of an idiot."

"Thank you." A half smile, fast and then obliter-ated, replaced by the set and hard features of a man about his work. Carboni offered a hand to help Car-penter climb inside. There were two lines of benches in the interior, running against the sides, and the woman rested in a corner far from the door. Illumina-tion came from a single bulb protected by steel mesh. Carboni felt in his waist and produced his short-barreled pistol and handed it without comment to an escort who would sit away from the prisoner.

"You are armed, Carpenter?"

"No." A blush, as if he had displayed an inade-quacy.

The van drew away, slowly at first, then speeding forward, and the echo of the sirens in front and be-hind bathed through the shallow interior.

"Come and join me."

Carboni, a hand against the ceiling to preserve his balance, had struggled across the heaving floor and subsided onto the bench beside the woman. Carpen-ter took a place opposite her. Tantardini traversed her eyes, gazing at them both, the indifference heavy.

"Franca," the policeman spoke as if it hurt to use her first name, as if afterward he would soap-rinse his mouth. "I am Carboni of the Questura. I am in charge of the investigation into the kidnapping of an English businessman, Geoffrey Harrison . . ."

"Am I to be accused of that too," she laughed clearly.

"Is every crime in Rome to be set against the terri-ble, the fearsome Tantardini?"

"Listen to me, Franca. Listen and do not interrupt . . ." The talk was fast and Italian, leaving Carpenter far from any understanding. His attention was held only by the calm, bright face of the woman. " . . . Hear me out. He was taken, this Englishman, by a Calabresi group. Now he has been removed from them, and he is in the hands of your boy, your Giancarlo."

Again the laugh, and the rich, diamond smile. "Battestini could not deliver a letter . . ."

"He has killed three men, he has moved Harrison half across the country." Carboni pierced her with his small pig eyes. The heat in the van was intolerable, and he mopped at his face with a stained handkerchief. "Battestini holds the Englishman in Rome and demands your freedom against his prisoner's life."

There was a trickle of wonderment and surprise. "Battestini had done all this?"

"On his own, that is what we believe."

Almost a chuckle. "So why do you come to me?"

"You are going to my office now. In little more than an hour, in eighty minutes, Battestini will telephone to that office. He has demanded that he should talk with you. We have agreed that this should happen . . ."

Carpenter, the eyewitness, watched the tightening of the woman's body, saw the muscles ripple against the cloth of her jeans.

" . . . He is very young, this boy. Too young. I tell you something very honestly, Franca, if any harm should come to Harrison, then Giancarlo will die where we find him."

"Why tell this to me?"

"You bedded him, Franca," the words ripped in distaste from Carboni's mouth. "You poured the gasoline on his calf love. He does this for you."

The van had lost its speed, telling the occupants that the built-up sprawl of north Rome had been reached, and the sirens bellowed with a greater ferocity their demand that a passage be cleared for the convoy. Carpenter watched the woman as she lapsed into silence as if pondering what she had been told. The blanket of warm air wrapped all of them, and there was a drain of sweat leaking from her hairline down across the finely chiseled nose.

"What do you offer me?"

"I offer you the chance to save the boy's life. He is not of your sort, Franca. He is not a man of the *Nappisti*, he is a boy. You will go to jail for many years, not less than twenty. Help us now and it would be considered at your trial, there would be clemency."

As if from instinct, the scorn dappled at her mouth before the softness of the woman's lips was resurrected. "You ask me to secure the release of the Englishman?"

"That is what we ask of you."

"And I will talk with Giancarlo?"

"You will talk with him."

Carboni looked hard into her, waiting for the response, conscious that he had committed much of his future to a conversation of a few minutes. Whitened skin, pale as the flesh of an underground creature, hair that was not greased and ordered, tired to exhaustion.

"He is very young," the woman murmured. "Just a boy, just a pair of clumsy little hands . . ."

"Thank you, Franca. Your action will be rewarded."

What had been settled Carpenter could not know. Carboni had leaned back against the discomfort of the rolling metal wall, and Tantardini sat very still except that her fingers played on the links of the chains that fastened her wrists. And she wasn't wearing a bra either. Bloody marvelous sight, and the blouse must have shrunk in the last wash. Wrap it, Archie. Carboni seemed happy enough, something would have been sorted.

The van traveled at steady speed toward the inner city.

* * *

Only when the last of them had retreated noisily through the low yellow gorse clumps beneath the pines did Violet Harrison open her eyes again. Too dark under the trees for her to see his fleeing back, but there were the sounds for a long time of his blundering feet and his calls for his friends. The pain in her body was intense, bitter and vivid, and there was a chill seeping against her skin. But the cold was nothing set against the agony of the wounds provided by the boy Marco and his friends. The worst was at the gentle summit of her thighs, on the line where the tan and the whiteness split, where the bruises were forming. She did not cry out, was beyond tears and remorse, her horizon set only on controlling the virulence of the aching. The scratches on her face were alive where the nails had ripped her cheeks as she had writhed and sought to escape from them, and the harshness of the ground dug deep into the weak slackness of her buttocks that had been pounded, battered, into the earth surface.

At first it had been right, as she had prepared it, as her fantasies had dictated.

She and the boy Marco had gone together from the heat of the beach to the shade of the pine canopy. A narrow path that flicked the gorse against her bared legs below the hem of the loose beach dress had led them to a place that was hidden, where the scrub formed a fortress wall of privacy. Swimming to the ground, she had slipped the dress over her head, an absence of words and invitation because everything was implicit and unspoken. First the bikini top, loosened by herself because his hands were jumping with nervousness, and then the cupping of her breasts till the boy was panting, frantic. Fingers leaping over her, and Violet Harrison lying back, willing him on, exposed. Fingers on the smoothness of her belly and reaching down and feeling for her and hunting for her, and she clutching at the dark curled hair on his head. That was when she had heard the giggles of the watchers, and she had started up, arms crossing her chest, and they had come like hyenas to a prey. One on each arm and Marco pulling her knees apart, cutting at her with the sharpness of his nails, and tugging at the slight cotton fabric of the bikini bottom. The sweet smile of respect lost from Marco's face, replaced by the bared teeth of the rampant rat. First Marco, penetrating and deep and hard and hurting her because she was not ready. And when he was spent, then the first friend came, and there was a hand across her mouth and her arms were spread for crucifixion. After the first friend, the second, and then Marco again, and nothing said among them. Just the driving of the hips and the gush of their excitement at the forbidden. Too good to miss, Marco's fortune. Right that it should be shared among his friends. The last had not even managed, and when she spat in his face and his friends jeered encouragement, he had raked her cheek and she had felt the warm blood sprinkle her skin. He had rolled away leaving only his eyes and those of the other two boys to perpetuate the violation.

The tears would be later, back at the flat, back at their home, when she thought again of Geoffrey.

She stood up on her weakened legs.

Out loud, "God help me that he should never know."

What if this were the time that he was preparing to die, what if this was the moment that he clutched at an image of Violet? What if it were now that he looked for her as she was walking on a path in strange woods, her clothes devastated, her modesty laughed over and splintered?

"Never let him find out, please God. Never."

She had not even spoken to him when he left the house that morning. She had lain in bed, her night-dress tight around her, aware of his movements in the flat, but she had not called him, because she never did, because they had only banalities to speak of.

"Forgive me, Geoffrey. Please, please."

Only if Geoffrey died would he never know. Only then would she be safe in her secret. And he must live, because she had betrayed him and was not fit for the weeds of the widow, for the hypocrisy of condol-ence. She must will him to live. A terminal patient of catastrophic internal illness sometimes comes back, al-ways there is hope, always there is chance. And then he will know, if the miracle is enacted, he will know.

Violet Harrison ran on the pine-needle rug. The pain of the wounds was subsidiary to the greater hurt of shame and humiliation. She skirted the trattoria, darkened and shuttered, and sprinted for the parking area. Her hand plunged into her bag, wrenched at the cosmetics in the search for the car keys. When she sat in the driver's seat, ignition fired, she trembled with the tears that had been stifled.

"Come home, Geoffrey. Even if no one is there. Come home, my brave darling, come home."

"Goodbye, 'arrison."

Giancarlo could barely see his prisoner against the dirt black of the earth pit.

"Goodbye, Giancarlo." A faint voice, devoid of hope.

"I will be back soon." As if Harrison needed to be reassured, as if all his ordeal was a fear of being alone with darkness. A slight stirring of warmth and the nudge of communication. Was the confidence of the boy failing, was the certainty sliding?

Giancarlo slipped away along the path, feeling with

his arms outstretched in front of him for the low branches. There was much time, there was no haste.

He had come so far, and yet where was the measure of his achievement? A bramble stem caught with its spikes at the material of his trousers. He tore himself clear. Had he advanced his claim to Franca's freedom? His ankle turned under a protruding root. The P38 dug at the skin of his waist, the acknowledgment that this was his sole power of persuasion, his only right to be heard and known in the great city to the south, basking in its summer evening.

The breath of darkness had eddied into the courtyard of the Questura. The headlights and roof lamps of the convoy from the Rebibbia gleamed out their urgency as they swung through the archway from the outside street into the parking area. More shouting, more running men, more guns as the van was backed toward an opened door that led directly to the cell corridor. Among those who worked late in the city's police headquarters there were many who hurried down the internal staircases and craned from the upper windows that they might catch a brief glimpse of "La Tantardini." They were rewarded sparsely, a flash of the color of her blouse as she was manhandled the few feet from the van steps to the entrance of the building, and disappearance.

Carboni did not follow her, but stood in the center of the courtyard among the reversing, straightening cars that jockeyed for the last parking places. Archie Carpenter stood a few feet from him, sensing that the policeman preferred his own thoughts for company.

She had been long gone from their sight when Carboni threw off the spell, turned to look for Carpenter. "You would not have understood what passed between us."

"Not a word, I'm sorry."

"I have to be brief . . ." Carboni began to walk toward the principal entrance to the building, ignoring the many who watched him as an object of interest now that the woman was gone. "The boy will telephone at eight. I have to trace that call. I must know the location from where he telephones. To trace the call I must have time. Only when he talks to Tantardini will he gabble on. He will talk to her." Carboni's face was cut with anxiety. "I have told her that if Harrison is harmed, then we will kill Battestini wherever we find him, that if she cooperates, then clemency will be shown her in the courts."

"Which you have no power to guarantee."

"Right, Carpenter, no power at all. But now they have plenty to talk of, and they will use quickly the time that the engineers need. I have no other option but reliance on the trace procedure."

Carpenter spoke quietly, "You have one other option. To free Tantardini for Harrison's life."

"Don't joke with me, Carpenter, not now. Later when it is finished."

They stopped at the outer door of Carboni's office. The retort was rising in Carpenter's throat, but he suppressed it and thought for the first time how ludicrous to these people was the proposition that seemed straight and clear and commonsense.

"I wish you luck, Mr. Carboni."

"Only luck . . . you are mean with your favors, Englishman."

They entered the office and Carpenter was quick to appraise the mood, sensitive to the atmosphere of downed heads, flattened feet, gloom and frustration. This was Carboni's own team and if they were not believing in success, then who was he to imagine in his mind the incredible. Carpenter watched as Carboni moved among the hastily installed desks and tables and the teleprinters in the outer room, speaking softly to his men. He saw the line of shaken heads, the mournful mutters of the negative. Like he's going round a cancer ward and nobody's carrying the good news, nobody's lost his pains, nobody thinks he's coming through. Poor bastard, thought Carpenter.

Carboni expended a long, powered sigh and slumped to the chair behind his desk. With a sense of theater, of tragedy, he slapped a hand onto the cream-colored telephone receiver in front of him.

"Call Vellosi. Get him to come here. Not the same room as this . . . but ask him to be close." He rubbed at the weariness in his eyes. "Bring her up now, bring Tantardini."

The child fled from the raw, opened hand of his mother.

Nimble on his feet, he dodged the swinging blow, scattered the posy of wild flowers onto the stone slabs of the kitchen floor, and scampered for the corridor that led to his bedroom.

"All afternoon I've been calling you from the house . . ."

"I was only in the wood, Mama." He called shrilly in his fright from the sanctuary of his room.

"I even went and bothered your father in the field . . . he called too . . . he wasted his time when he was busy . . ."

"Mama, in the wood, I saw . . ."

His mother's voice boomed back, surging to him, as in falsetto she mimicked his small voice. "I saw a fox . . . I saw a rabbit . . . I followed the flight of a hawk. You'll have no supper tonight. Into your night clothes . . . sick with worry you had me."

He waited, trying to gauge the scale of her anger, the enormity of his fault, then wheedled in justification. "Mama, in the woods I saw . . ."

She bit her interruption back at him.

"Silence your chatter, silence it and get yourself to your bed. And you'll not sit with your father after his supper. Not another sound from you or I'll be in after you."

"But Mama . . ."

"I'll be in and after you."

"Good night, Mama, may the Virgin watch over you and Papa tonight."

The voice was small, the fluency broken by the first tears on the child's smoothed-down cheeks. His mother stabbed with her upper teeth at her lower lip. It was not right to shout at a small child. He had so few to play with and where else was there for him to go but to the woods or to the fields with his father? Better when he started school in the autumn. But she had been frightened by his absence, and she consoled herself that her punishment of her only little one was for his own good. She returned to the preparation of her man's supper.

Throughout the city and its suburbs the security net was poised. More than five hundred cars and trucks and riot vans were on the streets. They wore the colors of the *Primo Celere*, and the *Squadra Volante* and the *Squadra Mobile*. Others were decorated in the royal blue of the *carabinieri*. There were the unmarked cars of the undercover men, and SISDE, the secret service. The agencies of government poised to spring should the engineers of the Questura basement provide reference from which Giancarlo Battestini telephoned. Engines ticking idly, watches and clocks repeatedly examined, machine guns on the back seats of cars, on the metal floors of vans. A great army, but one which rested till the arrival of the orders and instructions without which it was a helpless and useless force.

On the fifth floor of the Questura, in the control center, the technicians had exhausted the lights available on their wall map for marking the position of their interception vehicles. A clock creeping on twenty hours had silenced conversation and movement, leaving only the mindless hum of an air-conditioner system.

Grim-faced, wearing his years, Francesco Vellosi strode from the central doors of the Viminale to his car which waited at the apex of the half-moon drive. The men who were to escort him to the Questura fidgeted in the seats of the cars that would follow. As he settled in the back seat he was aware of the clatter of the loading of weapons. From an upper room the Minister watched him go, then resumed his tiger pacing of the carpet. He would hear by telephone of the night's developments.

Nothing to impede Giancarlo, a fierce moonlight to guide his way. A stream of cars on the road. Of course there would be cars, for this was a resort of the Roman summer, and there was nothing extraordinary that a driver would find with a youth with the long hair of a student, the T-shirt and jean uniform of the unemployed. On the road he did not flinch from the blinding beams of the headlights. On down the hill he walked till he could see the still reflection of the lights of the trattorias and bars playing on the distance of smooth water. On down the hill, with only occasional stolen glimpses at the slow-moving hands of his watch. The fools with their wives and girls, they would know of Giancarlo Battestini. Those who rushed past him in their impatience in their cars, they would know of him tomorrow. Tomorrow they would know his name and roll it on their tongues and savor it, and try to ask how, and try to ask why.

The pavements beside the lake were filled with

those who drifted in aimless procession. They did not
look to the boy. Safe in their own lives, safe in their
own businesses, they ignored him.

At the *ristorante* the booth with the telephone was
empty. He darted his eyes again to his watch. Patience, Giancarlo, a few more minutes only. He collected the *gettoni* from the knot in his handkerchief
where they had been segregated. Noise and purchased
happiness crept from the interior. Where he stood,
hemmed in by the glass walls of the cubicle, he could
see the mouths that burst with pasta, the hands grasp-
ing at the wine bottles, the bellies that rocked over
the table tops. Tomorrow they would not shriek in
their gusts of laughter. Tomorrow they would talk of
Giancarlo Battestini till it consumed them, till it
burned them, the very repetition of the name. His
name.

The child's father came to the stone-walled, tin-
roofed farmhouse when there was no longer light for
him to work his fields. A tired, sleep-ridden man looking for his food and his chair and his television and
his rest.

His wife chided him for the late hour, played the
scolder, till she kissed him, light and pecking, on a
hair-roughened cheek; to her he was a good man, full
of work, heavy in responsibility, a loyal man to his
family, who depended on the long-drawn-out power
of his muscles to make a living from the coarse hillside
fields. His food would soon be ready and she would
bring it on a tray to their living room where the old
television set, provider of black and white pictures,
sat proudly on a coarse wooden table. Perhaps later, if
he had not already drifted to sleep, the boy could sit
with him, for her anger had evaporated with the passing of her fear at his absence.

He had not replied when she told her man of the

time their child had returned and the punishment exacted, just shrugged and turned to the sink to wash
away the day's grime. She held sway over the domestic routine and it was not for him to challenge her authority. Hearing him safely settled she hurried to her
stove, lifted the big metal saucepan down, and
drained the steaming water from the pasta, while
through the opened doorway blazoned the music of
the opening of the evening's news program. She did
not go to watch beside her husband; all day the radio
channels had shown themselves obsessed with an
event from the city. City people, city troubles. Not
relevant to a woman with stone floors to be scrubbed
daily, a never-filled purse, and a distant, difficult
child to rear. She set the pasta on a plate, doused it in
the brilliant red of the tomato sauce, flecked it with
the grated cheese, and carried it to her man, flopped
in his chair. She could take satisfaction from the con-
tented smile on her husband's face, and the way that
he shook off his weariness, sat himself upright, and
the speed with which his fork drove down into the
lengths of the brilliant butter-coated spaghetti.

On the screen were photographs of a man with
combed hair and a knotted tie and the smile that read
responsibility and success, replaced by those of a boy
whose face showed confrontation and fight and the
trapped gaze of a prisoner. There was a picture of a
car and a map of the *mezzo giorno* . . . She stayed
no longer.

"Animals," she said, and returned to her kitchen and
her work.

At one hundred and forty kilometers an hour, Violet
Harrison careened along the dual highway of the Rác-
cordo.

Her handbag lay on the seat beside her, but she did
not bother to winkle out the square lace handkerchief

with which she might have dabbed her puffed, tear-laden eyes. Only Geoffrey in her thoughts, only the man with whom she lived a rotten, neutered life, and who now, in her fear, she loved more than she had ever before been capable of. Commitment to Geoffrey, the boring little man who had shared her home and her bed for a dozen years. Geoffrey, who polished the heels of his shoes, brought home work from the office, thought marriage was a girl with a gin waiting at the front door for the return of the frontiersman husband. Geoffrey, who didn't know how to laugh. Poor little Geoffrey. In the hands of the pigs, as she had warmed and nestled close to a stranger on a crowded beach, and watched the front of his costume and believed that prayers were answered.

Beyond the grass and barriers of the divider, cars rushed past her, swallowed in the night, blazing headlights lost as fast as they had reared in front of her. The lights played on her eyes, flashed and reflected in the moisture of her tears, cavorted in her vision as tumbling cascades and aerosols of lights and stars.

That was why, beyond the Aurelia turnoff from the Raccordo, she did not see the signs beside the road that warned of the approaching end of the dual highway, did not read the great painted arrows on the road surface. That was why she was oblivious to the closing lights of the fruit truck bound for Naples.

The impact was immense, searing in noise and speed, the agony howl of the ripped metal of the car. A fractional moment of collision, and then the car was tossed away, as if its weight were trifling. The car rose high in the air before crashing down, destroyed and unrecognizable, in the center of the road.

The face of Geoffrey Harrison, its lines and its contours, was frozen in his wife's mind in the final broken seconds of her life. The sound of herself speaking his name was bolted to her tongue.

There was much traffic returning at that time from the coast. Many sitting behind their wheels would curse the unseen source of the lines that built on either side of the accident, and then shudder and avert their faces as they witnessed in their lights the reason for their delay.

In front of Carboni's desk, Franca Tantardini sat on a hard, unprepossessing chair. She was upright, taking little notice of the men who bustled around her, gazing only at the window with its dark abyss and undrawn curtains. The fingers of her hands were entwined on her lap, the chains removed. More like a waiting bride than a prisoner. She had not replied when she had first come into the room and Carboni had taken her to a corner and spoken in his best bedside hush beyond the ears of his subordinates.

Archie Carpenter's eyes never left her. Not the sort of creature that he had handled when he was with Special Branch in London. His career spanned the years before the Irish watch, before the bombers came in earnest. Not much color in those days for Carpenter who was concerned with the machinations of the far-out shop stewards, the Marxist militants, and that old source of inspiration, the Soviet Trade Delegation from Highgate. His had been the old Branch, the archeological specimen that withered and died in its ice age before learning the new techniques of the war against urban terrorism. The guerrilla fighter was a new phenomenon for Archie Carpenter, something experienced only through newspapers and television screens. But there seemed to be nothing special in the woman, nothing to put her on the pedestal. Well, what do you expect, Archie? A Che Guevera T-shirt, the hammer and cycle tattooed on her forehead?

The telephone rang on Carboni's desk.

Difficult really to know what to expect. Criminals the world over, all the same. Whether it's political, whether it's material. Big, fat, bouncy kids when they've the air of freedom to breathe. Miserable little bastards when the door closes behind them, when they've twenty years of sitting on a blanket.

Carboni grabbed at the receiver, snatching it from the cradle.

Thought she'd have more fight in her, from the way they cracked her up. Belt it, Archie, for Christ's sake.

"Carboni."

"The call that you have been waiting for, Dottore."

"Connect it."

The light bulb had been removed from the telephone booth. In the half dark Giancarlo watched the second hand of his watch moving slowly on its path. He knew the available time, was aware of the ultimate danger. With one hand he held the telephone pressed hard against his right ear, the noise of the *ristorante* stifled.

"*Pronto,* Carboni." A voice fused in metallic interference.

"Battestini." He had used his own name, chipped at the pretense.

"Good evening, Giancarlo."

"I have little time . . ."

"You have as much time as you want, Giancarlo."

The sweat rivers ran on the boy's face. "Will you meet the demands of the Nuclei Armati Proletaria . . . ?"

The voice cut back at him, smothering his words. "The demands of Giancarlo Battestini, not of the *Nappisti.*"

"We stand together as a movement, we . . ." He

broke off, absorbed in the motion of his watch, ticking on its way, edging toward fiasco.

"You are there, Giancarlo?"

The boy hesitated. Forty seconds gone, forty seconds of the two minutes that was required for a trace.

"I have demanded the freedom of Franca . . . that is what must happen if 'arrison is to live . . ."

"It is a very complicated matter, Giancarlo. There are many things to be considered." There was an awful, deadening calmness in the response. A sponge that he hit at but could not mark.

Close to a minute gone.

"There is one question only, Carboni. Yes or no . . . ?"

The first hint of anxiety broke in the distorted voice, the noise of breathing mingled with the atmospherics. "We have Franca here for you to talk with, Giancarlo."

"Yes or no, that was my question."

More than a minute gone, the hand on its second arc.

"Franca will talk to you."

All eyes in the room on the face of Franca Tantardini.

Carboni held the telephone mouthpiece against his shirt, looked deep and far into the woman, and saw only the blank, proud, composed eyes, and knew that this was the ultimate moment of risk. Nothing to read from her mouth and from her hands that did not fidget, showed no impatience. Total silence, and a leaden atmosphere which even Carpenter, without Italian language, could sense and be fearful of.

"I trust you, Franca," barely audible the words as Carboni's hand with the telephone stretched out toward the responding arm of La Tantardini.

There was a carelessness now in her smile. Almost

human. Long, slender fingers exchanged for the fatty,
stumpy grip of Carboni's fist. When she spoke it was
with a clear and educated voice, no roughened edges,
no slang of the gutter. The daughter of a well-placed
family of Bergamo.

"It is Franca, my little fox . . . do not interrupt me.
Hear me to the finish . . . and little fox, do as I instruct you, exactly as I instruct you. They have asked
me to tell you to surrender. They have asked me to
tell you that you should release the Englishman . . ."

Carboni permitted his eyes, in secrecy, to float to
his watch. One minute and twenty seconds since the
call was initiated. He saw the image of activity in the
Questura basement. The isolation of the communication, the evaluation of the digital dialing process, the
routing of the connection back toward its source. He
strained forward to hear better her words.

"You have asked for my release, little fox. Listen to
me. There will be no freedom. So I say this to you,
Giancarlo. This is the last . . ."

It was the action of a moment. Franca Tantardini
on her feet. Right arm high above her head, the fist in
clenched salute. A face riven with hatred. Muscles of
the neck bulged.

". . . kill him, Giancarlo. Kill the pig. *Forza la proletaria. Forza la rivoluzione!* Giancarlo, *la lotta con-
tinua* . . ."

Even as they were rising to their feet, the men
about her, struggling to reach her, she had moved
whiplash fast toward the receiver on Carboni's desk.
As she wrenched at the telephone, tearing its cord
from the wall fitting, they pounded her to the ground.
The little men of the room kicked and punched at the
unresisting body of the woman while Carboni and
Carpenter, separated by the melee, and on their different sides of the office, sat stock-still and assessed the
scope of the catastrophe.

"Take her back to the Rebibbia, and I want no marks on her . . . none that can be seen." A terrible ice-cold in his voice, as if the shock wave of betrayal had broken Giuseppe Carboni.

Another telephone ringing. He picked it up, placed it to his ear, and dropped his weight onto an elbow. As he listened he watched Franca Tantardini half carried, half dragged, take her leave of him. Carboni nodded as information was given him, offered no gratitude for the service.

"They say, from the basement, that I had told them they would have a minimum of two minutes to find the trace. They say that I gave them one minute and forty seconds. They say that was not sufficient. I have failed your man, Carpenter, I have failed your man."

Carpenter spat back at him. "They gave you nothing?"

"Just that it was from the north of the city . . ."

Carpenter stood up and walked toward the door. Wanted to say something vicious, wanted to let the frustration go, and couldn't find it in himself. Not to kick a dog, not one that's already limping, that has the mange at its collar. Nothing he could say. Grown men, weren't they? Not kids who could bully. All adults, all trying, all confronted by the same cancer that was eating deep and ravenously.

"I'm going around to Charlesworth's place. The embassy fellow. You can reach me there . . . till late."

"I will be here."

Of course he would be. Where else for him? No embassy duty-free Scotch for Giuseppe Carboni, no shutting out of the problem with eight percent proof to drown its life away. Carpenter let himself out, didn't look back at Carboni, and walked off down the corridor to the staircase.

Through the connecting door and into the inner sanctum marched Francesco Vellosi. Uninhibited hatred on his face, brutal and devastating, informing Carboni that he had heard the words of Tantardini.

"I told you to be careful, Carboni, I told you."

"You told me . . ."

A strand of sympathy shone. "Anything?"

"With the time available, nothing of substance, nothing that matters."

Their arms around each other's waists, in mutual consolation, the two men walked from the room to the wire cage elevator for the fifth floor.

They would saturate an area of slightly more than three thousand five hundred square kilometers. Viterbo in the north to La Storta in the south, the western limit would be the coastal town of Civitaveccia and the eastern line would be the Roma-Firenza autostrada. Formality, the task provided by the basement technicians. Too great an area for a manhunt, too great an area to lift the man's bowed shoulders.

As they emerged from the elevator, Vellosi said softly, "They will crucify you, they will say she should never have spoken to the boy."

"It was the best chance to make him talk for longer."

"Who will say that? You will be torn apart, Carboni, the entertainment of the wild dogs."

Arms still around each other, faces close, Carboni looking up and Vellosi down, eyes meeting. "But you will be with me, Vellosi."

Only a smile, only a tightening of the fist in the material of Carboni's shirt, as they came to the operations center.

The child's head, wearing the winning smile, drifted around the kitchen door.

"Mama," the plaintive call. "Can I sit with Papa?"

"You were a bad boy today."

"I'm sorry, Mama . . ."

She had no stomach for the fight, was pleased the child had come from his room, exorcising her shame that she had lost her temper and tried to strike him. God knows they both worshiped their son.

"Papa is tired." She heard the distant steady snore from her man's throat, the warm food cossetted in him, the burned energy of the day seeking replacement. "You can sit with him, but don't you bother him, don't you wake him . . ."

The child waited for no more hesitation from his mother. He raced in his light bare feet, his loose pyjamas flowing, through the kitchen and into the living room.

His mother listened.

"Papa, are you asleep? Papa, can I tell you what I saw in the wood? Please, Papa . . ."

She slapped the towel across her hands, summoned herself across the room in a cloak of annoyance, and hissed through the doorway at the sofa where the child snuggled against his sleeping father.

"What did I say to you . . . that you were not to wake him. Another word from you and you go to your bed. Leave Papa alone. You talk to Papa in the morning."

"Yes, Mama, can I watch the program?"

A concert flickered on the aged screen, the harmony of the notes suffering from the distortion of the set. She nodded her head. That was permitted, and it was good for the boy to sit with his father.

"But don't you wake Papa . . . and don't you argue when I call you for bed."

18

The sounds of Giancarlo returning carried to Geoffrey Harrison from far away. The arrival was blundering and clumsy, as if silence and stealth were no longer of importance. The noise spread through the quiet of the wood where there was nothing to compete with the snapping of branches, the crushing of fallen leaves. He would not be able to see the boy's face when he came, would not be able to recognize the mood and the danger. A blessing or an accidental wound? Better to know when the boy was still far from him, better his news while the creature was still distant.

They say some men die well and others die badly. Harrison remembered when he was a kid and he'd read in a magazine stories of executions by law in a jail. They said some had screamed and some walked with head high, some were carried and some went unaided and thanked the men around them for their courtesy. What bloody difference did it make? Who looks at a skinned pig hanging from a butcher's hook and says, "That pig would have died well, you can see it on his face, brave bugger, well done." Who looks at the carcass and thinks of its going?

You'll crawl, Geoffrey, grovel on your knees, because that's the way you are. The bender and the compromiser. Have to be, don't you? Because that's the way you do business, and you're good at business, Geoffrey. That's why International Chemical Holdings sent you here, sent you to lie on your side with the hair growing on your face and the smell from your socks and pants, and the hunger in your belly, and the pain at your wrists, and a kid coming to kill you. Crawl, Geoffrey, play the lizard scuffing on his stomach through the deadwood. That's the way of commerce. Know when you can fight and when you can lose, and if it's defeat then turn the cheek and summon the sweet words and save something for the shareholders. Bloody shareholders. Fat women in Hampstead, poodles and jewels, apartments with lifts, and deceased husbands. For you, you bitches, for you I'm lying here, listening to him coming.

There were the moments for escape, Geoffrey. In the car, plenty of them, each time you stopped . . . God, do we go through all that again? It's a big grown-up world, Geoffrey. Nanny isn't here anymore. No one to save you but yourself. Why isn't little Giancarlo messing his knickers, why isn't he frightened that his time is coming? Because he believes in something, idiot. It's a faith, it has a meaning to him.

And Geoffrey Harrison has no creed.

Who does Geoffrey Harrison fight for? What principle?

Where is his army of companions who will weep if one of their number falls?

Another bloody casualty, Geoffrey, and there will be a public sadness in Head Office, and a few will scratch their heads and try and remember the chap who went aboard because it paid more. But don't expect there's going to be any wet on the blotting paper, any stains on the ledgers, any flags pulled down.

Remember the bar at the Olgiata Gold Club. Red faces and long gins. Men who were always right, always knew. Remember the bar of the Golf Club when Aldo Moro was cringing for the world to see and pleading in the letters to his friends for government capitulation to preserve his life from the Red Brigades.

Despicable behavior. The man had no dignity.

What you'd expect from these people.

Only have to go back to the war, in North Africa, show 'em a bayonet and you've more prisoners on your hands than you can feed.

What a wonderful wallowing security, membership of the Golf Club. They'll make hay of you, Geoffrey. The man who came back for nine holes after he'd been on his knees with the tears on his cheeks and the sobbing in his throat, and pleaded and held the legs of a boy half his age.

Got to fight 'em, show 'em there's going to be no nonsense. That's the way to beat the scum.

Giancarlo was very close, and his voice pierced the darkness.

"They want you dead, 'arrison."

Harrison wriggled and dragged at the wires, tried to turn to face the boy. Managed a few inches.

"What do you mean?"

"They do nothing to save you."

"What did they say?"

"They tried only to use up time so that they could trace the call."

"What did Franca say?" The questions from Harrison blurted at the center of the shadow above him.

"Franca told me to kill you. She said they would not release her. She told me to kill you . . ."

A whisper from Harrison. The breached corn sack, from which the grain spills. "Franca said that?"

It's a bloody dream, Geoffrey.

"I'm not your enemy, Giancarlo. I've done nothing to hurt you." And where was the bastard's face, molded in the blackness. How could you crawl before a boy with no face, how did you win him with your fear and your misery? "I've never tried to harm you . . ."

"Franca said I was to kill you."

"For Christ's sake, Giancarlo. I'm no enemy of the Italian proletariat, I'm not in the way of your revolution."

"You are a symbol of oppression and exploitation."

"It's like you're reading out of the telephone book, they don't mean anything, those words. You can't take a life for a slogan."

The same dripping voice, the same cruelty in the unseen eyes. "There can be no revolution without blood. Not just your blood, 'arrison. We die in the streets for what we believe is a just struggle. We face the living death in the concentration camps of the regime. Twenty years she will exist in Messina . . ."

"Don't talk to me about other people." The dream clearing, the nightmare fading. "It helps you not at all, not if you kill me. You must see that, Giancarlo, please say you can see that . . ."

"You are pathetic, 'arrison. You are of the middle class, you are of the multinational, you have an apartment on a hill . . . should you not defend that way? Should you not defend that exploitation? I despise you."

The silence fell fast because the killing words of the boy struck far. Harrison lay still and heard the sounds of Giancarlo dropping to sit on the ground a dozen feet from the bunker. Man and boy, they drifted to their own thoughts.

Crawl to him, Geoffrey. It's not the Golf Club's life, forget the humiliation. That he couldn't grovel, what a thing for a man to die over.

Shrill little words and a voice he did not recognize as his own. "What do I have to do, Giancarlo? For you not to kill me, what do I have to do?"

The Judas movement, Geoffrey. The betrayal of his society. The boy had read him, that he belonged nowhere, was a part of nothing. "Answer me please."

Endlessly the boy waited. The wave rolled back from the beach, then gathered itself in white-crested accumulation, burst again, shattering with force on the sand. The reply of Giancarlo.

"You cannot do anything."

"Afterwards I will say what you have told me to say."

"Franca has ordered it, you cannot do anything."

"I will go to the newspapers and the radio and the television, I will say what you want me to . . ."

The boy seemed bored, as if wishing the conversation terminated. Could the man not understand what he was told? "You chose a way for your life, I have chosen mine. I will fight against what is rotten, you will prop it up. I do not recognize the white flag, that is not the way of our combat."

Harrison was crying, convulsing, the great tears welling in his eyes, dribbling on his cheeks, wetting at his mouth. "You take a pleasure in it . . ."

There was a sternness in the boy. "We are at war, and you should behave like a soldier. Because you do not I despise you. It will be at nine o'clock in the morning. You have till then to become a soldier."

"You horrid, repulsive little bastard . . . they'll give you no mercy . . . you'll die in the fucking gutter."

"We ask for no mercy, 'arrison. We offer none."

Quiet again in the forest. Giancarlo spread himself on the leaves. He pushed with his hands to make the surface more even, wriggled onto his side so that his back was turned on Geoffrey Harrison, and beneath a ceiling of moonlight, flecked by the high branches, settled himself. For a few minutes he could hear the foreign sounds of his prisoner's choking sobs. Then he found sleep and they were lost to him.

The sun of the day and the food of the evening ensured the farmer's sleep, and his rest was escape from the worries that burgeoned his life. The price of fodder, the price of fertilizer, the price of diesel for the tractor could all be shut out only when his mind was damp and at peace. His child stayed silent, close to the rise and fall of his father's chest, and waited with a concentrated patience, fighting off his own tiredness. Beyond the doorway the child heard the sounds of his mother, and they spurred his stillness as he lay fearful that any stirring on the damaged springs of the sofa would alert and remind her that he was not yet in his small bed.

Mingled with the music were the mind pictures that the child drew for himself. Pictures that were alien and hostile.

"Come on in, Archie."

"Thank you, Michael." Didn't slip off the tongue that easily, not the Christian name, not after the hard words. Charlesworth stood in the doorway with a loose shirt on him, no tie, and slacks and sandals. Carpenter fidgeted at the door in his suit.

"Come on into the den."

Carpenter was led through the hall. Delicate furniture, a case of hardback books, oil paintings on the wall, a vase of tall irises. Do all right, these people . . . stop bitching, Archie, drop the chip off your shoulder. You can't blame people for not living in Motspur Park, not if they've the choice.

"Darling, this is Archie Carpenter, from Harrison's head office. My wife, Caroline."

Carpenter shook hands with the tall, tanned girl presented to him. The sort they bred down in Cheltenham, along with fox hunters and barley fields. She wore a dress held at the shoulders by thin straps. The wife back in the semi would have had a fit, blushed like an August rose, no bra and entertaining.

"I'm sorry I'm late, Mrs. Charlesworth. I've been at the Questura."

"You poor thing, you'd like a wash."

Well, he wouldn't have asked for it himself, but he'd worn a jacket all day, and the same socks, and he stank like a hung duck.

"I'll take him, darling."

An older man was rising heavily from a sofa. Washing could wait, introductions first. Charlesworth resumed the formalities. "This is Colonel Henderson, our military attaché."

"Please to meet you, Colonel."

"They call me 'Buster,' Archie. I've heard about you. I hear you've a straight tongue in your head, and a damned good thing too."

Carpenter was led to the peace of an outer bathroom. Time for him as he stood in front of the sink to examine the sentry row of deodorant sprays on the windowsill, enough to keep the embassy smelling sweet for a month. And books too. Who was going to read classical Greek history and contemporary American politics while having a squat? Extraordinary people. The reek of public school and private means. He washed his hands, let the day's grime dribble away, pushed a washcloth round the back of his neck. Long live the creature comforts. Soap and water and a waiting gin.

They sat around in the lounge, the four of them, separated by carpets and marble flooring and sprouting coffee tables. Carpenter didn't resist the demand that he shed his jacket, loosen his tie.

"Well, tell us, Archie, what's the scene at the Questura?" Charlesworth setting the ball rolling."

"I think they've screwed it . . ."

"For that poor Mr. Harrison . . . ?"

Carpenter ignored Caroline Charlesworth. What did they want, a coffee morning chat with the neighbors, or something from the bloody horse's mouth?

"Tantardini got her hands on the telephone too early in the game for the trace people. Told her boy to chop Harrison, then pulled the connection. The call was still at the switchboard but the boy had the message. He rang off, and that's about it."

Charlesworth was leaning forward in his seat, glass held between his two hands. The honest and earnest young man, he seemed to Carpenter. "She gave a specific instruction for the boy to kill Harrison?"

"That's the way Carboni put it. 'I have failed your man,' those were his words. Biggest bloody understatement of the day."

"He's a good man, Giuseppe Carboni." Charlesworth spoke with enough compassion for Carpenter momentarily to squirm. "It's not easy, not in a country like this. Right, Buster?"

The Colonel swirled his whisky round the glass. "We had full powers in many places, what you'd call nowadays totalitarian powers, in Palestine and Malaya and Kenya and Cyprus. Here the legacy of prewar fascism is that the security forces are kept weak. But for all that we had it didn't do us a great deal of good."

"But that was far from the great Mother Britain," Carpenter interjected impatiently. "This is different, this is behind their own doorstep that they're being whipped. Carboni excepted, they're ambling about like bloody zombies . . ."

"They're trying, Archie," Charlesworth intervened gently.

"I wouldn't care to make a judgment on their efficiency if I'd been here just a few hours." The Colonel cut at the air, the swinging of the old cavalry saber.

Carpenter put his hands above his head, grinned for a moment, dissolved the tempers. "I'm outnumbered, outflanked, whatever . . . so what I want to know is this . . . when they say they'll chop him, when Battestini says it, do we take that at face, is it gospel?"

Caroline Charlesworth started from her chair. The plea to be excused from the blunt assessments. "The dinner won't be more than a few minutes."

"You answer that, Buster," Charlesworth said. "It's the pertinent question of the evening."

The hard, clean eyes of the veteran fixed on Carpenter. "The answer is affirmative. When they say they'll kill, they're good to their word."

"Black tie job?"

"I repeat it, Mr. Carpenter, they're good to their word."

Caroline Charlesworth appeared from the kitchen doorway. The food was ready. She led, the men followed. In the dining room Carpenter saw the wine on the table, the port and brandy on the sideboard. There was solace to be found here, escape from a hideous and crippling mess.

Late into the evening, the child's mother came at last for him. With a sweep of her hand she hushed his protest, and swept him up so that he sat on her hip as she took him from the side of his father. It was done quickly and expertly and the farmer seemed as unaware of the child's going as he had been of his presence. She nuzzled her nose against her son's neck, saw the fight that he had to keep his eyes open, and chided herself that she had left him for so long. She carried him to his room.

"Mama."

"Yes, my sweet." She lowered him into the bed.

"Mama, if Papa wakes soon, will he come to see me?"

"You will be asleep, in the morning you will see him." She pulled the coarse sheet to his chin.

"I have to tell him what I saw . . ."

"What was it, a wild pig, the big dog fox . . . ?" She watched the yawn break on the child's face.

"Mama, I saw . . ."

Her kiss stifled his words, and she slipped on her toes from the room.

At this time of the evening it was the work of the *agente* to make a final check of the cell doors after the prisoners held in maximum security had finished communal recreation and were consigned for the night to their individual cells. His pracitce was a quick glance through the peephole and then the sliding of the greased bolt. Others would come after him when the lights were dimmed to make the last muster call of the night.

The *agente* had found the paper, folded once, on the mat at the front door of his home. A small piece, ragged at an edge where it had been torn from a note pad. There was a penciled number on the outside flap that was immediately relevant to the *agente*. Three digits, the number of the cell of the Chief of Staff of the *Nappisti*.

When he reached that door, the *agente* pushed it a few inches, tossed the paper inside, crashed the bolt home, and was on his way. Any colleague who might have seen him would not have been aware of the passing of the message.

The *capo* abandoned his weekly letter to his mother in the hill city of Siena, saw the paper and slipped from his chair to gather it.

L'amministrazione dice non per Tantardini.

No freedom for Tantardini, it was as he had said. What he had anticipated, because the Englishman was of insufficient importance. Inevitable, but better that way, better if the ultimatum were to expire, the gun were to be fired. The strategy of tension they called it in the Roman newspapers, the creation of intolerable fear. The death of the enemy created fear, something not achieved by negotiation and the making of deals. Better if the Englishman were killed.

But who was the boy, Battestini? Why had he not heard of a youth who could implement so much? The radio in his cell had told him the police held the opinion that the boy worked alone . . . remarkable, outstanding . . . and the commentator called him the lover of Franca Tantardini and expounded that this was the reason for the boy's action. Who in the movement had not been the lover of Franca Tantardini? How many of the *Nappisti* in this same cell had not taken comfort from hours spent strangled by the arms and legs of Tantardini, taken pleasure from the flesh and fingers of the woman? His table lamp lit a mirthless smile. Perhaps it was the boy's first time, and he believed he had made a conquest. If it was the first time, the boy would climb a mountain for that woman, perhaps he'd die for Tantardini. Certainly he would kill for her.

When the ultimatum was met he would issue a communiqué in his own name, from inside the walls of Asinara. Courage, my child. We love you, we are with you. But why had he not been told of this boy?

Mosquitoes slipped through the opened window of the farmhouse parlor and turned their incisive attention to the arms and neck of the resting man. Instinctively he slapped the side of his face in irritation, and in his growing consciousness there was the drone of their wings, the rising surge of their attacks. He started up, blinked in the flicker light of the television, and heard the sounds of the kitchen through the closed door, water running, the quiet clatter of dishes and tins. He scratched savagely at the bitten skin where the mark had grown enough for him to gouge a sharp trickle of blood, he rubbed the back of his hand into his eyes, then headed for the kitchen. Time for him to be going to bed, time for him to encourage her to follow.

His wife put her finger across her mouth, the call for quiet, and pointed to the half-opened doorway that led to their son's room. A tall, broad-shouldered woman, red-faced, dark hair pulled to an elastic band, thick bare arms and a faded apron. She had been his woman since he was seventeen, and he had shyly courted her with the encouragement of her parents who knew of the farm that he would inherit.

"The little one is sleeping?"

She worked at the final flurry of the day's sink work. "It's taken him long enough, but he's nearly there."

"Did he tell you where he'd been?"

She slopped warm water from a kettle into the bright plastic sink bowl. "In the woods, where else?"

"What kept him there?" He was well tired, yearning for his bed, and there was much hay to be moved by trailer in the morning. Perfunctory conversation, and made only because she was not ready to follow him to their spacious, heavy, oak wedding bed.

"He saw something, he said."

"What did he see?"

"I don't know . . . something. He wanted to tell you about it. I said that it would keep till the morning. Perhaps it was a pig?"

"Not this far down the hillside, not a pig," he said softly.

She sluiced at the pan in which she had made the sauce for the pasta.

"You have much more to do?" he asked.

"I have to wash some socks, then it is finished." She smiled at him, kindly, dark-eyed.

"I'll say goodnight to the boy."

The frown crossed her face. "Don't wake him, not now. He's dead to the world, don't wake him now."

"I'll see his bedclothes aren't on the floor."

When he had gone, she could muse as she doused the socks in water that her man loved his boy child as the most precious thing in his life. God be blessed, she thought, that if we were to have but one child it should have been a boy. Someone for him to work for, someone for him to dream would one day take the running of the farm. She worked quickly, and with the soap lathering in a sea of bubbles among the wool. Shirts she would do in the morning, after the chickens had been fed.

"Mama."

She turned abruptly in response to the strained voice of her man. He stood at the kitchen door, his face dazed and in shock, his hand resting loosely on the shoulder of his son.

"You've woken him." The petulance rose in her voice.

"You never asked him what he had seen?" The farmer spoke hoarsely.

"A fox, a rabbit, perhaps a heron, what difference does it make, what difference at this time?" She bridled, before her senses responded to the mood he set. "What did he see?"

"He found a red car hidden in the bushes beside the small field and the wood. He has a toy, a toy car that your mother gave him last Easter, the one he plays in his bed with. He said to me that the toy was the same as the car that he had found. His toy is a red Fiat *Uno Vente Sette*. They showed the car on the television, the car for the foreigner who was kidnapped. Fiat *Uno Vente Sette*, and red . . ."

"A red *Uno Vente Sette*, there would be half a million . . ." her hands were drawn from the water, wiped nervously at her apron. There should be no involvement, not with something hostile.

"He found a man who was tied."

"The boy dreams. It is a world of his own."

"He saw a youth come, with a gun."

She stammered, "It's not our business."

"Dress him."

Her eyes wide, her lips moving in fear, she attacked in protection of her child. "You cannot take him there, not in the darkness, not if you believe that he has seen these things."

"Get his clothes and dress him." It was an order, a command. She did not resist and scurried to the child's room for his day clothes.

From the hallway the farmer took a thick sweater and the small-bore shotgun that he used for pigeon and rabbit when he went with his neighbors to shoot on a Sunday morning. From a nail high on the back door to the yard he unhooked a rubber-coated flashlight.

Together they dressed their son.

"You remember Mama, what Father Alberti said, at the Mass after Moro. He said these people were the anti-Christ. Even Paulo Sesto they rejected, even the appeal by him that Moro should be spared. They are the enemies of the church, these people, they are the enemies of all of us. You remember what Father Alberti said? On the television it was spoken that they would kill the foreigner tomorrow morning. We have to go, Mama, we have to know what the boy has seen."

They slipped the child's shirt and coat and trousers
over his pyjamas, drew on his boots over his bare feet.
The mother's hands fumbled and were slower than
her man's.

"Be careful, Papa, be careful with him."

The father and his son walked out of the door and
into the night. She followed the passage of the flashlight before the bend in the lane obscured its light,
and then she sat at the kitchen table, very still, very
quiet.

The wine had gone and the port after it and Caroline Charlesworth had fled the scene for her bed. The
three men sat around the table and the ash and cigarette ends made their mole hills in the coffee saucers.
They'd been over all the ground, all the old and tram-
pled paths. The issues of principle and pragmatism
were digested and spat back. The debate on negotiation had been fought with anger and spite. And then
the brandy had taken its toll and soaked and destroyed the attack of Carpenter and the defense of
Charlesworth and the attaché. They were resting now
and the talk was sporadic. Geoffrey Harrison was no
longer principal, replaced by the rate of income tax,
church aid to the Patriotic Front of Rhodesia, decad-
ence on the streets of London. The familiar fodder for
Britons abroad.

Michael Charlesworth stood up from the table,
murmured something about calling to check the embassy, and moved unhappily away from the safety of
the chairs.

"He's a damn good man," Carpenter had problems
with the words.

"Damn good," growled Buster Henderson. "You're
right you know, a damned good man."

"I've given him some stick since I've been here."

"Wouldn't give a hoot. Knows you've a job to be getting on with. A damn good man."

"I've never felt so bloody useless, not in anything before."

"I once did a stint at G 2 Ops. Shut up in a bloody office, out in Aden. We had a couple of Brigades in the Radfan, tribesmen bashing. Damn good shots they were, gave our chaps a hell of a run for their money. I couldn't get clear of my desk, and my brother-in-law was up there with a battalion. Used to rub it in with his signals, wicked devil. Used to get me damned cross, just talking and not doing. I know how you feel, Carpenter." The weathered hand surged again for the bottle's neck.

Neither man looked up as Michael Charlesworth came back into the room. He paused, and watched Henderson refilling the glasses, slopping brandy on the polished wood surface.

"You'll be needing that, Buster, I've just heard something awful . . ."

His voice attracted, mothlike, the eyes of his guests.

". . . it's Harrison's wife. Violet Harrison, she's just hit a lorry on the Raccordo. She's dead. Ran slap into a lorry. Killed outright, head-on collision."

The bottle base crashed down onto the table and trembled there in tune with the hand that held it. Carpenter's fist shot for his glass and dashed a saucer sideways, spewing ash on the white crocheted mats.

"Not bloody fair." The Colonel spoke into the hand that masked his face.

"I made them repeat it twice, I couldn't believe it." Charlesworth still standing.

Carpenter swayed to his feet. "Could you get me a taxi, Michael. I'll wait for it downstairs." He didn't look back, headed for the front door. No farewells, no thanks for hospitality. Going, getting out, and running.

He didn't call the elevator, kept to the stairs, hand
on the support rail, the fresh air freezing at the alcohol.

God, Archie, you've screwed it now. Throwing the
shit at everyone else but not yourself. Laying down
the law on how everyone else should behave. Ran out
on the poor bitch, Archie, hid behind the prim chintz
curtain and clucked your tongue and disapproved.
Bloody little pharisee with as much charity as a weasel up a rabbit burrow. Preaching all day about getting Geoffrey Harrison back to his family, but he
hadn't shut the door and seen there was a family for
the bastard to come home to. What had Carboni said?
"I've failed your man." Join the club, Giuseppe, meet
the other founder member.

He fell into the back of the taxi. Gave the name of
his hotel and blew his nose noisily.

The dog fox crept close to the two sleeping men.
With a front paw it scratched the P38 a little farther
from Giancarlo and its nose worked with interest at
the barrel and the handle before fascination was lost.

Four times the fox went over the ground between
Giancarlo and the pit, as if unwilling to believe there
was no food remnant to be rifled. Disappointed, the
animal moved on its way, along the path that led to
the fields and hedgerows where mice and rabbits and
chickens and cats could be found. Abruptly the fox
stopped. Ears straight, nostrils dilating. The noise that
it heard was faint and distant, would not be felt by
the men who slept, but for a creature of stealth and
secrecy it was adequate warning.

A dark shadow, flitting comfortably on the path,
the fox retraced its steps.

The farmer had laid the shotgun on the ground and
knelt at the front of the car. The flashlight was in the

boy's hands, and the farmer cupped his hands around it to minimize the flare of the light as he studied and memorized the number plate. Not that it was necessary after he had seen the prefix letters before the five numbers. RC, and the television had said that the car had been stolen from Reggio Calabria. Cunningly hidden too, a good place, well shielded by the bank and the bushes and the trees. He rose to his feet, trying to control his breathing, feeling his heart battering at his chest. He switched off the flashlight in the boy's hand and retrieved his gun. Better with that in his hands as the wood threw out its death hush. The farmer reached for the hand of his son, gripping it tightly, as if to provide protection from a great and imminent evil.

"Two men were in the wood?"

He sensed the nodded response.

"Where was the path to their place?"

The boy pointed across the car's hood into the black void of the trees. By touch the farmer collected with his fingers three short fallen branches, and made an arrow of them that followed his son's arm. He put his hand on the boy's shoulder and they hurried together from the place, back across the fields, back to the safety of their home.

19

Giuseppe Carboni was dozing at his desk, head resting lopsided on the folded arms that were his pillow.

"Dottore . . ." the shout of excitement and pounding feet boomed in the outer corridor.

Carboni flicked his head up, the attention of the
owl, his eyes large in expectation. The subordinate
surged through the opened door, and there was a
gleam and an excitement at his face.

"We have the car, Dottore . . ." stuttered out, because the thrill was great.

Chairs heaved back, files discarded, telephones
dropped, men hurrying in the wake of the messenger
of news gathered at Carboni's desk.

"Where?" Carboni snapped, the sleep shed fast.

"On the hill below Bracciano, between the town
and the lake."

"Excellent," Carboni sighed, as if the burden of At-
las were shifted.

"Better than excellent, Dottore. A farmer found the
car . . . his son, a small boy, took him to the place,
and he thinks the boy watched Battestini and Harrison in the wood in the day . . ."

"Excellent, excellent . . ." Carboni gulped at the fetid air of the room which had taken on a new freshness. He felt a weakness in his hands, a trembling at his fingers. "Where is Vellosi . . . ?"

"At the communications center. He said he would not return to the Viminale tonight."

"Get him."

The room had been darkened, and now Carboni moved to the door and rammed down the wall switch and the response was blinding light in the room, all bulbs on the chandelier illuminated, sweeping away the shadows and depressions.

"The liaison officers of *carabinieri* and SISDE, get them here too . . . within ten minutes."

Back at his desk, moving with uncommon speed, he pulled from a drawer a large-scale map of the Lazio region. His aide's pencil raked to the green plot of woodland dividing the built-up gray shades of the town of Bracciano from the blue tint of the Lago de Bracciano. Carboni, without ceremony, relieved him of his pencil and scratched the crosses on the yellow road ribbons for the perimeter that he would throw around the boy and his prisoner. Seal the road to Trevignano, the road to Anguillara, the road to La Storta, the road to Castel Guiliano, to Cerveteri, to Sasso, to Manziano. Seal them tight, block all movement.

"Has the farmer alerted them at all . . . is there that risk?"

"He was asked that, Dottore. He says not. He went with his son to the car, identified it, and then returned home. He left the child there and then he walked to the home of a neighbor who has a telephone. He was careful to walk because he feared the noise of a car would startle the people in the wood, though his farm is at least a kilometer away. From the house of his neighbor he telephoned the *carabinieri* in Bracciano . . ."

"The *carabinieri* . . . they will not blunder . . ." Carboni exploded, as if success was so fragile, could be snatched from him.

"Be calm, Dottore. The. *carabinieri* have not moved." The aide was anxious to pacify.

"You have them, Carboni?"

The direct shout, Vellosi striding into the office, hands clapping together in anticipation. More followed. A *carabinieri* colonel in pressed, biscuit-brown uniform, the man from the secret service in dark suit with sweat stains at the armpit, another in shirtsleeves who was the representative of the examining magistrate.

"Is it confirmed, the sighting . . . ?"

"What has already been done . . . ?"

"Where do you have them . . . ?"

The voices rose, a gabble of contradiction and request.

"Shut up," Carboni shouted. His voice carried over them and silenced the press around his desk. He had only to say it once, had never been known to raise his voice before to equals and superiors. He sketched over his knowledge and in a hushed and hasty tone outlined the locations he required for the block forces, the positioning of the inner cordon, and his demand that there should be no advance into the trees without his personal sanction.

"The men best trained to comb the woods are mine . . ." Vellosi said decisively.

"A boast, but not backed by fact. The *carabinieri* are the men for an assault." A defiant response from the *carabinieri* officer.

"My men have the skills for close quarters."

"We can get five times as many into the area in half the time . . ."

Carboni looked around him, disbelieving, as if he had not seen it all before, heard it many times in his years of police work. His head shook and rocked in anger.

"If is, of course, for you to decide, Giuseppe," Vellosi smiled, confident. "But my men . . ."

"Do not have the qualities of the *carabinieri*," the colonel clipped his retort.

"Gentlemen, you shame us all, we discredit ourselves." There was that in Carboni's voice that withered them, and the men in the room looked away, did not meet his gaze. "I want the help of all of you. I am not administering prizes but seeking to save the life of Geoffrey Harrison."

And then the work began. The division of labor. The planning and tactics of approach. There should be no helicopters, no sirens, a minimum of open radio traffic. There should be concentrations before the men moved off on foot across the fields for the inner line. Advance from three directions, one force congregating at Trevignano and approaching from the northeast, a second taking the southern lakeside road from Anguillara, a third from the town of Bracciano to the west to sweep down the hillside.

"It is as if you thought an army were bivouacked in the trees," Vellosi said quietly as the meeting broke.

"It is a war I know little of," Carboni replied, as he hitched his coat onto his wide shoulders. They walked together to the door, abandoning the room to confusion and shouted orders and ringing telephones. Activity again and welcome after the long night hours of idleness.

Carboni hesitated and leaned back through the doorway. "The Englishman who was here in the day, I will take him with me, call him at his hotel." He hurried to catch Vellosi. He should have felt that at last the tide had turned, the wind had slackened, and yet the doubt still gnawed at him. How to approach by stealth, through trees, through undergrowth, and the danger if they did not achieve surprise. The thing could be plucked from him yet, even at the last, even at the closest time.

"We can still lose everything," Carboni said to Vellosi.

"Not everything, we will have the boy."

"And that is important?"

"It is the trophy for my wall."

They destroy us, these bastards. They coarsen our sensitivities, until a good man, a man of the quality of Francesco Vellosi believes only in vengeance and is blinded to the value of the life of an innocent.

"When you were in church, Francesco, last night . . ."

"I prayed that I myself, with my own hand, might have the chance to shoot the boy."

Carboni held his arm. They emerged together into the warmed night air. The convoy stood ready, car doors opened, engines pulsing.

The damp of the earth, rising through the leaf mattresses, crawled and nagged at the bones of Giancarlo, till he writhed in irritation and the refuge of sleep fell from him. The hunger bit and the chill was deep at his body. He groped across the ground for his pistol and his hand brushed against the metal of the barrel. *P trent' otto.* Sometimes when he awoke in a strange place, and suddenly, he needed moments to assimilate the atmosphere around him. Not at this awakening. His mind was sharp in an instant.

He glanced at the luminous face of his watch. Close to three. Six hours to the time that Franca ordered for the retribution of the movement on Geoffrey Harrison. Six hours more and then the sun would be high, and the scorch patterns of the heat would have flung back the cold of darkness, and the wood would be thirsting for moisture. Two or three of them there

would have been with Aldo Moro on this night. Two
or three of them to share the desperate isolation of the
executioner as he makes ready his equipment. Two or
three of them to pump home the bullets, so that the
blame is spread . . . blame, Giancarlo? Blame is for
the middle class, blame is for the guilty. There is no
blame for the work of the revolution, for the struggle
of the proletariat. Two or three of them to take him to
the beach by the airport fence of Fiumicino. And they
had had their escape route.

What escape route for Giancarlo?

No planning, no preparation, no safe house, no car
switch, no accomplice.

Did Franca think of that?

It is not important to the movement. Attack is the
factor of importance, not retreat.

They will hunt you, Giancarlo, hunt you for your
life. The minds of their ablest men, hunting you to
eternity, hunting you till you cannot run farther. The
enemy has the machines that are invulnerable and
perpetual, that invoke a memory that there has been
great sacrifice.

And there is advantage in the killing of 'arrison . . . ?

Not for your mind to evaluate. A soldier does not
question his order. He acts, he obeys.

The insects played at his face, nipping and needling
at his cheeks, finding the cavities of his nostrils, the
softness of his ear lobes. He swatted them away.

Why should the bastard 'arrison sleep? When he was
about to die, how could he find sleep? A man with no
belief beyond his own selfish survival, how could he
find sleep?

For the first time in many hours Giancarlo summoned the image of his room in the apartment at seaside Pescara. Bright posters on the walls of Alitalia
views, the hanging figure of the wooden Christ, the

thin, framed portrait from a color magazine of Paulo Sesto, the desk for his school books where he had worked in the afternoon after classes, the wardrobe for his clothes where the white shirts for Sundays hung ironed. Insidious and compelling, a world that was lit and conventional and normal. Giancarlo, who sat beside his mother at meals, and wanted in the evenings to be allowed to help his father at the shop. A long time ago, an age ago, when Giancarlo was on the production line, held in the same precise mold as the other boys of the street. 'arrison had been like that.

The ways had parted, different signposts, different destinations. God . . . and it was a lonely way . . . terrifying and hostile. Your choice, Giancarlo.

He slapped his face again to rid himself of the insects and the dream collapsed. Gone were the savors of home, replaced by a boy whose photograph was stuck with adhesive tape to the dashboards of a thousand police cars, whose features would appear in a million newspapers, whose name drew fear, whose hand held a gun. He would never see Franca again. He knew that and the thought ripped and wrenched at him. Never in his life again. Never again would he touch her hair and hold her fingers. Just a memory, a recollection to be set beside the room in Pescara.

Giancarlo lay again on the ground and closed his eyes.

Up the Cassia, northward from the city, headed the convoys, lights flashing, sirens rising.

The riot wagons of the *Primo Celere*, the Fiat trucks of *carabinieri*, the blue and white, prettily painted cars of the *polizia*, the unmarked vehicles of the special squads. There were many who came in nightclothes to the balconies of the high-rise apartments and watched the stream of the participants and felt the thrill of the circus cavalcade. More than a

thousand men on the move. All armed, all tensed, all
drugged in the belief that at last they could assuage
their frustration and beat and kick the mosquito that
hounded them. At the village of La Storta where the
road narrowed and was choked, the drivers hooted
and blasphemed at the traffic police and demanded
clearance of the chaos, because all were anxious to be
in Bracciano when dawn came.

Past La Storta, on the narrower Via Claudia with its
sharp bends between the tree lines, Giuseppe Carboni's car was locked into a column of trucks. A quieter, more sedate progress because now the sirens were
forbidden, the rotating lights doused, the horns unused. Archie Carpenter shared the front seat with the
driver. Vellosi and Carboni were behind among the
bullet-proof waistcoats and the submachine guns,
taken from the trunk before the departure from the
Questura.

Water dripped from Carpenter's hair onto the collar
of his shirt and down the back of his jacket, the remnant of his shower after the telephone had broken the
total, drink-induced sleep that he had stumbled to.
Now that he was awake, the pain between his temples
was huge.

A boring bastard, she'd called him. A proper little
bore. Violet Harrison on Archie Carpenter.

Well, what was he supposed to do? Get her onto the
mattress in the interests of ICH, take her on the
living-room carpet . . . ?

Not what it was about, Archie. Not cut and dried
like that. Just needed someone to talk to.

Someone to talk to? Wearing a dress like that, hanging out like it was going out of fashion?

Wrong, Archie. A girl broken up and falling down,
who needed someone to share it with. And you were
out of your depth. Archie, lost your lifebelt and

splashing like an idiot. You ran away, you ran out on her, and had a joke with Charlesworth, had your giggle. You ran because they don't teach you about people under high stress in safe old Motspur Park. All cozy and neat there in the mortgaged semis, where nobody shouts because the neighbors will hear, nobody has a bit on the side because the neighbors will know, where nobody does anything but sit on their arses and wait for the day when they're pushing up daisies and it's too late and they've gone, silent fools and unremembered. She needed help, Archie. You galloped out of that flat as fast as your bloody legs would take you.

A proper little bore, and no one had ever called him that before, not to his face.

"Did you hear about Harrison's wife, Mr. Carboni?" Spoken offhand, as if he wasn't concerned, wasn't involved.

"What about her?"

"She was killed in a car crash, late last night."

"Where was she?" The puzzlement was ringing through Carboni's preoccupation with the procedures of the coming hours.

"Out on what's called the Raccordo."

"It is many kilometers from where she lives."

"She was driving home, she was alone," Carpenter spewing it out.

"No one with her, no friends with her . . .?"

"So, if we get the man out, that is what we have to confront him with," a light, chilled laugh from Vellosi. "Incredible, Carboni, when a man's cup is overfilled . . ."

"It is criminal that in this time a woman should be alone." A distaste hung in Carboni's words.

"I suppose no one thought about it," said Carpenter dully.

At the junction to the lake road they saw the stationary rows of trucks and vans parked on the grass verge. They passed lines of walking men in uniform, and the headlights glinted on the metal firearms, and there were glimpses of cordons forming in the fields. The car winged on down the steep hillside before turning hard to the right along a weeded driveway with a military barrier and concentration of elderly brick buildings awaiting them. Carpenter tried to lose the load of self-pity and stared about him as the car stopped.

The doors snapped open, Carboni was out quickly, and mopped himself and turned to Carpenter. "It used to be a flying boat station, long before the war. It is a place now just for dumping the conscripts. They maintain a museum, but nothing flies. But we are close to the wood here and we have communications." He took Carpenter's arm. "Stay near to me, now is the time for you to wish me well."

They were swept through the ill-lit door of the administration block, Carpenter elbowing to keep contact with the bustling Carboni, and on into a briefing room. Hands out to greet Carboni, hugging and rubbed cheeks, a clutch of bodies around him, and Carpenter relegated to a chair to the back while the policeman found sufficient silence to make a short address on his plan. Another surge of the men in suits and uniforms and battledress and Carboni, the emperor of the moment, was speeding for the doorway. They won't stop for you, Archie. They won't hang about for that bloody Englishman. Carpenter shoved and pushed, winced as a Beretta holster dug at his stomach, and won his way to Carboni's side. In the wedge at the door Carboni smiled at him, looking up, perspiring.

"I have made a great decision. The antiterrorist unit demanded the right to lead, so did the *carabinieri*.

Both thought they were best fitted. I have satisfied everybody. The *carabinieri* will come from the north, Vellosi's men from the south. I am an Italian Solomon. I have sliced Battestini in two."

Carpenter stared coldly at him.

"Allow me one levity, I have nothing else to laugh at. At any moment Battestini may kill your man, he may already have done so. We are going forward in the dark, we are going to stumble in the dark through the wood."

"You're not waiting for daylight?"

"To wait is to take too great a risk. If you pray, Carpenter, now is the moment."

They were out of the building.

Muffled, subdued orders. Men in the bleak half-light hitching over their heads the heavy, protective clothing that would halt all rounds other than high velocity. The cock and loading of weapons. Ripples of laughter. Feet tramping away into the last remnants of the night. Should have a bloody stirrup cup, Archie, and a red coat, and a man to shout "Tally Ho!"

The group, with Carboni at its heart, set off toward the road. Walking beside him was a short, firm-bodied man who wore torn trousers and boots and a thick sweater, who carried an old shotgun broken and crooked, farmer's style, across his elbow, and who held the hand of a small boy.

From the hard, bare mattress of her cell bed, Franca Tantardini heard the soft-soled footsteps in the outside corridor. A bolt was drawn back, a key inserted and turned, and the man who had been her interrogator let himself in.

He smiled at the woman as she lay with her head propped on her clasped hands, her golden hair spilling on the one pillow.

"I have some news for you, Franca. Something that you would wish to know."

Her eyes lit at first, then dulled, as if her interest betrayed her before the discipline triumphed.

"I should not be telling you, Franca, but I thought that you would wish to hear of our success."

Involuntarily she half rose on the bed, her hands forsaking her neck, propping her now.

"We know where he is. Your little fox, Franca. We know where he hides, in what wood, close to which village. They are surrounding the place now. At first light they will move in on your little fox."

The light from the single bulb behind its casing of close mesh wire hit down at the age lines of her face. The muscles of her mouth flickered.

"He'll kill the pig first."

The interrogator laughed softly. "If he has the courage, when the guns are around him."

"He'll kill him."

"Because Franca told him to. Because Franca from the safety of her cell ordered it. His pants will be wetted, his hand shaking, guns around him, aimed on him, and he is dead if he does what Franca has told him."

"He will do as he was ordered."

"You are certain you can make a soldier from a bed wetter, that was what you called him, Franca."

"Get out," she spat her hatred.

The interrogator smiled again. "Let the dream be of the failure, Franca. Goodnight, and when you are alone think of the boy, and think of how you have destroyed him . . ."

She reached down beside her bed for the canvas shoes, snatched at one, and hurled it at the man in the open doorway. Wide and high, and bouncing back from the wall. He chuckled to her and grinned.

She heard the key in place, the bolt thrust across.

* * *

The noise of Giancarlo twisting from his side to his back drifted Geoffrey Harrison from sleep. As soon as he woke the hurt of the wire at his wrists and ankles was sharp. The first, instinctive stretch of his limbs tautened the wire, dug the knots into the flesh of his wrists and ankles. A man who awakens in hell, who has purchased a great vengeance. Nothing but the bloody pain, first sensation, first thought, first recollection.

God, the morning that I die.

The mental process became a physical happening, and his body curled to a fetal position of fear. No protection, nothing to hide behind, nothing to squirm to. The morning that I die. He felt the tremble and the shudder take him, and the awareness was overwhelming. God, the morning that I die.

The first precious beginnings of the day were seeping into the wood. Not the sunlight, but its outriders in gray pastel which permitted him to detect the lines of the nearest tree trunks. This morning, with the birds singing, at nine o'clock. Another shape, suffused and vague and hard to alert himself to, as Giancarlo rose and stood above him and looked down. Giancarlo, called by Harrison's movements and inspecting the fatted goose of the feast.

"What time is it, Giancarlo?" He could hear the watch ticking on his wrist, could not see it.

"A little past four . . ."

The little bastard had learned the role of jailer, thought Harrison, has taken the courtesy of the death-cell attendant. The hushed tone, and "Don't you worry lad, it doesn't hurt and it's quick." The warm eyes of sympathy. Well, that never helped a poor lad who was going to swing at nine. What do you know about that, Geoffrey? I read it. That was other people, Geoffrey, and half the fucking population saying, "And a damn good thing too." That's for a criminal. "No sympathy" and "Deserves all he's getting." That's for men who've shot policemen and raped kids. That's not for bloody Geoffrey Harrison.

"Did you sleep?"

"Only a little," Giancarlo spoke simply. "It was very cold on the ground."

"I slept very well. I didn't dream."

Giancarlo peered down at him, the definition growing at his face with the slowly coming light.

"That is good."

"Are you going to get some food?" Could have kicked himself when he'd said it, could have spat on himself.

"I am not going for any food . . . not now . . . later, later I will eat."

Cheaper to feed one. Should have your calculator here, the one beside the desk in the office, the one you use for all the arithmetic of ICH, then you'd know the boy would only be shopping for one, and how many lire he would save that way. Only for one, only one mouth. Not on the bloody bread list, Geoffrey, because you'll be past food, past caring about the ache in your guts.

Geoffrey Harrison's voice rose in crescendo, down the paths of the wood, high with the birch branches, fluttered the thrushes and blackbirds.

"Don't hurt me, Giancarlo. Please, please, don't hurt me . . ."

He was answered, far back, from the shadows among the trees, distant and beyond sight, answered by the rampage of a dog's bark.

And in the wake of the bark was the drumming of feet and the crash of branches swept aside.

An avalanche, circling and nearing.

Giancarlo had crouched, bent double at the sound of the dog. At the noise of the approach of men he

surged toward Harrison, pulled him to the limit of the
wire, and flung himself into the gap between his prisoner and the earth roof where the roots had taken the
ground high out of the pit. He panted for breath,
wriggled to get lower, held the gun at the back hair of
Harrison's head.

"If you shout now you are dead."

The gun squirming against his neck. Harrison
played his part, the one he was familiar with. "Run,
you little fool. Run now."

He could sense the shock of terror in the boy, im-
parted through their clothes, body to body, flesh
warmth, through the quivering and pulsing of the
blood veins. Didn't know why he spoke, only that this
is what he would have done. This was his way. Avoid
contact, avoid impact, stall the moment, the life-style
of Geoffrey Harrison.

"If you go now you have a chance."

He felt the boy drive deeper into the pit, and then
the voice, small and reeded.

"I need you, 'arrison."

"Now, you have to go now." Father and mother,
didn't the little bugger understand? Time for running,
time for ducking, time for weaving.

"If I go now, they will kill me."

What was he supposed to do? Feel sorry for the little pig? Wipe his bottom for him, clean his pants out?

"We stay together, 'arrison. That is what Franca
would have done."

The man and the boy, ears up, lying in the shallow
hole and listening.

Around them, unseen among the trees, an army
advanced, clumsy and intimidating in its approach,
breaking aside the wood that impeded its progress,
bovine in its determination. Closing on them, sealing
them, the net tightening. Fractured and splintered
branches in front and behind them, stamped leaves

and curses of discomfort to right and left. And the baying of dogs.

Harrison turned his body from his side, a ponderous movement, then twisted his neck farther until he could see the face of the boy. "It is too late, Giancarlo." He spoke with a kind of wonderment, astonished because the table was turned and the fear exchanged. "You had to go when I said."

"Shut up," the boy spat back at him, but there was a shiver in his voice. And then more slowly, as if the control were won with great effort, "That is not our way."

Carboni with his pistol drawn, Vellosi trailing in one hand a submachine gun, Carpenter keeping with them, all were running in their own fashion down the narrow path, spurred on by the shouts of the advance, and the roars, fierce and aggressive, full and deep-throated, of the police attack dogs. They sprinted on the shadowed surface, buried in the surreal dawn mist that ebbed between the tree towers.

Archie Carpenter saw the shape of the *polizia* Vice Brigadiere materialize from the foliage at the pathside, rising to block Carboni and Vellosi. The stampede stopped, men crouched about them and struggled to control the heaving of their lungs that they might be quieter. The trees were infested, the undergrowth alive. Static from the portable radio, whispered voices, garbled replies. A council of war. Grown men on their knees, huddled to hear, the weapons in their hands. Birds shrieked in flight.

"Carpenter, come close," Carboni called, his voice blanket-shrouded. "The dogs heard voices and barked. They are about a hundred meters from us. We are all around them but I do not wish to move farther till there is light. We wait for the sun."

"Battestini, will he pack it in, will he give himself up?"

The big sad eyes rolled at Carpenter, the shoulders heaved their gesture, "We have to try. If the spell of Tantardini is still on him . . ."

Left unsaid because Carpenter mouthed his obscenity and understood.

"We wait for the sun." Carboni turned away, resumed the hush of conference.

This was where it all ended. In a damp wood with mud on your shoes and dirt on the knees of your trousers. Right, Archie. Where the family picnickers might have been, or boys with tents, or a kid with his condom and his girl. Only the method and the style to be decided. To be determined only whether it was champagne or a mahogany box. You're within rock-throwing distance of him, Archie. You could stand up and shout and he'd hear you. A few seconds running, you're that close. God, the bastard can't shoot him now. Not now, not after all this. Not after Violet.

The dawn came steadily, imperceptibly, winnowing behind the trees and across the leaves, cloaking the men who peered forward and fingered the mechanisms of their firearms. Drawn out, mocking their impatience, the light filtered into the wood.

20

Thrusting its brilliance, the dart of a lance, the first sun ray pierced the wall of trees. The shaft picked at the ground in front of the fallen trunk, faded in the eddy of the branches and then returned. The sharpness held sway over the gray, shadowed light.

The moment of ultimate decision for Giancarlo Battestini. Move now or be damned and finished, vulnerable to the sniper's aim, naked to the gas and nausea cartridges, open to the bone-splintering bullets of the marksmen. His hands furtive, he reached for the wire at Geoffrey Harrison's ankles, swore at the skill of his own knot, and with difficulty loosened it. By the collar of the shirt he pulled his prisoner close to him and back down into the pit that the wire tied to the wrists and the roots would have more play. Easier now to unfasten, the work of a few seconds.

"What are we doing, Giancarlo?"

A grim, set smile, "We go on another journey, 'arrison."

"Where are we going?"

Busy with his work, scraping together the strands of wire, Giancarlo muttered, "You will know."

The boy bound together the length of wire that he
had used on Harrison's legs to the piece now trailing
from his wrists.

"Kneel upright."

Harrison stretched himself to the extent of the pit,
wriggled and turned his ankles to restore the flood of
circulation, and slowly raised his head above the rim.
He lifted his shoulders, tautened his spine, and grimaced at the stiffness remaining from his trapped
night's sleep. Giancarlo looped the wire around the
front of his chest, then snugged it behind his own
back, drew it beneath his armpits and then again to
Harrison's wrists. Pressed hard against his arm, the
boy entwined the knot that closed them together,
linked them as one. With a hand he pulled Harrison's
shirt from the waist of his trousers and the metal pistol barrel was formidable against the skin of the small
of Harrison's back. The front gunsight carved a
scratch line in the flesh as Giancarlo armed the
weapon.

"It is a light trigger, 'arrison. When we start you
should not talk, you should not slip. My finger will
barely have to move, you understand?"

Harrison nodded, the questions stifled in his throat,
choked on his tongue. No more compulsion to ask
questions. Just a new horror, and what value explanation? Just a new abyss, and he was plunging.

"We stand up, and carefully."

They straightened as one, the vibrations mingled,
and Giancarlo pressed his head against Harrison's
shoulder.

But your legs don't work, Geoffrey, been tied too
long. You'll slip, you'll bloody stumble . . . and then
the bloody trigger goes. How far does the finger
move, how far . . . quarter of an inch, eighth of an
inch . . . ? Concentrate, you bloody fool. One leg forward, put it down slowly, ease the weight onto it,

stop, put the other foot forward, test the balance, stop again, put the next foot forward . . .

Harrison looked around him, blinked in the air, drank in its freshness, felt the stale breath of Giancarlo. A certain sort of freedom, a certain sort of release. Breathing something other than the odor of the earth. Nothing moved at the front, but there would be an army there, concealed, close and waiting. The voice bellowed behind his ear.

"Is Carboni there?"

Ahead of them was the path that they had walked down the previous morning, long ago, separated by infinite time. The route that Giancarlo had used to get his food and to drift down when he went to the telephone in the darkness, and it was the way the child had come.

The stream of the sun caught the three men square as they came forward on the path. They wore their badges of nationality, their flags for recognition. A short, rolling man at the front, balding, sallow. One behind him who held a submachine gun diagonally across his waist, hair combed, the trace of a clipped mustache at his upper lip, his silk tie somber. The last was a stranger, clothes of a different cut, hair of a different trim, rounded shoulders and a pallor not of the Mediterranean. Two Italians and an Englishman. Harrison felt the weakness at his knees, the shake at his thighs and shins that was irresistible. The bastards had come. Long enough about it.

"I am Carboni."

The words echoed in the trees.

Harrison felt the boy stiffen, readying himself. The last great battle, striving for strength and steel stamina.

"Listen, Carboni. This is your 'arrison, this is your foreign dirt. I have tied him to me, and against his back, behind his heart, I have the P38. It is a hair trigger,

Carboni, tell your criminals, tell your gunmen that. If they shoot, my finger will move on the trigger . . . you are listening, Carboni? If you hit me, 'arrison is dead. I am going to walk down the path, I am going to walk to my car. If you want 'arrison alive, you do not impede me."

Harrison was aware that the pressure of the circled barrel grew in his back, the impetus growing for movement.

"I am going to move forward. If you want 'arrison, stay back."

"What does he say?"

Carboni did not turn toward Carpenter and his sharp anxiety. He gazed on down the path at Harrison and Giancarlo. "The boy has the gun at Harrison's back. He says it is hair-triggered. He wants to drive away from here . . ."

Vellosi, in English, because that was the language of the moment, "Giuseppe, he doesn't walk out of here."

"Then Harrison dies."

"The boy cannot leave here," the spitting whisper of the cobra.

"I am here to save Harrison." Confusion, catastrophe ravaging at Carboni.

"If he walks out of here, Battestini, if he leaves the wood, he has disgraced us. One boy and he has beaten us . . ."

"I have to save Harrison," Carboni wavering, torn and pulled and tossed.

"Italy we have to save . . . think, Carboni, the implications if the boy walks clear. One against so many, and he wins because we have no courage."

Violet Harrison, dead and mangled on her back in a plastic sack on the morgue slab, incised for autopsy, viewed by pathologists. And Geoffrey Harrison to lie beside her with a pencil hole in his back and a cavity large enough to fit a lemon into at his chest. Get off your arse, Archie Carpenter. Get into the big boy's league. Your man out there, Archie, so get off your bloody arse and get walking.

A short jab of his elbow and Archie Carpenter was past Carboni and Vellosi. Three quick strides and he was clear of them . . . and who was going to run forward to pull him back?

"Watch the boy, Carboni, watch the boy and be ready."

Giancarlo watched him come. Saw the purposeful clean steps eat into the dividing distance. Nothing to read from the face of the man, nothing that spoke of danger and risk, nothing from which to recognize his emotions. The command to halt, the shout, was beyond the boy. Fascinated, spellbound. And the light caught at the man's face as he passed between two trees and there was no glimmer of fear. A man with a job to do, and getting it over with, and wearing a crumpled suit.

Giancarlo felt his hand on the pistol butt cavort with the weapon. He could not hold it motionless.

Francesco Vellosi spun on his heel, raking the trees and bushes behind him till he saw the *carabinieri* sergeant with the rifle, kneeling and in cover. His fingers snapped for the man's attention and he tossed the submachine gun toward him, gestured for the rifle and caught it as it was thrown to him. The rifle slipped to his shoulder. Rock-steady, unwavering, and the needle of the front sight rested centrally in the V of the rear attachment by his right eye. The line was on a small part of Giancarlo Battestini's head that was visible to him.

The void cut, the gap halved, Archie Carpenter spoke. Almost surprised to hear his own voice. Brisk and full of business.

"Geoffrey Harrison. I'm Archie Carpenter . . . does this Battestini speak English?"

No preamble, dominate from the start, the way they taught them far back, the Metropolitan Police drill on approaching an armed man.

He saw the half head on Harrison's shoulder, an unfinished ventriloquist's dummy, dumped on a perch, lacking a body. Harrison's lips moved and then his tongue brushed against them, the moisture glistening. Poor blighter's at the limit.

"He does."

Still moving, still hacking and cutting at the intervening space. Carpenter called, "Giancarlo . . . your name, right? . . . I've come for the gun."

Edging his way forward, slower steps as the distance capsuled, and the spots and the beard on Giancarlo's face were sharp and visible, and the color at his eyes was dark and haunted. Ten yards short and the scream from the boy.

"Stop, no closer."

"Just the gun, Giancarlo, just give it to me." But Carpenter obeyed and now stood his ground, fair and square across the path. Saw the sweat on the boy's forehead and the tangled skeins of his hair, and the yellowed teeth.

"You move aside, you give us room . . ."

"I'm not moving. I'm here and I want the gun from you."

Where did you get it from, Archie, which silk hat? Out of the door of her flat, out of the staircase of a high building, out of a woman past her breaking point. Ran once, not again. Once was enough to turn the shoulder, not ever again.

"If you do not move, I shoot . . ."

"Empty threat. I don't move, you don't shoot."

Who'd know you, Archie? The girls in the office, in the typists' pool? The men in the pub off the evening

train from the city? The neighbor who borrowed the
lawn mower alternate Saturday mornings? Who'd
know Archie Carpenter in a wood at Bracciano?

"I have the gun at his back . . ."

"I don't care where you have the bloody thing. I
don't move, you don't shoot. It's easy, a ten-year-old
knows that."

Stretching the boy. Out into the risk area, out into
the storm. Watch the eyes, Archie, watch the blinking
and the uncertainty and the fidget. Traversing and
hesitant, the fear's building. The bully when he's outnumbered, when the other kids come back to the
playground. Careful, Archie . . . Gone past that
place, off Mum's knee, playing it the grown-up way.

"You do not believe that I will shoot . . ."

"Right, Giancarlo, I don't believe it. I tell you why.
You're thinking what happens if you do. I'll help you,
I'll tell you. I strangle you, boy. With my hands I
strangle you. There's a hundred men out there behind
me that want to do it. They won't get near you, you'll
be done by the time they reach you."

Carpenter held him unswervingly. Never left the
eyes of the boy. Always there when he turned back,
always present. Lowering over him, heavy as a snow
cloud, absorbing the hatred.

"I've no gun, but if you fire on Harrison, I'm on
you. You've trussed yourself, silly boy, that's why I'll
get you. I used to be a policeman, I've seen people
that have been strangled. Their eyes come half out of
their head, they shit themselves, they wet their legs.
That's for you, so give me the gun."

You never saw anyone strangled in your bloody life,
not ever. Steady it, Archie. Turn it over. Possible that
the physical isn't the soft belly of the boy. Don't make
him play the martyr, don't put coal on that fire. What
else gets to a psychopath?

"I'm going to start walking, you cannot take him

from me . . ." Giancarlo holding his defensive line. The rout not accomplished. "Get out of our way."

Harrison gazing at Carpenter, like he doesn't know what's happening, like he's out on his feet. Best bloody way. Who's going to tell Geoffrey Harrison? Who's that one down to? Archie Carpenter going to do it? Well done, Geoffrey, we're very pleased you've come out of this safely . . . excellent show . . . but there's been a bit of bother while you've been away . . . well the missus, actually . . . but you understand that, Geoffrey, good lad, thought you would. . . .

Throw in the big one, Archie. Go for broke. All the chips on the green cloth, into the center of the table.

"I saw your woman last night, Giancarlo. Raddled old bitch. Bit old for a boy, wasn't she?"

He saw the composure break on the boy's face, saw the anger lines form and knit on his forehead.

"I wouldn't have thought a boy would be interested in a workhorse like that."

The blood was running fast to the boy's cheeks, the flush rising under his skin, the eyes slitted in loathing.

"Do you know what she called you when they interrogated her? You want to know? A little bed wetter. Franca's opinion of lover boy . . ."

"Get out of my way." The words came fast and weighted by Giancarlo's fury.

Carpenter could see the nausea rising in Geoffrey Harrison's face, the eroded self-control. Wouldn't last much longer, wouldn't sustain the supreme effort. Batter on, Archie, belt the little bastard.

The sound of the voices carried easily among the trees. Carboni had eased his pistol from the jacket pocket and it hung from his fingers as a token of participation. Beside him Francesco Vellosi still stood, eye at the gunsight, tight in anticipation, ignoring the fly that played at his nose.

"Why does he say these things?"

Vellosi never strayed from his aim. "Quiet, Giuseppe, quiet."

"How many others have there been, boy, do you know? I mean, you weren't the first were you?"

"Get out of my way . . ."

Not much longer, Archie. Hold your ground and it's disintegration time, spitting collapse. Forgetting where he is, and what he's here for, like we want him to be. Don't run now, Archie, just round the corner is the Shangri-La that you came for. Almost at the fingertips, almost there to touch.

"They'd all been there, boy, every grubby finger, every sweaty armpit in the movement, did you know that . . . ?"

He's rising, Archie. The slimed creature forced out of the deep water. Coming for you, Archie. Hold the line, sunshine. Come on, Archie bloody Carpenter from Motspur bloody Park, don't let old Harrison down now, not when he's flaking, not when Violet's on her back and cold. Watch him, watch the struggle in the shirt. The gun comes next. You'll see the barrel, you'll see the fist on it, and the finger that's lost behind the trigger guard. Hold the bloody line, Archie.

"I wouldn't have done what you've done, not for a cow like that. You know, Giancarlo, you might even have got the scabs from her . . ."

Carpenter laughed out loud, shaking in his merriment, confronting his fear. Was laughing as he saw the pistol emerge from behind Harrison and raised at him as fast as a snake strikes. Looked into the torture of Giancarlo's face, sucked at the agony. Well done, Archie, you made it, sunshine. First time in your bloody life, across the finish line and in front.

The gun was coming, bright with menace from beneath a winter sea. The pistol showing, sharp and tooled, and aiming.

The one shot, the whiplash crack.

Carpenter was on the ground, thrown backward, the involuntary reflex, on his face a splitting smile.

Harrison staggered, legs weak and resisting his efforts to withstand the weight of the smitten Giancarlo dragging down the wire that wrapped their waists. Blood on Harrison's face, dripping, and a mess of brain matter and no hands free to clear the sheen of destruction from his eyes.

Carboni recoiled from the explosion behind his ear. He pivoted toward Vellosi, gazed at him and saw the grim pleasure spreading like an opening flower on his companion's face.

And then the running.

Men rising from their hidden places, careening over fallen branches, bullocking through undergrowth. Carboni joined the herd as if time now was at last special. Francesco Vellosi dropped the rifle barrel with deliberation, bent down and picked up the single brass cartridge case and pocketed it. He turned and with an easy movement tossed the gun back to its owner, the *carabinieri* sergeant. Revenge exacted. He walked, tall and proud, toward the huddle that was gathering around Geoffrey Harrison.

With a knife a policeman sliced through the wire that held Harrison to Giancarlo Battestini. The body of the boy, shed of its support, slumped to the ground. One half of his face was intact, unblemished and waxen; the other was obliterated, removed as if in tribute to the marksmanship and the brutal power of the high velocity bullet. Freed, rubbing hard at his wrists, Harrison dived away from his helpers, turned his back on them and vomited into the dried grass at the edge of the clearing. They gave him room, respected him.

Archie Carpenter pulled himself to his knees, rose unsteadily to his feet, and clamped his fingers together to hide the shaking that gripped them. He stood aside, a stranger at a party.

When Harrison came back to the group, he spoke simply, without idiocy. "What happened . . . I don't know what happened . . ."

Vellosi pointed across the clearing to Carpenter. "This man was prepared to offer his life for yours," he spoke gruffly, and then his hand slipped in support to Harrison's armpit. "He gave himself to Battestini that you should be saved."

Their eyes met in a fleeting moment, then Carpenter turned his head from the deep puzzlement of Harrison's gaze and seemed to those who watched him to shrug his shoulders as if an episode had ended, a man had done his work and needed no praise or thanks. Studiously, Carpenter began to wipe the clinging leaves and sticks from his back and his trousers.

They moved from the clearing. Vellosi and Harrison setting the slow pace at the front, Carboni busy and bustling behind them, Carpenter trailing. Harrison did not look round for a final glimpse of Giancarlo's body, stumbled away, reliant on the strength of the hand that helped him. They moved at cortège speed and the route along the path was lined with the unsmiling faces of the men in uniform who held rifles and submachine guns and who did not flinch from the hurt on Harrison's face. They masked their feelings, those who stared, because death was recent and the devastating speed of the violence had stripped from them the elation of victory.

"I didn't understand what he was doing, this man Carpenter."

From behind Harrison's shoulder, Carboni spoke. "He had to get the pistol from your back, he had to produce the pistol against himself if your danger were to be taken. That was why he taunted the boy. He gave the opportunity to Francesco. Francesco had a half face to shoot for. That there was the chance was because of Carpenter."

Carboni still walking, swung his head toward Carpenter, saw only a shaded half smile, a tint of sadness.

"My God . . . God help us." Harrison walked with his eyes closed, led as a blind man on a street pavement. He struggled for his words, confronting the shock and exhaustion. "Why was another life . . . why was another man's life less important than mine?"

"I don't know," said Carboni.

"Get me home please, get me to my wife."

The quick light of warning flashed between the policeman and the head of the antiterrorist squad. Carboni stopped and grabbed surely at Carpenter's sleeve and drew him forward. The procession had stopped. The four men were in a group, a huddle of shoulders, and those in uniform faded back, abandoning them.

"You have something to tell your man, Archie," Carboni spoke in a whisper.

"Charlesworth can . . ."

"No, Archie, for you, it is your work."

"Not here . . ."

Wriggling, Archie, sliding in the mud stream, seeking to extricate himself, and Harrison peering into him, unshaven face close, bad breath reeking. Come on, Archie, this is why you saved him, this is the moment you preserved him for. Can't slip the buck to Charlesworth, can't push it away. It's now it has to be said, and it's you that has to say it.

"It's about Violet, Geoffrey . . ." Carboni and Vellosi watched the shame driving up on Carpenter's face, realized the bewilderment creeping again into the man whose arms they held.

"What about her?"

"Violet . . . Geoffrey, I'm sorry."

"Where is she?" The shriek coming from Harrison, the embarrassment flowing into Vellosi and Carboni.

A sudden coldness from Carpenter, as if from this came his protection, as if his face could be hidden by chilled words. "She's dead, Harrison. She piled into the back of a lorry last night. She was alone."

Vellosi and Carboni hurried forward, half-carrying, half-dragging the weight of Harrison between them. Carpenter detached himself and hung back. Nothing more to be said, nothing more to be done. The speed of the group quickened, past the man who stood with the broken shotgun and the small boy, past the field hedgerows, on down to the road. They slid Harrison into the back of Carboni's car, Carboni followed him, clapped his hands and the driver accelerated away.

His arm hanging from Carpenter's shoulder, Vellosi watched the car spin around the first curve.

"You did well, my friend."

"Thank you," said Carpenter.

The sensational new paperback
from the author of *My Mother/My Self*

MEN IN LOVE

by NANCY FRIDAY

Nancy Friday, who probed the secret world of women's fantasies in *My Secret Garden* and the mother-daughter bond in *My Mother/My Self*, now explores in depth the uncensored fantasies of thousands of men—and is amazed by what she discovers!

"Courageous. Moving."—*The Washington Post*

"A labor of love for all humankind. Nancy Friday is still on the cutting edge."—*The Houston Chronicle*

A Dell Book $3.50   (15404-9)